STALKING BRIDGET

As she clicked off her cell phone, Bridget noticed something down the alley. A dark figure darted from behind a recycling bin into a doorway. Bridget held on to the cell phone and moved toward the recycling bin. Behind the bin, she saw a shadowy alcove with a door and a window—both closed.

There was no sign of anyone in the alcove. The darting figure she'd seen must have been her imagination. But then she glanced down at a puddle by the alcove stoop. There were wet footprints all around the stoop—and on the pavement by the bin.

It wasn't her imagination. Someone was just there.

Biting her lip, Bridget reached for the door handle. Her hand was trembling. The hinges squeaked as she started to open the heavy door. She didn't have to open it more than a few inches to see the wet footprints on the dusty cement floor inside.

Bridget froze. She realized if she didn't get out of there right now, she could be as dead as Olivia and Fuller.

Bridget backed away from the door and watched it close. Her heart racing, she retreated toward the sidewalk at the end of the alley. As she headed back toward her car, her cell phone rang. She clicked on the Talk button. "Hello?"

"Bridget?"

She didn't recognize the voice on the other end. "Yes?"

"Why didn't you open the door?"

"What?" But then she suddenly realized what he meant.

"Why didn't you step inside, Bridget?" he whispered. "I was in there, waiting for you. . . ."

Books by Kevin O'Brien

Published by Kensington Publishing Corporation

KEVIN O'BRIEN

THE LAST VICTIM

PINNACLE BOOKS
Kensington Publishing Corp.
http://www.kensingtonbooks.com

PINNACLE BOOKS are published by

Kensington Publishing Corp.
850 Third Avenue
New York, NY 10022

All Kensington Titles, Imprints, and Distributed Lines are available at special quantity discounts for bulk purchases for sales promotions, premiums, fund-raising, and educational or institutional use. Special book excerpts or customized printings can also be created to fit specific needs. For details, write or phone the office of the Kensington special sales manager: Kensington Publishing Corp., 850 Third Avenue, New York, NY 10022, attn: Special Sales Department, Phone: 1-800-221-2647.

Pinnacle and the P logo Reg. U.S. Pat. & TM Off.

ISBN: 0-7860-1662-0

First Pinnacle Books Printing: September 2005

10 9 8 7 6 5 4 3 2 1

Printed in the United States of America

This book is for my editor and friend,
John Scognamiglio

ACKNOWLEDGMENTS

Many thanks once again to my editor, John Scognamiglio, who got this book off the ground and got me off my ass to write it. Thanks also to my other friends at Kensington Books, especially Doug Mendini, who is *a little bit of terrific,* and Robin Cook, who rocks.

Another great big thank you goes to Meg Ruley, Christina Hogrebe, and the folks at the Jane Rotrosen Agency.

I'm grateful to my Writers Group pals and fellow authors, who worked with me on this book. Thank you, Soyon Im, Dan Monda, and Garth Stein. My thanks also go to my dear friend Cate Goethals, who also put a lot of time into this book, and helped whip it into shape.

Thanks also to my neighbors at the Bellemoral, who are incredibly supportive, especially Kate Debiec, Cathy Johnson, and David Renner; the gang at Broadway Video; some wonderful customers; and my pals, Paul, Tony, Sheila, Chad, Tina, Larry, Danielle, and Tiffany. And how could I not thank my local book store? Thank you, Michael Welles and all the cool people at Bailey/Coy for always pushing my books.

For their friendship and support, I want to give another great big thank you to Lloyd Adalist, Dan ("Well, on a scale from 1 to 7, I'm about a G") Annear, Marlys Bourm, Terry and Judine Brooks, Kara Cesare, Anna Cottle and Mary Alice Kier, Tom Goodwin, Val Hockens, Ed and Sue Kelly, Elizabeth and Kate Kinsella, Megan Leonard Fleischel, Judy O'Brien, John Saul and Michael Sack, Dan and Doug Stutesman, and George and Sheila Stydahar.

A huge thank you goes to my pal Tommy Dreiling.

Finally, thanks to my wonderful family, Adele, Mary Lou, Cathy, Bill, and Joan.

CHAPTER 1

Desperation time.

The singer-pianist had just wrapped for the night, and the bartender announced last call. The bar would be closed within the hour. Not good.

Olivia Rankin didn't want to go home alone tonight, and the way things were looking, that was just what would happen.

The cocktail lounge at the top of Seattle's Grand Towers Hotel was all sleek metal and polished mahogany—with a sweeping view of the city and harbor lights. Very ritzy. Eleven-fifty for a cosmopolitan. But at least it came with a fancy little silver bowl of mustard-flavored pretzels.

Sitting at the bar in a sexy wraparound pale green dress, Olivia once again scanned the Crown Room and decided the pickings were pretty slim.

Olivia was thirty-eight, with short-cropped, platinum-blond hair and a perpetual tan—thanks to regular sessions at the tanning booth. Though attractive, she figured there was room for improvement, and planned to lose twenty pounds by December. Once meeting that goal, she'd reward herself with a Botox session. Lately, her face was looking like a road map—especially around the eyes. Years of partying had caught up with her. On her birthday, a friend had sent her a card, which hit a little too close to home. On the front of the card was a cartoon of a woman holding a champagne glass. It said: *Happy Birthday! The Years Have Been Good to You . . .* Inside was the punch line: *. . . But Those Weekends Have Really Taken a Toll!*

Olivia ordered a third cosmopolitan. She'd come to the Crown Room alone, hoping she would meet a better class of guy there. If she was lucky, she would end up with some guest at the hotel, and he'd let her spend the night. She wouldn't turn her nose up at a room service breakfast in the morning either. The Grand Towers was pretty damn swanky. And it beat spending the night at home—alone.

It wasn't so much that she was lonely. She was scared.

During the last week, some strange, disturbing things had happened to her. While undressing for bed Wednesday night, she'd caught a man peeking through her window. Olivia didn't get a good look at his face. By the time she'd thrown on her robe and come to the window, all she saw was a tall, shadowy figure sprinting away from the town house. The next night, Olivia saw someone dart by her kitchen window. It scared the hell out of her. She immediately called the police. Two cops came by, asked a lot of questions, then gave her some tips on home security and how to start up a neighborhood watch. Useless.

Then two nights ago, she woke up from a sound sleep, and immediately knew someone was in the house. She reached for the light on her nightstand, but hesitated. She didn't want him to know she was awake. So she lay there in the darkness, afraid to move. She listened to the floorboards creak and told herself it was the house settling or the wind or something else totally harmless. After a while, her eyes adjusted to the darkness. She focused on the bedroom door, which she'd left open a crack. If she stared at it too long, the shadows played tricks, and the door seemed to move on its own—ever so slightly. Still, she couldn't close her eyes or look away.

Olivia remained paralyzed under the covers until dawn,

when she heard the *Seattle Times* delivery person tossing the newspaper on her front stoop. She crawled out of bed, then checked the living room, kitchen, bathroom—and even the closets. Nothing unusual, nothing out of place.

She desperately needed some coffee, and put some water on to boil. When she wandered back to the living room, she noticed something. Her photo album was in its usual spot on the coffee table, but it was open. She'd had a couple of drinks before going to bed, and couldn't remember whether or not she'd looked at any pictures.

The kettle's shrill whistle sounded, and she hurried back into the kitchen. It wasn't until after she'd had a few sips of coffee that Olivia thought to glance through the album. Three photos were missing, pulled out of their clear plastic sleeves. If someone had actually broken into her home last night, it didn't make sense that he'd steal a few photographs of her and nothing else. She thought about calling the police again, but what good would that do?

Olivia wondered if she might actually know this stalker. Was he someone from the gym, or the supermarket? Maybe he was a customer at the chiropractors' office where she worked. A lot of creeps came through there.

Whoever he was, she had a feeling he'd just gotten started in some kind of weird courtship of her. And it would only get worse.

That afternoon, Olivia bought a package of bullets for an empty gun, which she'd been keeping in the back of her closet for years.

The loaded gun was now in the glove compartment of her car, parked in the underground garage at the Grand Towers Hotel. She liked having it around—for insurance.

Funny, it took this stalker to make her realize how alone she was. She'd lived with several different men over the years, but since she'd moved to Seattle a year ago, there hadn't been anyone who lasted beyond a few dates. It had been pretty lonely. Hell, she couldn't even keep a cat; she was allergic.

If she went home alone tonight, she probably wouldn't sleep a wink. Her prospects didn't look so hot either. The bar would be closing within the hour. Frowning, Olivia planted an elbow on the bar and sipped her cosmopolitan.

"Hey there, honey. Why so glum?"

Olivia stared down at her drink for another moment. Part of her clung to the impossible hope that the smoky-whiskey voice belonged to a tall, handsome hunk. Maybe he'd spend the night with her, and this would be the start of something terrific.

When Olivia looked up from her near-empty glass, she couldn't hide her disappointment. He was a short, balding, ape of a man. He wore a red Izod short-sleeve shirt that looked painted on. He was very muscular—with a coat of black hair on his arms. He had hair coming out of his ears, too. In fact, he looked as if he had hair everywhere except on the top of his head.

He leaned against the bar and gave her a smug smile. "Whaddya say, honey? Can I buy you a drink?"

"I'm not your *honey*," Olivia muttered. "Besides, you're out of luck. It's past last call."

"There's no last call at my place," he said. "I have a bottle of scotch there."

"Well, go home and drink it," she replied, fishing for some cash in her purse. "Try some other woman in the bar, okay?"

He laughed. "Feisty. I like that. Are you feisty in bed too?"

Olivia waved at the bartender, then slapped two twenties on the countertop. She didn't look at the creepy little man. "I'll ask you nicely," she said, staring straight ahead. "Would you do me a big favor and leave me the hell alone?"

"Oh, c'mon, honey," he purred. "You can't mean that."

"I sure do. So go haunt somebody else. Okay?" She continued to avoid eye contact with him.

"Fucking bitch," she heard him growl. She caught his reflection in a mirror behind the bar as he walked away. He had the meanest, most hateful look on that ugly-ape face of his.

The bartender came by and took her money. Then a few moments later, he returned with her change.

Olivia defeatedly slid off the bar stool and started toward the elevator. She saw the creepy little ape of a guy waiting there. Olivia stopped dead.

She didn't want to ride down to the lobby with him—not alone. But she was saved. A handsome, well-dressed black couple stepped out of the bar area right after her. They headed toward the elevators.

Olivia followed them. Out of the corner of her eye, she could see the obnoxious man glaring at her. She refused to look in his direction. The elevator door opened and she stepped aboard.

The couple got in after her, and then the ape-faced man followed. He squeezed past the twosome and stood next to her.

Olivia kept ignoring him. She figured he wouldn't say anything rude to her in front of the couple. The handsome black man was a head taller than him and looked as if he could tear him apart.

"Oh God, I left my cell phone in the bar!" the woman exclaimed.

Her boyfriend grabbed the door before it slid shut, and she hurried out of the elevator. He tailed after her. The door began closing right behind him.

Olivia made a run for it.

The little man grabbed her arm. She recoiled, but he had a very strong grip.

The door shut. The elevator started its descent.

He was grinning at her. His eyes had a crazy, intense look. Olivia noticed a squiggly vein on the side of his forehead.

"Let go of me!" she snapped.

He chuckled, then released her. "I just didn't want the door to slam on you, honey."

Olivia backed away—until she bumped against the polished brass wall.

"I was afraid it would smash in that cute, fat little face of yours," he said, touching her cheek.

Olivia shrank into the corner. She eyed the lighted buttons on the panel by the elevator door. They still had another thirty floors to go. She thought about pressing the alarm button.

Just then, he stepped between her and the door. He glanced up and down at her. Grinning, he brushed his fingertips against her blond hair.

"Stop that," Olivia shuddered. "Get the hell away from me. I mean it." She looked up toward the ceiling. Where was the camera? Didn't most hotel elevators have cameras in them?

The little man was still stroking her hair. "Whether you like it or not," he whispered, "I'm going to fuck you."

Just then, the elevator stopped and the door opened.

The man backed away from her. He frowned at the tall, handsome stranger who stepped on from the eighteenth floor. The tall man wore a brown leather aviator jacket. He nodded politely at Olivia.

She felt such utter relief. As the door shut, she cleared her throat. "Excuse me, sir?" she said, her voice a little shaky.

The handsome stranger turned to smile at her.

Olivia shot a look in the direction of the crude little man. "This guy has been bothering me," she said. "Would you mind staying with me until the valet gets my car?"

The tall stranger glared at the creepy runt. He grabbed him by the collar of his Izod shirt and shoved him against the wall. Olivia gasped. The elevator shook a bit at the sudden tussle. "You son of a bitch," the handsome man growled. "Are you harassing this lady?"

The ape-faced man held up his hands, sort of a half-hearted surrender. "Hey, it's cool, buddy. Relax."

Olivia's rescuer turned to her with a reassuring smile. "Don't worry, Olivia. He won't bother you anymore."

She caught her breath and smiled back at him. She was so

grateful for his intervention, it took her a moment to realize something was terribly wrong.

Olivia stared at the man. "How do you know my name?" she whispered. She looked over at the short, hairy guy and wondered why he was smirking.

"He's not going to hurt you," the tall stranger said. He stepped between her and the elevator door. "No, Olivia. Hurting you is *my* job."

The door opened at the lobby.

Suddenly, the short man came behind her and slapped his hand over her mouth. Olivia tried to scream. Only a muffled whimper emerged. She struggled desperately, but the ape-faced man was too strong for her. Olivia thought he'd snap her neck.

She caught a glimpse of the empty lobby. No one could see her—or save her. The man in the aviator jacket blocked her way out. He jabbed the button for the basement level.

"It'll be easier for you, Olivia, if you just give in," he whispered.

Olivia helplessly watched the elevator door shut.

Preston McBride started out the evening thinking he would get laid.

He'd met Amber (her last name hadn't come up in conversation) at a kegger party at the house of some buddies near the University of Washington campus. Preston was in his junior year, studying business administration.

Amber wasn't in college. She'd dropped out of high school a couple of years back. When she told this to Preston while nuzzled against him in a smoky, sweltering living room full of people, she seemed to be bragging. With a pink streak in her blond hair and her pierced nostril, she struck Preston as a free spirit. At one point, when she squatted down to pump the keg and refill her beer, he noticed a tattoo of a dragon on her lower back. He couldn't help noticing her terrific body too. The front of her black T-shirt was stretched to its fiber limit. After an hour of screaming at each other over the noise, he heard her say: "I think you're cute. Can we get out of here and go some place?"

They made out in his car for nearly two hours. Preston's roommate was away, and he suggested they go back to his apartment. But Amber had another suggestion: "I know it's September and all, but I'm hot. Aren't you? Let's go swimming. I've always wanted to make love on a beach at dawn."

A half hour later, they were lost, driving around, trying to find the Denny-Blaine Beach. Apparently, Kurt Cobain used to meditate in the park there, and Amber wanted to visit the stomping grounds of the late rock legend. They never did find the place.

Birds were chirping and only the first light of dawn appeared on the horizon when Preston parked the car near a deserted Madison Park beach. With apartment buildings on both sides of the shoreline strip, and a quaint row of shops a stone's throw away, the beach wasn't exactly ideal for skinny-dipping and making love—even at this predawn hour. Some bushes camouflaged them at this end of the shore. Farther down, there was a beach house, a couple of lifeguard towers, and park benches staggered along the water's edge, spaced out every few feet. Preston imagined people would be coming here soon for their morning run, or for a cup of coffee on one of the benches, or maybe—like Kurt Cobain—some morning meditation.

Preston felt cold—and terribly self-conscious—as he began to undress. He was still in his white briefs when he tested the water with his foot. Freezing.

He looked over at Amber, squirming out of her panties. For a moment, she stood before him naked, her long blond hair fluttering in the wind. Her lithe body was so white against the dark water. She swiveled around, and let out a shriek as she scurried into the surf. Preston stared at the dragon tattoo above her perfect ass.

He shucked down his briefs, then ran in after her. The water was like ice, but he didn't care.

Amber wrapped her wet, cold, slippery arms around him. She was laughing and shivering. He felt her bare breasts pressing against his chest. Her nipples were so hard. He kissed her deeply.

With a squeal, Amber pulled away and splashed him. Then she swam out toward deeper water. Preston swam after her. But she splashed him again. He got water in his eyes and stopped for a moment. Standing on his tiptoes, he kept his head above water as he rubbed his eyes. He could hear her giggling and catching her breath.

When Preston focused on her again, Amber was dunking under the surface and swimming the length of the beach. He realized that if they were going to have sex, she planned to make him work for it. Once again, he started after her. She was a fast swimmer, with a good lead on him. "Come and get me!" she called, then dove below the surface again.

Preston was in over his head and had to tread water. Suddenly, he felt something brush against his leg. It felt slick. He wasn't sure if it was a fish or a piece of seaweed or what, but it gave him the creeps.

Preston shuddered. He quickly swam toward the shore—until he was standing in shallow water, up to his chest. Then he glanced around to see where Amber had gone. He no longer heard her laughing and splashing. He didn't see anything breaking the water's slightly rippling surface.

He felt a sickly pang in his gut. Preston told himself that Amber was screwing around with him. He glanced over to where they'd undressed. In the distance, he could see the piles of clothes near the shoreline. He turned and looked out at the deep water again. Nothing.

Preston tread closer to the shore. The cold air swept over his wet, naked body, and his teeth started chattering. He gazed over at the opposite side of the beach from where they'd shed their clothes. In the darkness—and the distance—he hadn't noticed anyone there earlier. But now Preston saw someone sitting on one of the park benches.

"Amber?" he yelled. The water was just below his waist.

Suddenly, something squirmed behind him in the water. Before he had a chance to turn around, he felt it grab his ass. Preston let out a howl, then swiveled around.

Amber sprang up from under the water. She was laughing.

Preston felt as if his heart was about to explode in his chest. But he managed to laugh too. He grabbed her and pulled her toward him.

With a finger, Amber traced a line from his chest down his lean torso. She drew a little circle around his belly button, gently tugging at the hair there. Amber grinned at him, but then her eyes shifted away—to something past his shoulder. "Who's that?" she asked, frowning. "Is she staring at us?"

Preston glanced back at the person on the park bench. He moved a bit closer. He could see now, it was a woman. She hadn't budged an inch—not even when some birds came and perched on the bench with her. She seemed to be sleeping. Her legs were spread apart in an awkward, sort of boneless way. Her green wraparound dress was bunched up to her thighs, and a huge dark stain ran down the front of it.

"Who the hell is that?" Amber repeated. Covering her breasts, she crept closer to the shore—toward the sleeping woman. "Oh my God," she whispered.

Shivering, Preston covered himself up as well. He stared at the woman slumped on the bench. Had she been in the water? Her face was shiny, and her short, platinum-blond hair was matted down on one side.

Amber let out a shriek that must have woken up half the residents of the apartment building nearby. The birds flew away. One grazed the woman's head, but she didn't move at all.

Several lights went on in the building—including an outside spotlight. It illuminated the ripples on the surface of the lake.

Now Preston could see the gun in the woman's hand. Now Preston realized the woman's face and hair weren't dowsed with water.

It was blood.

Sunlight sliced through the blinds in his studio loft. He'd been up all night, and had lost track of the time. That often happened when he was painting.

He favored classical music while working on his art. Wagner was on the stereo, cranked up to *Twilight of the Gods, Funeral March*. The orchestration was rousing. He felt goose bumps covering his near-naked body.

He wore only a pair of snug black boxer-briefs as he put the finishing touches on his latest masterpiece. His lean, chiseled body was flecked with several different-colored paint smudges. It was almost as if he'd become one with the canvas.

A tracklight from above illuminated the painting. On either side of the easel stood a pair of tall, cathedral-type candleholders he'd bought in Paris. The candles were almost burned down to stubs. It was his own fault they burned so fast. Every once in a while, he'd take one of those tapers out of its ornate holder, then tip it over his chest. The hot wax splattering on his skin gave him a delicious little jolt of pain that kept him going.

He was exhausted, having been up the last thirty-plus hours. He wasn't sure how long ago they'd left Olivia Rankin on that park bench by Lake Washington. But he could still smell her flowery perfume on his skin—along with the oil paint and his sweat. The combination of scents was arousing; it smelled of sex.

His drive from Seattle to Portland had taken three hours. He'd arrived home at dawn, then immediately shed his clothes and gone to work on his masterpiece. He wasn't going to bed until he finished.

The painting was of Olivia, sitting on that park bench by the shoreline—just as they'd left her.

In his one and only art show—given in a Portland café nine years ago—a critic commented that his work was "derivative of Hopper with its vivid colors, heavy shadows, and melancholia." He didn't sell anything at that exhibition, and he didn't have another art show. But he didn't change his style either.

Olivia Rankin's "death scene" was indeed full of intense colors, shadows, and pain. And it was almost finished.

To his right, he had a cork bulletin board propped on an easel. It was full of location photos he'd taken last week: the beach at Madison Park, the beach house and park bench. Working from these "location shots," he'd completed the background and the setting—right down to the DO NOT FEED THE WATER FOWL sign in the far right of the painting—a couple of days ago. All that remained was filling in Olivia. He'd done preliminary sketches from pictures he'd taken of her while she was out shopping—and again when she ate lunch in the park. She'd been an oblivious subject. Those photographs and his preliminary sketches were also tacked to the bulletin board—along with three snapshots he'd stolen from her photo album a few nights ago.

He stepped back and admired his work. He'd captured Olivia's blank, numb expression as she sat there with a bullet in her brain. He was proud of himself for that little gleam of moonlight reflecting off the gun in her hand. He used the same method—adding just a few slivers of white—to make the blood look wet.

He'd decided to call the piece *Olivia in the Moonlight*.

Absently, he ran his hand across his chest—over the sweat and the dried flecks of candle wax and paint. His fingers inched down his stomach, then beneath the elastic waistband of his under shorts.

The telephone rang.

Letting out a groan, he put down his paintbrush and started across the room. His erection was nearly poking out of his underpants.

He passed a wall displaying several of his other masterpieces. There was a painting of a woman floating facedown in a pool; a vertigo-inducing picture of a man falling off a building rooftop, a businessman sitting at his desk with his throat slit; a naked woman lying in a tub with her wrist slashed open; and several other "postmortem portraits." Some of the subjects in these paintings appeared to have died accidentally or committed suicide; but all of them had been murdered. He'd killed them all for money—and for the sake of his art.

He grabbed the phone on the fourth ring. "Yes?"

"Did you get any sleep yet?" his associate asked. "Or have you been painting all morning?"

"I'm just finishing this one," he answered coolly. "What do you want?"

"We have another job—for the same client."

"How soon does it have to be done?" he asked. "I need time to prepare, and I won't be rushed."

His associate let out an awkward chuckle. "Relax, you'll have time. The client likes the way you work."

He said nothing. Of course the client liked his work. He was an artist, and they were commissioning him to create another masterpiece. To him, each one was special. Each murder, each painting.

"Call me later and we'll set up a meeting," he said finally. "I can't talk right now. I'm painting."

"God, you're a quirky, kinky son of a bitch." His associate let out another uncomfortable laugh. "You and your *artistic temperament*."

The artist just smiled and gently hung up the phone.

CHAPTER 2

A CORRIGAN FOR OREGON sticker was plastered across the back bumper of a minivan on the shoulder of Interstate 5 near Longview, Washington. The vehicle's left rear tire was flat.

Alongside the van, a pretty woman with auburn hair knelt on a CORRIGAN FOR OREGON cardboard banner while she changed the tire. She didn't want to dirty her sleeveless Versace "little black dress." So far, she was successful in her efforts. Except for her hands, there wasn't a smudge on her.

Bridget Corrigan didn't have the time to wait for Triple-A to show up. She was thirty-eight years old, and had changed a few flats in her time. She'd gotten past the worst part—unscrewing the damn near impossible-to-budge lug nuts. With the minivan jacked up on one side, she removed the deflated tire.

It was almost one o'clock on a sultry Indian summer afternoon. Cars and trucks on the interstate whooshed by at seventy miles an hour.

"Ms. Corrigan is running about a half hour late today," Bridget's assistant, Shelley, was saying into her cellular phone. She stood on the gravel area off the road's shoulder, a few feet behind her boss. Shelley was a petite woman in her sixties with wiry gray hair and a cute, pixyish face that defied her age. She had to shout over the traffic noise. "Yes, I'm sorry. I know it's inconvenient, but Ms. Corrigan was held up at the Children's Hospital this morning."

Bridget set the spare tire in place and started screwing on the lug nuts. "What were you giving them with the Children's Hospital excuse?" she asked, once Shelley clicked off the line. "That was two mornings ago. Why not just tell them the truth—that I have a flat?"

"Because they never would have believed me," Shelley said, consulting her notebook. "Car trouble is the oldest and worst excuse in the book. Besides, who's going to begrudge you changing around your schedule to accommodate some sick kids?"

Working the lug nut wrench, Bridget threw Shelley a shrewd grin. "You're the one who should be in politics, you big liar."

"You'd lie too if you had to deal with that broom-riding witch of a chairwoman I just had on the horn. But she shut the hell up as soon as I mentioned the Children's Hospital." Shelley dialed another number on the cell phone, and her voice took on a sudden, perky, professional air. "Hello, this is Shelley Bochner, assistant to Bridget Corrigan. Is Ms. Vogel in? Yes, thank you, I'll hold."

The flat tire was taking an estimated twenty-five-minute bite out of their itinerary. While Bridget manipulated the jack and lowered the minivan, Shelley made three more calls reshuffling their afternoon appointments. Bridget picked up the CORRIGAN FOR OREGON banner on which she'd been kneeling. There were indents on the thick cardboard, and some dirt smudges on the picture of Bridget's twin brother, Brad.

Bradley Corrigan was running for the state Senate against the ultrarich, ultra-self-serving Jim Foley. So far, it was a very tight race.

In the last eight weeks, Bridget had become vital to her brother's campaign. She'd been all over the state, canvassing for Corrigan.

Bridget was baffled—and somewhat amused—by her sudden status as a Very Important Person in Oregon. Until recently, she'd quietly gone about her business: married fifteen years to an attorney, Gerry Hilliard; mother to two terrific boys, David, thirteen, and Eric, eight; and a teacher (part-time) of Spanish at a girls' private high school. She led a fairly ordinary, predictable life. The spotlight had always belonged to her twin brother, the rising star in state politics. That was Brad's domain, not hers.

Yet now, Bridget Corrigan was profiled and quoted in newspapers. At least a couple of times a week lately, the local TV news showed her on the campaign trail for her brother. Reporters wanted her opinions on everything from global warming to the crisis in the Mideast to the latest trends in fall fashions. Suddenly, she mattered.

This afternoon, Bridget was scheduled to talk at an elementary school, a high school, and then at a "Garden Tea" for a women's club. All of these commitments were in Astoria, Oregon. At Bridget's request, Shelley had set up the appearances a couple of days ago—and reshuffled some others. Bridget had given no explanation for suddenly changing her itinerary, but she needed an excuse to be near Longview, Washington, today. She was attending a function there that had nothing to do with her brother's campaign.

"I'm putting you to work here," Bridget called to her assistant—over the traffic noise. She was standing by the deflated tire on the roadside. "Manual labor this time. Help me put this lousy flat in the back."

"Another call just beeped in," Shelley replied. "Saved by the bell." Then she spoke into the phone: "Corrigan-for-Oregon campaign, this is Bridget Corrigan's line, Shelley Bochner speaking . . . Oh, hello! I'm peachy, thanks . . . Yes, she's right here. Just a minute." She handed the phone to Bridget. "It's the future senator of Oregon."

Bridget put a hand over her other ear to block out the highway noise as she spoke into the phone. "Hey, Brad. What's up?"

"Oh, I'm stuck in traffic on the way back from speaking to some environmentalists in Eugene."

"How did it go?" she asked.

"They loved me."

"Huh," Bridget said. "Then I gather you didn't tell them your wife drives a gas-guzzling SUV and owns a mink coat."

"No, that didn't come up in the course of my visit, and screw you," Brad replied. "What's up with you, Brigg?"

"Meets, greets, talks, and photo ops. I have a grade school, a high school, and a women's club—all in Astoria. But we're running late. Shelley and I just had a flat on the interstate, believe it or not."

"A flat? Did anyone stop to help?"

"Not a soul. I tried to get Shelley to take her top off—thinking someone might pull over—but she refused." Bridget winked at her assistant, who just shook her head and laughed. Shelley was trying to lift up the discarded, deflated tire without getting her hands dirty, and she wasn't having much luck. Bridget took the phone away from her ear for a moment. "That thing weighs a ton, Shell," she called. "Wait just a sec, and we'll lift it together."

"So—where are you right now?" Brad asked.

"We're just outside Astoria," Bridget lied. Out of the corner of her eye, she caught Shelly frowning at her. Bridget turned away. "Anyway, I think I just broke my record for changing a flat. I shouldn't be gabbing here on the roadside. We need to motor. So—is the barbecue still on for Dad's birthday tonight?"

"Yeah. Janice wants me to make sure you're bringing your salad with the homemade croutons and sweet-and-sour dressing."

"The salad's a go," Bridget answered. "And so am I. See you at six-thirty."

"Knock'm dead in Astoria, Brigg. Love ya."

"Love you too, Brad," she said. Then Bridget clicked off the line. She handed the cell phone to Shelley, who gave her a dubious look.

"So—we're just outside *Astoria* now?" she asked, sticking a thumb over her shoulder at a sign along the highway: LONGVIEW EXIT—1 MILE. "I think you're about sixty miles off."

Bridget shrugged evasively. "Let's get this tire in the back."

Together, they lifted up the deflated, dirty tire and carried it toward the back of the minivan. "So what's the story with this secret trip to Longview?" Shelley asked. "You know, you never explained to me why I had to change all your appointments for today. What's the mystery?"

"It's no mystery," Bridget replied, a slight edge in her voice.

Shelley let out a grunt as they hoisted the tire into the minivan. "Well, you're sure acting mysterious about it. Why did you tell your brother that we were in Astoria?"

Bridget wiped her forehead with the back of her hand, then shut the van's rear door. "Let's just file this under Kindly Butt Out. Okay?"

Shelley's eyes narrowed at her for a moment; then she nodded. "Yes, ma'am," she muttered, her voice almost drowned out by traffic noise. "You're the boss." She headed toward the passenger side of the minivan.

"I didn't mean to snap at you, Shell. I—" Bridget bit her lip. A truck whooshed by. Shelley couldn't hear her.

Bridget started for the driver's side. Why didn't she tell Shelley the purpose of this side trip to Longview? Hell, Shelley was headed there with her. She'd know in a few minutes what this was all about.

But she wouldn't know the whole story. She wouldn't know the real secret.

Before climbing into the car, Bridget glanced down at her dirty hands. She thought about Lady Macbeth: *Out Damn Spot.*

Bridget opened the vehicle door. Shelley sat on the passenger side, wiping her hands with some Wet Ones they kept in the glove compartment for emergencies.

"I'm sorry, Shell," Bridget said. "I'm a little tense today. I didn't mean to—"

"Oh, shut up," Shelley said, waving away her apology. "I love working with you, Bridget. Sometimes I'm just too damn nosey for my own good." She offered Bridget the container of Wet Ones. "Here. Clean yourself up."

Bridget paused before climbing behind the wheel. She plucked a damp tissue from the dispenser and began to work away at the grime on her hands.

As much as Bridget rubbed and rubbed, she had a feeling her hands would never be completely clean.

He had Bridget Corrigan in the telescopic sight of his bolt-action .35 Remington rifle. It was practically an antique. In fact, Charles Whitman, the University of Texas Tower sniper, used the same make of rifle back in 1966 to kill fifteen people and wound thirty more.

It was still perfect for a sharpshooting sniper. He'd killed before with it.

Through the telescopic sight, he watched Bridget Corrigan standing by the driver's side of the minivan. She was wiping off her hands. She had no idea that the right side of her pretty face was caught in the crosshairs of his sight. With just the slightest adjustment—tilting the barrel down a mere half inch—he could shoot her in the chest. But then he wouldn't be able to see the blood on that sleeveless black dress of hers. She should have been wearing white.

He'd found the perfect sniper's nest: in back of a deserted, old Burgerville restaurant on a side road across the interstate from where Bridget Corrigan and her friend were parked. He hid behind some bushes along a chain-link fence. There in the shrubbery, he'd come upon a small opening that looked right down at her. The spot seemed made to order. Incredible luck. From this point, he could shoot both Bridget and her pal, then be on the road before the first car stopped to help them.

For a while, he'd thought his luck was working against him. Early this morning, before first light, he'd planted three nails under the rear tire of that minivan in Bridget Corrigan's driveway.

He'd parked across the street and a couple of houses down the block from her gray cedar shaker with the white shutters. Through the telephoto lens of his camera, he'd watched Bridget Corrigan put her two brats on the school bus. She was dressed in a sweatshirt and jeans. She gave them each a hug, and mussed the little one's mop of brown hair. Then she held up the bus for a few moments while she dashed back into the house and ran out again. She waved a baseball glove, which she tossed—with dead-on accuracy—to her older one, who was standing in the doorway of the school bus.

He imagined how devastating it would be for those two young boys if their mother was killed. He smiled at the thought. It made him feel so powerful. Perhaps he would spare them the sorrow of losing their mother. Perhaps the humane thing to do was kill them too. Kill the cat and drown the kittens.

An hour later, she emerged from the house in that sleeveless black number, looking damn sexy. And she didn't even seem to be trying.

He followed her in the minivan to the Corrigan-for-Oregon campaign headquarters. All the while, he expected the tire to give out. It was one of his little quirks. He liked to see them vulnerable and helpless. Stranded. He'd pulled this trick before with some of his other subjects.

But the tire didn't show any sign of deflating during the two and a half hours she was inside the campaign headquarters. Nor did it collapse after Bridget and her skinny little pal came out of the storefront office and climbed into the minivan. He followed them on the interstate for over an hour until—finally—the tire gave out. He watched the minivan rocking up and down on the mangled tire; then she pulled off the road. At last, he could see her helpless and stranded.

Not so. After he'd sped to the next exit and located this spot, he'd seen how she changed that flat tire—with the same quick, no-nonsense efficiency in which she'd retrieved her son's baseball glove. No damsel in distress was she. He had to admire Bridget Corrigan a little bit. She might not be so easy to kill. But then, he liked a challenge.

From his sniper's nest, he watched her finish cleaning her hands. Then she ducked inside the minivan. Pulling away from the scope of his .35 Remington, he observed with his naked eye as Bridget Corrigan's minivan merged back onto the interstate. He lowered his rifle.

Just as well, he thought. Yes, he could have shot and killed her any time within the last twenty minutes. There had been several opportunities. But this was just a little flirtation, a dry run, something to whet his appetite.

Bridget Corrigan wouldn't be taken down on the roadside by his sniper's bullet. That wasn't how he wanted to paint her.

Her hands on the steering wheel, Bridget watched the road ahead. She knew this area.

She also knew her assistant pretty well. At the moment, Shelley seemed a bit too quiet and serious. She'd taken a few more phone calls while Bridget drove, but didn't strike up any conversations with her. Though she'd waved away Bridget's apology earlier, she was probably still a little hurt. And Bridget still regretted getting snippy with her.

She wasn't used to being someone's boss. Most of the time, she treated Shelley like a coworker and friend, not an assistant. Bridget wasn't much for barking orders at people. "You're like Martha Stewart in reverse," Shelley once told her. "You're just so mellow, considerate, and easy to work with. I think you'll have to start taking some bitch pills if you expect to survive in the political arena."

That had been a couple of months ago, when Bridget had just started campaigning for her brother. Maybe she'd changed since then. Maybe she was indeed becoming a bitch.

Shelley glanced out the passenger window and remained silent while Bridget navigated through traffic in the center of town.

"This is Main Street here," Bridget said finally. "There's a Les Schwab Tire place about three stoplights down—on the left. Could you do me a huge favor and call them? See if we can get a new tire in a half hour. We shouldn't put more than fifty miles on this spare. Then, if you don't mind, Shell, you can take in the car while I'm at this thing. And when they're done, you can swing by and pick me up." Bridget glanced at Shelley. "If you're still talking to me, that is. Again, Shell, I'm sorry to snap at you earlier—"

Shelley cut her off. "Oh, please, get over it." She pulled out her cell phone. "Go on a guilt trip with someone else. My feelings aren't hurt. You were right. It's none of my business what we're doing here." She dialed a few numbers, then asked for the number for Les Schwab Tire Service on Main Street in Longview.

Bridget pulled into the parking lot of a pristine-looking red-brick estate with white shutters. Amid the neatly trimmed hedges by the house was a sign: SHOREWOOD FUNERAL HOME.

Shelley clicked off the phone and announced that the tire service center could accommodate them.

"Thanks, Shell," Bridget said, stopping in front of the funeral home's main entrance. With a sigh, she shut off the ignition, then handed the keys to her. "I don't know why I've been so secretive about this. It's just that Brad didn't want me rescheduling a lot of commitments for this personal thing—so I'm doing it on the sly."

"Who died?" Shelley asked. "If you don't mind my asking."

"An old high school friend," Bridget said, soberly. "I haven't seen her in twenty years."

"She was pretty young," Shelley remarked.

Bridget gazed out at the funeral home. "She was living in Seattle. Apparently, a few days ago, she went to the beach in the middle of the night, sat down on a park bench, and shot herself in the head."

CHAPTER 3

Bridget leaned over the sink in the ladies' room at Shorewood Funeral Home. She'd gone directly to the lavatory without stopping by the viewing area. She knew where the restrooms were in Shorewood Funeral Home. She'd been there before.

Her hands still felt grimy from changing the tire. The Wet Ones hadn't done the trick. She needed soap and water. She also needed to be alone for a minute.

As she stood in front of the mirror, drying off her hands with a paper towel, Bridget started to cry. She couldn't help it. Olivia's death had brought back all these old feelings.

She and Brad had grown up not far from here, in the little town of McLaren. Bridget knew this funeral home, because her mother's wake had been held here. With the flood of memories, Bridget should have expected a few tears to escape.

Olivia had been in the same circle of friends with Brad and Bridget during high school. She'd been the party girl, the daring one. Bridget lost track of how many times she'd seen Olivia drunk. She'd even held back Olivia's hair for her on one occasion while Olivia threw up. But the very next day, Olivia—as always—was ready to party again. She was crude and funny and uninhibited.

It was hard to imagine Olivia committing suicide.

Then again, Bridget hadn't seen Olivia since the summer after graduation. The Corrigans moved sixty miles away to Portland—just after Bridget and Brad had started college. They'd always been reluctant to return. They'd lost touch— almost on purpose—with their former high school friends.

Bridget understood why Brad didn't want to go to this memorial—and why he didn't want her attending it. "What's past is past," he'd said. "I've put that chapter of our lives behind me. You should too."

Still, she'd needed to come. And now that she was here, Bridget wondered if any of the old gang would show up.

She wiped her eyes and blew her nose. After fixing her makeup, Bridget stepped out of the lavatory and started toward the wake area.

The viewing room was full of floral arrangements, strategically placed around the Mission-style furniture. The polished mahogany casket at the end of the room was closed. Understandable, since Olivia was supposed to have shot herself in the head. About forty people stood around the room.

Bridget spotted Olivia's mother, a slightly dowdy, dishwater blonde who showed all the traces of having been very pretty once. Bridget remembered Mrs. Rankin just turning that corner to frumpiness when Olivia was in high school— around the time Mr. Rankin packed his bags and disappeared. In Olivia's obituary, Mr. Rankin wasn't even mentioned.

Mrs. Rankin caught her staring. "Bridget?" she said. Her eyes were red-rimmed, and she gave her a pale smile. "Bridget Corrigan?"

Bridget stepped up to Olivia's mother and shook her hand. Then she placed her other hand over Mrs. Rankin's.

"That's the double handshake." Brad had taught her a few weeks ago how to greet different people at rallies. *"The double handshake is for when you want to show some extra*

warmth or empathy. . . ." At the time, Bridget thought her brother was a major-league political phony for teaching her these gestures. But now they came to her naturally. She wondered if perhaps they'd been there all along—and Brad had just labeled them—or had she become a bit of a political phony herself?

"I was so sorry to hear about Olivia, Mrs. Rankin," she whispered.

"Thank you," Olivia's mother said, with a raspy voice. "You know, I recognized you the minute I saw you, Bridget. Whenever you're on TV, I tell my friend Rosemary, 'That's Bridget and Brad Corrigan. They were good friends of my Olivia.' " She glanced around. "Where's Brad?"

"Oh, I'm sorry, Brad couldn't make it," Bridget said. "But he sends his condolences. We're both so sorry about— what happened."

Mrs. Rankin sighed, and her eyes welled up with tears. "I—I simply don't understand. I was just talking with Olivia a little over a week ago, and she said everything was fine. It doesn't make any sense that she'd take her own life."

Bridget squeezed Mrs. Rankin's hand. What do you tell a mother who has just lost her only child? Why didn't Brad ever tutor her in that?

Then someone else approached them. "Thank you for coming all this way, Bridget," Mrs. Rankin said.

Bridget nodded and stepped aside. As she turned away, she suddenly locked eyes with a tall man she didn't recognize. He was handsome, with a pale complexion and black hair. He wore a blue blazer, black tie, and khakis. He smiled— just slightly. Had she seen him somewhere before? Did she know him? His direct gaze and that smile seemed almost impertinent. Bridget numbly stared back at the man and watched his smile fade.

"Bridget Corrigan?" she heard someone say.

She turned and saw someone who was undeniably familiar. "Fuller Sterns?"

But Fuller Sterns's goofy-cute face was about the only

thing that looked the same from when they were in high school together. His long, wild, uncombed brown hair was now trimmed short around the sides and back—and receding badly. Fuller had been a loud, husky teenager—with a voracious appetite for beer, junk food, pot, and pranks. Now he was a pale, overweight man in a dark gray suit.

"Bridget," he said, approaching her. "Christ, you look exactly the same!"

"You too!" she lied. She hoped he was lying as well, because she'd spent her high school years feeling plain, unattractive, and robbed-in-the-womb of good looks by her twin brother.

She gave Fuller an awkward hug, then pulled back to look at him. "Thanks for telling me about Olivia. I got your phone message just yesterday. Sorry I didn't get a chance to call you back."

"I left a message with Brad too. I didn't hear back from him either."

She gave him a tight smile. "So—how've you been? Are you married?"

Fuller rolled his eyes. "Twice burned, and up to my neck in alimony payments. You ain't gonna see me head down the aisle again soon, no, thanks. I'm in finance, and the ex-wives spend it almost quicker than I can make it. Otherwise, I'm hangin' in there."

Grinning, Fuller looked her up and down. "I don't have to ask about you. I live across the river in Vancouver and get the Portland TV stations. You and Brad are always on the news. Sorry I can't vote for him, but tell that son of a bitch he has a fan in Washington State. He isn't here, is he?"

"No, Brad couldn't make it. Has anyone else from our graduating class shown up?"

Fuller frowned. "If they have, they're invisible, because I haven't seen them. And I've been here since this thing started." He shrugged. "Then again, it's been twenty years since graduation. A lot of people have moved away, lost touch."

"Had you seen Olivia recently?" she asked.

Fuller quickly shook his head. "No, I—huh, no. I haven't seen Olivia in years."

"But you knew that she'd died," Bridget said.

"Yeah, well, I—I just caught the obituary, that's all."

Eyes narrowed, Bridget stared at Fuller. He seemed to be lying—or at least, concealing something.

"I thought I should come here, y'know?" he said. "Pay my respects and all that. What about you? Did you talk with Olivia recently?"

Bridget sighed. "No, I'm one of those people from twenty years ago who moved away and lost touch." She worked up a smile. "But it's good to see you again, Fuller."

He let out a weak chuckle. "Huh, how about that twin brother of yours? I should have known he'd end up running for senator—or even president. He was like that in high school too." Fuller reached into his suit jacket and handed her a business card. "Listen, tell Brad to give me a call, okay? I tried to get a hold of him last week. Left a couple of messages, but I guess he's such a big shot now, he won't return my calls."

"Well, you know, Brad's really busy. He—"

"Hey, I'm just giving you shit," Fuller interrupted. "But seriously, tell him to call me. Okay? The number's there on the card."

Bridget didn't ask him why he wanted to get in touch with Brad. Ever since junior high school, people had used Bridget to get to her popular brother—in one way or another. Along with people giving her messages to pass on to Brad, there were the ones—both guys and girls—who pretended to like her so they could get closer to Brad. She didn't exactly like it, but she'd been accustomed to it. She'd learned long ago not to care, and rarely questioned what people wanted from her brother.

"I'll pass this on to him," Bridget said, slipping Fuller's business card into her purse.

Past Fuller's left shoulder, she noticed the man with black

hair staring at her again. But as soon as her eyes met his, he looked away.

She touched Fuller's arm. "Behind you to your left—around two o'clock—there's a good-looking man with black hair. He's standing by the lamp with the Tiffany shade. Do you know him?"

Fuller casually looked over his shoulder. "The dude with the blue blazer?"

"Yes," Bridget whispered. "He keeps staring at me like he knows me."

"Huh, he looks vaguely familiar, but I'll be damned if I know who the hell he is."

Bridget caught the stranger stealing another glance her way. Maybe he was a reporter, or he recognized her from TV. Was he a friend of Olivia's?

Fuller glanced at his wristwatch. "Well, hey, I'm gonna split. I need to get back to work." He kissed Bridget on the cheek. "Listen, I mean it, tell Brad to call me. I really want to talk with him. Okay?"

She nodded. "Sure thing, Fuller. Good to see you again."

He patted her arm, then headed for the door.

Bridget turned toward the dark-haired stranger again. But he wasn't there. She glanced around the room. She didn't see him at all. It was as if he'd vanished.

Yet, somehow, Bridget still felt his eyes on her.

CHAPTER 4

"I can't believe you went to her wake," Brad said. "You know how much I didn't want you attending that thing."

"Are you sending me to bed without any supper?" Bridget asked wryly.

Brad was barbecuing steaks on the grill in the backyard. Bridget stood over the picnic table, fixing skewers of cut vegetables. It was starting to get dark—and chilly—earlier now, so Bridget was wearing a sweater.

Brad and his wife Janice's house was a big, four-bedroom, beige brick monstrosity built in the early nineties. The backyard was surprisingly small. A couple of Japanese maple trees and a spruce interrupted the well-manicured green carpet of a lawn. On one end stood a swing set and monkey bars for Brad and Janice's daughter, Emma. Brad had also installed a small court area with a stand and a basketball hoop. He, David, and Eric had just played a round of HORSE before he started grilling the steaks.

Janice was in the kitchen, and the boys were now in the den, watching a new DVD on the big-screen TV with their grandfather. It was one of Bradley Senior's favorite movies, and their birthday present to him, *The Magnificent Seven.*

Bridget had picked it out and written the card for the boys to sign: *To Our Magnificent 77-year-old Grandfather . . .* The windows to the den were open, and Bridget could hear Elmer Bernstein's familiar theme music stirring.

She set the vegetable skewers beside the steaks on the grill.

"So—are you going to call Fuller or what?" she asked her brother.

"I'm going to 'what,' " Brad grunted, watching his steaks. He turned one over with his tongs. "I have no desire to get back in touch with Fuller Sterns—or anyone from that group."

Bridget shrugged. "Well, he seemed pretty adamant about wanting you to call. He mentioned it twice."

"I don't care if he repeated it like a broken record, I'm not calling him." Brad sighed, then flipped over another steak. "Did you talk to anyone else at this thing?"

"Just Mrs. Rankin." Bridget winced a bit. "Actually, I noticed one guy who kept looking at me. I don't know who he was. He might have been a reporter or a friend of Olivia's. He seemed to recognize me."

"Swell," Brad grumbled. "Jesus, Brigg, I asked you as a favor not to go. I don't understand why it was so necessary for you to attend this thing."

"For the exact same reason you were so determined *not* to go," she replied. "I want to put that chapter of our lives behind me, Brad. I thought it might bring me some closure. You and I may not talk about what happened at Gorman's Creek, but that doesn't mean I—"

"Hey," he hissed. He gave a cautious glance at the kitchen window. "Keep it down."

Bridget shot a look toward the kitchen, where Brad's wife was mashing the potatoes. She turned to her brother. "You mean, Janice doesn't know?"

Brad shook his head. "And I don't see any reason why she should ever know." He frowned at her. "Don't tell me you spilled your guts to Gerry."

"Of course I did," she whispered. "I told him before we got married. He was going to be my husband, for God's sake. I didn't want to keep any secrets from him."

"Well, that's terrific," Brad grumbled. "Now Gerry has probably spilled everything to that bimbo he's shacked up with."

Bridget turned the vegetable skewers again. Her face felt hot as she stood near the grill. "I sincerely doubt it," she said. "Gerry would have nothing to gain by sharing it with Leslie. I told him fourteen years ago, and neither one of us has mentioned it since."

Maybe Gerry had forgotten about it. But she certainly hadn't. And she knew her brother thought about the incident at Gorman's Creek as much as she had in the last twenty years. But Brad refused to talk about it.

Even a couple of days ago, when they'd discussed Olivia's death and the memorial service, they'd spoken in an unacknowledged code, never referring to Gorman's Creek or what had happened there. But Olivia had been part of it—along with Fuller Sterns.

Bridget stared at her brother. He was clenching his jaw.

"More than anything right now," she said steadily, "you'd like me to shut up about Fuller, Olivia, and the whole damn mess, wouldn't you?"

With the barbecue fork, Brad took the steaks off the grill, then transferred them to a plate. "Yes," he whispered, not looking at her. "Yes, please."

Bridget watched him carry the plate of steaks into the kitchen.

"Oh, those look great," she heard Janice say.

"Are you Mommy's little helper with the potatoes?" Brad was asking his daughter. "Hey, guys!" he called to her sons. "There are a couple of root beers with your names on them in the refrigerator. Take an intermission. Dinner's on."

He was such a terrific uncle to her boys. Hell, Brad had rescued all of them. Only seven months ago, Bridget had thought her life was over.

She remembered how it had come as a total shock to her. If anyone would have asked at the time, she would have told them that she and Gerry had a good, solid marriage. When Gerry had made reservations for them at Giorgio's on a Tuesday night, Bridget had thought he was trying to put a little romance back in the marriage.

Things between them had become somewhat routine— but comfortable. With David and Eric in school, she'd taken a part-time job teaching Spanish at a girls' private academy. She loved teaching. A lot of the girls regarded her as a smart, older-sister type, and they often went to her for advice. Bridget liked to think that she made a difference in a few young lives. The job wasn't overwhelming at all, only twenty hours a week. Gerry, on the other hand, was a workaholic. She'd become accustomed to him frequently staying late at the office and traveling so much. Gerry was getting a spare tire around his middle, and she was plucking her gray hairs. But they were still an attractive couple, and the sex was good—whenever they had time for it.

For their night at Giorgio's, Bridget wore a sexy red off-the-shoulder dress Gerry liked. And Gerry looked dapper in his gray Armani suit.

He broke the news to her over the appetizers: "I'm sorry. I can't keep this up. I—I don't want to be married anymore."

It took Bridget a few moments to realize he was serious.

"I've told you about Leslie, the paralegal at work," he continued. "But I didn't tell you that she and her boyfriend broke up months ago. She and I found out that we had a lot in common. I realized you and I have been—just *coasting* for the last couple of years. I sort of stopped *feeling*. But Leslie brought the *feelings* back in me. We didn't mean for anything to happen—"

"Stop," Bridget whispered. She grabbed her purse and abruptly pulled away from the table, spilling her glass of wine. She ran to the ladies' room and ducked into one of the stalls. Bridget thought she was going to vomit, but she fought it.

She lowered the toilet seat lid and sat down. She couldn't

stop trembling. Then, all of a sudden, Bridget fell on her knees, lifted the lid, and threw up.

She couldn't believe he'd sprung this news on her at Giorgio's. He must have figured she wouldn't make a scene. They'd just ordered their entrees, for God's sake. She was destroyed. Did he really expect her to sit there and calmly eat dinner with him?

Bridget went directly from the ladies' room to the parking lot and climbed into Gerry's merlot-colored Mercedes. He loved that damn car. Bridget rarely drove it, but had the extra set of keys in her purse just the same. For a few moments, she thought about driving herself off a cliff in it. If not for her sons, she might have.

Instead, she drove home, carefully parked the merlot Mercedes in the driveway, then used her key to leave a long, deep, solitary scratch-mark from the driver's door to the front bumper. It felt good—for a moment. Then she just felt silly and stupid.

She told David and Eric their father was called away on a business meeting. Good thing too, because Gerry never came home that night.

Bridget didn't want to be one of those scorned wives who constantly complained to her kids about what a shit their father was. She kept thinking about the scratch-mark she'd left on Gerry's Mercedes, and told herself not to act impulsively, because she could cause some irreparable damage.

Gerry telephoned her the next day—from his office. They set up a time to sit down together with the boys and break the news to them. "Well, what exactly are you going to tell them?" Bridget asked pointedly. "I should warn you, if you start talking about your 'feeling' issues—or lack thereof—I may throw up again. I mean, what is it you want, Gerry? A trial separation, some time alone, or—"

"It's like I told you last night," he interrupted. "I don't want to be married anymore. I think we should get a divorce."

When he said those words, it was like a sudden kick in

her stomach. Bridget couldn't get her breath, and all the while, she thought about how stupid she was. She'd let him sucker punch her twice—with the same line. *He doesn't want to be married anymore.*

That was exactly how he worded it to David and Eric in the living room three nights later.

To Bridget's amazement—and Gerry's utter humiliation—the boys didn't seem too disturbed by the announcement that their dad was moving out. David and Eric were accustomed to his being away quite often. Their uncle Brad was more like a father to them than Gerry was. Twelve-year-old David's main concerns were staying on at the same school, keeping his room in this house, and remaining close to his friends.

Gerry assured his sons that their routines wouldn't be changed at all. In fact, he'd probably see *more* of them than before.

This, of course, was a total lie.

Bridget and the boys didn't see more of Gerry. In fact, they hardly saw him at all. But Bridget was constantly in touch with Gerry's attorney—the best at his firm. Gerry and his lawyer had brilliantly seen to it that he paid only the bare minimum requirements of child support and alimony. Bridget's attorney suspected that for the past few weeks, Gerry had been secretly transferring a sizable portion of savings into Leslie's bank account. And now, Bridget couldn't touch it. This was just the start of a long, messy, bitter divorce.

Bridget got the house, her lovely gray cedar shaker with the white trim—and the lovely mortgage. Her oldest son was traumatized by the mere prospect of moving. And because David was upset about it, Eric became upset too. But they couldn't afford to stay on there. Hell, Bridget wondered how she could even pay her attorney fees.

She went to the principal of the private girls' school where she taught, and asked to be hired full-time. She loved the work and figured there was no harm in asking for a salary increase as well. She hadn't figured on being told that they had to lay her off next year due to budget cuts.

So—Bridget started the summer applying for unemployment, talking to a real estate agent about selling the house, enduring a double dose of resentment from her sons for even *thinking* of such a thing, and developing a sudden backache, which her doctor said was due to stress.

That was when Brad said he needed her help. At the time, he was trailing significantly behind Jim Foley at the polls. Brad was ambitious and driven—with a genuine desire to help the poor and middle class. It didn't hurt that he was young and very handsome. Some members of the press likened him to Robert Kennedy. Of course, none of those press members were associated with the two local TV stations or the major newspaper Jim Foley had in his pocket.

On a Thursday in early July, Brad was scheduled to speak at an outdoor rally. They expected about five thousand people to attend—a high number of them Spanish-speaking. Oregon's Latino community had more than doubled in the last two years, and a majority of them were in lower income brackets. These were Brad's voters. He needed his sister to translate for him at the rally.

Brad's wife, Janice, had lent her a very elegant, lightweight Donna Karan suit for the rally. The creamy yellow color complemented Bridget's auburn hair. She'd worn the suit before—at a dinner for Gerry's firm—and she'd gotten raves for it.

But at the last minute, Bridget changed into a pink oxford blouse and khaki skirt that she'd worn her last day of teaching. Instead of wearing Janice's white gold and sapphire broach on the lapel of the Donna Karan jacket, Bridget put a CORRIGAN FOR OREGON button on her shirt, and she rolled up her sleeves.

"*That's* what you're wearing?" Brad asked, when she climbed into the back of his limo with him. He'd had his driver swing by and pick her up for the rally. "What happened to Janice's yellow outfit?"

Brad was dressed in a dark blue Brooks Brothers suit, a gorgeous, muted blue and black tie, and a crisp white shirt.

Her brother was an impeccable dresser. He looked very handsome with his early summer tan and his thick brown hair slicked back.

Bridget shrugged. "Well, I figured, this is a rally—not tea at Buckingham Palace. It's informal. These are 'regular folks.' I need these people to like me and relate to me—so they'll listen to me."

"Huh, why not just wear an old T-shirt and cutoffs?" he said sarcastically. "Jesus. . . ."

Bridget was about to tell him to go to hell. But she swallowed hard and turned toward the window. Her brother was asking for her help, and she'd let him down. "I can go back and change," she started to say.

"Forget it," he grumbled. "We're running late as it is."

Then the car phone rang, and Brad got online with someone from his campaign. Bridget didn't talk to him until they pulled into a VIP parking area behind some Winnebagos and trailers. Once he was off the phone, she started pointing to people walking toward the grounds. "See her? Cutoffs and a T-shirt . . . another one in a T-shirt . . . another T-shirt. It's hot out there. Do you see *one* woman in a dress or suit? Do you see *one* man in a tie?"

Brad glared at her, then sighed and loosened his tie. "You're right. I'm a horse's ass."

Ten minutes later, when Brad Corrigan took the stage, he wasn't wearing a tie or a suit coat, and his sleeves were rolled up.

While Bridget translated in Spanish for him, she spoke passionately and often prefaced Brad's remarks by saying: "My brother wants you to know . . ." or "My brother is concerned about . . ."

It made all the difference in the world. From years of teaching, Bridget knew how to work a crowd, and her Spanish was excellent. Each time Brad paused after saying something, he got a polite spattering of applause; but Bridget's translation of the same comments drew enthusiastic cheers, whistling, and clapping. The crowd obviously loved her.

The TV stations and newspapers not controlled by Jim Foley reported that Brad Corrigan had unveiled a new secret weapon in his campaign: his twin sister. Bridget started making more and more appearances with him, advising him, and editing his speeches for him. Soon, she was on the campaign payroll, earning twice as much as she'd made teaching.

By late August, Brad was neck and neck with Jim Foley at the polls. And Janice Corrigan was pregnant. Ordinarily, that might have helped win votes. It certainly wouldn't have hurt them if Brad's beautiful, blond, pregnant wife was at his side throughout the campaign. But Janice had endured a difficult pregnancy with their only child, four-year-old Emma, so the doctor had ordered her to rest. No active campaigning for Janice.

Bridget had become Janice's stand-in for dozens of dinners, fund-raisers, and personal appearances. And she was amazingly good at it.

The irony and strangeness of the situation didn't escape her. She'd become sort of a surrogate wife for her twin brother, and he'd become something of a substitute dad to her sons.

"C'mon, guys, turn off the movie," she heard Brad saying over *The Magnificent Seven* theme music.

Bridget remained outside the house—by the warmth of the grill. She listened to them in the kitchen. She heard her younger son, Eric, excitedly telling his uncle about part of the movie: ". . . and he threw the knife faster than the other guy could draw his gun, and it stuck him right in the chest. You shoulda' seen it, Uncle Brad."

"I've seen it—about a dozen times, sport. Hey, let's go find out what Grandpa wants to drink. C'mon, pardner. Later on, you're gonna help me with the cake, aren't you? Seventy-seven candles. We'll need the fire department here. . . ."

A terrible sadness swept over Bridget as she listened to them. Her brother sounded so happy, yet she knew he carried around the same pain and anguish that she did. He'd carried it around for twenty years. Like her, he'd been haunted by a crime they'd committed back in high school. Even with all the good he intended to do for people, it wouldn't wash away that sin. That stain wouldn't go away.

Bridget took a deep breath and wiped her eyes. She carefully picked the vegetable skewers off the grill and stacked them on a plate. Then she put on a smile and carried the plate inside.

"They should have done a survey on this back in the fifties," Bradley Corrigan Sr. said. He sat—slightly hunched over—at the head of the table. He erratically cut into his steak as he talked. He was still a handsome man—with his lean build, blue eyes, and a head of wavy white hair. "Back in fifty-five, if someone sideswiped a car late at night with no one around, I'll bet you seven out of ten people would stop and leave a note or call the cops or take some kind of responsibility for their actions. But nowadays . . ." Bridget and Brad's father dropped his fork to raise his hand and point a finger. He stabbed at the air. "Nowadays, you can bet your hindquarters that only three out of ten would even bother to stop. People have no accountability nowadays. If they can get away with it, they figure they didn't do anything wrong. They rationalize, and say the other guy's insurance will pay for everything. Or maybe they just consider it a 'close call,' because no one was around to see what they did. Everyone's morals have gone down the porcelain convenience. You can get away with murder and still consider yourself a good person—so long as you don't get caught. People just don't give a damn about personal integrity anymore. It's like they have a made-to-order filter for their consciences."

"Jesus, Pop," Brad said, dabbing his mouth with a napkin. "Who put a coin in you?"

"Dad, I don't know if that's necessarily true," Bridget said. She sat near the other end of the table. "I think what you're saying applies more to politicians than regular people—"

"Well, I for one totally agree with you, Dad," Janice piped in. She got up from the table and took her plate. Brad's pretty, blond wife was only in her first trimester, but she wore an oversized blouse that made her appear more pregnant than she was. "I think that's the kind of thing you should use in some of your speeches, Brad."

Bridget helped Janice clear off the table. Then they prepared the birthday cake, settling for two rows of seven candles. Bridget imagined her father having a stroke as he tried to blow out seventy-seven candles.

In fact, she'd noticed that he looked rather frail tonight. Maybe he was showing signs of stress from the campaign. He'd made only a few personal appearances, but he took each new poll result, every commercial for Foley, and every little upset so seriously. It had long been his dream to see his only son become a senator.

He'd been such a powerful force in their lives. Their mother had been kind of a cold fish. So their dad was the one Bridget and Brad used to run to for encouragement or whenever they were in trouble. He was the one who always forgave them when they screwed up. And he never hesitated to kiss them or give them a hardy hug.

Their father had taught them to chase after their dreams. He instilled in them—especially Brad—a fierce sense of competition. Brad became an outstanding athlete, and Mr. Corrigan rarely missed one of his games when he was in town. If he seemed more wrapped up in Brad's every move than in Bridget's, she didn't really mind. There was less pressure for perfection in Brad's shadow. Her father's expectations weren't as high for her. But Bridget never for one minute thought her dad loved her any less than he loved Brad.

Their father was a very handsome and robust man. He'd started out with nothing, and become a millionaire by his thirtieth birthday. One of his investments was ownership of a lumber and recycling mill outside McLaren. He often traveled to New York to meet with investors—and to Washington, D.C., to talk with environmental lobbyists. Whenever he came back home from these long trips, young Bridget and Brad painted and posted WELCOME HOME signs on the lawn of their large Tudor home. Sometimes, they even posted the placards up and down the block.

Now the posters and banners in their neighborhood were for his son, the candidate for senator.

As Janice brought the cake into the dining room, Bridget looked at her father, seated at the end of the table, his grandsons on either side of him. He had that slightly startled expression elderly people sometimes get. Bridget noticed some food stains down the front of his gray cardigan, and remembered he used to be an impeccable dresser. In lieu of a napkin, he had a dish towel in his lap. It too was food-stained.

She thought about how she used to throw her arms around him and hold him tightly. If she tried that now, he'd probably break.

Still, he managed to blow out all his candles. He cracked some jokes with her boys, fawned over Emma, and flirted with his pregnant daughter-in-law. He ate his birthday cake, then nodded off five minutes after returning to *The Magnificent Seven*.

Bridget shared the sofa with her dad and David, who sat between them. With his eyes closed, his face drawn and slightly ashen, her father almost looked dead. David kept nudging him every few minutes. "Hey, Grandpa, you're missing it," he'd say. Then Bradley Senior would awaken with that feeble, startled look, and he'd nod off again within moments.

"David, let him sleep, for God's sake," Janice hissed from her easy chair across from them—after David's third attempt to wake up his grandfather. "You're annoying *everyone*. Just be quiet and watch the movie."

If Brad were in the room, he might have said something or made a joke to cut the tension. But he was taking a phone call in his study. Bridget said nothing. She didn't see any point in getting into a snit over it.

Wordlessly, she slid her arm around David. She felt his body stiffen up; then after a moment, he shifted away and leaned forward, elbows on his knees. He didn't say a word for the rest of the movie.

"Honey, Aunt Janice didn't mean to snap at you tonight," she told him later, when they got home. She was carrying Eric, who had fallen asleep in the car. He was eight years old, and not a light load.

David hung up his jacket on one of the hooks on the wall by the kitchen door. "It's okay," he muttered.

With his thick brown hair, wiry build, and brooding good looks, he was a dead ringer for his uncle at that age. But there was still a slight, sweet gawkiness to him that reminded Bridget of herself at thirteen.

"Well, it's not okay," Bridget replied. "I think your feelings were hurt. But you know, when women get pregnant, their hormones go out of whack, and they can be awfully snippy—for no apparent reason. That's what happened tonight with Aunt Janice."

"It's no big deal, Mom," he mumbled.

Bridget struggled to take off Eric's jacket while still holding him. David helped her. "You know Aunt Janice loves you," she whispered.

David just rolled his eyes, then nodded. He hung up his brother's jacket.

"God, he's getting too big for this." Bridget shifted Eric in her arms.

"I'll take him, Mom," David said. He tapped his brother. "C'mon, butt-face, I'm giving you a piggyback ride."

"Piggyback," Eric murmured, his eyes still closed. But he put his arms around David's shoulders.

"You shouldn't call your brother a butt-face," Bridget said, hovering behind David as he carried Eric up the stairs.

"Ah, he likes it. Don't you, butt-face?"

"Yeah, it's cool," Eric murmured sleepily.

You know, sometimes Aunt Janice is a real butt-face,

Bridget wanted to say. Yet she let the subject drop while David helped her get Eric ready for bed.

At first glance, Janice was pretty and poised, the dream wife of any man running for public office. But Brad's wife had an icy, snippy side that Bridget knew too well. There had always been a bit of tension between Janice and her. Bridget chalked it up to jealousy. Janice once told her: "You'll always be closer to Brad than any woman or man. Hell, you shared the womb with him."

Perhaps to compensate for her perceived second-place status with her husband, Janice was disgustingly solicitous of Bradley Senior. She kept saying that she would be giving him a grandson, because *it felt like a boy*, and some idiot astrologer had told her she would have a son. *Bradley Robert Corrigan III.* Bridget's dad lapped it up. Besides, he and Janice had something in common: a relentless determination to see Brad become senator. As far back as Brad and Janice's engagement, Bridget remembered another family barbecue—at her father's place. While Brad had been outside, grilling the dinner, his fiancée and father had sat in the kitchen, discussing his future life in politics. They'd had his career all mapped out for him.

Bridget had turned from the stove to stare at them. "Will you both still love Brad if he ends up managing a video store or something like that?"

Janice had given her a cool, condescending smile. "But he doesn't want to manage a video store *or something like that*. He's going into politics."

And go into politics he did.

Bridget had never expected to be drafted into the political arena too. But now she was in it up to her neck. She had a long day ahead tomorrow—including some campaign-related breakfast at eight in the morning.

As she got ready for bed, Bridget paused in front of her dressing table mirror. A snapshot she kept lodged in the bottom corner of the mirror frame was missing. It was a recent photo of Eric and her. Bridget hadn't gotten around to buying a frame for it yet.

She glanced behind the dresser to see if the photo had fallen back there. No sign of it. Yet the snapshot had been on the mirror this morning. She figured Eric or David must have come in and taken it for some reason.

Bridget continued to undress. She had no idea that neither one of her sons had set foot inside her bedroom all day.

Bridget lifted her head from the pillow and squinted at the clock on her nightstand. Two-fifteen. She needed to look halfway presentable for her breakfast gig in less than five hours. And it was a photo op, no less. *Crap.*

Bridget had been tossing and turning since midnight. So many things were going through her head. Maybe Brad had been right. Maybe she shouldn't have gone to Olivia Rankin's wake. Perhaps that flat tire had been a sign telling her to turn back. If she hadn't attended the wake, maybe she would have fallen asleep tonight without a hitch.

It had been strange, seeing Fuller Sterns after two decades. She wondered why he was suddenly so anxious to speak with Brad. Did it have anything to do with Olivia's death? Or Gorman's Creek? Brad actually *talking* about Gorman's Creek tonight—though briefly—was something of an unsettling milestone, a reminder that their tired old sin couldn't be completely erased.

Bridget threw back the covers and climbed out of bed. "Damn it," she muttered, putting on her robe.

She wandered down the stairs to the kitchen, where she poured herself some brandy. For a while, after Gerry left, she'd come to rely a bit too much on the stuff at bedtime. But she'd kicked the habit, figuring if something happened to one of the boys late at night, she would have been useless. It had been months since she'd dipped into the brandy supply.

However, at the moment, Bridget figured one shot wouldn't kill her.

She took her brandy into the TV room, a large, wood-paneled area off the dining room. There was a brick fire-place, and on the wall, framed family photographs. Bridget had taken down only one photo—of Gerry and her on their wedding day. All the other photos of Gerry remained.

At one end of the room was a huge picture window that looked out to the backyard. Bridget caught her reflection in the darkened glass as she stepped into the room, carrying the drink in her hand. With her robe on and her hair a mess, she looked like a lush.

Suddenly, she realized there was another image in the darkened glass. It seemed to move and merge with her own. They looked like dancing ghosts. Bridget stopped dead. There was a man in her backyard—staring at her.

Gasping, she dropped her glass of brandy. It shattered on the floor—by her bare feet.

Bridget ran across the room and flicked on the light switch. A couple of floodlights went on in the backyard. Trying to catch her breath, she anxiously studied the illuminated yard, but didn't see anything. The man had disappeared. Or maybe he was just hiding.

She hurried into the kitchen and reached for the phone on the wall. That was when she saw someone dart past the window in the kitchen door.

"Oh my God," she whispered. She was thinking about her sons, asleep upstairs. Bridget grabbed the phone and dialed 9-1-1.

Her heart was racing, and the two ring tones seemed to last forever until the operator answered: "Police Emergency."

"Yes," Bridget said, steadily. "My name is Bridget Corrigan, and I'm at 812 Greenwood Lane. I need to report a prowler."

"Is he in the house now?" the operator asked.

"No—at least, I don't think so," she replied. It suddenly occurred to her, what if there were two of them?

"Let me confirm that address," the operator said. "Eight-twelve Greenwood?"

"Yes, that's correct," she replied into the phone. Bridget felt something warm and wet under her bare feet. She looked down at the tiled floor, and realized she was standing in blood. She'd cut her feet on the glass.

"Hold the line, ma'am," the operator said.

"I can't," she argued. "This—this phone isn't cordless. My two sons are asleep upstairs. I need to go up there and make sure they're okay—"

"We have a patrol car in your vicinity," the operator said. "Can you describe the prowler?"

"Um, about six feet tall, medium build." Bridget glanced toward the kitchen windows, then down the hall at the front door. "I didn't see his face, but he was wearing a leather jacket. Listen, I can't stay on the line. I have to check on my sons—"

"I need you to hold on, ma'am," the operator said. "Just—please, hold on. . . ."

CHAPTER 5

"Did this guy try to get into the house?" Brad asked in a hushed voice.

Bridget sipped her coffee. "No," she muttered. "No sign of an attempted break-in. Whoever he was, the police couldn't find him."

Brad frowned. He shared the sofa with her. He wore a T-shirt and slacks, but no shoes or socks. He'd been changing his clothes when Bridget started telling him why she'd only gotten two and a half hours of sleep the previous night.

They were scheduled to speak at a party luncheon at the Portland Red Lion. The hotel had given them a hospitality room—with two extra phone lines and a fax machine, all of which never stopped ringing. The hotel had also provided them with a tray full of sweet rolls and an ice chest crammed with soft drinks. A large coffeemaker was brewing, and the aroma filled the large burgundy-and-beige room. The TV set was on at a low volume. Two members from Brad's staff—along with Bridget's assistant, Shelley—kept running in and out of the suite.

Bridget rubbed her forehead. "Anyway, the police didn't leave until about four this morning—"

"Brad, sorry to interrupt," said his assistant, Claudio, a

handsome black man with a buzz cut and glasses. He handed Brad a fax. "Here are the figures you wanted on the state unemployment rate for August."

"Thanks, Claudio," he said. He glanced over at his other assistant, Chad, and Bridget's assistant, Shelley. They were both on the phone. He turned back to Claudio and gave him a tight smile. "Listen, could you guys give us a couple of minutes alone?"

While Shelley, Chad, and Claudio stepped out of the suite, Brad stole a sip of Bridget's coffee. "You should have called me, Brigg," he said. "Are the boys okay?"

"Oh, they're okay. They slept through the worst part." She shrugged. "I didn't call, because I didn't want to wake you up. No reason the *two* of us should feel like the walking dead today." Bridget sipped her coffee. "At first, the police seemed to think I was crazy. But I'd turned on the sprinkler before we left for your place last night, and switched it off when we got home. So the ground was still damp. They found footprints all around the house. Looked like the same set, they said."

"But the cops found absolutely no sign of an attempted break-in?"

"No, thank God."

He leaned closer to her. "Well, I think this might've been one of those things that come with the territory when you're on TV. These snoops with nothing better to do have been sneaking up to our house for months now. Last week, we caught two women—and their *kids*—trying to peek into our front window. There were five of them, for God's sake. And—get this—when Janice asked them to leave, they got all huffy with her."

Bridget frowned. "But do you have them coming up to your windows in the middle of the night?"

"Twenty-four-seven." Brad sighed. "Still, I hate the idea of you being there alone with the boys while these idiots are coming up to the house. I'll see if I can get the precinct to put an extra patrol on your block. Are all your locks working? Is the house alarm system up to snuff?"

Bridget nodded. "The cop was asking me the same thing this morning. I had it all upgraded when Gerry left, remember? Anyway, the police were very thorough and . . ."

Bridget trailed off as she caught a glimpse of Brad on the muted TV set. It wasn't a flattering photo of him—and bad pictures of her brother were hard to find. "Hey," she said, grabbing the remote. She turned up the volume. "God, you look horrible. Is this a new Foley commercial?"

"Oh Lord," Brad grumbled. "Yes. I've already seen it."

"Brad Corrigan wants to take away your fishing rights," the announcer was saying. Brad's photo dissolved over a scenic shot of a boy fishing with his father. The circle-with-a-slash symbol was slapped over this idyllic image—punctuated with a somber drumbeat on the sound track. "Corrigan's proposing a bill to outlaw fishing in certain sections of the Willamette River, and that's just not right."

"And that's just bullshit," Brad growled at the TV.

A crestfallen blond-haired boy with a fishing reel over his shoulder turned toward the TV viewer with tears in his eyes. "I won't be able to go fishing with my dad anymore," he lamented.

"C'mon, Brad, why won't you let that kid go fishing with his daddy?" Bridget asked.

"Because the fish in some areas of the Willamette are poisonous, due to all the pollution," Brad said. "I don't want to outlaw *fishing*. I'm trying to get the river cleaned up so people won't die when they eat the fish they catch there. But Foley—"

"I know all that," Bridget cut in, waving away his explanation. "You're preaching to the choir. Quiet, I want to hear this."

Another shot of Brad—looking angry—came on the TV screen. "Brad Corrigan is also proposing a bill that could shut down dozens of plants and factories in Oregon. Thousands could lose their jobs." The slash-through-a-circle symbol struck an image of a factory with smokestacks against a gorgeous sunset. Then they showed footage—probably from the forties—of smiling factory workers filing into a building. The same slashed circle lingered over their happy faces.

"Don't tell me," Bridget said to her brother, eyes on the TV. "This has something to do with you wanting stricter standards for employee safety and for industrial waste disposal. Am I right?"

"Bingo."

"I don't want my daddy to lose his job," said another tearful child—a little black girl with her hair in braids.

Jim Foley appeared on the screen. Wearing khakis and a denim shirt with an open collar, he sat on the edge of a desk. The ruggedly handsome, gray-haired sixty-year-old looked very relaxed and accessible. A regular Joe. He had a warm smile and appeared to be a tall man—in very fit condition.

Actually, Jim Foley was a multimillionaire, the former CEO of a huge intermobile corporation. He stood five eight in his stocking feet, and beneath those casual clothes he wore a man's girdle. But few people knew that. Jim Foley had paid one of the West Coast's most prominent marketing firms to advise him on sharpening his TV-image—to compete with the handsome and charismatic Brad Corrigan. Thanks to marketing experts, makeup, and crafty camera angles, Jim Foley came across as tall, stoic, friendly, a little bit gruff and a little bit sexy—a cross between Harrison Ford and Tom Brokaw.

"There are over a hundred reasons why you shouldn't vote for Brad Corrigan," Jim Foley said to his TV viewers. "But I'll give you just one reason—your children."

"Who wrote this?" Bridget said. "It's terrible."

"Wait a minute," Brad said. "Here comes the trademark sign-off."

Foley smiled into the camera. "I'm your friend, Jim Foley, and I want to be your senator."

"With friends like that, who needs enemas?" Bridget remarked, shaking her head. "I can't believe you let him get away with all those distortions and lies." She clicked off the TV.

Brad took a folded white button-down shirt out of a plastic bag from the cleaners. "I've discussed it with Jay, and he says I'm better off not acknowledging Foley's bullshit."

Jay Corby was Brad's campaign manager, a slick huckster and a bit of a control freak. Bridget often thought Jay underestimated their opponent. Foley had interests in two local TV stations, a radio station, and a major newspaper in Portland. The distortions he broadcast weren't being contradicted by anyone.

Bridget sighed. "If you don't challenge him on these lies, the thousands and thousands of people who see him on TV will take what he says as gospel. I can't believe you're letting him get away with this."

"Oh, this is nothing," Brad replied. "I think Foley's just warming up for now. The campaign hasn't even *started* to get dirty yet."

Bridget said nothing. She watched her brother retreat into the bathroom.

Brad had gained his popularity from endless personal appearances and word of mouth. The independent weeklies in Portland, Salem, and Eugene were behind him. It was only from the small press—along with several Internet sites—that people got the truth about Jim Foley.

While Foley was CEO of Mobilink, Inc., the company got away with violating dozens of ecological, safety, and antidiscrimination laws. Before caring so much about "our children" in his current ad campaign, Foley consistently rejected proposals for employee pregnancy-leave benefits and on-site day care facilities.

Under Foley's regime, the company avoided paying any state or federal income taxes for four years—thanks to some crafty manipulations of their books. Certainly helping matters were Foley's close ties to the current incumbent senator, Glen Eberhart. Foley had been a huge contributor in Eberhart's last campaign. Foley had also used his media connections to downplay a scandal last year when Eberhart's drug habit was uncovered. The senator, who suffered from chronic back pain and obesity, had been buying addictive painkillers and diet pills from a black market supplier for months. Foley's press and Eberhart's followers quickly forgave the senator for violations that would have landed some poor, anonymous *nonwhite* man in jail for at least two years.

Wisely, Eberhart chose not to run for office again—and he endorsed the candidacy of his buddy, Jim Foley.

Before retiring from Mobilink, Foley persuaded the board of directors to give him a nine-million-dollar bonus—in addition to his secured pension of $2.5 million a year. Then one of the last things Foley did as CEO was manipulate the books again and reward his board of directors with bonuses—while taking away the retirement and unemployment benefits for three-quarters of Mobilink's workforce.

There was a story about Jim Foley speaking informally to a group of clerks during a tour at one of Mobilink's terminals. It was after lunch, and Foley must have been drunk or very full of himself at the time. In his short talk, Foley compared himself to a proud Indian warrior chief, who would keep riding and riding his horse until it was dead, and then he would eat it. "You people are like my horse," he concluded.

One clerk, a nine-year employee named Mike Nuegent, ceremoniously spat in his face. Two more quit on the spot. Mike Nuegent mysteriously died later when he plunged from the roof of an abandoned apartment building. The police ruled his death as a suicide.

Brad hired a couple of investigators to determine if the "horse" story was true. No one would go on record. Witnesses had been threatened or harassed. Even Mike Nuegent's widow wouldn't be quoted. Off the record, Mrs. Nuegent was certain her husband had been murdered.

It was clear to those who bothered to think beyond what the Foley media machine told them: Jim Foley would treat the people of Oregon as he had the bulk of Mobilink's work-force. Only big business, special interest groups, and *Jim Foley* would benefit from his winning the Senate race. The rest of the state would be screwed.

Foley based his campaign on bringing back "family values" and lowering taxes. He even claimed that God wanted him to be Oregon's senator. He'd given up drinking and found Jesus at just about the time he'd gone into politics. His campaign speeches were often sprinkled with references to God, morality, or the power of prayer.

Divorced during his Jim Beam days—and now remarried to a Good Christian Woman nineteen years younger than himself—Foley couldn't reproach the "family values" of his opponent. Brad Corrigan was married to the same woman for eleven years with one child and another on the way. Moreover, Brad was devoted to his father—and to his twin sister and two nephews. He was untouchable.

Almost.

Brad said he was pretty certain Foley had investigators digging into his and Bridget's past for something that might discredit them. Bridget had known as much when she went to Olivia Rankin's funeral service yesterday. Yet she'd gone anyway—against Brad's objections. Now she wished she hadn't. Could that dark-haired stranger who had been staring at her during the service be working for Foley? And if he was a Foley spy, how much did he already know?

The phone rang, but Bridget didn't make a move to answer it.

Brad stepped out of the bathroom. He was straightening his tie. "Maybe you should bring the troops back in," he suggested.

"In a minute," Bridget said soberly. She waited until the phone stopped ringing.

Eyes narrowed, Brad stared at her.

"I want to apologize," she said finally.

He let out a little laugh. "What for?"

"You didn't want me going to Olivia's wake, but I went

anyway. I was being selfish, trying to—exorcise my own demons from twenty years ago, and what happened at Gorman's Creek."

He glanced toward the door, then gave her a wary look. "Brigg—"

"Maybe I was rebelling against you," she continued. "I'm not totally sure of my motives now. But I know, it was a bad decision to go. I hate the idea that one of Foley's spies could easily have followed me there."

Brad sat down next to her on the sofa. "Please, shut up," he whispered in her ear. He patted her arm. "We didn't check this room for bugs. And we've been scheduled to speak here for a month now. That's plenty of time for Foley's tribe to have set up some kind of *eavesdropping* party. Get my drift?"

Frowning, Bridget glanced around the hotel room, then finally stared down at the burgundy carpet. "Oh God, Brad," she murmured. "I wasn't even thinking about that. I'm so sorry."

He put his arm around her. "No, I should be apologizing to you. I keep thinking about what happened to you last night. If you weren't helping me with this campaign, you wouldn't have these creeps coming up to your house, peeking in your windows at three o'clock in the morning."

Brad hugged her, and she held on to him for a moment. Then the phone rang again.

Sighing, Brad got to his feet, went to the door, and called in Shelley, Chad, and Claudio from the hotel's hallway. Within a few moments, the hospitality suite was under siege again—with phones ringing, people talking over one another, and hotel staff and campaign volunteers going in and out. Then someone let in a few reporters and photographers. "It's hold-on-to-your-purse time," Bridget whispered to her assistant. That was their private, not-so-funny joke, referring to a similar scene weeks ago in another crowded hospitality room, where Shelley's purse had been stolen.

"No kidding," Shelley replied, under her breath. She had her purse tucked under her arm. "It's like the ship-cabin scene in that Marx Brothers movie. All that's missing is the maid and the manicurist."

Camera flashes were going off. Someone thrust a microphone in front of Bridget's face. "When you were just kids together, Bridget, did you ever think your brother would grow up to run for senator?" a perky blond reporter asked.

"Oh, as far back as grade school, I figured he was headed for great things," Bridget responded, putting on a smile. "Brad was always very popular—with everyone. He was president of this and that, captain of practically every team. Even our teachers adored him. I lost track of how many times my teachers asked me, 'Why can't you be more like your brother?' If Brad wasn't such a wonderful guy, I'd have hated him."

"And Brad was there for you when your husband left you, wasn't he?" the reporter asked.

"Um, yes, he was." Bridget managed to keep smiling. She didn't want to go into details with this reporter about her marriage failing. Bridget nervously glanced around the crowded room, and hoped the woman would change her line of questioning.

Among all the people, she saw a man standing against the wall—near the doorway. He stared back at her. It was the black-haired man from Olivia's wake.

The reporter was asking her another question, but Bridget didn't hear it. She'd locked eyes with the man across the room. He smiled a bit—that too-familiar smile. A chill rushed through Bridget.

Had he been the one peeking into her window at three o'clock this morning? Did he have the same little smile on his handsome face when he was watching her then?

"Bridget?" the reporter was saying. "Ms. Corrigan?"

A camera flash went off, blinding her for a moment.

She rubbed her eyes, then glanced toward the door again. He wasn't there.

"Are you all right, Ms. Corrigan?" the reporter asked.

Bridget got to her feet, then anxiously glanced around the

room. At least twenty people filled the hospitality suite. The black-haired man was no longer among them.

By the darkroom's faint red light, he studied the sheet of Kodak paper in the pan full of solution. The image of Bridget Corrigan's face slowly emerged on the white paper.

He'd taken several candid shots of her in the hospitality room, and a dozen more during the luncheon speech. She'd translated Brad Corrigan's words for the Spanish-speaking attendees, which made up less than 5 percent of this audience. In fact, most of the Spanish-speaking people in the room were on the wait staff. He'd found himself a nice shadowy spot, an alcove near the waiter's bus station, where he watched the proceedings. He used his telephoto lens to get a good look at her.

Bridget Corrigan seemed uncharacteristically edgy and distracted. She even flubbed a Spanish phrase while translating. He knew, because a couple of busboys laughed quietly, and he asked them why. She kept looking out at the audience, her eyes shifting from side to side.

He had a feeling she was searching for him in the crowd—and the notion amused him.

He took the photograph out of the developing solution, then set it beside the others he'd taken of her today. They were damn good—even better than the snapshot he'd stolen from her dresser mirror while she and her brats were at her brother's house last night.

Sweeping aside a heavy black curtain that blocked out any accidental light, he opened the darkroom door. He'd left the television on in his studio. They were broadcasting the local news. On his way to the refrigerator, he passed by several of his paintings, his postmortem portraits.

On TV, they were talking about the election: ". . . the latest polls show Corrigan now in a slim lead with forty-three percent of the votes. But Foley isn't far behind with forty-one percent, and sixteen percent still undecided. Brad Corrigan spoke at a party luncheon today at the downtown Portland Red Lion . . ."

The artist loaded a glass with ice, then poured himself some scotch.

"KJLU's Paula Dwoskin spoke with the candidate's sister . . ."

He heard her voice and turned toward the TV.

"Oh, I think my brother will win," Bridget Corrigan was telling a reporter at the luncheon.

The artist raised his glass of scotch as if to toast her.

"I have to think my brother will win," she continued. "Otherwise, I'm very afraid about what's going to happen to this state—to our middle- and lower-income families, our environment, the education of our children, our safety, and our basic human rights."

She looked amazingly pretty—considering she'd been up all night. He touched his TV screen, caressing her cheek.

"When I think about what's at stake," Bridget Corrigan said, "I get very scared."

At five o'clock on a Thursday morning in early October, twenty-nine-year-old Loreen Demme's alarm clock went off. She wasn't accustomed to getting up this early in the morning. But she had promised a friend that she would pick her up at the airport. The flight was due in at 6:10. Loreen crawled out of bed, then put some water on to boil for coffee. She headed back toward the bathroom to brush her teeth, but as she passed by the bedroom, she saw the unmade bed. She was cold and half-asleep, and couldn't resist just another minute under the covers. One more minute. She wouldn't nod off. And even if she did, the kettle whistle would wake her up. Wouldn't it?

It didn't.

Loreen Demme and two of her neighbors died in the fire. Eleven other neighbors were rushed to the hospital with burns and smoke inhalation. Loreen lived on the second floor of a five-story apartment building. The fire destroyed over half of the El Teresa Apartments' seventy units, occupied mostly by low-income families. One hundred and ninety-three people were suddenly homeless. Many of them were among Portland's Spanish-speaking populace.

"Brad wants you to drop everything this afternoon," Shelley said, leaning against Bridget's office doorway.

The Corrigan-for-Oregon headquarters used to be a Honda dealership. Two dozen desks for volunteers occupied what was once the automobile showroom. Bridget had one of eight salesmen's offices—with windows looking out to the main room. CORRIGAN FOR OREGON posters and banners were on display everywhere—especially in the huge parking lot outside.

Bridget's office had an old, beat-up metal desk, a brand-new computer, a framed photo of David and Eric, a philo-dendron plant, and room for little else. But she loved it.

She looked up from her computer. "What's going on?"

"You know that apartment building fire this morning?" Shelley asked, folding her arms.

Bridget nodded. "The El Teresa."

"The gym-cafeteria at Sacred Heart Grade School has been set up as a temporary shelter. They have clothes, cots, blankets, and food for about a hundred people, a lot of them families. A lot of them do not *hable inglés*—if I'm saying that right. They need volunteers to fix sandwiches and serve up dinner this afternoon. Your brother wants to volunteer you."

"Well, bless his heart," Bridget said dryly.

"Brad said he or Janice could pick up the boys from school. Meanwhile, he's trying to round up a camera crew to go over to Sacred Heart . . ." Shelley trailed off as one of the volunteers, Wes Linderman, passed behind her.

Wes was in his early twenties with straight, pale blond hair and the tall, broad-shouldered build of a basketball player. He was also a spy for Jim Foley. Bridget and Shelley had figured him out early in the campaign, but after consulting with Brad, they'd decided to keep him on. They didn't want any more "volunteers" like Wes infiltrating campaign headquarters. They fed Wes just enough correct ~~harmless~~ information to keep Foley happy. And every once in a while, when they wanted to totally mislead Foley about a strategy, Shelley, Bridget, or someone else in-the-know would share with Wes some misinformation in the form of gossip. It worked like a charm. Bridget didn't like having a Foley spy always wandering around just outside her little office, but at least they had control over the situation.

"Hi, Wes!" Shelley called over her shoulder.

"Oh, hi," he said, lumbering toward his desk.

"My, what big ears you have," Shelley muttered under her breath. She stepped inside Bridget's office and shut the door behind her. "Anyway, Jay Corby is trying to round up a camera crew to go over to Sacred Heart School with you."

Bridget rolled her eyes. "If Jay wants to send a crew over there to film me volunteering, I guess I can live with that. But I won't *arrive* there with them, that's just plain obnoxious. I know where Sacred Heart School is. Do me a favor and find out what time they want the volunteers to come by."

"Will do," Shelley said. She glanced out Bridget's office window—toward the main room full of volunteers. "Hmmm, our pal Wes is at his desk and on the phone already. I'll bet he's telling someone at Foley HQ where you'll be this afternoon. It's a good photo op. Foley would be a fool to pass it up. Huh. You might just get to serve up some supper with Jim Foley."

A short, copper-haired dynamo of a woman named Roseann was in charge of fixing dinner for the one hundred recently homeless people. The fifty-something woman made Bridget feel welcome, then immediately got her an apron and put her to work, fixing ham and cheese sandwiches in Sacred Heart School's kitchen. When the camera crew arrived, Roseann didn't make a fuss. Bridget insisted Roseann and the other volunteers pose with her in still shots. Later, Bridget also insisted the crew put their cameras in the coach's office, and help set up tables in the gym.

They broke out the cameras again while Bridget served up the chicken noodle soup. The line for food wound around the gym. It slowed down at her spot, because some people recognized her and wanted to talk. She was also one of the few volunteers who spoke Spanish, so people often stopped to ask her about the food—or about the bathroom and sleeping facilities. Bridget did her best to answer their questions and keep the line moving.

She had served about forty people when Jim Foley showed up—with his own camera crew and a couple of guys in business suits. Foley was dressed in a denim shirt and jeans. He had his sleeves rolled up, ready to go to work. Apparently, Wes had gotten through to Foley headquarters.

Roseann was too busy trying to get the dinner served. So Foley stood around for about fifteen minutes—getting in the way while he discussed something with the two business-types. At one point, they flagged down Roseann and consulted with her.

She broke away and made a beeline to Bridget. "Can you believe it?" she muttered. "They want us to move the entire food table to the other end of the gym, because the lighting is better over there. He'll *photograph* better over there."

"What did you say?" Bridget whispered, filling another soup bowl.

"I told the son of a bitch to shut up, put on an apron, and hand out sandwiches—or get the hell out of here."

Five minutes later, Jim Foley, wearing a chef's apron, was standing beside Bridget, giving out ham sandwiches. It was Bridget's first meeting with Foley. She said hello.

He gave her a brief, patronizing smile. "Well, well, we have someone from the Corrigan camp here too," he said. "Isn't that nice? Brad sent his sister over. Good to see you."

Then he tried his charm on the newly homeless. "Hi, Jim Foley, nice to see you," he'd say, giving some tired, despondent person a wrapped sandwich. Or: "Hi, Jim Foley, God bless," and, "Hi, Jim Foley, I'm saying a prayer for you tonight." All the while, flashbulbs popped and video cameras rolled.

Bridget was in no position to criticize. She had a camera crew too. But they hadn't pushed people aside to get a good shot. And they'd been there for two and a half hours.

"Hi, Jim Foley. Here you go. God bless."

The plump young Latino woman with the pretty face had two toddlers at her side. She didn't accept the sandwich he offered. She looked so exhausted, and scared. *"¿Tiene mostaza este sandwich?"* she asked timidly.

"Take it," he said, shaking the wrapped sandwich at her. "It's good. Don't hold up the line. C'mon."

"¿Tiene mostaza este sandwich? Mi hijo es alergico a la mostaza," she said.

Visibly frustrated, Foley turned to Bridget.

She gave him a little smile and spoke to the woman in Spanish. The young mother broke into a grin and nodded. She took three sandwiches from Foley, said, *"Gracias mucho,"* then put them on her children's trays and her own. She moved down the line, and she and Bridget spoke to each other in Spanish. All the while, Foley stared at them with his lip curled.

"What was *her* problem?" he asked indignantly—once the young mother and her children moved on.

"She just asked if there was mustard on the sandwich, because her son is allergic to mustard," Bridget said. "I told her there wasn't."

"What about just now when she was talking with you?"

"Oh, she was thanking me. She also asked if I was with you. And I told her no, I wasn't with you at all."

She thought Foley might laugh. Instead, he gave her an icy, imperious look and went back to handing out sandwiches. "Hi, Jim Foley, God bless you . . ."

There were still people in line when Foley glanced at his wristwatch, consulted his men in the business suits, then took off his apron. He tracked down Roseann and had his cameramen get it on film as he shook her hand. Then he hugged her. Roseann looked a bit startled.

Foley's cameramen started filing out, but he and his two friends in the business suits turned and approached Bridget. "I just wanted to say, it was nice to meet you, Bridget," he said, shaking her hand.

"You too, Jim," she said, relieved he didn't hug her too. "It was fun working alongside you."

He stepped up closer to her. "I can see why they're saying you're Brad's secret weapon. Talking in Spanish to so many of these good people. Very impressive. You're a smart girl, aren't you? And pretty. You're almost too good to be true—just like your brother."

"Thank you, Jim." She reached for the soup ladle again. "Well, I'm holding up the line. I should get back to work now."

He winked and touched her arm. "You put on a good show, Bridget. Still, everyone has their secrets, right? I know you and old Brad have a skeleton or two in the Corrigan closet. I can almost hear those bones rattling. Can't you?"

Bridget gently pulled her arm away. She stared at him, eyes narrowed. "What exactly does that mean, Jim?"

"Oh, you know what it means, Bridget," he said, giving her another wink. "You don't need a translation."

Then he turned and walked away.

CHAPTER 6

"Oh, say, can you see, by the dawn's early light . . ."

When she was a kid, Bridget used to think the lyrics were "Jose, can you see . . ." As she sang, she tried to enunciate correctly so it didn't sound funny. She was standing on a pitcher's mound, belting out the National Anthem—God help her. And God help anyone who was listening.

The bleachers at Harrison High School's playfield were nearly filled. About two hundred people had come to see the Little League baseball game. Most of them—including Bridget—hadn't expected a media event. They hadn't known there would be a camera crew and a local TV personality, Skip Stevens of *Northwest Tonight*, on hand. Skip was in his late forties, with chiseled features and a helmet of perfectly coiffed blond hair. Everyone was surprised when he trotted up to the pitcher's mound with a microphone in his hand. He introduced himself, put in a plug for his show, then—much to Bridget's chagrin—announced that while this was a bipartisan event, "We have a partisan celebrity in the crowd today, Bridget Corrigan, whose twin brother just happens to be running for senator of Oregon."

Bridget put on a smile, got up from her seat in the third row of bleachers, and waved to the crowd. Had she known there would be a camera crew, photographers, and this jack-ass from Channel 6 asking her to take a bow, she'd have put on some makeup this morning. At least her hair was clean—though a bit windswept. And she looked presentable in her Irish knit sweater and jeans. She didn't feel totally humili-ated.

She got a polite smattering of applause from the crowd, along with a couple of wolf whistles. Then Skip Stevens chimed in again: "We've seen her on TV, translating her brother's speeches into Spanish. But did you also know that Bridget has a terrific singing voice? With us today, we have Tony DeCavalero, one of the finest, most-famous accordion players in the country. . . ."

A short, dark, chubby man, wearing kelly-green pants and a yellow windbreaker, lumbered up from the dugout to the pitcher's mound. He carried his accordion—and played a few bars of "Take Me Out to the Ball Game."

"You can hear Tony Tuesday through Sunday nights at Mama Pageno's Italian Café in downtown Portland," Skip said. "We're in for a special treat today, folks, because Tony will open our game with a rendition of our National Anthem on his accordion. Now, if we could only persuade Bridget Corrigan to provide the vocals. Bridget?"

Wide-eyed, Bridget shook her head. She was so stunned and embarrassed. And Lord, she didn't even want to think about the utter humiliation her son, David, probably felt at that moment.

Skip had stirred up the crowd, and they cheered her on. Reluctantly, Bridget got to her feet, then made her way from the bleachers to the pitcher's mound, where Skip Stevens and the short man with the accordion were waiting for her.

Bridget figured Brad—or his campaign manager—had something to do with this surprise. They'd turned David's Little League game into a photo opportunity/media event. Though she had a smile plastered across her face, Bridget was seething inside. She and Brad were attending a fund-raiser later tonight, and once she got him alone, she was really going to let her brother have it. What nerve. It was bad enough they were doing this to her, but did they have to screw around with David's baseball game? Brad could have at least warned her. Did he have any idea how difficult the National Anthem was to sing? All those high notes in the "rockets' red glare" section. And with a creaky accordion backing her up, no less.

Bridget hadn't sung in public since a drunken karaoke night session at a party with Gerry six years ago. Before that, she'd sung a number from *Candide* at a college recital her senior year. Still, despite an uncertain start, she managed to hit the right notes and belt out a fairly rousing version of the National Anthem.

The applause was enthusiastic. And much to her relief, David, standing by the dugout with his teammates, was also clapping. He didn't seem too embarrassed. Bridget got a peck on the cheek from Skip Stevens, and shook hands with the accordion player. She blew a kiss to the crowd, then retreated to her spot in the bleachers' third row.

The video crew recorded her every move, and she noticed several people who had brought cameras to their sons' game were now taking *her* picture. It was beyond her why they wanted a snapshot of someone they barely knew—just because she was on the local news from time to time. Still, several people in the bleachers were moving down the aisle with their cameras for a good shot of her. Bridget put on her sunglasses, then did her best to pretend they weren't there. By the end of the first inning, she'd managed to pretty much block everything out—even the camera crew—and concentrate on David's game.

"Bridget?" said someone standing to her right.

She ignored him and held up her index finger. "Just a minute, okay?" she said, eyes on home plate. "My son's at bat."

She moved forward—to the edge of the seat. David played second base, and wasn't up to his usual game today. A grounder had gotten past him and he'd thrown a wild ball at the first baseman, botching a double play. Bridget figured the cameras—along with that surprise pregame show—had unnerved him. Now he stood at the plate—having tallied up a ball and two strikes. From the crowd, he got a chorus of cheers and jeers—more than any other batter so far. Bridget kept thinking it was unfair David should have all this extra pressure heaped on him. She blamed herself—and Brad.

Biting her lip, she watched the pitcher wind up and let loose a fastball. David swung the bat and *connected*—thank God. Bridget got to her feet and studied the ball as it soared toward left field—directly into the glove of the opposing team's left fielder. *Damn it.*

Frowning, she plopped back down on the bench.

"Bridget?"

She sighed and glanced up. Fuller Sterns was staring back at her. The once loudmouth party boy appeared nervous and tentative. He wore a baseball hat to protect his nearly bald head from the overcast sun. "Fuller?" she said. "What are you doing here?"

He hesitated. "Could I sit down?"

Bridget slid over on the bleacher bench and made a spot for him. She was suddenly aware again of the people watching her—and the camera crew. "Um, do you have a son playing in the game?"

He quickly shook his head. "No, I knew you'd be here, so—"

"*You knew* I'd be here?" she asked, eyes narrowed at him. "What? Are you following me or something?"

"No, I read that you'd be here. It was on Brad's campaign Web site."

She blinked. "What?"

He nodded. "They listed your schedule today, all your public appearances. They said you'd be singing the National Anthem at your son's Little League game. Harrison High School playfield at one this afternoon, the Web site said."

Bridget couldn't believe it. People logging on to Brad's Web site knew before she did that she'd be singing the

National Anthem at David's Little League game. Was her every move being broadcast? No wonder she had strangers peeking into her house at three in the morning. It took a minute for her to swallow her anger and address her old high school classmate. "So, um, why are you here, Fuller?"

"Well, I haven't had much luck getting a hold of your brother. I mean, I've left several messages for him the last couple of days. Have you spoken with Brad? It's like I told you at Olivia's wake, I really need to talk with him."

Bridget sighed. "Fuller, I'm sorry—"

"I don't mean to ambush you like this," he continued. "But it's easier to connect with you. You're more accessible than your brother. I guess you've always been—even back in high school. Anyway, if you could please ask him to call me—"

"I've already tried, Fuller," she gently interrupted. "Brad just doesn't want to talk to you. I'm sorry. Maybe if you told me what you want to see him about . . ."

"It has to do with Gorman's Creek," he whispered.

Bridget stared at him for a moment, then shook her head. "If that's the case, Brad definitely won't talk with you. Remember the agreement we all made twenty years ago—not to talk about it—ever? He still feels that way."

"Listen, Bridget," Fuller said, frowning. "I lied the other day when I said I hadn't seen Olivia since graduation. A couple of weeks ago, she called me—out of the blue. Suddenly, after twenty years, she wanted to get together. She practically insisted on it. I'll be honest, I know how Brad feels about seeing me, because I felt the same way about getting together with Olivia. But she talked me into meeting her for coffee."

"What did she want?" Bridget asked.

"I found out at the Starbucks. She needed money. She said she had 'information to sell,' stuff that would rip the lid off what went on at Gorman's Creek."

Bridget glanced around to see if they were being watched. No one was taking her photograph, and the camera crew seemed focused on the game for the moment. She turned to

Fuller, and her voice dropped to a whisper. "You mean Olivia was blackmailing you?"

"That's what I thought," he replied. "But it didn't make any sense. After all, Olivia was just as culpable as any of us for what happened. If she went public with it, she'd be ratting on herself. But Olivia insisted this wasn't blackmail, and she used that phrase again: she had 'information to sell.' Apparently, she found out something that happened at Gorman's Creek, something none of us are aware of. Olivia said several people would be happy to pay for this information."

Bridget wasn't sure what that meant. Did Olivia intend to divulge their secret to Brad's political opponent? Jim Foley would have paid dearly for what she could tell him.

"Olivia and I met last Sunday," Fuller continued. "She drove down from Seattle. I promised her, when the banks opened the next day, I'd wire her five thousand bucks. And that's just what I did."

"You gave her five thousand dollars? Why, for God's sake?"

"I needed to find out what she knew," Fuller said. "For a measly five grand, wouldn't you have done the same thing? Maybe she discovered something about where the body went. I mean, hell, I don't know about you, Bridget, but a week doesn't go by without me thinking at least once or twice about what happened back there at Gorman's Creek. And I get sick to my stomach every time."

Bridget understood exactly what he meant.

"Anyway, after I wired her the money, she called to set up another meeting. She didn't want to give out this information on the phone, she said. So she promised to drive down from Seattle and meet me the next day. We were supposed to get together on Tuesday. That was the morning she shot herself."

"Did you talk to the police or anybody about this?" Bridget asked.

He let out a laugh. "What, are you crazy? You think I'd

tell the police about a meeting I was supposed to have with a dead woman—so we could discuss a crime we committed twenty years ago?"

An older man on the bench in front of them glanced over his shoulder in their direction.

Bridget nudged Fuller. "Keep it down," she whispered. "People are watching. Huh, in fact, *one person in particular* is making it his avocation to watch me."

"You mean, like a stalker?" he asked.

"Brad said it comes with the territory when you're in the newspapers and on TV," Bridget explained under her breath. "But I think this guy might be more, I don't know, *sinister*."

Fuller just gave her a slightly dubious stare.

"You think I'm paranoid, don't you?" she said, restlessly shifting on the bleacher bench. "Well, this guy was peeking into my windows at three o'clock the other morning. The police confirmed it. There were footprints all around the house. And I don't mind telling you, it really scared me."

"I believe you, Bridget," he murmured. His face looked ashen. "I believe you, because the same goddamn thing has been happening to me."

From the far corner in the top row of the bleachers, he watched them—like God.

Fuller Sterns and Bridget Corrigan were deep in conversation. He'd been carefully observing them for the last ten minutes—ever since Fuller sat down beside the senatorial candidate's sister. Though he only saw their faces in a quarter profile, every once in a while Bridget Corrigan would glance around or peek over her shoulder. She had a nervous, guarded look on her pretty face. What with the camera crew and all these spectators, maybe she didn't want to be seen talking to Fuller Sterns. Or perhaps what Fuller was telling her made her uncomfortable.

He watched a plump woman waddle down the aisle and unwittingly interrupt Bridget's and Fuller's furtive discussion. She seemed to babble on, while Bridget smiled and nodded patiently at her. The woman pointed to someone else in the bleachers, then seemed to indicate to Bridget that she would be right back.

As soon as the lady left, Bridget whispered something in Fuller's ear. He got to his feet, worked his way down the aisle, then ducked behind the bleachers.

From his spot on the top row, he turned and watched Fuller head toward a side entrance to the high school.

Bridget Corrigan remained seated. The woman descended on her again—this time with another, older, chubby lady. The two of them seemed to talk Bridget's ear off. After a few minutes, Bridget got up and shook both their hands, then moved down the aisle and disappeared behind the bleachers.

With a grin, he turned and watched her hurry into the high school. She ducked into the same side door Fuller Sterns had used just a few minutes before.

"Fuller?"

Bridget stood alone in the darkened, windowless corridor. Behind her was a display case full of dusty old trophies and team photos of young men who were now either middle-aged or dead. In front of her were the restrooms—along with the janitor's closet.

The janitor's son was on David's Little League team. Whenever a game was held at the high school playfield, the janitor always unlocked the side door so people could use the bathrooms. But he never switched on the hallway overhead lights. Bridget wasn't sure if it was to save electricity or discourage people from abusing his open restroom policy. Whatever the janitor's reason, it made for a gloomy, slightly creepy corridor. The brightly lit washroom always seemed so stark and white in contrast to that dim hallway.

Bridget squinted as she opened the door to the boys' room. "Fuller? Are you in here?" she called, not stepping over the threshold. There was no response, only a steady hum from one of the pipes.

She backed away from the doorway. Had Fuller misunderstood when she asked him to meet her here?

No other door to the high school was open. This was the only way in. The three classrooms and the door at the end of this corridor were usually locked. Where else could he be?

She couldn't have been more than five minutes with that woman and her mother. She wondered if Fuller had grown impatient waiting. Or had something happened to him?

"Fuller?" she called again. This time, her voice echoed in the vacant, dark hallway.

She opened the door to the girls' room and stepped inside. Her footsteps clicked on the tiled floor. "Fuller? You in here?" she whispered. Nothing. It was a long shot anyway.

With a sigh, Bridget turned and started out of the restroom. She saw a shadow sweep across the wall—then a man, reflected in the glass of the display case.

She gasped, then swiveled toward the exit. Fuller was staring at her. For a moment, his face was in the shadows.

"Bridget?"

A hand over her heart, she caught her breath. "God, you scared the hell out of me."

"I figured you'd be a while with those gasbags, so I stepped out for a smoke," he explained. She could smell the cigarette smoke on him as he stepped toward her. He grinned, the same goofy smile he had back in high school. "A little jumpy, huh? Well, so am I. Like I started to tell you, I have a stalker too. And I'm not on TV, I don't have any relatives running for senator, and I'm not pretty. So I'll be damned if I know why this creep is following me around or what he wants."

"He isn't, by any chance, the same dark-haired man I pointed out to you at Olivia's wake, is he?"

Leaning against the display case, Fuller shrugged. "I'm not sure. I still haven't gotten a good look at the guy. But he's pulled the same shit on me that he's pulling on you, peeking inside my house at night. I called the police on him, but he was gone by the time they showed up. Cops didn't do much, useless as tits on a bull. Of course, I couldn't give them much to go on with a description of this joker. All I could see was that he was a tall white guy, wearing one of those leather, y'know, bomber jackets."

"The man outside my house the night before last was wearing a bomber jacket," Bridget murmured.

"Yeah? Well, when this clown shows up again, I'll be ready for him. I own a gun, a forty-five."

"When did you first notice this stalker?"

"Hmmm, I thought I saw someone in my backyard the day I was supposed to meet Olivia the second time."

"You mean, the day after she shot herself?" Bridget asked.

He nodded glumly. "Yeah. So—does Brad have someone tailing his ass? I mean, you and I both have this guy shadowing us, maybe he's watching Brad too. Maybe he's stalking each one of us who were at Gorman's Creek. We should track down Cheryl Blume and see if someone's following her around too."

"Is that why you're trying to get in touch with Brad—to find out whether or not someone's been following him?" Bridget frowned at her old high school classmate. "Gorman's Creek was over twenty years ago. Why in the world would someone be stalking us *now*—after all this time?"

He shrugged. "I don't know. Maybe Olivia stirred something up. Olivia told me she had 'information to sell.' Well, Brad's loaded. Olivia knew that. She didn't say anything to me. But I'm wondering if she gave the same sales pitch to Brad. Maybe she told him what she didn't have a chance to tell me. I forked over five grand for that scoop. I'd like to know what she found out. Maybe it'll mean I could sleep a little better at night."

"Believe me," Bridget said, "if Olivia met with Brad—or if he had any new information about Gorman's Creek—my brother would have told me."

"Are you sure?" Fuller pressed. "Could you ask him for me, please?"

She sighed. "All right. I'll ask him tonight and get back to you, Fuller."

Suddenly, the side door opened, and a shaft of light poured into the hall. A woman, holding her toddler daughter by the hand, paused in the doorway. She stared at them.

Bridget quickly grabbed Fuller's hand and shook it. "Thanks so much. I'll be sure to tell my brother that he has your support. It was nice meeting you."

"Thanks," Fuller said, a bit bewildered.

The woman and her daughter moved toward the restroom. Bridget smiled as she passed them in the corridor. She headed for the exit.

"That's the lady who sang before Andy's baseball game," she heard the woman tell her daughter. "She's on TV . . ."

In a daze, Bridget walked through the playfield's parking lot, toward her car. Fuller had left shortly after they'd spoken inside the high school. She'd returned to her spot in the bleachers and watched David redeem himself by hitting a double in the second-to-last inning. Still, his team had lost—their final game of the season. But that didn't stop them from going out for a post-game pizza. A teammate's mother had promised to drive David home by six o'clock.

Eric was at an all-day birthday party. He was getting a ride home at five-thirty.

So Bridget was alone with her thoughts. She wondered what kind of "new information" Olivia had discovered about Gorman's Creek. Or was that merely some sort of fake bait Olivia had used to lure Fuller, so she could snag five thousand dollars? Well, the bait certainly worked. Bridget suddenly thought of something that made her stop in her tracks. Why would someone who had just made herself an easy five thousand bucks decide to put a bullet in her head? And how many women committed suicide that way? Bridget wasn't up on all the statistics, but she was pretty certain women usually chose pills, razor blades, or carbon monoxide over bullets when it came to taking their own lives.

All at once, a blast from a car horn made her jump. Bridget realized someone was honking at her to get out of the way. She gave a contrite wave and stepped aside.

Retreating to her car, Bridget opened the door and climbed behind the steering wheel. She sat there for a few moments, still lost in thought.

If Olivia had really uncovered something new about what had happened at Gorman's Creek, apparently she'd decided to take the secret to her grave. Who was to say why she'd killed herself? Bridget hadn't known Olivia very well—not even back in high school. Olivia was more Brad's friend than hers. The same was true of the others at Gorman's Creek. Technically, they were Brad's friends.

As she sat alone in the parked car, Bridget thought of all the high school games she'd attended by herself, both home and away games, in which her twin brother was the star player. Football in the fall, and basketball, winter through spring. It wasn't so much that Bridget was full of school spirit. She simply needed to be there for her brother. Most of the time, she drove to the games by herself, sat by herself, and went home by herself. Brad usually had some post-game party with his teammates and their girlfriends. He often asked Bridget to come along, but they weren't her crowd. They merely tolerated her presence from time to time because she was Brad Corrigan's twin sister. And Bridget, in turn, put up with them because they were her brother's friends. Actually, most of them were jerks.

"They're not jerks," declared Kim, her best friend in high school. "They're assholes—in jerks' clothing."

Kim Li was a chain-smoking, slightly punk Korean-American with a high IQ and a low tolerance for just about everyone else at McLaren High. Try as she did, Bridget could never persuade Kim to attend a game with her. Kim was one of the first girls at the school to put a primary-color streak in her hair—and a lot of people were shocked. Olivia Rankin once asked Bridget why she hung out with such a "freak."

"I'm just lucky, I guess," was Bridget's response.

Bridget always felt like an outsider herself, someone on the fringe. She got the impression from her high school peers that her sole worth was wrapped up in being the twin sister of the most popular guy in their class. A lot of girls tried to be Bridget's friend, but most of the time, they were merely using her to get close to Brad. She always saw through them early on.

But Kim didn't care that much about Brad. "Oh, your brother's gorgeous," she said. "He's an incredible athlete, very sweet, and smart as a whip. Plus he has a cute ass—as much as that grosses you out to hear it. Still, c'mon, you must know that just about every girl in the class—and a few guys too—would love to jump his bones. Maybe that's why I'm not getting a case of thigh-sweats over him. The last thing in the world I want is to be like everyone else."

Kim was the only true friend Bridget had. And in some ways, Bridget felt better off than her brother. Despite having a throng of friends, admirers, and hangers-on, Brad wasn't particularly close to any of them. The most popular guy in class didn't have a best friend. He used his popularity in a way that some people become generous with money. For biology class, he chose the class "fag," Ricky Savan, as his lab partner, and people stopped picking on Ricky. At school functions, Brad often paired off with one of his far-less-popular classmates for an entire afternoon.

One of those chosen was Zachary Matthias, a likable "geek," whose baby fat, bad glasses, and chipped, gray front tooth didn't deter Kim from having a little crush on him. Brad had "bonded" with Zachary during a school picnic.

"I asked Zachary what your brother and he talked about," Kim later told Bridget as the two girls walked home from school. "Zach said Brad basically 'interviewed' him the whole time. He said he was really flattered to have the attention of the 'coolest guy in class' for three hours, but he walked away from that picnic not knowing Brad Corrigan one bit better than before."

"What's that supposed to mean?" Bridget asked indignantly.

Kim shrugged. "I don't know. Maybe he's implying that your brother is more interested in finding out what makes people tick than actually connecting with them. Why else would Brad choose to spend so much time in private pow-wows with so many class nobodies and also-rans? And I'm proud to count myself among them, I might add."

Bridget figured Brad was merely trying to make them feel good about themselves. The most popular guy in class was showing interest in those people who didn't quite fit in, and it must have made them feel special. Brad was a champion for the underdog, always trying to do good.

"I think Zach would rather have spent three hours at the picnic with *you*," Kim said. "He's got such a crush on you, Bridget. It's so unfair, because you don't even like him that much, and I think he's really cute."

"Oh, I like him okay," Bridget muttered, hugging her schoolbooks to her chest. But Zach Matthias wasn't her type. Besides, she was in love with David Ahern. Blond-haired, blue-eyed, and brooding, he was a senior who hung around with Brad from time to time. Bridget got all tongue-tied and ditsy whenever he came over to the house. He wasn't part of the pack who had latched on to Brad. David and Brad usually went off by themselves whenever they got together—hiking, swimming, long drives to Portland or along the Columbia River. Bridget didn't know much about David, except that his mother had died when he was eleven. This, of course, endeared him to her even more. She pumped Brad about him. Typical of guys, Brad couldn't tell her much about his friend: "Well, he's just, y'know, a nice guy. Reads a lot, likes movies. He's really interested in astronomy. I don't know what else I can tell you."

"He's as gay as a maypole, and you're totally wasting your time," Kim maintained. She often spent her weekends with an aunt in Seattle, and had a lot of gay friends there. "I can read all the signs. He's cute, dresses nice, and I see the way he sometimes looks at your brother—though obviously, you and Brad don't see it. I highly recommend you get a crush on a guy who likes girls."

But Bridget didn't want to hear it. David barely knew she was alive, but she worshiped him. On a Friday morning in mid-October, when both their parents were out of town, Brad mentioned to Bridget that David Ahern was coming over to the house for pizza and a movie. And no, Brad didn't mind if she wanted to join them. The Corrigans had a VCR, and David wanted to rent *On the Waterfront*. Bridget was ecstatic. She spent the afternoon in the library looking up *On the Waterfront*, so she could make all these intelligent statements about the movie: "Did you know that this picture won eight Oscars? This was Eva Marie Saint's first movie. Did you know that it was shot in Hoboken, New Jersey? Have you ever been to New Jersey, David?"

She spent over an hour picking out just the right clothes for a "casual" look. Bridget rarely wore makeup, but she made an exception that night. It was while she was gingerly applying her mascara that she noticed a note to herself—taped to the bottom of her dressing table mirror: *Babysit— The Shieldses @ 8, Fri, 10/19.*

"Oh, crap!" she groaned. "No, no, no!"

Bridget tried calling Mrs. Shields to cancel, but the line was busy. She tried several times—right up until a quarter to eight. But she kept getting the damn busy signal. Bridget waited around as long as she could, but David didn't show up. She didn't even get to say hello to him and let him see how cute she looked.

Bridget walked the six blocks to the Shieldses' house, where she would be looking cute for nine-year-old Andy Shields. His toddler sister, Danielle, was probably already asleep. Danielle's bedtime was eight o'clock. So basically, Bridget's job would be keeping Andy entertained for the next few hours.

She hoped and prayed something would happen to get her out of babysitting for that little brat tonight.

Actually, she wasn't being fair to Andy. He was a cute, skinny kid with red hair and a goofy face. He wore these ugly madras shirts all the time. And he loved his green Converse All-Star high-tops. Bridget often teased him that he "dressed like a dork." Still, he was sweet and easy to get along with. He liked to draw and had given Bridget a pencil sketch he'd done of her. It was awful, but she'd kept it anyway. Tonight, they would probably watch TV and play Monopoly. He was big into Monopoly too. She would send him to bed at eleven.

Later, Mr. Shields would drive her home, and she would probably miss David again. Damn it. Why couldn't she get a break? Was it too much to hope that she'd get to the Shieldses' house and find nobody home?

Instead, as she turned down the block and approached the Shieldses' small brick Tudor, Bridget noticed all the lights were on inside. And outside, a police car was parked in their driveway.

The front door had been left open, and as Bridget came closer to the house, she could see Mr. and Mrs. Shields through the screen door—in the living room. Mrs. Shields, a thin woman with short, wavy red hair, was sitting on the sofa, quietly talking with a policeman. Mr. Shields paced back and forth while he spoke into a cordless phone. "Yes, well, thank you," he was saying—a bit loudly. "And please . . . please, call us if you hear anything. . . ."

Bridget always thought he was handsome in a bookish way—*bookish* because of his glasses. He was an accountant. He must not have changed his clothes since coming home from work. He wore a blue suit, and his tie was loosened.

"And listen," he said into the cordless phone, "if you can't get through to us, just leave a message with the police, okay? Thanks a lot."

Bridget hesitated before knocking on the side of the screen door. Spotting her, Mr. Shields suddenly stopped pacing. She nodded and gave a tentative little wave to him on the other side of the screen. "Hi, Mr. Shields," she said nervously. "It's me, Bridget. Is- -everything okay?"

Mrs. Shields and the cop stood up. Andy's father hurried to the door and flung it open. "Jesus, I'm sorry," he muttered. He reached into his pocket. "We should have called you, Bridget. Mrs. Shields and I aren't going out tonight. We won't need you, but thanks. You can go back home."

Bridget thought of David Ahern, and realized she was getting her wish. She started to smile a little. But then she saw the torment in Mr. Shields's eyes. He was holding out two five-dollar bills for her. His hand trembled. "Here, let me give you something for your trouble—"

"What happened?" she whispered. "Is Andy okay?"

"He's missing," Mr. Shields replied, his voice cracking. "He and two other boys in his class—the Gaines twins, Robbie and Richie—they wandered off during recess at school today, and no one has seen them since. I've been on the phone with just about everyone from his class. You haven't heard anything, have you?"

Bridget numbly shook her head. "No. I'm—so sorry."

"See if she can't sit with Danielle for a while," Mrs. Shields said, plopping back down on the couch.

"Would you mind, Bridget?" Mr. Shields asked. He held on to the screen door and moved aside to let her in. "Danielle won't go to sleep. I think she senses something wrong here. Could you read her a story and keep her occupied until she drifts off?"

"Of course," she murmured, heading for the stairs.

The phone rang, and Mr. Shields stopped to answer it. He waved her on. "Hello?" he said into the phone. "Yes, thanks for calling back. Andy was wearing a navy blue jacket with a zipper up the front, madras shirt, green sneakers . . ."

Bridget continued up the stairs by herself, passing through the darkened hallway to Danielle's room. The little girl's door was halfway open. Bridget slipped into the room, which had been decorated with a *Sesame Street* motif. There was wallpaper with *Sesame Street* characters on it, a Cookie Monster bedspread, and a five-foot, stuffed Big Bird standing in the corner. A lamp on the dresser had a heat-activated shade that rotated and cast moving shadows across the wall—colorful stars and birds. The three-year-old with curly red-hair lay quietly in her bed and stared at Bridget.

"Hi, Dani," she whispered, stepping closer to the bed. "Your mom and dad wanted me to read you a story, so I came all the way over from my house to do just that." She pulled a chair near the bed, then glanced at the books by the nightstand. "What did you want to hear, Dani?"

The little girl just stared at her with those big, innocent blue eyes. "Where's Andy?" she asked in a sleepy voice.

Shrugging, Bridget reached for a book. "I don't know where Andy is," she replied. "He's with some friends. He should be home soon. What do you think of this story? *Betty, the Bashful Bumblebee.* I don't know about you, but I'm sure interested. Should I read it?"

Bridget didn't even get halfway through the book before Danielle was nodding off. Lulling Andy's little sister to sleep was easier than she'd thought it would be. The hardest part was lying to her about Andy coming back. While she read aloud from the children's book, Bridget pretended not to hear Mrs. Shields crying downstairs. The sound drifted through the vent.

Bridget sat at Danielle Shields's bedside for a few more minutes, watching the colorful shadows sweep across the wall, and listening to adults talking down in the living room. Between the phone ringing and whispered conversations, Bridget only caught snippets:

". . . bringing in the state police," the cop said at one point.

"Andy has never run away before," according to Mrs. Shields. "Nancy Gaines said the same thing about Richie and Robbie. They're good kids."

Later, the phone rang again, and Bridget listened to the policeman mumbling for a few moments. Then she heard him tell Mr. and Mrs. Shields: "We have someone who says they saw three boys wandering down Briar Court around twelve-thirty this afternoon. That's a cul-de-sac. They were headed toward Gorman's Creek, the witness said. From the description she gave, it sounds like Andy and the Gaines twins."

Bridget waited another couple of minutes; then she tip-toed out of Danielle's room. From the darkened corridor, she peeked into Andy's room. His desk light was on. She stared at the neatly made bed and wondered if Andy would ever sleep in it again. On the wall, between a couple of *Indiana Jones* posters, were several of Andy's drawings. He'd told her that he wanted to be an artist when he grew up.

Bridget heard someone coming up the stairs, and she quickly stole out of Andy's bedroom. She met his father at the top of the stairs.

"Danielle's asleep now," she whispered. "Is there anything else I could do to help? I could fix you and Mrs. Shields something to eat—a couple of sandwiches—"

"No, thanks, Bridget," he said. "I don't think either one of us could eat right now. I'll drive you home."

"Oh, you don't have to bother. I can walk—"

"That's okay," he said with a pale smile. "I need to step out for a minute. And I'll feel better making sure you get home okay."

Mr. Shields said nothing as he drove the six blocks to Bridget's house. She was reluctant to break the silence. She hated the tiny, most-selfish part of her that was excited to spend some time with David Ahern after all. Then Bridget stole a glance at Mr. Shields at the wheel. He was in profile as he watched the road ahead. The streetlights moved across his face, and she saw a tear on his cheek.

He pulled into the driveway and stopped the car at the stone walkway that led to the front door.

"I'll say a prayer for Andy," Bridget whispered. "Though I—I'm sure he's okay, Mr. Shields."

Nodding, Mr. Shields took off his glasses, then wiped his eyes. "Thanks so much, Bridget," he said with a raspy, broken voice. "You take care now, sweetheart."

"G'night, Mr. Shields," she said. Bridget climbed out of the car and started up the walkway. But a strange sound made her stop in her tracks. It was a muffled wailing, like a wounded animal. Bridget turned and looked back at the car. Mr. Shields was slumped over the wheel, crying inconsolably. Those awful, painful sounds were coming from Andy's father.

Retreating up the walkway, Bridget unlocked the front door and slipped inside. She could hear the TV on in the den, and recognized Marlon Brando's voice. "Brigg, is that you?" Brad called.

"Yes, it's me," Bridget called back to him. She paused in the foyer for a moment. "But I'm going right out again."

She knew David Ahern was sitting there with her brother in the den. All she had to do was stick her head in and say hello. But she didn't deserve to see him. She didn't deserve to benefit in any way from what had happened to Andy Shields.

Grabbing a jacket from the front hall closet, she turned and stepped out the door again.

Bridget watched Mr. Shields's car back out of the driveway, then pull away down the road. She headed in the opposite direction—on foot. It was a chilly fall night. Dried, fallen leaves scattered along the sidewalk with the light wind. Many of the trees along the walkway were bare. Their branches hovered over her like spindly claws. Bridget hiked up the collar to her jacket. She hadn't noticed how cold—and creepy—it was on her way to the Shieldses' house earlier. But then she'd had David on her mind.

Now she was thinking about Andy Shields. She glanced at her wristwatch. Andy and the Gaines twins had been missing for nine hours now. If the boys didn't show up by tomorrow morning, everyone in town would be racking their brains to remember if they'd seen any strangers along Main

Street or by the grade school today. McLaren was the kind of small town where most everybody knew everybody else.

Bridget stopped at Briar Court, the dead-end street where Andy and the Gaines twins were last seen. Heading down the road, she spotted three police cars parked at the turn-around by the Fesslers' house—and the start of Gorman's Creek.

The Fesslers' place was a large, mountain-cabin-style house, all dark wood and stone with big windows and balconies jutting off practically every room. The entire back of the house was on stilts, so it hung over the wooded ravine. It might have been gorgeous once, but the Fesslers had let the place go. The house desperately needed a paint job—and someone to trim back all the foliage and trees that threatened to swallow it up.

The trail through Gorman's Creek started on the Fesslers' property—by their driveway. Anyone choosing to brave that crude pathway had to pass by the dark, neglected house. The Fessler family—like Gorman's Creek—was the subject of rumor among the townspeople. They said the Fesslers—and the deep, winding, wooded ravine behind their house—were cursed.

Mr. Fessler—or Loony Lon, as some called him—was a widower, and had been confined to a wheelchair for years. His daughter, Anastasia, was about fifty, very high-strung, and still lived at home. Apparently, she'd attempted suicide several times. The son, Lon Junior—or Sonny—was the town Boo Radley. He could be seen riding along the streets of McLaren on his old Schwinn bicycle, looking unkempt and unshaven, with his red hunting cap and an old merit badge from his Boy Scout days hanging from a string around his neck.

It seemed fitting that the Fesslers were the unofficial gate-keepers to Gorman's Creek. Bridget had heard the stories of murder, suicide, and madness. She figured most of them were made up, local legends and spooky tales to keep people off the Fesslers' private property—and away from Gorman's

Creek. But the legends also lured some people—mostly curious teenagers—to that forbidden path by the Fesslers' home.

At the end of the long, sometimes treacherous trail was a pond perfect for skinny-dipping or lovemaking. Olivia Rankin claimed it was an ideal spot for a "drunk and dunk" on a hot summer night. Olivia, Fuller Sterns, and others had enjoyed a few private, impromptu parties at that swimming hole—until one night when Anastasia Fessler called the police on them. The cops nabbed Olivia, Fuller, and two others while they were skinny-dipping in the Gorman's Creek pond. A couple of days later, a barbed-wire fence went up at the beginning of the pathway. But enterprising explorers could still find a way around that fence.

Bridget guessed that Andy Shields and the Gaines twins must have found a way. She stared at the thick, dark forest, illuminated in areas by beams of light that broke through the trees. It was an eerie, unsettling sight. The police were in there with flashlights, searching for the three missing boys.

Bridget glanced over at the Fesslers' house, and all the dark windows. Except for Sonny's sojourns on his bicycle, they didn't go out. Were they asleep already? Or perhaps Lon, Anastasia, and Sonny were in the back of the house, watching the strange light show in the forest.

She'd babysat for the Shieldses enough to know that Andy wouldn't have disappeared like that deliberately. He wasn't an adventurous kid. His idea of a terrific time was sitting at home and drawing. Bridget thought of Andy and his sweet, goofy smile. She thought about the picture he'd drawn for her, and she started to cry.

"Hi, young Corrigan girl," someone whispered.

Startled, she spun around and gaped at Sonny Fessler. She almost didn't recognize him without his hunting cap. His blondish gray hair looked greasy and unwashed. He wore a ratty old cardigan sweater, a graying T-shirt, and flared corduroys that hit him a couple of inches above the ankles. His milky blue eyes were guileless as he smiled at her.

"Oh, hi, Sonny," Bridget managed to say, a hand over her

heart. "You scared me." She wiped her eyes. Some people were afraid of Sonny, because he was so strange. Or they made fun of him. But Bridget always treated him like a normal person.

"Did you hear what happened?" he asked. "The police are looking for some boys who are lost. I found out about it on my police scanner. I listen to all the police reports. It's really interesting. Do you think those boys might be dead?"

She shook her head. "I don't know, Sonny. I hope not."

"The police might have to issue an all points bulletin so they can find a murderer," Sonny whispered. He crept toward the pathway's edge. "Look at all the footprints the police left. I've read up on the FBI. You know, they can trace a criminal by his footprints at the scene of a crime. But it's too late now. The policemen wrecked it. Now they really won't be able to tell if anyone bad was here."

Bridget gazed out at the darkened ravine. The broken beams of light were moving farther and farther away.

The investigation at the cul-de-sac began to attract others. When a few Briar Court residents came down the block to see what was happening, Sonny Fessler quietly slipped inside his house. There were others with CB radios, who listened to police reports, and they showed up too. Within an hour, two state police cars arrived, followed by three local TV news vans.

Bridget turned and started for home. But then a reporter stuck a microphone in front of her face. She recognized the thin, pretty blonde from a Seattle TV station's eleven o'clock news.

"Hello, I'm Gina Gotlieb from KIXI Four TV. Can I ask you a few questions?"

Bridget numbly stared at her. "Um, sure."

"Do you know any of the three boys reported missing?"

Bridget looked at the camera trained on her—and the man behind it. Then she turned to the reporter and nodded. "Um, I babysit for Andy Shields. I was over there tonight—"

"Wait a minute," the woman interrupted. "Ted, keep tapıng," she said over her shoulder. Her eyes narrowed at Bridget. "Are you Bridget Corrigan? Are you the young woman Dennis Shields took home tonight in his car—before his accident?"

"Accident? What are you talking about?"

"Mr. Shields ran his car into a telephone pole on his way back from dropping you off at your house. Haven't the police talked to you yet? Didn't you know?"

Bridget just shook her head.

"He was admitted to Longview General Hospital twenty minutes ago in critical condition. Do you have any comment? Do you think he might have run into that phone pole intentionally?"

Bridget kept shaking her head. She backed away, but the reporter jabbed the microphone closer to her face. "Do you think it was intentional?" she pressed.

"No, I don't know," Bridget heard herself say. "I don't think he would do something like that on purpose. He—he was upset and worried about Andy's disappearance, but there's still a chance Andy and the Gaines boys are all right. Isn't there?"

Another TV reporter got in on the act, and he threw a barrage of questions at her too. Then a policeman and some plainclothes detective insisted she give them a statement. Bridget told them what she'd told reporters: Mr. Shields had been worried about his son, but she didn't think he'd tried to kill himself.

Finally, they let her go. Bridget fled the mob scene that had taken over the quiet, little cul-de-sac. She practically ran home. She found Brad and her crush, David Ahern, anxiously waiting for her. The police had come by, and there had been several phone calls—from Mrs. Shields, reporters, and some of their classmates. They'd shown a news teaser on TV about the three missing boys, and she was on it. What was going on?

Bridget stared at David's handsome face. It was the first time he ever appeared genuinely interested in her. But she shook her head at him and her brother. "I don't want to talk about it," she muttered. "It's almost eleven. You can watch it on the news." Then Bridget retreated upstairs.

She didn't watch herself on TV, but snippets of her being interviewed kept running on news broadcasts all weekend. She'd mentioned that Andy was a sweet, thoughtful boy who wanted to be an artist. The three boys were still missing on Monday morning, when Bridget went back to school. The newspapers reported Mr. Shields had suffered several fractures and lacerations in the car accident. He remained hospitalized in stable condition.

It seemed everyone at school wanted to talk to Bridget that day—about Andy Shields, and what it was like being interviewed, and what she saw at the Shieldses' house that night. People who had barely known she was alive were suddenly fawning over her. That day, she got a taste of what it was like to be popular, and she hated it. Bridget no longer envied her brother his status at school.

That day, when one of her classmates didn't answer during attendance count, Fuller Sterns cracked, "Kurt's missing. He's pulling an Andy Shields." And people laughed. During lunch hour, Olivia Rankin approached Bridget and asked if she was scared: "Aren't your folks still away? Isn't it just you and Brad at home? I mean, Richie and Robbie Gaines are missing, maybe dead. What if someone is out there killing twins? Aren't you worried?"

For a while after that, Bridget didn't mind being a mere peripheral member in Brad's circle of friends. It was all right with her if she didn't get invited to certain parties. And she didn't mind driving to and from Brad's football and basketball games by herself.

Looking back, she saw that had been good training for single motherhood. Hell, even when she and Gerry were together, he rarely attended their sons' school events and Little League games.

The high school parking lot had emptied out, and Bridget realized that she'd been sitting in her parked car for several minutes now. She started up the engine, then pulled out of the lot and headed for home.

She thought of something Fuller had said to her in the high school hallway: "You and I both have this guy shadowing us, maybe he's watching Brad too. Maybe he's stalking each one of us who were at Gorman's Creek. . . ." All the way home, Bridget kept checking her rearview mirror.

Once she got inside the house, she locked the door behind her. She knew it was silly, but Bridget decided to put her worries to rest. She checked every room and every closet to make sure she was alone.

The last closet she examined was a tiny storage room by the den. Along with board games and sports equipment, there were boxes of keepsakes. Bridget took out an old Bon Marche box full of high school memorabilia. Sitting by the sliding glass doors, she opened up the box and sifted through the birthday cards, old photos, and certificates.

Bridget found what she was looking for, and her hand began to shake as she held it up. The sketch Andy Shields had made of her was clumsy, but the rough, near-cartoon image did indeed look a bit like Bridget in her high school years. He'd made her look like a nice girl.

That had been back at a time when she could still think of herself as nice.

Bridget's eyes filled with tears. Sighing, she put the drawing back in the Bon Marche box. Then she wiped her eyes and stared out the window. She could see some of the footprints outside the house—from when the police were investigating around there the night before last.

She remembered something Sonny Fessler had said to her that evening Andy and the twins had disappeared: "You know, they can trace a criminal by his footprints at the scene of a crime. But it's too late now. The policemen wrecked it. Now they really won't be able to tell if anyone bad was here."

CHAPTER 7

Bridget heard a noise. For a moment, she thought she was in bed—and someone was trying to get into her room. Then she realized that she'd fallen asleep on the sofa in the den. It was one of those unplanned afternoon naps that had her waking up so tired and disoriented, she felt as if a truck had hit her.

Bridget sat up. Outside, the sun had just set, and only a vestige of light came through the den's windows. She reached over toward the end table and switched on the lamp.

Then she heard the noise again. Someone was at the front door, trying to get in.

A panic swept through her. Bridget got to her feet. It sounded as if someone was manipulating the lock. Just a few seconds ago, she'd felt so groggy, but now she was wide-awake and alert. Her heart was racing.

Bridget moved toward the front hallway. The entire house had grown dark while she'd napped. She was reaching for the foyer light switch when the doorbell rang.

Who would ring the doorbell—after trying to break in?

She didn't flick on the light. She didn't want the person to know she was home. She stared at the door. The bell kept ringing and ringing. It couldn't be David. He had a key to the back door, and always used that. Eric always rang the bell first—even when the door was wide open. He liked ringing the bell. So Bridget knew neither one of her sons was on the other side of that door. Whoever it was tried to trip the lock again, and he rattled the knob.

Bridget stood frozen in the darkened hallway. The ringing stopped—so did the grinding sound of the lock being manipulated. After a few moments, she was still afraid to move.

The mailbox slot in the door opened and a set of eyes stared at her.

Bridget gasped, and backed away.

"Brigg?" she heard her brother yell. "Brigg, what the hell is wrong with you?"

She sighed, then trudged to the door and unfastened the dead bolt. She opened the door. "You scared the crap out of me," Bridget told her brother. "That's what's wrong with me. What are you doing here?"

She hadn't been expecting to see Brad until later tonight. She was supposed to swing by his house and drop David and Eric off with Janice. Then she and Brad were going on to a black-tie fund-raiser for his campaign. At this point, she didn't feel too terrific about leaving her boys with Janice and her raging hormones; and she wasn't exactly dying to attend this stupid party-for-the-party tonight.

Brad stepped into the foyer. He held a videocassette in his hand. "I need to speak with you alone, Brigg," he said glumly.

"You sound ticked off," she observed.

Brad's handsome face tensed up, and he shrugged.

"Well, I need to chew you out as well, you jerk." She turned and started toward the back of the house. "So—knock this around while I go to the bathroom," she called over her shoulder. "I don't know if it was Jay Corby's brilliant idea or yours, but I'd like a little warning before I'm forced to sing the National Anthem in front of two hundred and fifty people." Bridget ducked into the bathroom and slammed the door shut.

When she emerged a couple of minutes later, she found Brad in the den. Scowling, he stared at something on TV. It took Bridget a moment to realize he was watching a video-tape of David's Little League game that day.

"You know, Brad, I didn't appreciate having David's ball game turned into a media-event photo-op for your campaign," she declared, standing by the TV with her arms folded. "Also I didn't appreciate being yanked out of the stands to sing the National Anthem for the crowd. And by the way, I kind of butchered it—"

"I saw the footage," Brad said, sitting down in the easy chair's ottoman. "You did fine."

"I was in shock, for God's sake. And the camera crew you—or Jay—sent there, what was that about? It totally threw off David's game. It's bad enough you exploited me without warning, but did you have to drag David into the act? He was in the spotlight too, you know. That's a lot of pressure you piled on him today. The worst part is—you didn't ask, you didn't even warn us. You just sent Skip Stevens and a film crew over—like party-crashers—so you could turn a Little League game into a Corrigan-for-Oregon event. Talk about tacky. I'm surprised people didn't boo."

Brad's cell phone rang. He shut it off, then sighed. "Okay, maybe we should have asked you first—and David too," he muttered. "Jay wanted footage of a Little League game, for a commercial. It's to soup up my all-American image. I think they're splicing me in later or something. Jay wanted you in it too. I'm sorry. I didn't mean to cross a line."

Bridget frowned. "Well, you didn't cross it. Jay did. Huh, *Mr. Slick*, the great showman. I should have known he was behind that farce this afternoon. So, anyway, what did you want to talk to me about?"

Brad's glum expression was nearly identical to his sister's. From the ottoman, he barely glanced up at her. He just nodded at the TV screen. "I wanted to ask you about this," he said.

She turned and saw herself on the TV, sitting with Fuller

Sterns in the bleachers. The cameraman must have moved behind a post to take the footage, because she hadn't noticed him at the time.

"That guy you're with looks like Fuller Sterns—with a few more pounds and a lot less hair," Brad murmured. "Am I right?"

Staring at the TV, Bridget nodded.

"Why in God's name did you meet with him, Brigg?" he asked quietly. "You knew I wanted to put as much distance as possible between us and him. Yet there you are, chatting with Fuller Sterns. Did he call you up and arrange a meeting? Or did he—"

"He *ambushed* me," Bridget cut in. "Just like your buddy Skip Stevens ambushed me. I had no idea Fuller was going to be there. But he knew exactly when and where to find me—thanks to your Corrigan-for-Oregon Web site. That's the other bone I have to pick with you. I can't believe my personal comings and goings are posted on that Web site. Don't I have any privacy at all?"

"Well, it's not like they're listing when you plan to take a trip to the crapper—or to the Safeway or the hair salon," Brad said in his defense. "The stuff listed in there is from the itinerary you submit every week to campaign headquarters. You blocked off this afternoon for a Little League game—"

"I didn't tell anyone where the game was. How did they know?"

"It's Jay's standard operating procedure. If you or I block out some time, and one of us is going to a public event—a game, fair, supermarket opening, whatever—it's a potential public appearance. They look up where and when. Nobody expects us to make a speech or anything. But being seen in public can make a difference. It might mean taking a bow or waving to a crowd, shaking a few hands—"

"Or singing the National Anthem for a crowd of two hundred and fifty?" she pressed. "It's a total invasion of my privacy."

"Well, I okayed that policy with Jay a while back. Maybe

we should have discussed it with you in detail." He shrugged. "I honestly figured you were willing to give up some of your privacy when you agreed to campaign with me. I mean, that comes with the territory. But if you want to put up some restrictions, some boundaries, I certainly understand."

She sighed. "Well, for now, I'd just like a little advance warning. And maybe Jay Corby can *ask* before he decides to arrange an ambush while I'm doing something with one of my boys."

"Fair enough," Brad replied, nodding.

Neither one of them said anything for a moment. Then Brad glanced at the TV, and he let out a loud sigh. "So—Fuller tracked you down today. What did he want?"

Bridget sat down in the easy chair and told him about their conversation. She watched her brother bristle as she mentioned Gorman's Creek, and again as she told him about Olivia offering to "sell new information" to Fuller before she committed suicide.

"Sounds like extortion," Brad said finally. "I wouldn't have given her a dime. Fuller was an idiot to fork over five grand."

"But that wouldn't make sense," Bridget argued. "Olivia couldn't have blown the whistle on Fuller, or any of us, not without ratting on herself. She must have found out something that none of us knew about. That's the only logical explanation. But I'll tell you what can't be explained away so easily. Why would Olivia put a bullet in her brain—just two days after she got the money she wanted?"

Frowning, Brad shook his head. "I don't know. Maybe she was in some other kind of trouble. Olivia was crazy back in high school. I guess she hadn't changed much."

"Did she try to contact you?"

"Yeah, I think she left a message a couple of weeks ago. But I didn't return the call."

"Why didn't you tell me?" Bridget asked. "For God's sake—"

"Because I didn't think it was important. Jesus, I get messages all the time from people we used to know. In the past month, I've gotten messages from Olivia, Fuller, Nancy Abbe from grade school, Rachel Porter, Margaret Freeman—and Zach Matthias. Remember him? Nice guy, Coke-bottle glasses?"

Bridget just nodded. "Yeah, my friend Kim had a crush on him."

"I don't have time to return all those calls. I know it sounds heartless and unsentimental, but I don't. You know how crazy my schedule is."

"So you won't call Fuller back," she said.

He nodded. "Bingo."

"Aren't you at all curious about this new information Olivia uncovered?"

"No, because I think it's bullshit."

"They never found the body," Bridget whispered. "Maybe she discovered something about that."

"And maybe she was just trying to squeeze a few grand from Fuller," Brad replied. He turned away from her.

"Fuller said that someone's been following him. From his description, it could be the same man who was outside my house the night before last."

"Fuller was a major pothead back in high school," Brad grunted. "He probably still is. That stuff makes you paranoid. He was always nuts too—just like Olivia. You were smart not to get too close to them in high school. They were more trouble than they were worth. I don't know what Fuller is trying to pull right now. Hell, for all we know, he could be working for our friend Jim Foley. I don't trust him."

Bridget said nothing. Brad was being stubborn—and a bit stupid. But he was always that way when it came to the incident at Gorman's Creek. Twenty years ago, he'd made everyone swear that they wouldn't discuss it, that they'd forever put it behind them. To have all this coming up now—during his election campaign—must have been terribly unnerving for him.

"Well," she said finally, "I guess you have enough on your mind right now. You don't need—"

Bridget didn't finish. Something she saw on the TV silenced her. She leaned forward, eyes on the screen. "Go back . . . rewind it . . ." she told her brother.

He pressed the remote, and the picture moved backward, scanning the crowd in the bleachers.

"Stop!" Bridget said, staring at the screen. "Stop it there."

Brad hit Pause, and the tape froze on the image of a handsome, black-haired man, sitting in the bleachers. His face was just slightly out of focus. Bridget hadn't noticed him at the game.

She pointed to the man on the screen. "Do you know that guy?" she asked her brother. "Have you seen him before?"

Brad squinted at the TV. "He looks a little familiar."

"He was also in our hotel room yesterday—and at Olivia's wake."

"Maybe he's a reporter," Brad murmured.

"What would a reporter be doing at Olivia's wake?" Bridget asked. "I didn't tell anyone I was going there. I didn't tell a soul."

Her brother gazed at the slightly blurred image on the TV screen, and he just shook his head.

It took him nearly a whole day to recreate on canvas all the details in the billboard at the side of Garrett Road. BRAKE FOR COFFEE! it said in scripted red letters, alongside a smiling cartoon coffee mug with little arms and legs. The jaunty little mug was waving—supposedly to the driver. DELICIOUS FOOD! the sign exclaimed. DONNA'S DINER, 24-HOUR CAFÉ—EXIT 1/2 MILE. He'd decided the cartoon mug on that billboard would be one of the focal points of his next masterpiece. It would look very ironic smiling down on a twisted wreck of a car on the roadside beneath it.

He'd already put on the canvas the little slice of lonely

highway—and the dark, cloudless sky. But he hadn't painted a corpse yet. He wasn't sure how that would look. There might be only a little blood, or perhaps it would be all over the place. There might even be a decapitation. He wouldn't know until it actually happened. He had to be patient.

He'd made some preliminary sketches of the car. On his bulletin board by his easel, he'd posted several photos he'd gotten off the Web. They were of cars demolished in wrecks—deadly head-on collisions.

All of the cars were BMWs.

He knew the car type, but how it would look after the wreck was still to be determined.

He would know soon enough.

"Brad is out there shooting hoops in his tux, for God's sake," Janice said. She held Emma in her arms. The child had blond hair and fair skin like her mother. Janice wore one of Brad's striped shirts—untucked so it camouflaged her belly.

The boys—along with Brad—were yelling and laughing in the backyard. The fund-raiser dinner was in a half hour, but Brad always seemed to make time for his nephews—even if it meant tossing around the basketball in his tuxedo for a few minutes.

"You want to hear the infuriating part?" Bridget offered. "I'm pitted out just from nerves and the drive here, and he won't even break a sweat out there."

Janice didn't laugh. She seemed genuinely miffed. She just frowned at Bridget, while bouncing Emma in her arms.

Bridget stood by the front door. She had her hair up and wore a floor-length, black satin mandarin dress with a rich, wine-colored flower design throughout. Around her, she clutched a black satin stole. She gave her sister-in-law a contrite smile. "Listen, Janice, if the boys get to be too much, don't hesitate to call my cell. I have it in my purse. I'll come

running over and take them off your hands. In fact, I'd welcome any excuse to cut out of this black-tie bore-fest early."

Janice set Emma down. "Honey, why don't you go back
to watching TV. Okay? I'll join you in a minute."

Bridget watched her niece scurry toward the rec room.
Then she glanced at Janice, who was glaring back at her.
"What's wrong?" Bridget asked. "Do I have lipstick on my
teeth or something?"

"No, you look fine," Janice answered coldly. She clutched
the stairway newel post. "Brad told me about your discussion this afternoon."

Blinking, Bridget just stared at her. Janice wasn't supposed to know about Gorman's Creek.

"What did he tell you?" she asked numbly.

"He said you weren't too happy about them taping David's
Little League game this afternoon. And I guess you had to
sing the National Anthem for the crowd too."

Bridget smiled and rolled her eyes. "Oh God, I was in
shock. You should have heard me trying to warble through
those high notes. The whole time, I kept thinking—"

Janice cut her off. "Yes, it must have been very traumatic.
How awful for you. I'm really surprised at how selfish you
can be, Bridget. If you think your private life is so important,
why did you agree to work for Brad? You know, he did you a
huge favor hiring you. You were jobless, practically homeless. He saved you—and the boys—and this is the thanks he
gets."

Bridget shook her head. "Janice, I—"

"This campaign is everything to him—and to your dad,"
Janice continued. "If it's such a terrible imposition on your
precious privacy, if you're not going to do your part, then I'll
step in. I'll go against my doctor's orders and take the campaign trail with my husband. So what if it puts my unborn
child's life in jeopardy? I'll do what needs to be done!"

Stunned, Bridget said nothing. She watched her sister-in-
law swivel around and march toward the recreation room.

She decided not to say anything to Brad. But before they left together, she went to the backyard and pulled David aside. "Remember what I told you about women when they're pregnant?" she whispered. "They get a little crazy?"

With a wary look, David nodded. He held on to the basketball.

"So listen, if Aunt Janice snaps at you—or even if it's just a repeat performance of what happened the other night with her getting snippy—I want you to call me on my cell. Okay? I'll come pick you guys up."

David nodded again. "Okay, Mom," he said. Then he went back to shooting hoops with Eric.

As Bridget and Brad took off in his BMW, Janice was all smiles, waving at them from the front door.

"I keep thinking about what you told me this afternoon," Brad said, after they'd started down the street. He had his eyes on the road.

Bridget was about to say, *No kidding, Janice just bitched me out about it.*

But then Brad continued. "It makes me nervous that this guy is following you around. If he's not a reporter, who is he? I mean, do you think he could be a spy for Jim Foley? I wouldn't be the least surprised if Foley hired some goon to tail you."

Bridget watched him pull onto a lonely, dark highway called Garrett Road. "What if this guy isn't at all connected to the campaign?" she asked. "What if he's after something else entirely?"

"Like what?"

"Maybe he's after me—or the boys," she heard herself say.

Brad glanced at her for a second, then turned his attention to the road again. His grip seemed to tighten on the steering wheel of his BMW. "We ought to hire you a bodyguard—at least, for the time being. Just until we figure out who this guy is, and what he wants."

Bridget glanced in the side rearview mirror. She imagined this man following them right now. She noticed only two different sets of headlights behind them on Garrett Road. She also saw a billboard near the exit ramp to Brad's house. It had been there for years. BRAKE FOR COFFEE! it said in red letters, alongside a cartoon coffee mug. DELICIOUS FOOD! DONNA'S DINER, 24-HOUR CAFÉ—EXIT 1/2 MILE.

Though she'd driven to Brad's house countless times, there were occasions when Bridget felt a bit uneasy on this lonely, two-lane highway. Garrett Road wasn't very well lit— and never very busy, the perfect spot for one of those man-in-the-backseat stories. She was always afraid of having a breakdown somewhere along that isolated road. The DONNA'S DINER sign always gave her a sense of comfort, because it meant she wasn't far from the turnoff to Brad's house.

But tonight, she felt no relief spying the DONNA'S DINER sign. They were driving away from it.

Bridget gazed at the dark highway ahead. She couldn't shake this feeling of foreboding. Something horrible was starting to happen. Or perhaps it had actually started twenty years ago in Gorman's Creek, and been dormant all this time—until Olivia's strange suicide.

Bridget had a feeling things would only get worse. And relief was nowhere in sight.

CHAPTER 8

"I'm dead," Bridget muttered, as she buckled her seat belt.

"Ibid," Brad said, starting up the BMW.

It was a quarter after midnight. The black-tie fund-raiser had been a success. But all the smiling, handshaking, and effort at being charming had worn Bridget out. And the whole time, she'd been on edge, scanning the ballroom to see if that dark-haired stranger was among the attendees.

Bridget hadn't seen him. She'd half-expected another ambush from Fuller Sterns tonight. Fuller had paid Olivia five thousand dollars for some "new information" a while back; it stood to reason he'd cough up the money for this three-hundred-dollar-a-plate dinner tonight. If he was so anxious to talk with Brad, that would have been a smart way to get an audience with him. But Fuller wasn't there.

Then again, Fuller was never the sharpest tool in the shed.

As Brad pulled out of the Convention Center lot, Bridget leaned back in the passenger seat. She remembered how stupid and insensitive Fuller could be.

She recalled that afternoon they'd found Andy Shields and the Gaines twins. Fuller, Olivia, Brad, and she were all driving back from a field trip. Brad's girlfriend, Cheryl, wasn't there. She was sick or something that day. The juniors had spent the day at the state capitol in Olympia. Brad, in true form, had paired off with Marty Richter, the fattest, loneliest kid in their class; and then he'd talked with a nerdy-looking security guard for an hour.

Most of the juniors had gone to Olympia by chartered bus, but Brad and his group were too cool for the bus. Fuller had driven Brad and Olivia in his beat-up Imperial convertible. Brad had asked Bridget if she wanted to ride back with them.

Fuller drove like a maniac. But it was fun, sitting in the back of his convertible with the wind whipping through her hair on that sunny October afternoon. Olivia was on the CB radio, flirting with truckers, and everyone was laughing. Then someone patched through with a police bulletin. They'd discovered three bodies in the rail yard at the old Oxytech plant.

"Jesus, that's right near here!" Fuller exclaimed. He got on his CB and started asking different truckers if they could give him directions to the plant, which had been closed for a few years.

Biting her lip, Bridget suddenly felt cold—and scared. Andy and the Gaines twins had been missing for five days. The police had combed through Gorman's Creek to no avail. Photos of the missing boys were posted all over town. The flier-bulletins had been distributed as far north as Seattle— and south to Portland. According to reports, the police had no leads.

But now, they'd just found three bodies near a deserted chemical plant.

"Maybe we can get there before the cops cover them up," Fuller said eagerly.

"I don't want to do this," Bridget piped in. "I babysat for Andy. If it's him they found, I don't want to see his body. I—"

"So don't look," Olivia interrupted. "No one's gonna make you."

Brad patted her arm. "We probably won't be able to get near the place anyway," he whispered.

But Fuller made contact with someone who knew the plant. In the backseat, all Bridget could hear from the CB radio was a lot of static and some muffled mumbling.

Within minutes, they were off the highway and driving through a little hiccup of a town—then beyond, to an abandoned railroad station.

Bridget prayed this was all a mistake. For the last few days, she'd been clinging to an impossible hope that Andy Shields and Robbie and Richie Gaines were still alive. Maybe the police bulletin about the three dead bodies was a false alarm or something. Certainly, there would have been squad cars or TV news vans around here by now.

Instead, they were alone—in an area that might have been thriving twenty years before. Now it was desolate and isolated. Only a handful of tank cars sat in the railroad yard, all of them old, rusty, and deteriorated. Across the street was a boarded-up café.

They found a dead-end road with a dilapidated, weather-beaten sign, OXYTECH CORPORATION, INNOVATION FOR TOMORROW, TODAY! The lettering was faded, almost illegible. Cutting through a scrawny forest, the road to Oxytech was full of potholes. Bridget felt every bump in the backseat of the huge, old car. Through the skinny, leafless trees, she could see a couple of silos from the plant. Just beyond a barbed-wire fence and a ditch, the railroad tracks ran along the roadside.

Fuller finally slowed down as they reached an open gate. The potholes and cracks in the pavement became worse as they approached the plant. Bridget felt carsick. She was grateful when Fuller finally stopped for a second.

In the shadow of the two tall silos was a long, one-story, brick warehouse. All of the windows were broken or boarded up. The wind swept through the cavities of the building and made a strange howling noise—almost like distant screaming. Torn plastic shades billowed out from some of the dark windows.

"This is bullshit," Fuller said, disappointed. "There's nobody here."

Bridget let out a sigh. She just wanted to go home.

"Damn it," Olivia said. "I thought we were gonna be on the news."

"This totally sucks," Fuller said, banging the top of the steering wheel.

Brad tapped him on the shoulder. "Hey, dumb-ass," he said, pointing to the rusty railroad tracks that eventually curved around to the other side of the silos. "Try following those tracks—over there."

The car lurched forward, and Fuller followed the tracks to the back of the warehouse. The tracks dipped into a gully, and Bridget lost sight of them—until Fuller got close to the guardrail at the edge of the concrete drive. Then she could see the rail yard below. There were some old tank cars on the tracks, mere rusted-out shells. Bushes and tall weeds had grown through gravel and around the rails.

As Fuller drove around to the back of the silos, Bridget saw two police cars ahead of them.

"Oh, Jesus," Brad murmured.

Fuller slowed down. Along with the wind whistling through that old building, now Bridget could hear some muffled gibberish on a static-laced squad car radio. One of the cops was standing by his patrol car with the door open. He frowned at them and immediately started shaking his head.

Fuller came to a stop. "Fuckin' A! Look!" he said, pointing down at the rail area.

Without thinking, Bridget looked.

Not far away, three policemen stood over something piled up near a clump of bushes by the edge of the rail yard. It took Bridget a moment to realize they were the corpses of three young boys. They were all barefoot. Whoever had killed them must have taken their shoes and socks so they wouldn't run away.

Two of the bodies were facedown in the gravel and weeds. The third was lying faceup across one of his friends—so their bodies formed an X. Bridget recognized Andy Shields's red hair and his madras shirt—untucked and covered with dirt and dried blood. His face was just brown skin stretched over a skull.

Tears stung her eyes. "God, no," she whispered.

Brad pulled her toward him. She buried her face in his shoulder. But it was too late. She'd already seen it.

"Oh, gross!" she heard Olivia say.

"Is that the Shields kid?" Fuller was asking. "Is that him?"

"It's Andy, isn't it?" Brad whispered, still holding her.

Bridget just nodded against his shoulder.

"It's Andy Shields," Brad said soberly. "Okay? Satisfied? Now you've seen what you wanted to see, Fuller. So let's get out of here."

"Fuck that," Fuller retorted. "We're sticking around until the TV reporters arrive. I want to be on the news tonight."

"You kids need to leave—right now!" the cop yelled. Bridget lifted her head from Brad's shoulder to see the stocky policeman lumbering toward them. He was shaking his head and waving them away. "You have no business being here. You heard me! O-U-T, out!"

"You can't make us go," Fuller shot back. "It's a free country. We can stay here and look if we want to."

"But we don't want to stay and look, you moron," Brad grumbled. "C'mon, Fuller. Let's get the hell out of here. Bridget's sick, and I want to go. Just do what the cop is telling you."

"You're on private property," the policeman said. "Turn this car around and head back the way you came."

"Hey, this is almost like police brutality—"

"Do as he says," Brad growled, smacking Fuller's shoulder with the back of his hand. "C'mon, get moving, goddamnit . . ."

Fuller got moving. "I don't know what your problem is, Corrigan," he grumbled while turning the car around. A siren wailed in the distance. "We're gonna miss all the excitement. Shit, I mean, Bridget could have identified the Shields kid for the cops. We should go back—"

"We're not going back, and Bridget has seen enough," Brad replied evenly. "Sometimes, you're a real idiot, Fuller."

Driving away, they passed an ambulance and two more police cars on that dead-end road. As Fuller drove by the train station, a TV news van sped past them and turned down the plant road. He continued to complain that they were missing one of the biggest stories to hit McLaren in years.

Bridget said nothing for the rest of the way home.

Looking back on that afternoon, she could understand why Brad now wanted nothing to do with his old friend Fuller.

The mandarin dress was pinching a bit, and Bridget shifted in the passenger seat of Brad's BMW. They'd just pulled onto Garrett Road. Brad picked up speed. Bridget noticed Brad's face tense up as he glanced in the rearview mirror. "What's wrong?" she asked.

"Maybe you've got me paranoid," he said. "But I think this car has been following us ever since we left the Convention Center."

Bridget glanced in the passenger-side mirror. About ten car lengths behind them, she saw an SUV. It was the only other vehicle on Garrett Road.

"Does that SUV look familiar?" Brad asked. "Could it be your stalker, the guy we saw on the ball game tape?"

"I don't know his car," Bridget said, squinting at the mirror. "It could be." She felt the BMW slow down, and shifted her gaze to the dashboard. The needle moved from forty-five to thirty. "What are you doing?" she asked.

"I want to see if he passes us," Brad replied. "If he hangs back there, it means he's following us."

Bridget glanced over her shoulder. The headlights in back of them loomed closer for only a moment. The SUV seemed to keep pace with them, still about ten car lengths behind.

Bridget turned forward. They passed an exit—and a speed limit sign: 50 MPH. Brad was going thirty, and the SUV was still lingering behind them on the dark highway. "Okay," Bridget said edgily. "Now what?"

"Hold on," Brad said.

The BMW picked up speed, and Bridget watched the speedometer needle shoot up to sixty-five. She braced her hand against the dashboard. In the side mirror, she watched the SUV's headlights become like little pinpoints—but for only a few moments. Then they grew brighter, closer. The SUV started closing the gap between them.

"Oh no," Bridget murmured. She checked Brad's speedometer again. He was going seventy-five miles an hour.

"Better call the police," he said. "Is your cell phone in your purse?"

Trembling, Bridget dug the cellular out of her little black clutch.

The SUV switched on its high beams, and started tailgating them.

"Jesus Christ," Brad whispered.

Bridget started to dial 9-1-1, when suddenly the SUV swerved into the next lane and passed them.

"Corrigan sucks!" yelled a college-age guy from the passenger window. He flipped them the bird. "Corrigan's a fag! Foley rules!"

Then the SUV let out a roar as it raced ahead of them. Brad slowed down. "Forget the police," Brad muttered. "I think they were just protesting my Corrigan-for-Oregon bumper sticker. Huh, typical Foley fans."

Bridget clicked off the line. She watched the SUV tear down the highway in front of them. On its back door was a bumper sticker: JIM FOLEY, MY FRIEND, MY SENATOR. The taillights of the SUV disappeared in the night.

With a sigh, she put the phone away.

Ahead, Bridget noticed the sign for Donna's Diner, which meant they were getting close to Brad's house.

She felt a little better.

* * *

"Where's your aunt Janice?" Bridget asked.

Sitting on the sofa in Brad's den, David held the remote control in his hand. Beside him, his toddler cousin, Emma, was asleep, and still wearing the little denim outfit she'd had on earlier tonight. Ensconced in the nearby easy chair, Eric was also sleeping. On the TV, Vanessa Redgrave was frozen in midsentence as she talked to Tom Cruise.

"Aunt Janice got tired and went to bed a couple of hours ago, so I put in this DVD," David explained. "I think it's almost over. Can I watch the rest? Please?"

Brad gingerly lifted Emma off the couch. She whimpered, then nestled her face in his shoulder, drooling on the lapel of his tuxedo jacket. Brad didn't seem to mind. Nor did he seem very concerned that his wife had gone to bed and left her—still dressed in her day clothes—and in the care of her young cousin. He patted Emma on the back and glanced at the TV. "That's *Mission Impossible*. I recognize that scene on the Eurostar with Vanessa Redgrave and the laptop. Let him watch the rest. It'll only be a few minutes."

Brad headed up the stairs with Emma.

Bridget waited a moment before asking David in a whisper: "Wasn't Aunt Janice feeling well?"

David hesitated before pressing the remote. He shrugged. "I dunno. She just said she was tired and went to bed."

"Was she okay with you and Eric tonight? I mean, she didn't get mad at you guys or anything, did she?"

David shook his head.

"Okay, thanks, sweetie," she said. "Finish your movie." She collected a couple of glasses and a bowl with the remnants of greasy microwave popcorn in it.

Bridget carried everything into the kitchen. Dirty dishes and an empty pizza delivery box sat on the counter by the sink. Bridget put an apron over her dress and went to work on the dishes. Among them was a highball glass—with lipstick marks on it. She wouldn't have paid any attention to the glass, only something looking like bourbon was at the bottom of it. She sniffed the glass. Bourbon, all right.

Maybe that explained why Janice had been "tired," leaving the dishes undone and her daughter downstairs with the boys.

She wondered what her sister-in-law was thinking, consuming hard liquor while she was pregnant—and under a doctor's strict orders to "take it easy." Was she drinking on the sly? Did Brad have any idea? Perhaps he turned a blind eye to it.

Back when she was getting to know Janice, Bridget remembered thinking that Brad had found a girl *just like the girl who married dear old Dad.* Maybe that notion was even more on target than she'd figured.

Maggie Corrigan—like the daughter-in-law she'd never know—was blond, regally pretty, and aloof. In contrast to her husband, who showered the kids with affection, she had a stiff way of tilting her head to receive a kiss on the cheek from one of them. And she always had some reason to squirm out of a hug: "You're wrinkling my dress," "It's too hot for that," or "For God's sake, Bridget, stop hanging on me."

Bridget and Brad were raised by a constant, rotating crew of nannies and housekeepers. They'd just get used to one woman; then her mother would fire her and hire another. So they came to depend very much on each other—especially during those periods when their father was away on business.

Whenever their father came home, their mother would go off for a weekend shopping trip in Seattle, or she'd spend a few days at her parents' estate in Lake Oswego, near Portland. Mr. and Mrs. Corrigan were rarely together under the same roof for a sustained period.

The only times Bridget remembered her mother showing much interest in her were on Sundays, when the family went to church. They had to be dressed immaculately, not a hair out of place.

The Corrigans were, no doubt, the richest family in McLaren—with the nutty, reclusive Fessler clan running a not-too-close second. They seemed as healthy and normal a family as the Fesslers seemed weird. And Mrs. Corrigan was McLaren's classy, elegant, unofficial First Lady. She was deeply involved in several local charities and women's clubs. They seemed to take up more and more of her afternoons and evenings as Brad and Bridget got older.

Bridget had no idea what her mother did during her club excursions. But she noticed that her mother often returned from those meetings totally exhausted. She'd barely make it up the stairs to the master suite for a nap. They had an intercom in the master suite, and Maggie would often buzz the kitchen and instruct the housekeeper to have dinner brought to her room. Sometimes, neither Bridget nor Brad would see her again until the next day.

One afternoon, Bridget returned from school to find no one home. That wasn't so unusual. Brad was at basketball practice; her mother had a club meeting; her dad wasn't due back from a business trip until tonight; and the housekeeper had the day off. Bridget killed an hour dancing to Duran Duran, pumped up on the stereo, and then watching a bad talk show on TV. When the housekeeper had the day off, it was up to Bridget to fix dinner, and she was procrastinating.

At around five-fifteen, the phone rang, and she picked it up. "Hello?"

"Hi, Bridget? It's Debi Donahue from next door."

"Oh, hi, Mrs. Donahue."

"Bridget, I just wanted to make sure everyone was okay. I got back from the market a couple of minutes ago and noticed your mom's car smashed into the tree near the end of your driveway."

"What?" Bridget murmured. "You're kidding . . ."

But Mrs. Donahue was serious. Bridget ran out of the house and saw her mother's Mercedes wrapped around a tree near the end of the driveway. The front bumper and hood were a tangle of twisted, exposed metal. The driver's door was open, and there didn't seem to be anyone inside. Beneath the car was a puddle of greenish fluid.

It took a moment for Bridget to notice the rumpled, bloody thing lying on the section of lawn on the other side of the driveway—halfway toward the house.

"Mother?" she screamed. "Mom?" Bridget ran to her mother, who wasn't moving. She lay facedown on the grass. She must have crawled out of the car, and passed out halfway up the driveway.

Bridget carefully turned her over. She winced at the huge gash on her mother's forehead. Blood matted down her blond hair and stained the front of her pretty, pink Chanel suit. Now it was dirty and torn. She wore only one shoe.

Bridget could see that her mother was still breathing.

"You really kept your head, sweetheart," her father said later—in the hospital's parking lot. "I'm very proud of you."

"All I did was call an ambulance," Bridget replied, shrugging.

Heading toward the car together, he put an arm around her. "You also left a message on my pager and another at my office," he said. "And you phoned the tow company to haul the car away. I'd say you can be counted on in a crisis, Brigg."

Her mother had sustained a broken arm, multiple fractures and lacerations, and they'd put twelve stitches in her forehead. She had to spend the next couple of nights at Longview General Hospital.

Brad had left a message at home that he was having dinner out with a couple of teammates. He wouldn't be home until about ten o'clock. He still didn't know about the accident.

Bridget paused under a light in the parking lot. She stared at her father, who stopped walking too. "Is she an alcoholic?" Bridget asked.

Her father took his keys out of his pocket, then studied them. He nodded. "She's sick, Brigg."

"How can they let her drink so much at these committee meetings? Are they all drinking like that? Or is it just her?"

He kept looking down at his keys. "She hasn't attended a club or committee meeting for a couple of years now," he muttered. "She's been driving out here and going to the bar at the Red Lion. She sits and drinks and drinks, and . . . well, after that, she doesn't hold herself responsible for what happens—or who she ends up with."

"What do you mean?" Bridget asked.

"She's sick," he repeated. "It's a miracle she didn't smash up the car until now. You don't know how many times I've had to call in favors to have different DWI charges dropped. Some of those 'trips to your grandparents' she took were really stays in clinics so she could dry out. Interventions. But nothing we've tried seems to work."

He unlocked and opened the car door for her. Bridget climbed inside and unlocked the door for her father. He got behind the wheel, but didn't put the key in the ignition. He stared out the windshield.

"What . . ." Bridget hesitated. "What did you mean earlier when you said Mother didn't feel responsible for 'who she ends up with'? Do you mean she's been . . ." Bridget trailed off.

Her father nodded. He finally started up the car, then pulled out of the lot. "I'm sorry, Brigg," he said. "This isn't the kind of discussion a father should be having with his daughter. Far from it."

"Does Brad know?" she asked quietly.

"No, and I don't want you saying anything to him. Please, Brigg. He mustn't know." Her father stopped at a traffic light, and he turned to look at her. "I shouldn't have told you. I guess I'm just tired. I've covered your mother's tracks and cleaned up her mess the best I could these last couple of years. And you know why, Brigg? So your brother's future won't be hurt by any of this. He has a chance to do something really great. He can be a congressman or senator—or even president. We can help make that happen, sweetheart. Promise me you won't say anything to Brad about what I've told you tonight."

"I promise," Bridget said, obediently.

The traffic light turned green, but her father didn't notice. He was still staring at her. "And promise you won't discuss what you know with anyone else. This can't get outside the family, Brigg."

The driver in back of them honked his horn, but her father didn't even flinch. His eyes were locked on hers.

"I promise, Dad," she said.

They started moving again, and Bridget stared at the road ahead. She thought about her mother and the type of person she might "end up with" after too many drinks. "Has Mother been . . ." Bridget hesitated. "When you said she was sick, did you mean from the drinking? Or is she sick with something else?"

Eyes on the road, her father frowned. "What are you talking about?"

"She—she doesn't have AIDS, does she?"

"Not that I know of," he grumbled.

"Well, aren't you worried, Dad?" she asked gently. "I mean, not only for her, but she could be passing a lot of stuff on to you—"

"That's not going to happen," he muttered

"What makes you so certain?"

"Your mother hasn't let me touch her since you kids were born."

"What?" Bridget murmured.

"Your mother thought having babies was just about the worst hell a woman could go through. And I gave her twins. She never forgave me for that."

Bridget turned toward the window. She'd always wondered what they'd done to make their mother so cold toward them. Tears filled her eyes. "That explains a lot," she whispered finally.

"I guess that's something else Brad doesn't need to know about," her father said.

"I won't say anything to him," she replied, still staring out the window. Then she added under her breath—in a slightly

wounded tone: "After all, we have to think about Brad's future."

She almost hoped her father had heard her. If he had, he
didn't say anything.

True to her word, Bridget didn't breathe a word to Brad.
In regard to their mother's accident, he totally swallowed the
story that she'd simply overshot the driveway. Her stay in the
hospital was longer than they'd anticipated. They'd dried her
out again, and conducted a series of tests. They discovered
extensive liver damage.

The doctors sent Mrs. Corrigan to a group of specialists
at the Dennison Clinic in Bellevue, Washington. She began
spending more time there than at home. Brad and Bridget's
father often stayed at a hotel—near the clinic. For Mrs.
Corrigan's brief reprieves at home, she always went back to
drinking on the sly and fired one nurse after another.

Brad turned a blind eye to it. He believed the "official"
diagnosis of his mother's illness: liver cancer. At least, that
was the story everyone got. It was one reason their father
stuck so close to the Dennison Clinic. He had the doctors
and nurses in on the cover-up. Cirrhosis or cancer, it was just
a label.

The label won their family a lot of sympathy. And as if
Brad needed to be more popular, that was exactly what happened. Sitting alone at those basketball games, Bridget would
often hear people around her talking about her brother—always about how well he was playing, how cute he was, and
Oh, it's so sad, his mother has cancer.

She and Brad became accustomed to being alone in that
big Tudor house for days—sometimes weeks—at a time. By
their junior year, they didn't need the housekeeper staying
with them. Bridget did most of the shopping and cooking.
She was grateful whenever one of Brad's pals decided to
spend the night—especially if it was her crush, David Ahern.
An extra person in the house gave her a better sense of security. There were times she couldn't help feeling scared and
vulnerable in that large house.

One of those times was during the week Andy Shields and the Gaines twins went missing. Bridget kept remembering something Olivia Rankin had said: "What if someone is out there killing twins? Aren't you worried?"

She slept with a bat at her bedside. Every night, she double-checked the doors to make sure they were locked. McLaren was a little town where no one bothered locking their doors. But the murders of those three boys changed that.

Andy Shields and Robbie Gaines had their throats slit. One of the newspapers used an off-the-cuff description a policeman on the scene had given: "They were cut from ear to ear," he'd said. "Like each one had been given a second smile." Richie Gaines had been strangled, and there were rumors he'd been sexually assaulted as well. They never did find the boys' shoes. And they never found the killer—or killers.

Bridget attended Andy Shields's memorial service. The closed-casket wake was held at Shorewood Funeral Home.

Within a few months, she would be there again—for her mother's funeral. Most of the town showed up to pay their respects. Bridget talked to dozens of people who thought her mother was the epitome of grace and elegance. The church—along with the viewing room at Shorewood Funeral Home—was filled with floral arrangements. Over three thousand dollars was donated in Mrs. Corrigan's name for the American Cancer Society.

They'd stuck with the cancer story. Bridget's father even managed to get it put on the death certificate. He was protecting Brad—and his future.

Bridget had kept her promise to her father, and never said anything to her brother about what really killed their mother.

Now, she studied the highball glass from which her pregnant sister-in-law had been drinking. Bridget decided it wasn't her business to say anything to Brad about it.

She finished up the dinner dishes Janice had left—with

one exception. She took off the apron, then brushed a few stray threads from the front of her black-and-wine mandarin dress.

Bridget left the highball glass—with its lipstick marks and bourbon smell—on the counter, just where she'd found it.

If Brad decided to turn a blind eye, she wasn't going to make it easy for him.

"Brad?"

"Yeah, hello, Fuller," said the voice on the other end of the line.

Fuller rubbed his eyes and squinted at the clock on his nightstand. "Jesus," he said, sitting up in bed. "It's one o'clock in the morning." He cleared the phlegm out of his throat, then checked the caller ID on the phone base: *No listing.*

"Sorry if I woke you—"

"You don't sound like Brad. Where are you calling from?"

"I'm calling from a pay phone. And if I don't sound like myself, it's because I've been making speeches all night and I'm tired. The reason I'm calling is I want you to stop bothering my sister."

"You wouldn't return any of my calls," Fuller explained. "I had no other way of getting in touch with you. Did Bridget tell you—"

"Not over the phone," he cut in. "Come meet me."

"Now? What, are you high?"

"No, I'm tired, and I want you off my back. It's now or never. I don't want to be seen talking with you, and no one here knows me. I'm at an all-night café near my house. Do you know where Donna's Diner is?"

The old Volkswagen minibus seemed to come out of nowhere.

With this elusive creep following him around for the past

week or so, Fuller was constantly on his guard. When he'd left his house and got behind the wheel of his BMW at ten minutes after one o'clock in the morning, he'd brought along his cell phone and his gun. He'd thrown on a sweatshirt and a pair of jeans for his meeting with Brad Corrigan. All the while, he wasn't quite sure whether he'd really been talking on the phone with Brad—or some imposter. Fuller had watched news clips of Brad Corrigan speaking, and he knew his voice. This guy on the phone had sounded different. Still, who else but Brad would know that he'd been talking with Bridget?

Fuller hadn't seen anyone lurking around his house as he'd backed out of the driveway. On his way to the interstate, he'd repeatedly checked his rearview mirror. He knew where Donna's Diner was—about twenty minutes from his house. He'd rolled down his window and cranked up an oldies station to keep from nodding off.

He'd been listening to Blondie's "Rapture" while pulling off the interstate and onto Garrett Road. One moment, there were no other cars on the lonely, dark highway; then, suddenly this old Volkswagen minibus was behind him. Had it been waiting for him—with its lights off—along the roadside?

Fuller squinted in the rearview mirror. The minibus was about five car lengths behind him. From what he could tell, it looked like just one person in the vehicle—no passengers.

Fuller straightened up behind the wheel and pressed harder on the accelerator. The speedometer needle on his BMW shot to seventy. He checked the mirror again. The Volkswagen minibus was still with him, getting closer. He could even see the driver—a balding man who looked a bit like an ape. There was something dangling from his rearview mirror that kept catching the light. It was a reflective insignia of a sea serpent or a snake.

Fuller didn't see any other cars on the highway. "Shit," he murmured. "Where's a fuckin' cop when you want one?"

His foot pressed even harder on the accelerator—until he

was doing eighty-five miles an hour. The wind blasted through his open window. The old Volkswagen stayed on his tail. Then that simian shit-heel put on his high beams. The inside of Fuller's BMW was suddenly illuminated in a blue-white light.

"Son of a bitch," he growled. His heart was racing. Blindly, he reached for his gun on the passenger seat. Maybe if he held it up and waved it, the bastard behind him would back off. Fuller patted the seat cushion. He didn't feel anything. Finally, he glanced over at the passenger side for a moment. Something caught his eye, and it wasn't his .45. With the minibus's headlights illuminating his car, he noticed for the first time a half-full bottle of whiskey on the floor. "What the hell?" he whispered. Someone had planted it there. But why?

Fuller swallowed hard, grabbed his gun, and held it up. "See this, asshole?" he growled. "Want some?" He kept brandishing the gun. In the rearview mirror, he watched the ape in the minibus lag back a bit. Fuller smiled.

Up ahead, he saw a sign with a cartoon coffee mug. BRAKE FOR COFFEE! it said. DELICIOUS FOOD! DONNA'S DINER, 24-HOUR CAFE—EXIT 1/2 MILE.

He was almost there. Fuller let out a little laugh. The old Volkswagen minibus seemed to be lingering back now. If that was part of a setup, he would soon find out. He planned on taking his .45 into the diner. For now, he put the gun on the passenger seat. It was dark inside his car once more.

Fuller eased off the accelerator a bit, then checked his rearview mirror. He didn't see the minibus. "What the hell?" he muttered. The damn thing had disappeared just as quickly as it had snuck up on him.

Fuller realized he was veering off the road—toward a mass of trees that surrounded the DONNA'S DINER sign. He quickly straightened out the wheel and got back in his lane. He squinted at the mirror again, and finally spotted the old Volkswagen minibus, still following him—with its lights off.

"Jesus, what—" he started to say. But he didn't finish.

All at once, straight ahead, he saw a car in his lane, barreling toward him. Its lights were off too. But he barely had a moment to realize it was there, before the vehicle's high beams went on.

Fuller was blinded. He couldn't even see what type of car was coming at him. Through the open window, he heard an engine roaring. He caught sight of the Volkswagen minibus in his side mirror. It propelled forward, blocking the left lane.

Fuller leaned on the horn. But the oncoming car was relentless. He had no way out. Fuller slammed on the brakes and jerked the wheel to the right. Tires shrieked. He veered off the road—and felt the car tipping over. "Jesus, no!" he yelled.

The car was spinning. Flying. Through the windshield, he saw the trees—only they were upside down. He was soaring straight toward them.

Fuller Sterns didn't see another thing after that. Only blackness.

He had to admit something to himself about his new painting.

It just wouldn't match what had actually happened only a few hours ago. There was no way he could recapture the excitement of the crash, the adrenaline rush he got from playing that game of chicken with the BMW and putting his own life on the line.

Stinking of sweat, he went to work on some sketches. He had to work from memory. He hadn't counted on the BMW flipping over like that. All those car-crash photos he'd downloaded were a waste. The wrecked BMWs had been upright in those shots. The joke was on him.

Nor did he need those photos of Fuller Sterns he'd taken on the sly. The son of a bitch was buried beneath the car. All he could see of him was his arm—sticking out the crumpled window. The way it poked out of the dark opening, the bloody limb didn't seem connected to anything. He wondered whether or not the arm had been severed.

He wanted to capture that same sense of uncertainty when he painted the lifeless arm. He liked the juxtaposition of the smiling cartoon coffee mug on the billboard and the wrecked car below it. He was calling this one *Brake for Coffee*.

He still had a lot of work to do. Yet his mind was already on his next job, his next masterpiece. This one coming up would bring him immense satisfaction. It would be carefully staged—with a lot less room for surprises and error. He'd have more control over everything.

And besides, he always enjoyed it so much better when he got to paint a woman.

CHAPTER 9

"I thought maybe we could do this without getting our lawyers involved," Bridget said.

Gerry nodded over his coffee cup. They'd met at a Starbucks in Portland's trendy Northwest District. All the tables were taken, so they sat at the counter-bar. On the wall in front of them were newspapers, hanging by clothespins on a line—for the customers to read.

Bridget had chosen the Starbucks this Tuesday morning so their meeting wouldn't turn into a shouting match. She'd been a few minutes late, and found her estranged husband with his nose in one of the newspapers.

She hadn't seen Gerry since their last meeting three weeks before—and that had been with the lawyers. This time around, she noticed he looked pretty handsome, damn him. He'd lost some weight, and must have gotten some sun recently. His curly gray-brown hair had a touch of blond in it. He wore a tan suit, some designer label, and a tie that matched his blue eyes. Bridget wore a pale green suit that he'd always liked. She hated the part of her that still needed to look attractive for him. But she wasn't trying to lure him back, she just wanted him to kick himself for letting her go.

She'd gotten a double espresso, brought it back to the counter-bar, and climbed up on the stool beside his.

"I need to ask you for a favor, Gerry," she said. "I'd like you to spend more time with David and Eric. I'm talking beyond the every-other-weekend schedule, which—well, you haven't been too terrific at keeping."

He put down his coffee cup and eyed her warily. "You told me this was going to be a *friendly* talk. I already explained why I couldn't take them last time. I had a client in Palm Springs—"

"I understand, really," she cut in. "I just think the boys, especially David, they need a father figure. They miss you, Gerry."

He let out a cynical laugh. "Don't bullshit a bullshitter, Bridget. They don't miss me. They have a father figure with their uncle Brad. He walks on water as far as they're concerned. Always has. How can I compete with that?"

Bridget didn't say anything. She just sipped her coffee. She knew what Gerry was talking about. She'd grown up in her twin brother's shadow, and had long, long ago stopped trying to compete with Brad.

"Brad will be busy for the next few weeks," she said. "It's crunch time with the campaign. They'll be demanding more of my time too. It would be nice if you could look after David and Eric some nights—and weekends. I don't want to leave them alone. And I don't want to leave them with Janice."

He smirked a bit. "You and Janice still maintaining a policy of mutually polite contempt?"

Bridget shifted on the stool. She didn't want to confide in him about Janice snapping at her the other night—or about the possible drinking on the sly. Bridget gave her estranged husband a pinched smile. "I plead the Fifth, counselor," she said.

He laughed. "Some things never change."

"So—about the boys . . ."

"Well, I can't make ironclad guarantees here, Bridget," he

said. "I'll try to be available. But c'mon, in a pinch, can't David and Eric look after themselves? After all, David's fourteen—"

"He's thirteen," Bridget cut in. "And I don't want to leave them alone in the house. I have this—*stalker* situation, and I'd just as soon—"

"Wait," he said. " 'A stalker situation'? What are you talking about?"

She frowned down at her coffee cup. "Oh, it's probably some nut who saw me on TV, or maybe a reporter. Brad thinks he might be a spy for Foley—hoping to catch me in a *compromising position* or something. Whatever. This guy has been showing up in different places I've been, and the other night, someone was lurking outside the house at three in the morning. It might have been the same man, but I'm not sure."

Gerry hunched toward her. "My God," he murmured, putting his hand on her arm. "Did you call the police?"

Gently pulling her arm away, Bridget nodded. "Yes, and they came by. It's okay, really. It's nothing you should worry about."

She hated that concerned look on his handsome, tanned face. It made her think for a moment that he cared. Worse than that, it made her miss him. Bridget sipped her coffee. She couldn't look at him. "So—you'll help with the boys?"

He nodded. "Of course. Just give me some advance notice when you might need me. I want to spend more time with them. Really." He patted her hand. "You know, I still care, Bridget. I do."

Again, she pulled away from his touch. "How's Leslie?" she asked coolly.

"Leslie's fine," he answered. He drank his coffee, then set the mug down on the counter. "Well, I'll take that last question as a cue to get out while the going's good. You can count on me to help with the boys. Take care, Bridget." He climbed off the stool and started toward the exit.

"Gerry?" she heard herself say. When he glanced back at her, Bridget worked up a smile. "Thank you," she said. "I mean it."

He nodded, then walked out the door.

Bridget slumped a bit in the stool. She'd almost let herself become vulnerable with him just now. And she couldn't afford that.

She suddenly felt so alone— -and very self-conscious. With a sigh, Bridget turned toward the wall and tried to look interested in the newspaper page hanging on clothespins. It was yesterday's newspaper. The local news section was in front of her. She read the headline to an article near the bottom of the page:

VANCOUVER MAN DIES IN BIZARRE CAR ACCIDENT
Unexplained "Rollover" Occurred on Portland Highway

A name in the first sentence of the article caught her eye. "My God," Bridget murmured.

A Vancouver businessman, Fuller Sterns, 38, died when his BMW rolled over on Garrett Road, Highway 17, in Portland early Sunday morning. There were no witnesses to the accident, which one Portland policeman described as "a mystery."

"It appears as if the car rolled over at a high speed," said Officer Lawrence Blades, one of the first to arrive upon the scene, after a passing motorist reported the wreck at 1:53 AM on Sunday. "It's possible he might have fallen asleep at the wheel or swerved to avoid a deer. But we won't know for sure without further investigation. There are a lot of unanswered questions here. . . ."

Bridget pulled the newspaper section from its clothespins and tore off nearly half of the front page. Hunched over the counter-bar, she continued reading the article. She kept shaking her head over and over again. She couldn't believe Fuller was dead.

And she refused to believe it was an accident.

* * *

"I didn't know anything about it," her brother said on the other end of the line.

The cellular phone to her ear, she stood by an alley next to the Starbucks. People were passing by her on the sidewalk—within earshot. So Bridget stepped deeper into the alley, then stopped by a stack of plastic crates. A chilly autumn wind kicked up. Fallen leaves and bits of trash rolled along the cracked cement.

"According to this article, he was killed on Garrett Road," Bridget said. "That's right by your house. Was he on his way to meet you? Did you have some kind of appointment with him?"

"God, no," Brad replied. "At that hour? Besides, I had no interest in meeting with him. You know that."

"Well, it doesn't make any sense—Fuller's car flipping over in the middle of the night, alone on that old highway. Even the newspaper called it 'bizarre.' This was no accident, Brad."

"Brigg, I can't really talk about this right now. I—"

"But aren't you concerned?" she asked.

"Brigg, I can't talk right now—period. I have people here."

"Okay, okay. I'll talk with you later."

As she clicked off the cellular, Bridget noticed something down the alley. A dark figure darted from behind a recycling bin into a doorway. It happened so quickly, Bridget wondered if her eyes were playing tricks on her. She didn't hear a door shut. Maybe it was just a large piece of debris that flew by.

Bridget held on to the cell phone and moved toward the recycling bin. Behind the bin, she saw a shadowy alcove with a door and a window—both closed. The heavy-looking metal door had rust streaks. The window beside it was cracked and dirty—with crisscross wiring inside the glass. The dark room inside must have been a storage area. Someone had leaned a few old, tall wooden planks against the other side of that window. Beyond them, nothing was visible, just a murky blackness.

There was no sign of anyone in the alcove. Bridget told herself that the darting figure she'd seen must have been her imagination.

But then she glanced down at a puddle by the alcove stoop. She noticed wet footprints all around the stoop—and on the pavement by the recycling bin.

It wasn't her imagination. Someone was just there.

A chill swept through her. Bridget glanced over her shoulder for passersby at the end of the alley. No one. But after a few moments, finally, a woman walked by with her dog.

Bridget took a deep breath, then turned toward the alcove again. She stared at those footprints on the pavement—so much like the footprints around her house last week.

She took another step toward the door. She told herself that if she screamed, somebody would hear. She switched on her cell phone again, then dialed 9 and 1. She could dial the last digit in a matter of seconds.

Biting her lip, Bridget reached for the door handle. Her hand was trembling. The hinges squeaked a bit as she started to open the heavy door. She didn't have to open it more than a few inches to see the wet footprints on the dusty cement floor of that dark little room.

Bridget froze.

She realized that if she didn't get out of there right now, she could be as dead as her old high school friends, Olivia Rankin and Fuller Sterns.

Bridget backed away from the door and watched it close by itself. Her heart racing, she retreated toward the sidewalk at the end of the alley. All the while, she felt as if someone might grab her from behind, cover her mouth, than drag her back into that creepy storage room.

She didn't feel safe until she was standing on the side-walk—near the Starbucks entrance. Catching her breath, she stared back at the alley. No one had been chasing her. Except for some leaves and debris blowing in the wind, there wasn't any sign of movement.

Several people passed her on the sidewalk. Bridget kept studying the alleyway.

"Hey, 'Corrigan for Oregon'!" someone said.

Bridget turned toward a couple passing by on the sidewalk. The man was tall, blond, and Nordic-looking. He had his arm around a pretty Latino woman. *"Voy a votar por tu hermano,"* the woman called.

Bridget managed to smile. "I'm voting for your brother," the woman had said. *"Gracias!"* Bridget replied. *"Seria un buen senador. ¡Corre la voz!"*

They both waved at her and kept walking, arms around each other.

Bridget watched them stop two storefronts down from Starbucks. The man put a coin in a newspaper dispenser, then pulled out a *Portland Examiner.*

Bridget opened her purse and took out the article she'd torn from yesterday's newspaper. She read the last paragraph again:

> *Sterns was married to April Binneman from 1995 to 2001, and to Candice Percy from 2001 to 2003. Both marriages ended in divorce. He is also survived by a sister, Dorothy Sterns Howland, of Beaverton, OR. A memorial service has been scheduled for Tuesday, September 28, at 11 AM at Immaculate Heart of Mary Church in Beaverton.*

Bridget checked her wristwatch. It was 9:50. She could make it to Beaverton in plenty of time.

As she headed back toward her car, Bridget wondered—for the second time within ten days—if she would see any former classmates at the funeral of her old high school acquaintance. Would someone be there who could explain why this person was dead?

Once again, Bridget remembered something Fuller Sterns had said to her when she last saw him alive: "You and I both have this guy shadowing us . . . Maybe he's stalking each one of us who were at Gorman's Creek."

As Bridget ducked inside the car, her cell phone rang. She figured it was Brad, calling her back. She didn't bother checking the caller number. She clicked on the Talk button. "Hello?"

"Bridget?"

She didn't recognize the voice on the other end. "Um, yes? Who's calling?"

"Why didn't you open the door?"

"What?" she asked.

But then she suddenly realized what he meant.

"Why didn't you step inside, Bridget?" he whispered. "I was in there, waiting for you."

For a moment, she couldn't talk. "Who—who is this?" she finally asked. "Who are you?"

She heard a click on the other end of the line.

CHAPTER 10

Fuller must not have had many friends. Only the first few front pews of Immaculate Heart of Mary Church were occupied. Bridget sat alone in a middle pew. Dressed in her pale green suit, she felt slightly out of place among the mourners. So far, she didn't see anyone from her old high school class.

An antique-bronze casket sat in the middle of the aisle—near the gap in the communion railing. It was an old church, with an arched ceiling and a stone floor. Very little light came through the stained glass windows, yet on the walls, the murals of the saints appeared sun-faded. Dark wood latticework was practically everywhere—the pulpit, communion rails, the sides of the pews—giving the place a seedy grandeur. On its own, the organ made a low humming noise, probably a draft creeping through the pipes. An emaciated old priest presided over the painfully slow service. Every reading, every move he made seemed so deliberate and prolonged.

Bridget had found the church without a problem. Thanks to her campaigning across the state, she knew her way around the major cities and several small towns.

She kept thinking about that disturbing phone call, and what *might* have happened in the alleyway. She wondered if her stalker was taking his surveillance to a new level. Before, he'd merely been *watching* her. Was it a cat-and-mouse game now? Or perhaps, this was someone entirely different.

Either way, she could no longer put off finding a bodyguard. She also needed to sit down with her sons and tell them about this situation. Maybe this guy was hanging around their school. She hated upsetting David and Eric. She didn't want them constantly looking over their shoulders for someone in the shadows. But she couldn't let them blithely walk into harm's way. They had to know what was happening.

And so did she.

She hoped someone at this memorial—one of Fuller's friends or a family member—could tell her what wasn't in yesterday morning's newspaper. Perhaps someone among this congregation knew where Fuller was headed at two o'clock on Sunday morning.

During communion, Bridget got a look at Fuller's younger sister, Dorothy, who stepped out from the front pew and headed up to the communion rail. Her hands were folded in prayer. She wore a black wraparound dress that accentuated her sticklike figure. Her blond hair was pulled back in a little ponytail, making her long face and big teeth seem even more prominent. Bridget remembered her when she was a slightly bratty little girl and everyone called her Dottie. She had been in the same class with Andy Shields and the Gaines twins. Fuller often referred to her as "the little shit," and sometimes, "horse-face." Bridget wondered if they'd ever gotten along. Throughout the funeral mass, thirty-one-year-old Dorothy maintained a pious expression, but—from what Bridget saw—she didn't shed a tear.

Once outside the church, Fuller's sister dropped the piety and smoked a cigarette while she talked with some mourners.

An older woman recognized Bridget from TV, and began to tell her how wonderful Brad was. Bridget nodded politely and kept glancing back at Dorothy Sterns Whatever-Her-Married-Name-Was. For a moment, she and Dorothy locked eyes. With a sigh, Dorothy tossed her cigarette on the ground and stepped on it. Then she headed back toward the church doors.

Bridget excused herself from the old woman, then hurried after Fuller's sister. "Dorothy?" she called.

Dorothy stopped at the foot of the church steps. She turned and glared at Bridget.

"Dorothy, I'm so sorry about Fuller," she said. "I'm Bridget—"

"I know who you are," she interrupted. "I remember you. And I watch TV—so I know you, Bridget. And I think your brother is evil."

"What?" Bridget stared at her and shook her head. She figured Fuller must have told his sister that Brad had refused to see him.

"Your brother's disgusting," Dorothy sneered. "He's soft on gay marriage, which is a threat to the American family. And he wants to take away our Second Amendment rights."

"I'm sorry." Bridget let out a stunned little laugh. "Are you talking about him wanting to ban certain assault weapons?"

"Yes, that's what I'm talking about."

"Well, he's just talking about assault weapons. I mean, c'mon, Dorothy. Why would anyone need an Uzi to hunt deer or protect their home?" Bridget waved her hand as if to quickly dismiss what she'd just said. "But listen, listen, I don't want to get into a debate with you here. That's not why I came. I—"

"I'm voting for Jim Foley," Dorothy said, cutting her off. Then she turned and stomped up the church steps.

Bridget trailed after her. "Dorothy . . . Dottie . . ." she said. "I don't care who you vote for. Really. I'm not here to question your politics. I'm here about *your* brother, not my brother." Bridget lowered her voice as she stepped back inside the old church. She followed Dorothy Sterns up the aisle—toward the casket. Dorothy's high heels clicked against the stone floor.

"Fuller met with me a few days ago," Bridget continued. "He was—well, he was concerned about an old friend of ours—"

Dorothy stopped and swiveled around. "I don't know what you're talking about. And I really don't care. My brother and I hadn't spoken in quite some time. I arranged this memorial service for him because it's the Christian thing to do. Now, if you don't mind, I need to talk to the monsignor."

Bridget noticed the old priest coming from a side door near the altar. He slowly made his way toward the center aisle.

"Dorothy, I didn't mean to butt heads with you," Bridget said. "I read about Fuller's accident. I was wondering if the police got in touch with you. Have they found out anything? I mean, is it possible someone tampered with Fuller's car? I'm not asking this out of morbid curiosity. There's a valid reason why I'm bothering you about this. Dorothy, please . . ."

"You're right," Fuller's sister replied. "You're *bothering* me—and I'm in mourning. So would you leave me alone?"

She hurried to meet the old priest; then the two of them headed toward the side door. "Monsignor, I want to thank you for that lovely eulogy . . ." Dorothy Sterns was saying.

Bridget listened to the click-click of Dorothy's high heels—until Fuller's sister and the elderly priest exited through the side door. She could hear another door open and shut, then nothing—except that faint droning from the organ pipes.

Bridget suddenly realized she was alone in the drafty old church, just her and Fuller in his polished antique-bronze casket. She touched the edge of it and wondered what had really happened to him.

She glanced down the aisle toward the church doors. Bridget realized she wasn't alone with Fuller after all.

Dressed in a tie, blazer, and khakis, the black-haired man stood by the confessionals. At first, his face was shrouded by shadow, but then he came forward, and Bridget saw his eyes—fixed on her. He smiled.

Bridget stepped back and bumped into Fuller's casket.

She almost stumbled as she made her way around the coffin. She hurried to the side door near the altar, the same exit Dorothy and the priest had used. Pushing open the door, Bridget glanced back over her shoulder.

Her stalker paused by Fuller's casket. His hand lingered along the lid, and all the while he was staring at her. The smile had vanished from his face.

Bridget ducked into a dim, narrow corridor, then shut the door behind her. There was no lock on it. She saw two other doors at the end of the little hallway—one straight ahead, the other to her left. Bridget ran to the first door and reached for the knob. Locked. She pushed and pushed, but the door didn't budge.

She heard his footsteps on the church's stone floor. He was getting closer.

Bridget tried the door to her left. It swung open easily. But the room was dark and cluttered. She weaved her way around boxes of missals, acolyte candlesticks, and huge vases. She headed for the corner, hoping to hide in the shadows of a tall armoire. Then Bridget stopped dead.

She gasped at the tall man waiting for her there. He was in a monk's robe. It took a moment for her to realize she was staring at a life-size statue of St. Francis. In the darkness, the benevolent saint appeared slightly demonic. His nose had been chipped, and the bird he held in his hand was missing a wing.

Bridget was still trying to get her breath back when she heard a door yawn open—then close—down the corridor. She listened to the footsteps approaching.

She slid behind the statue. Past the piles of boxes and religious artifacts, she stared across the room at the door. She could feel her heart racing. She heard him try the next door down. He knocked softly.

To her left, within reaching distance, Bridget noticed an ornate brass candlestick poking out of an open box. She grabbed it. The thing was heavy. She hid the candlestick behind her back and watched the door open across the room. A shaft of light spilled across all the clutter. She stared at the tall figure in the doorway.

Bridget tightened her grip on the candlestick. She tried not to make a sound.

"Bridget Corrigan?" he whispered.

She didn't move. She didn't breathe.

"Is that you?" he asked.

Bridget couldn't tell where he was looking. She watched him feel around for a light switch on the wall. He found it. Suddenly the lights were on, and he was staring at her.

"Are you okay?" the man asked.

Bridget shrunk in the corner. "Who are you?" she demanded.

"I'm Zach Matthias," he said, taking a cautious step toward her. "You know, from McLaren High? Don't you remember me?"

She stared at the tall, lean, handsome man. It didn't make sense. She remembered chubby, sweet Zachary Matthias with his thick glasses and his chipped gray tooth. Except for the wavy black hair and creamy complexion, he didn't seem to be the same person. The Zach she knew in high school was slightly nerdy and gentle. This man, who had been stalking her ever since Olivia Rankin's wake, scared the hell out of her. Even his good looks were somewhat threatening.

Bridget didn't move from the corner. She kept a firm grip on the brass candlestick behind her back. "You're lying," she said finally. "I remember Zach, and you're not a thing like him."

He smiled. "Guess I should take that as a compliment. If I don't look the same, I owe it all to Weight Watchers, a fake front tooth, and laser eye surgery."

Bridget frowned at him. "Why are you following me around?"

"Following you around?"

"I saw you at Olivia Rankin's wake—"

"Yeah, I know," he said. "I wanted to talk to you there, but you kept avoiding me. I tried to smile at you, but you blew me off and went to talk to Fuller."

"Well, I—I didn't mean to *blow you off,*" she said. "I just didn't recognize you. Why were you there anyway? You were never very close to Olivia."

"Maybe. But she was a classmate. So was Fuller." He shrugged. "I didn't think you were that close to them either. I mean, weren't they more Brad's friends?"

Bridget ignored his question. "What were you doing the other day at the Red Lion Hotel—in Brad's and my hospitality room?" she asked. "And why were you at my son's Little League game?"

He frowned. "I'll tell you—if you get out of that corner. You're making me feel like Jack the Ripper here."

Chagrined, Bridget stuffed the heavy brass candlestick back in the open box. She stepped around the statue of St. Francis, but hesitated. "If I knew it was you earlier this morning," she said, looking him in the eye, "I would have opened that door."

He squinted at her. "What do you mean?"

"In the alley? Behind the Starbucks? Wasn't that you?"

"I still don't know what you're talking about."

She studied him. "No, you don't, do you?"

Bridget made her way around the stack of boxes and the religious artifacts, then met him by the doorway.

Zach offered his hand, and she shook it. He gave her a disarmingly cute, shy smile that reminded her so much of when he was a gawky teenager. "Hi, Bridget," he whispered. "It's nice to see you again."

From the corridor, they both stepped back into the old church and paused by Fuller's casket. "It's strange," Zach said. "Olivia and Fuller dying practically within a week of each other."

Bridget touched the side of Fuller's polished coffin. "Yes,

bizarre." She retreated down the aisle, and Zach walked alongside her. He stopped in the doorway—by a marble receptacle for the holy water. "I heard you earlier—with Fuller's sister," he said. "You were asking some interesting questions."

Bridget gave him a wary, sidelong glance. "I wasn't aware we had an audience." She knew he was Zachary Matthias from high school. He wasn't lying about that. Still, her guard was up.

"Well, it's not like I was eavesdropping," he said. "I was merely hanging around, hoping for an opportunity to come up and talk with you. Anyway, you were right to ask those questions. Some details about Fuller's accident have emerged in the last couple of days, stuff that wasn't in the newspaper."

"How do you know?" Bridget asked.

"I got curious and looked into it," he replied. "I talked to the cops and the coroner. Fuller Sterns had a gun in the car with him—along with a bottle of bourbon. It was smashed up from the accident. There was booze everywhere—except in Fuller's bloodstream. The coroner told me. Fuller was sober at the time of his death."

Zach glanced back at the coffin near the front of the church. "So where was he going at two in the morning with a gun and a bottle of bourbon in the car?"

Bridget kept thinking about the accident occurring on Garrett Road, so close to Brad's house.

"I talked to Fuller's neighbor yesterday," Zach continued. "This lady would have put Gladys Kravitz to shame. You know, the busybody on *Bewitched?* Her windows look right across to Fuller's house. And 'not that she makes a habit of minding other people's business, but she couldn't help noticing' that Fuller was home by eleven o'clock on Saturday night. She saw the light from the TV in his den until just past midnight. The old snoop even caught him getting ready for bed shortly after that." Zach frowned. "Then two hours later, Fuller smashed up his BMW on a lonely road—twenty miles away. Doesn't make much sense, does it?"

Bridget just shook her head.

"I keep wondering why he had the gun in the car with him."

Bridget shrugged uneasily. "Maybe he was scared."

"Maybe. Might explain the booze too. What's that old expression about booze? Dutch courage? Maybe he was going to meet someone he didn't want to face." Zach paused, and his eyes wrestled with hers. "Do you have any idea who that might be?"

Bridget shook her head. "Why should I?"

"Well, I saw you talking with Fuller at Olivia's wake, and then again at the Little League game. I didn't notice any kids here today, so my guess is the only reason he came to that game was to see you."

Bridget said nothing. She dipped her fingers in the holy water, then crossed herself. She headed through the vestibule and out the door. The afternoon sun was blinding after the church's gloomy interior.

Zach followed her. Stopping on the steps, Bridget fished her sunglasses from her purse and slipped them on. Then she turned to Zach. "You know, I asked you a few minutes ago why you were at that ball game. And I asked what you were doing in the hospitality suite at the Red Lion a few days ago. You still haven't answered me."

He gave her that disarmingly shy smile again. "Well, Bridget, I'm a reporter. I just started working for the *Portland Examiner*. If it seems like I've been following you around lately, I assure you, it's purely intentional. I'm doing a story on the election, a personal profile of the Corrigan twins."

"As told by an old acquaintance?" she asked, frowning. "The *Examiner* is blatantly pro-Foley."

He nodded glumly. "Yeah, I know."

Bridget felt as if he'd just punched her. She'd been talking to a pro-Foley reporter about Fuller and Olivia. If there was a connection between their deaths, he was on his way to finding it.

"So—I answered your question," he said. "Maybe you

can help me figure out what happened to Fuller. Why did he come to that Little League game? What did you two talk about?"

"No comment," Bridget replied.

She hurried down the church steps and headed for her car.

CHAPTER 11

She wasn't the type who drank in the middle of the afternoon, but Bridget could have used a cocktail when she returned home at 3:20 that day.

After Fuller's memorial service, she'd spoken at a Literacy Awareness event. All the while, she'd tried not to think about Zach Matthias, working for Foley's newspaper, asking questions about Fuller Sterns, and watching her every move. At least Zach hadn't shown up at the literacy event. And she'd managed to muster up enough poise to get through the proceedings.

After coming through the front door, Bridget settled for a Diet Coke and some barbecue potato chips. As much as a drink might have calmed her nerves, she didn't want to be like her mother.

She double-checked the locks on the doors and on the first-floor windows. David and Eric wouldn't be back from school for another half hour. Though it was still light out, Bridget didn't like being alone.

She now knew Zach Matthias was the man she'd noticed at the memorial services, at the game, and at the hotel. But what about the man she hadn't seen? He'd been waiting for her in the alley alcove, and he'd been lurking outside this house a few nights back.

How many nights ago had the exact same thing happened to Fuller Sterns? How many nights after that did he die in a strange, unexplained accident?

Bridget hadn't talked to Brad since that morning. She was miffed he hadn't had time to hear about Fuller's death. The news had seemed to shock him, but he hadn't cared enough to call back yet. No matter. She wasn't anxious to tell Brad that a former high school classmate was now working for a Foley rag and asking a lot of questions.

Still working on the Diet Coke, she dug her high school yearbook out of the storage closet, then plopped down on the sofa in the den. She cautiously glanced over at the picture window, where she'd first seen that man in her yard.

No one, just a lot of fallen leaves blowing in the wind, and a lawn that needed mowing.

With a sigh, Bridget opened the McLaren High yearbook, and turned to the class of '85 graduation portraits. She stopped on the M's page and stared at the photo of a young Zach Matthias in a coat and tie—the wild black hair, baby fat, thick glasses, and that sweet, guileless smile. Bridget could see why her old friend Kim had had a little crush on him. Under the portrait were his credentials:

ZACHARY L. MATTHIAS
"Zach"
Student Council; Yearbook Staff;
The McLaren Bobcat Gazette; French Club;
Teen Big Brothers; Glee Club; Bobcat Boosters.
Parting Words: *"Hello, I Must Be Going"*
—Groucho Marx.

Despite herself, Bridget smiled at his sentiments. Then her eyes wandered over to another portrait on the same page. She swallowed hard, and the smile ran away from her face.

The photo showed a plump girl with stringy brown hair and a superior look behind her glasses. For the photo-shoot, she'd dressed in a black T-shirt and a ratty old wide-knit sweater vest.

During the summer after graduation, that same photo had been posted all over McLaren and neighboring Longview in hopes that the missing eighteen-year-old would be found. In the flier-bulletin, they'd listed her name, height, weight, eye color, hair color, date of birth, and when she'd last been seen. There was also a contact number.

But in the McLaren High yearbook, the listing was more terse:

MALLORY MEEHAN
"Mallory"
Glee Club
Parting Words: *"To riseth above the crass and
common crowd is never easy."*
—M. Meehan

Mallory often broadcast to anyone who bothered to listen that she had an IQ of 141. "That's my 'intelligence quotient,'" she would add with haughty condescension. Despite her constantly reminding people of this, the story that stuck with Mallory for years was that she'd pooped in her pants during math class in the fifth grade. The students at McLaren High wouldn't let her forget it.

They might have been more kind if Mallory hadn't alienated everyone—including their teachers. Mallory often challenged them for not working hard enough—or knowing enough. The teachers retaliated by giving out a ton of homework assignments. Mallory was critical of her classmates too—almost vicious toward the slower ones.

Mallory Meehan wasn't one of those not-so-popular kids whom Brad befriended during a school outing. No, befriending Mallory was Bridget's mistake.

She thought Mallory was merely insecure and lonely. She

ried to be her friend. Kim said she was committing *social suicide.* "Not that I give the tiniest crap about what people in this school think of *me*," Kim told her. "But I know it matters to *you*. And if you get too chummy-chummy with Miss Pain-in-the-Ass Poopy-Drawers, believe me, no one will have anything to do with you."

But Bridget wanted to follow her brother's example and reach out to a less-popular classmate. She found it strange that Kim would object to her making friends with another extremely intelligent, above-the-crowd girl, someone very much like Kim herself. Bridget figured she was a bit jealous.

Mallory had her own theory: "I think she's a lesbian."

"No, she isn't," Bridget whispered. "Kim would have told me if she was gay. She wouldn't hide it. She knows it wouldn't make a difference to me."

They were huddled in a cubicle in the main room of the town library. Bridget imagined that the converted old mansion off Main Street in McLaren might become their after-school hangout. The library was a strange, unsuccessful melding of old-world charm with seventies-style utilitarian furnishings. Ugly metal bookcases were pushed against the elegantly paneled walls; track lighting was installed by a beautiful old chandelier; and a cheap black-and-brass fireplace insert had been stuck inside the handsomely manteled hearth. All the furniture was chrome and faux wood with orange and green imitation leather coverings. Two gray-cloth quad cubicles had been planted in the big room. Bridget and Mallory were crammed into one partition.

"I still say she's a lesbian," Mallory insisted. "She looks like one."

"Well, she isn't," Bridget said, rolling her eyes.

She tolerated Mallory because she was so damn fascinating. Mallory claimed she was writing an "exposé" of the whole town—like Grace Metallious did with *Peyton Place*. But Mallory wasn't going to change names, places, and dates. She was especially interested in murders, suicides, and missing persons cases. McLaren was a small, sleepy town, but it had had its share of the bizarre and macabre—even before the case of Andy Shields and the Gaines twins. And in nearly all of those stories, something horrible had happened in Gorman's Creek.

Bridget chalked the creepy tales up to local legend. If enough teenagers believed those vague, spooky yarns, they wouldn't trespass on the property. But Mallory claimed the stories were true. She had facts.

In 1932, a successful businessman, Henry Bowers from nearby Olympia, built a house overlooking the creek—on a piece of land named after one of the town's early settlers, Eli Gorman. The isolated cottage was meant to be a family retreat. But the Bowerses didn't have much time to enjoy their home away from home. The house was only a year old when most of it fell down the gulch during a horrible mud slide. The Bowerses' six-year-old daughter, Amy, was buried alive.

Another story about Gorman's Creek smacked of urban legend. Apparently, a teenage couple had gone skinny-dipping in the pond one summer night in the midfifties. They were still naked when their bodies were found. It appeared as if the boy had killed his girlfriend, then taken his own life. He'd hanged the girl from a tree limb, then disemboweled her. With a similarly fashioned noose around his neck, his naked corpse hung beside her—on the same branch. Their clothes—and a murder weapon—were never found.

"I've always found that tale tough to swallow," Bridget declared.

"Well, I'll show you—it's true," Mallory insisted. She peeked around the side of the cubicle toward the library's front counter. "It's in this article I want you to see—if that old queer behind the desk would hurry up and get the newspaper I asked for."

Bridget frowned. "Mallory, I really don't like—"

"Oh, I think he has it now," she interrupted, getting to her feet. She hurried toward the front counter. Bridget watched her mutter something to the slightly prissy, middle-aged Mr. Needler, who was the head librarian. Mallory scribbled on a

ign-out sheet, slapped down the pencil, and snatched the
ook off the counter. As she stomped back to the cubicle
ith her book, Mallory didn't see Mr. Needler frowning at
er.

"Look at this," Mallory whispered, plopping down in the
hair beside Bridget. She opened the book. It was a bound
dition of *Cowlitz County Registers* from January through
une, 1956. The *Register* was a weekly newspaper-magazine
or Longview and surrounding communities. The cover of
very issue was always some community event or a lighter-
ide news item: the Cowlitz County Teacher of the Year; a
'ub Scout Banquet; Cowlitz County Players presents *The
Aan Who Came to Dinner*; art shows; and pancake break-
asts.

Mallory furiously turned the pages. "This isn't about the
ouple who were found hanging from the tree, but they're
nentioned here. I haven't been able to track down an actual
tory on them. This stupid library doesn't carry any news-
apers before 1955. Oh, here it is." She paused to check an
ssue, dated June 7, 1956. Mallory turned a few more yel-
owed pages. Then she stopped and pointed to an article.

Alongside the story was a slightly blurred photo of a
miling, dowdy woman with dark hair and glasses. *Eloise
'essler, 49, left a husband and two children*, said the cap-
ion.

The headline read:

MCLAREN WOMAN FOUND DEAD
Tragic End to Two-Day Missing-Person Search

"Is this Sonny and Anastasia's mother?" Bridget whis-
ered.

Mallory nodded. "And Loony Lon's wife. Read on."

Biting her lip, Bridget read the story:

*The body of housewife Mrs. Eloise Fessler, 49, was
discovered on the bank of a small lake just a mile from*

her home in McLaren on Tuesday afternoon. She had been missing two days. Investigators on the scene are calling her drowning an apparent suicide.

Mrs. Fessler had recently been under a nurse's care after swallowing an overdose of sleeping pills. She disappeared Sunday morning, June 3, triggering a county-wide search.

Eloise Fessler was the wife of industrialist Lon Fessler, 51, and mother of two, Lon Jr., 22, and Anastasia, 19.

Authorities focused their search for Mrs. Fessler in a two-mile wooded ravine area behind her home. . . .

"Did you get to the part about Gorman's Creek yet?" Mallory asked impatiently.

"I'm just there," Bridget replied. "But they don't say exactly how she drowned."

Mallory whisked her hand over the page as if shooing away a fly. "Well, it's not in there. Loony Lon must have paid someone to leave out the details. Don't you know about it?"

Bridget shrugged. "I'd heard Mrs. Fessler drowned in that pond, but I never knew it was a suicide."

"Sure was." Mallory nodded emphatically. "She put on a big, heavy fur coat and walked the trail along Gorman's Creek. Back in the fifties, it wasn't so overgrown, because that used to be the Bowerses' driveway. Some of the property still belongs to the Bowers estate, the older sister of the kid who died in the mud slide. She inherited the place, but didn't want anything to do with it. The Fesslers are so nuts, they think the whole ravine is theirs. Loony Lon used to have a rowboat in that little lake. They even built a dock there. But old Lon had it torn down after Eloise killed herself."

"How did she do it?" Bridget murmured.

"She took the rowboat to the middle of the lake, then jumped in. The fur coat got all wet and dragged her down. found out from a couple of my mother's friends, who both grew up here. One of them was the sheriff's daughter. So

ave it on extremely reliable authority. They verified the
tory about the two teenagers as well. And it's mentioned
ight here. It's no urban legend, Bridget."

Mallory pointed to a paragraph near the end of the arti-
le. Bridget obediently read:

> The lake was the site of another tragedy in June,
> 1953, when the dead bodies of McLaren residents
> Frank Healy and Janette Carlisle, both 18, were dis-
> covered hanging from a nearby tree. The grisly scene
> reportedly shook several experienced lawmen. Author-
> ities ruled the deaths a murder-suicide, determining
> that Healy had killed his girlfriend, Carlisle, and then
> himself.
>
> Gorman's Creek, the ravine area and pond are on
> private property. McLaren police have announced their
> intention to prosecute trespassers to the fullest extent
> of the law.
>
> Funeral services for Eloise Fessler will be private.
> In addition to her husband and two children, she is
> also survived by a sister, Mrs. Sarah Ballard. . . .

"In the book I'm writing, I'm calling Gorman's Creek
he Devil's Gulch," Mallory bragged. "It's the only name
'm changing. After all, it's *cursed ground. Devil's Gulch* is a
etter name for the place, don't you think?"

Bridget shrugged. "Well, not really. *Devil's Gulch* sounds
ind of hokey to me, like some spot you'd visit on a tour of
)isneyland."

Mallory frowned at her. "I thought you—of all people—
vould understand. You knew one of the three boys who were
illed in that forest. You saw the dead bodies."

Bridget shifted in her chair. Suddenly, it seemed too hot
nd close in the little cubicle. "Well, except for someone
laiming they spotted Andy and the Gaines twins heading
)ward Gorman's Creek, no one ever said they were actually
illed there."

"I'm saying it," Mallory whispered. "I'm saying it now. I'll show you what I mean, Bridget. Let's go to Gorman' Creek. Let's do it now, before you get scared and chang your mind."

Bridget wasn't scared. She just found Mallory Meehan har to like. She was bossy, tactless, and overly critical of others

Walking alongside her, Bridget tried to overlook Mallory' many faults and quirks. After all, since early childhoo Mallory had been ostracized and tormented by her peers. N wonder she was a bit mean and difficult. To her credit, sh certainly was an interesting character to know bette *Eccentric*. Bridget had a feeling Mallory would indeed writ that book.

Still, as they headed down Main Street on that overcas spring afternoon, Bridget hated herself for hoping no on saw them together.

A car passed by, and someone stuck his head out the pas senger side. It took Bridget a moment to recognize Fulle Sterns. "Hey, Mallory!" he yelled. "You ugly piece of shit You suck!"

The car picked up speed, then turned a corner, its tire screeching.

"Oh, never mind him," Bridget said, giving her classmat a nudge. "He's a major asshole."

Mallory stared straight ahead with her haughty, superio look. "I don't know what you're talking about," she replied.

"I'm talking about Fuller Sterns," Bridget said. "He's jerk. He—" She stopped herself.

Mallory didn't seem to be listening. Had she actuall learned how to filter out the taunting and name-calling? Wa that possible? Bridget didn't say another word—for severa blocks.

As they headed down Briar Court, Bridget gazed at th Fesslers' house at the end of the street, and the dense fores beyond that. Above them, the skies were darkening, and th wind kicked up. Bridget shuddered. She didn't want to b stuck in the ravine if it started to rain.

"Don't you feel as if someone's watching us?" Mallory asked in a hushed tone. She nodded toward the Fesslers' house. All the lights were off inside.

"Oh, quit trying to creep me out," Bridget said, grinning. "The Fesslers are all pretty harmless."

"Huh, a lot you know," Mallory grumbled. "C'mon."

She led Bridget along some hedges around the Fesslers' side lawn to a gap in the barbed-wire fence. They slipped past the opening and started down a crude trail through the woods. The narrow, dirt path was muddy in spots. Rocks and exposed roots became obstacles along the way.

It had been years since Bridget had explored Gorman's Creek. Mallory forged ahead with the confidence of someone well acquainted with the terrain. Trees engulfed them, blocking out the sky. Branches swayed with the wind, and leaves rustled.

It was hard to imagine that this narrow path had once been a driveway to the Bowers family's dream house—before their dreams were destroyed. *Cursed ground*, Mallory had called it. Mrs. Fessler had taken this same trail to the pond, where she drowned herself. And one warm June night, thirty-odd years ago, a teenage Janette Carlisle had snuck down this path with her boyfriend, not knowing what he'd had planned for them.

There were ghosts in this forest. Bridget wondered if Andy and his two friends were among them.

It had been over a year since that night she'd stood at the end of the cul-de-sac, watching the policemen search these woods with their flashlights. They still hadn't found the person or persons who had murdered those boys.

Bridget wondered what Mallory planned to show her in these woods. How could she shed any light on the unsolved murders? Bridget remembered how all the boys' shoes and socks had been taken away. Had Mallory found them buried somewhere here?

"C'mon, the Bowers house is this way," Mallory announced. She veered off the path. The forest was so thick,

Bridget could only see Mallory in fragments—darting between the trees and shrubs.

"Hey, you know, Mallory," she called, a tremor creeping in her voice, "I thought you were going to show me something to prove Andy and his friends were killed out here." She weaved around bushes and small gullies, trailing after her guide. It seemed to be growing darker by the minute. "Listen, I've got burrs on my socks and I can tell it's going to rain. If you don't mind, I'd like to turn back. This isn't exactly my idea of a terrific time."

"Don't be such a scaredy-cat," Mallory called back to her. "C'mon over here."

Bridget maneuvered around the woods to a clearing, where Mallory stood. The trees in this small patch of land were dwarfed by all the others around them. The spot had been cleared for the Bowers house seventy-two years ago. But nature had taken back the land. Bushes had crept up through cracks in the concrete foundation that remained. A brick fireplace and broken chimney were weather-beaten and covered with mold. On the stone steps, spray-paint graffiti—probably from twenty years ago—was faded. Those steps had led to the Bowerses' front door; but now they didn't lead anywhere.

Bridget had explored Gorman's Creek back when she was a kid. She remembered stopping by these "ruins" with her friends. But she'd never really understood what had happened there, and what had been lost. Many others had been there before as well. Bridget noticed the old candy wrappers, empty soda pop bottles and beer cans where the Bowerses' living room must have been. A couple of the rusty, faded beer cans were so old, they had triangular punctures on the top—from can openers.

"Take a look down there," Mallory said, pointing to the creek below. "You can see what's left of the house. Darn, we should have brought binoculars."

Bridget came up beside Mallory, who stood a few feet from

where the ground sloped down to a plateau. Below that, the terrain took a sharp hundred-foot incline to the creek. They were gazing down at the treetops. Bridget moved closer to the edge so she could get a better look at the creek. She could hear the water rushing.

"Watch out," Mallory warned. "If you fall down there, I can't help you. I have vertigo. You know, acrophobia? I get nervous just standing this close to the edge."

Bridget made her way down the slight embankment toward the plateau. To keep from falling, she held on to bushes and the exposed roots of a tall tree.

"You're on your own, Bridget!" Mallory warned. "I'm not going down there."

Bridget wasn't listening. Between the trees, she could see a pile of rubble that had created a dam in the creek below. The stream ran over and around the wreckage, which after seventy years had almost become part of the terrain. Amid the debris, Bridget noticed planks of wood, half a window frame, an old, broken wicker chair, and even a child's rocking horse.

"What do you see?" Mallory called.

"You really should come down here," Bridget said soberly. "Take a look for yourself."

"No way," Mallory argued. "I told you, I have acrophobia. It's a *condition*. I don't like confined places either. I have claustrophobia too. What do you see?"

"Some of their furniture is down there," Bridget replied. She figured the rocking horse must have belonged to the little girl, buried in the mud slide.

"Most of the furniture that survived the fall got picked through, the good stuff anyway," Mallory said. "The Bowerses didn't want it, didn't want anything more to do with the place. The mud slide happened in the middle of the Depression, so a lot of bums made off with their stuff. I guess the word spread on the hobo trails that there were clothes and furniture here for the picking. That's how these woods first became dangerous for the townspeople and their kids There were always a couple of hobos around here ready to slit someone's throat for a few dollars."

Bridget had seen enough. She glanced around for an easier way to climb up from the bluff. She noticed a crude trail around the other side of a big tree that jutted out —almost diagonally—above the cliff. It looked ready to topple over—as the Bowers house had.

Approaching the tilted tree, Bridget spotted something in the ground—a trapdoor made of old wood planks, now covered with moss. A nearby shrub almost camouflaged it. Bridget squatted down for a closer look.

"Where are you?" Mallory called, panic in her voice. "I don't see you."

"I found something down here," Bridget replied. She noticed a rusty latch on one side of the door and a broken padlock on the other. Only God knew what was beyond the door, what was *nesting* in there. Bridget hesitated another moment, then reached down and tried to pull open the moss-covered door. It stuck at first, so she gave it another tug.

"What are you doing?" Mallory called. "You're making me nervous, Bridget."

The trapdoor let out a groan as Bridget pulled it open. She peeked into a little crawl space—about the size of a phone booth. It must have been a storage bin of some kind—for logs or coal. Bridget guessed it was about eight feet deep. She opened the door wider, and it let out another creak.

"What was that noise?" Mallory cried. "Oh my God, the tree's falling!"

For a moment, Bridget believed her. She dropped the lid to the storage space. The sudden noise—or something—made Mallory scream.

Bridget scrambled past the tree and up the slope. She stumbled. Rocks and chunks of dirt dislodged under her feet and flew down the precipice. Bridget scurried up the hill to where Mallory was standing with both hands over her mouth.

"What the hell are you screaming about?" Bridget asked, out of breath. She dusted the dirt off her jeans.

"I heard that weird, splintering noise," Mallory whined. "I thought the tree was tipping over."

"The tree's fine, stupid," Bridget replied, with a depleted laugh. "But you almost gave *me* a friggin' heart attack." She took hold of Mallory's arm to lean against her, but Mallory pulled away.

"Don't call me stupid," she snapped. "I'm smarter than you are. I have an IQ of 141."

Bridget saw tears in her eyes. "I didn't mean anything by it, Mallory. I even call my brother 'stupid' sometimes, and he's one of the smartest people I know."

"I thought you were going to get killed," Mallory said in a shaky voice. "And—and you're the only person in our class who's nice to me. I don't have any other friends."

Bridget felt so sorry for her at that moment. She couldn't think of anything to say. She smiled awkwardly, then shrugged. "Hey, listen, let's get out of here. Okay, Mallory?"

Mallory hesitated. She seemed reluctant to leave what was once the Bowerses' living room. "But don't you want to see the pond where Mrs. Fessler drowned herself? And the tree where that couple—"

Bridget was shaking her head. "I've seen the pond, Mallory. And I really don't want to look at the tree. I—I've seen enough. It looks like rain coming. I need to get home."

"I still haven't told you why I think those three boys were killed out here," Mallory offered as they forged their way back to the trail. "Want to hear my theory?"

Not really, Bridget was tempted to say. But she kept walking, and watched for tree roots, rocks, and other obstacles in her path.

"I already proved one part of my theory to you." Mallory dropped behind Bridget as the trail narrowed. "I screamed, a couple of times, and loudly too."

"Loud enough to wake the dead," Bridget muttered.

"But nobody came. Nobody heard me. There's no other place in this town where you could scream and scream, and no one would hear."

"That's no proof they were murdered in these woods," Bridget said. "Their bodies were found fifty miles from town. There are a lot of places they could have been killed between here and the old Oxytech plant. Lots of other places where no one could hear them screaming."

Bridget shuddered at the memory of seeing their dead bodies in the plant's rail yard. She didn't want to talk about this anymore.

"But the three of them were last seen walking toward these woods," Mallory argued. "And who lives at the beginning of the trail? The retard, that's who. He saw them—"

"Mallory, I really hate that term," Bridget growled, walking faster.

"Okay, but he's still not right in the head. And I'll bet he knows these woods better than anybody else. He could have killed them and hidden the bodies some place the police wouldn't find them."

Bridget thought of that crawl space she'd just stumbled upon. But she quickly shook her head. "Sonny Fessler is harmless."

"I'll bet those three boys thought the same thing."

"Have you ever seen Sonny behind the wheel of a car?" Bridget countered. "How do you think he got the bodies from here to that chemical plant fifty miles away? Do you think he used his Schwinn?"

"He could have had an accomplice who owns a car."

"Oh, please," Bridget groaned, not breaking her stride. "Sonny doesn't have any friends. He's just a sweet, simple, slightly off-beat guy. He's McLaren's Boo Radley. Didn't you ever read *To Kill a Mockingbird*? Sonny wouldn't intentionally harm anyone. You're way off, Mallory."

Bridget saw the barbed-wire fence up ahead, and thanked God she was almost out of there. She thought Mallory would

have been more sympathetic toward another friendless outsider. Instead, she seemed to have utter contempt for him.
Her accusations made no sense.

"I know he killed those boys," Mallory insisted. "I'm
going to prove it. And it'll be in my book."

"That's swell," Bridget muttered. She was looking at the
opening in the fence.

"I might have the whole book be about Gorman's Creek,"
Mallory said, trailing after her. "And I'll call it *The Devil's
Gulch*, like I said. It'll be a best seller, just you wait. It'll put
me above the crowd. . . ."

Bridget remembered that afternoon in the woods, and felt
a pang of regret in her gut. If she hadn't gone there with
Mallory Meehan that day, things would have been different.
Strange, how Mallory Meehan had been so obsessed with
Gorman's Creek, and that was where she would die.

Bridget stared at the quote under Mallory's portrait in the
yearbook: *To riseth above the crass and common crowd is
never easy.*

She heard the school bus pulling up in front of the house.
Then someone tapped on their car horn a couple of times.
Bridget glanced at her wristwatch: 3:45. Setting aside the
yearbook, she got up from the sofa and went to the front
door. Outside, the school bus was pulling away, and Brad's
BMW was just turning into the driveway. Eric waved at him.
And David had put down his schoolbooks to signal and di-
rect his uncle as if he were working in a plane hangar.
Watching him, Bridget cracked a smile.

Brad climbed out of the car, then hugged David and Eric.
He was wearing a suit and tie, but that didn't stop him from
horsing around with them on the front lawn for a couple of
minutes.

Finally, the three of them headed for the front door. The
boys, both out of breath, filed in first. Bridget gave them

both a quick kiss on the forehead. She threw her brother a wry smile. "To what do we owe the pleasure of your company?"

"I'm sorry I couldn't talk to you on the phone earlier," he said under his breath. "And I couldn't call you back. Something's come up. It's not a good idea to talk about Fuller Sterns over the phone- -or even in the house."

"What do you mean?" Bridget whispered.

"Uncle Brad, I want to show you my Power Rangers!" Eric interrupted. He grabbed Brad by the hand and started to drag him inside.

"Honey, not now," Bridget started to say. "Uncle Brad and I—"

"It's okay," Brad assured her. "We'll talk about this later."

"C'mon!" Tugging at his uncle's arm, Eric led him into the den.

Bridget shut the front door and wandered into the room after them. Eric already had Brad parked in front of the TV while he got out his CD-ROM game. David sat on the sofa with the McLaren High 1985 yearbook in his lap. "God, Mom," he cackled. "You and Uncle Brad had some really dorky-looking people in your graduating class!" He turned the book around and pointed to Zach's photo. "Who is Zachary Matthias? How nerdy can you get?"

"Actually, he was a very nice guy," Bridget said. "And I ran into him today—at the funeral of another high school friend."

Brad shot her a look.

She stared back at him, but kept talking to her son: "Zach is working for the *Examiner* now. He was at your Little League game on Saturday, David. In fact, I've seen him around a lot lately. I just hadn't recognized him. Turns out he's doing a story on me—for his newspaper."

Brad slowly shook his head.

Frowning, Bridget gave a secretive nod.

"Ugh! Who is Mallory Meehan?" David laughed. "Talk about a loser! Was she your friend, Mom?"

Bridget turned away from her brother, then sighed. "Yes, we were friends—for a very short time."

"What happened to her?" David asked.

Bridget didn't answer.

"She disappeared the summer after our senior year," Brad replied. "Isn't that right, Brigg? She disappeared, and no one ever knew what happened to her. Right, Brigg?"

Bridget didn't look at him. "I better get dinner on," she said quietly.

Then she headed toward the kitchen.

CHAPTER 12

With dusk creeping over the horizon, Bridget and Brad stood in her backyard. She was watering the bushes with the garden hose. Through the picture window, they could see David and Eric in the den, playing a video game on TV. Just a few nights ago, a stranger had been watching Bridget through the same window.

Brad said it wasn't safe to talk inside their houses or on their phones—not until they'd conducted a "sweep check" for bugging devices. Brad's campaign manager, Jay Corby, had a source on Foley's team. Jay's *source* was a spy—a *volunteer* at Foley campaign headquarters. Foley had planted Wes Linderman in the Corrigan-for-Oregon camp, so this was tit for tat. According to Jay's spy, Foley had investigators who uncovered some potentially damaging information about Brad's past. "No word on what it is," Brad explained. "But Foley was in his office dancing a jig over what they'd found. He must be waiting for the right time to spring the news."

"Do you think it might have anything to do with Gorman's Creek?" Bridget asked.

"I'm not sure. But I wonder if our pal Zach Matthias has a hand in this. You said he's with the *Examiner*? Foley has the *Examiner* kissing his ass. The son of a bitch could burn down an orphanage and *eat* the children, and the goddamn *Examiner* would still be singing his praises. I wouldn't be surprised if Foley put one of their reporters on his payroll. What exactly happened with you and *good old Zach* today?"

Bridget directed the hose on a hydrangea bush, and she told him about her day—all of it. She told him about meeting with her estranged husband, reading the article on Fuller's bizarre death, the incident in the alley, and finally, running into Zach Matthias at Fuller's funeral.

"I don't think Zach is the man who was in this yard the other night," she said. "And I don't believe he was in that alley this morning. I'm pretty sure it was someone else."

"I wouldn't be surprised if this *stalker* character works for Foley too," Brad said.

She frowned. "Why in the world would Foley hire someone to *stalk* me? What kind of strategy is that?"

"They're probably trying to get personal stuff on you, Brigg."

"Well, I have nothing to hide," she said, sighing. "Except the truth about something that happened twenty years ago." She gave the hose nozzle a twist and shut off the water. "Brad, sooner or later, we'll have to face up to what we've done. And I think we've run out of 'later.' " She tossed aside the hose. "There were five of us with Mallory that night at Gorman's Creek—"

Brad started shaking his head, refusing to listen.

"Five of us," Bridget repeated. She grabbed his arm. "You, me, Cheryl Blume, Fuller Sterns, and Olivia Rankin. Two weeks ago, Olivia contacted Fuller. She had new information about what happened at Gorman's Creek—"

"You know, we've already had this discussion—"

"Hear me out. Please. Two days after Olivia got a nice bundle of cash out of Fuller, she was found on a beach with a bullet in her head—an *apparent suicide*. It doesn't make sense."

He shook his head again. "A lot of suicides don't make sense. You have no idea why Olivia might have taken her own life."

"Yes, well, we can rule out money concerns, can't we?" Bridget retorted. "I don't think she killed herself, Brad. And I don't think Fuller's death was an accident. Zach has been looking into it, and from everything he told me, there's something awfully suspicious about that car wreck—like it was a setup. Fuller told me just a few days ago that he was being followed—watched. The same thing is happening to me. It could be happening to you too, Brad, only you're too busy to notice. You already have so many reporters and curiosity seekers on your tail, you might not see the one face in the crowd. Then again, I've never seen his face. Fuller said he never got a good look at his face either."

"I think you're shaken up," he said. "And that's understandable, considering what you've been through. But you're leaping to a lot of wrong conclusions here—"

"I am not, and you know it," she growled. Bridget snatched the hose off the ground, then dragged it toward the side of the house.

"Here, let me." He reached for the hose.

"I've got it," Bridget snapped, jerking the hose away from him. "At this point, I think the smart—the prudent—thing to do is track down Cheryl Blume. And if she's alive, if she hasn't recently fallen off some bridge or gotten hit by a car, maybe we can find out from Cheryl if someone has been following her around lately."

Brad shook his head again. "But with Foley's people watching our every move—"

"I'll do it," Bridget assured him. She dropped the hose by the side of the house and shut off the water. "I'll get myself a roll of quarters and call her from a pay phone. I'll be discreet—if I can track her down."

They'd lost touch with Cheryl—as they had the others. Cheryl had been Brad's girlfriend through most of their senior year. She'd been a prototype for Janice: pretty, blond, and a bit pushy. She didn't exactly lead Brad around by a ring in his nose, but at times it might have seemed that way.

"Do you know if Cheryl's parents still live in McLaren?" Bridget asked.

"Beats the hell out of me."

"Do you remember her parents' names?"

"Mike and Janet." His cell phone rang, and he automatically switched it off. "What do you plan to do about good old Zach?" he asked. "If he keeps picking away at this thing, he might just find out about Gorman's Creek—that is, if Foley's team doesn't already know about it."

Brad looked into the den and gave one of his nephews a little wave. "You'll have to keep him off course," he continued. "If Zach Matthias is working for Foley's newspaper, he can't be trusted."

Bridget frowned. "What exactly did you have in mind? I mean, what would you have me do?"

"Do whatever you need to do to keep him off track. The guy's poison, Brigg. He's poison."

"Order dessert for yourselves," Bridget said. She scooted out of the booth at the Mexican restaurant where she'd taken David and Eric for dinner. "Anything you want—except, Eric, you can't have the deep-fried ice cream."

"But, Mom—"

"No way," she said, cutting him off. "Last time you had that here, it gave you gross-out stomach, and I was up all night with you. Remember? Nix on the deep-fried ice cream. And stop kicking the table."

Frowning, her younger son stopped swinging his feet at the table leg.

"I'll be right outside, okay? I just need to make a couple of calls."

"Why don't you use your cell phone?" David asked, looking up from his dessert menu.

"Can't. The batteries are low. Behave yourselves, guys."

Bridget hurried to the cashier at the front of the restaurant, where she asked for three dollars in quarters. At home earlier, she'd gone through her change jar and come up with seventeen quarters. She figured she now had enough for a few long-distance calls. She'd already done a name/address search on Google.com and found nothing. She hoped to have better luck on the phone.

She ducked outside—to a pay phone by the front door. Through the window, she could see David and Eric in the booth. The waiter was taking their dessert order. Eric was kicking the table again.

Bridget rolled her eyes and dialed directory assistance for area code 564. She asked for Michael, Janet, or Cheryl Blume in McLaren, Washington.

"I'm sorry, there's no listing for any of those names," the directory assistance operator said.

She didn't have any luck finding Cheryl or her parents in Longview—or Vancouver, Washington. Bridget asked about some other cities.

"Ma'am, Portland is area code 503," the operator said. "For seventy-five cents, I can connect you. . . ."

Bridget ended up talking to an *M. Blume* in Tigard, outside Portland. The M was for Mildred, and she sounded like a cranky old lady: "No, I don't have any relatives in McLaren! Why in God's name are you bothering me?"

All the while, through the window, Bridget kept an eye on David and Eric. The waiter had arrived with their desserts, and now they were almost finished with them.

Working with yet another directory assistant in a third area code, Bridget had $2.25 left in her fist when they found a Michael and Charlotte Blume in Olympia, Washington. There was a chance that Mr. Blume had remarried—or perhaps it was Cheryl's kid brother, Mikey, who by now had to be about thirty.

Bridget took down the number, then deposited the rest of her quarters and dialed. She counted the ring tones. Through the window, she watched another waiter approach the boys' booth. David looked up and nodded at him. Bridget and the boys were regulars at this restaurant. She knew most of the staff, and chatted with them in Spanish. She didn't recognize this waiter, a tall, thin, pale man with wavy red hair. He wasn't dressed like the other waiters, who all wore white short-sleeve shirts and black pants under their red aprons. This guy had the red apron on over a dark shirt and khakis.

An answering machine clicked on the other end of the line. Over the recording, a young child recited the greeting—with considerable difficulty. Her parents kept coaching her in the background—and cracking up as the child fumbled over her lines. It was excruciating. Bridget prayed they were screening calls and would soon pick up the phone. She couldn't leave a message and ask them to call her, because Brad said her home and cell phones could be tapped.

She peered into the restaurant again. The red-haired waiter was still hanging by the booth, talking with David and Eric. Bridget wondered why he wasn't carrying a tray, and why he hadn't removed anything from the table.

Finally, she heard the beep on the other end of the connection. "Um, yes, hello," she said, eyes still on the tall, red-haired waiter. "I'm trying to track down a member of the Blume family who lived in McLaren. I went to high school with—"

There was a click on the other end. "Yes, hello? Who's calling?"

"Um, my name is Bridget. I'm trying to get a hold of someone who went to McLaren High with me."

"I went to McLaren High, and so did my older sister," the man said.

"Michael, I'm Bridget Corrigan. I was in Cheryl's class."

"Oh my God, this is a blast from the past." He chuckled. "Your twin brother's running for senator down in Oregon. He used to date Cheryl."

"That's right, on both counts. Is—um . . ." She hesitated. She was afraid to ask if Cheryl was all right. "How—is Cheryl doing?"

"Fine. At least she was doing great when I last talked with her a couple of weeks ago. She's single again. Lives down in Eugene. Why are you trying to track her down? A reunion or something?"

"Yes, something like that. Do you happen to have her phone number handy, Michael?"

Bridget was jotting down the phone number for Cheryl Blume Lassiter on Van Buren Street in Eugene, when she looked through the restaurant window for a moment. She didn't like what she saw. Ordinarily, it wouldn't have bothered her—especially if she'd known the waiter. But this stranger was still standing at their table, talking to her sons. David appeared a bit nervous, and he was shaking his head. The waiter reached over and patted Eric on the shoulder. Then he mussed his hair.

"I just saw Brad on TV yesterday," Michael was saying. "Some election coverage thing. We have a satellite dish and get the Portland stations too. Sure looks like a tight race down there. Tell me, does Brad—"

"Um, Michael, I have to go," Bridget said, looking through the restaurant window. "I'm sorry. One of my kids just got into something. Thanks so much for Cheryl's number. You take care."

She hung up the phone, stuffed her notepad in her purse, then swung open the door to the restaurant. As she made a beeline for the booth, the red-haired waiter glanced over his shoulder at her.

He quickly turned away and headed for the kitchen.

Obviously confused, her two sons stared up at her. Their empty dessert plates were still in front of them.

"Are you guys okay?" she asked.

"Yeah," David said. "Where were you?"

"What was that man saying to you?" she asked.

David shrugged. "I dunno—"

Bridget didn't wait for him to elaborate. She hurried toward the restaurant's kitchen. The double doors were still swinging back and forth as Bridget entered through them.

She saw the back door slam at the other end of the kitchen. A couple of cooks and a startled busboy looked at her from behind a stainless steel counter.

"¿Acaba de pasar corriendo por aqui un hombre de pelo rojo?" she asked them, which translated to: "Did a man with red hair just run through here? Do you know him?"

Bridget headed to the back door and opened it.

One of the cooks told her that a total stranger had indeed just raced through there—like someone was chasing him.

Bridget stared out at the back lot. The Dumpster was by the kitchen door, and it smelled of old meat and rotting fruit. Bridget caught a glimpse of a Subaru with its lights off—peeling out of the lot. The car disappeared around the bend.

Bridget could still hear its tires screeching in the distance.

"He said he heard you speaking Spanish to the other waiter," David explained. He sat on the passenger side—across from his mother. Eric was behind him, lightly kicking the back of his seat.

Hands on the wheel, Bridget watched the road ahead. "That's all? He was talking with you an awful long time."

David sighed. "He asked if we had a Spanish father. And big mouth back there says, 'No, our father's divorced.' So then the waiter asked if you had a Spanish boyfriend or something. I told him, no, and he asked some other stuff, like what grades we were in at school, and bla, bla, bla."

"The wader kept on axing if Mom has a boyfriend," Eric piped up from the back. Leaning forward, he stuck his head between the two front seats.

She shot David a look. "Is that true?"

"Yeah, he came back to it a couple of times."

Bridget sighed. "Listen, guys. As it comes closer to the election, you're going to get a lot of people coming up and asking you a bunch of stuff about me—and about Uncle Brad. You handled it well tonight. But from now on, just politely tell them to call my office or e-mail me at *Corrigan forOregon dot com*." She paused. "Better yet, just go by my old rule and don't talk to strangers. Okay?"

"Okay!" Eric replied in a singsong voice. He sat back again and recommenced kicking the back of his brother's seat.

"That guy with the red hair," David whispered. "He wasn't a waiter, was he?"

"No," she said under her breath.

"Then who was he, Mom?"

She stared at the road ahead. "I don't know, honey. Maybe a reporter, maybe somebody working for Foley, or maybe just some nut. I really don't know."

Beep.

"Hello, Bridget. This is Zach Matthias calling around eight o'clock, Tuesday night. I just wanted to say that I was glad we ran into each other today—despite the sad occasion. Um, I'm wondering if you might be free for lunch tomorrow. If tomorrow doesn't work out for you, maybe the next day?" He chuckled. "It wouldn't be an interview, don't worry. Anyway, my number is—"

Bridget switched off the machine. David came bounding down the back stairs. He stopped to grin at her. "Who's that? Sounds like he's asking you out on a date."

"It's an old high school friend," Bridget explained. "The 'dorky guy' from the yearbook, the one you were making fun of this afternoon."

"Sounds like a loser."

Bridget frowned. "Why aren't you doing your homework?"

"I just came down to get a Coke." He headed to the refrigerator.

Bridget sat down at the breakfast table. "As long as you're taking a break, do you have a minute? I need to talk with you about something."

David opened his Coke and plopped down across from her. "What's up?"

"Well, it has to do with what we were talking about in the car," Bridget said. "With the election coming up, you might have some more—strange encounters, like what happened to you and Eric tonight, or like last week, when we had the prowler outside and called the police. I don't want to alarm you, but just be extra cautious. Okay?"

He seemed to take her warnings with all the seriousness of being told he might have to take out the garbage more frequently in the week ahead. David shrugged. "Okay, sure, Mom." He started to get up.

"Honey, I'm sincere about this," she said, taking hold of his arm.

David sat back down.

"You're going to have people coming up to you," she continued. "You have to be extra, extra careful. So—if someone tells you he's a policeman, and he wants you to go with him, ask to see a photo ID. Don't let him just show you some badge. And even then, go to the nearest adult and tell them what's happening. Borrow a cell phone and call me—or Uncle Brad, or your father."

"I know that," David said. "I'm not dumb."

"No, you're not. But for the next few weeks, I don't want you—or Eric—going off anywhere by yourself. Stick with your buddies—and stick close to your brother."

Working up a smile, she squeezed his arm. "By the way, I'm very proud of the way you've been looking after Eric. Since your dad moved out, I've noticed how patient and sweet you've been with the little guy. He's very lucky to have a big brother like you. And I'm lucky to have you for a son."

"Oh, c'mon, Mom," David said, rolling his eyes. "Don't get all sappy on me. Give me a break."

She nodded and patted his arm. "All right, I just wanted you to know, I'm proud of you." Bridget sighed. "By the way, I met your dad for coffee this morning. He wants to spend some more time with you and Eric. So you'll probably be over there this week   for dinner or maybe even to spend the night. He really misses you guys."

David stared at her, deadpan. "Are you sure this was Dad, and not some guy who just looked like him?"

Bridget frowned. "Hey, cut him some slack. All right?"

David got to his feet. "Okay, Mom," he muttered. "I'll try." He kissed her forehead, then took his Coke and started up the back stairs.

Bridget got up and poured herself a glass of Chardonnay. Returning to the table, she grabbed her purse and fished out her notepad. She stared at Cheryl Blume's phone number. She couldn't call her from home. There was a pay phone at the 7-Eleven a few blocks away, but she didn't want to leave the boys alone at night—not even for a few minutes.

She'd have to try calling Cheryl in the morning.

With the wineglass in her hand, Bridget moved over to the answering machine at her desk near the back stairway. She played Zach Matthias's message over again. David was right: Zach was asking her out on a date. It was lunch, but it was still a date. Could it be that he had no ulterior motive? Seeing Gerry again this morning had reminded her of how lonely she was. And seeing Zach this afternoon had reminded her of when he was a sweet four-eyed geek with a crush on her. She still couldn't believe the transformation. He was so handsome. Could he still have feelings for her—after twenty years?

She knew from her own experience that it was possible. It had been over twenty years since she'd last set eyes on Brad's blond, blue-eyed, brooding friend, David Ahern. He was her first real crush, and he'd barely paid any attention to her. Yet she still had feelings for the guy, enough so that she named her firstborn David. No one ever made the connection. She'd told everyone that she'd just always liked the name.

Sometimes the sweet pain and longing she'd had for that young man in high school felt just as potent today. She still couldn't think about David Ahern without a little bit of regret. Bridget wished she knew what had happened to him.

She played Zach's phone message again: "... I just wanted to say that I was glad we ran into each other today—despite the sad occasion. Um, I'm wondering if you might be free for lunch tomorrow. . . ."

He sounded nervous—a bit like the old Zach. Or was that just an act? Had he figured out that she was lonely and somewhat vulnerable? Did he expect her to trust him and open up to him—simply because they'd known each other back in high school?

She thought of what her brother had said: "The guy's poison, Brigg."

Bridget swallowed hard. Her hand hovered above the answering machine for a moment. Then she hit the Erase button.

CHAPTER 13

Bridget switched off her bedside lamp. She'd already double-checked the locks on the front and back doors—along with the first-floor windows. Down the hall, the boys were asleep. It was 11:45.

It had been such a bizarre and emotionally draining day—from learning of Fuller's suspicious death to chasing down that red-haired man who had been talking with her sons in the restaurant. And there was Zachary Matthias too. She had such weird mixed feelings about him—attraction, apprehension, longing, and fear. He made her remember what it was like to have a crush on someone.

She should have known sleep wouldn't come easy tonight. She couldn't stop thinking about high school—and Fuller and Zach when they were young. She recalled those nights her junior year when David Ahern had stayed over. The very idea that he was sleeping down the hall from her always kept her wide-awake. She remembered once running into him in the hallway when he was on his way to the bathroom in the middle of the night. His blond hair was disheveled, and he wore only his white briefs. He didn't seem to care that she saw him, and even insisted that she use the bathroom first. Of course, she couldn't really do anything in there, not when he was using it next. All she did was wash her hands and straighten the towels on the rack.

With his clothes off or on, David Ahern always had the same effect on her. She got all tongue-tied around him and acted like an idiot. One of the most idiotic things she did—whenever he slept over—was steal his pillowcase in the morning and substitute it with one from the linen closet. She'd put David's pillowcase over her own extra pillow. Then she'd hug the pillow, smell his hair on it, and touch it against her bare skin. She'd hold on to the pillowcase as long as she could—long after his scent wore off. He had no idea how crazy she was for him.

David Ahern went away to college when she and Brad started their senior year at McLaren High. Brad still got together with him during Christmas, spring, and summer vacations. But after they moved to Portland, Brad lost touch with him. Bridget never saw David Ahern again.

Their mother died during their senior year. That was when Bridget and Brad had spent so much of their time alone in the house. And it was in the spring when Bridget had decided to reach out to Mallory Meehan. After a couple of sessions in the library and that trek through Gorman's Creek with her, Bridget had decided to avoid her. But Mallory kept calling anyway.

One evening a week before graduation, Mallory invited herself over to Bridget's house. Bridget never forgot how Mallory stepped into the front hall and looked around with awe. "God, your place is so big," she remarked. "My house is much smaller. But it's decorated nicer. Did your mother decorate this herself? She really should have had a professional do it. My aunt's a professional interior decorator, and she did our house."

Then she asked for a tour of the house and criticized the furnishings in every room. But she took a definite shining to a double-strand pearl necklace Bridget had inherited from her mother. It was one of the few pieces her father had let her keep. The rest of the jewelry had gone into a safety de-

posit box. The double strand of pearls was the only piece she
cared about anyway. Bridget kept the necklace in its original
jewelry box on her dresser.

Bridget didn't realize when she said good-bye to Mallory
later that afternoon, she was also saying good-bye to her
pearl necklace.

She discovered the empty jewel box the following day.
She phoned Mallory. "I know you wouldn't have stolen it,"
Bridget told her. "But—um—you might have picked it up
and put the necklace in your pocket for a second, then forgot
about it."

"What are you talking about?" Mallory said. "What necklace?"

"The one you were admiring, and asking about," Bridget
shot back. "What, do you have amnesia now?"

"Maybe your maid stole it," Mallory suggested.

"The maid hasn't been here in three days. The necklace
was there yesterday, Mallory. Besides me, you're the only
other person who's been in my room since yesterday. Just give
it back, and I won't raise a stink. It was my dead mother's,
okay?"

"I really don't know what you're talking about," Mallory
maintained.

So, along with acrophobia and claustrophobia, now klep-
tomania could be added to the list of Mallory's various "conditions."

Bridget phoned her again about the necklace. And again,
Mallory denied ever even having set eyes on it. Then Mallory
asked Bridget when she was going to invite her back to her
house again.

"Why?" Bridget retorted. "So you can criticize everything here and rip off some more family heirlooms?"

After that, Bridget no longer merely disliked Mallory
Meehan, she loathed her. Within two days, Bridget had a group
of classmates who shared her sentiments. Among them, her
brother.

On graduation night, after the dance, Brad and his girlfriend, Cheryl Blume, along with Fuller Sterns and Olivia Rankin, went to Olivia's house and got drunk on Boone's Farm wine in the basement rec room. Bridget wasn't in on it. She'd gone to the dance with Mark Easton, a hunk from the football team. Bridget had been so flattered when he'd asked her. But after telling him at the dance that she had no desire to hang around with her brother and his friends all night, Bridget found herself dropped off at home at half past midnight with a polite kiss on the cheek.

Apparently, things were a bit wilder in the Rankins' basement rec room. After both couples paired off and made out, Fuller snuck into Mr. Rankin's workroom and found a can of black paint and some brushes. Within an hour, Brad and Fuller were climbing the five-story water tower on the edge of town. Brad had taken off his tuxedo jacket and tied a plastic bag—filled with the paint can and brushes—to his belt.

By 3:20 AM, Brad and Fuller had painted BOBCATS CLASS OF on the side of the water tower tank. With Cheryl and Olivia coaching them from the ground, the boys got the block letters even and straight. No sloppy graffiti there. They were about to paint '85 when the girls noticed Mallory Meehan drive by in her mother's burnt-umber Plymouth Volare. It was hard to miss that old heap with the broken antenna. Plus, Mrs. Meehan's Volare was the only car to pass by at that early morning hour.

Mallory had told anyone who would listen that she had no intention of attending the graduation dance. She was celebrating her accomplishments by driving alone to the Pacific coast and meditating until dawn. Apparently, she hadn't lasted that long.

The Volare slowed down and Mallory poked her head out the window to gape up at Fuller and Brad. Then she suddenly hit the gas and sailed down the road.

Fifteen minutes later, Brad and Fuller had BOBCATS CLASS OF '85 FOREV painted on the side of the water tank, when two squad cars pulled up to the base of the tower.

The police caught Olivia and Cheryl smoking a joint, and

stopped Fuller and Brad before they could paint the ER in FOREVER.

Everyone went quietly—except for Cheryl, who became belligerent with the officers. They charged her with resisting arrest and placed her in a holding cell until her parents arrived at the station. Brad, Fuller, and Olivia were let go with the understanding that they had to return later that week and repaint the water tower tank. The cops went easy on them mostly because Brad's recently widowed father was such a powerful figure in McLaren. Besides, they liked Brad. Everyone did.

Cheryl, however, had to agree to forty hours of community service in order to have her charges dropped.

The group knew Mallory was the one who had called the police on them. They didn't need her mailing in an editorial to the *Cowlitz Country Register*, in which she pretty much ratted on herself. The published editorial was titled: IS VIRTUE THE ONLY REWARD FOR GOOD CITIZENSHIP? In her piece, Mallory wondered why the police didn't give out monetary awards to *vigilant citizens who report vandalism, thefts, and other crimes against our community. A grateful McLaren might have considered giving this good citizen at least one hundred dollars for notifying authorities about a vandalism being committed on one of the town's landmarks on graduation night last week.*

Fuller, Olivia, and Cheryl wanted revenge. But Brad saw no point in getting back at Mallory. He suggested they drop it, do their penance, and enjoy the rest of the summer. Though his friends continued to carry a grudge against Mallory, they went along with him.

Mallory's editorial also suggested if the police force offered better monetary incentives to vigilant citizens, many crimes could be prevented or solved. *The author of this editorial firmly believes that last year's murders of Andy Shields and Richard and Robert Gaines might be solved if a substantial reward was offered.*

Mallory's fixation over those unsolved murders hadn't diminished. In fact, one afternoon in late July, that obsession ran rampant, and she went a little crazy. Bridget witnessed it—along with a few other *good citizens* in the parking lot of Quality Foods in the center of town.

Bridget did the household shopping at Quality Foods at least twice a week. She was usually the only teenager in the place with a shopping cart full of food and other essentials.

That afternoon, she left the supermarket with four bags in her cart. She was walking a few paces behind Sonny Fessler, who had been in there talking to the ever-patient checkers. They were used to him coming in to chat quietly—always about the weather or what he'd had for breakfast and lunch that day. No one ever paid much attention to Sonny. But at times, an exasperated checker might say, "Sonny, I can't talk, we're really busy right now," or something along those lines. Sonny would nod, give a friendly wave, then shuffle out of the supermarket.

He'd bought a pack of Big Red chewing gum that afternoon. Bridget saw him slip it into his pocket as he wandered toward his Schwinn, parked at the bike rack in front of the supermarket. Despite the summer heat, he wore a flannel shirt and his hunting cap. The sweat ran down the side of his unshaven face. He bent down to work the combination on his bicycle lock.

"Hi, Sonny," Bridget said, pushing her shopping cart past him. "How are you doing?"

He looked up at her and nodded. "Hi, young Corrigan girl," he said, giving her a slightly startled smile. His teeth were yellowish brown.

"My God, Bridget!" someone screamed. "Why are you even talking to that retard? He's a murderer!"

Bridget glanced toward the parking lot. Mallory Meehan slammed the driver's door of her mother's Volare, slung her purse over her shoulder, and headed toward them. She wore madras shorts and a yellow T-shirt that had GENIUS written across the front. Her frizzy brown hair was all wild and unkempt, and she looked angry.

"You're a murderer, Sonny Fessler!" she yelled. "You butchered those three boys! I'm on to you!"

Sonny slowly straightened up and stared at her. He looked frightened and confused. Bridget noticed his lower lip quivering. His eyes filled with tears. "What?" he called back timidly.

Mallory approached, shaking her finger at him. "You heard me! I said I'm on to you—"

"Stop it!" Bridget shouted. "What the hell is wrong with you, Mallory? Leave him alone!"

People in the parking lot were staring.

"He's trying to act so innocent, but I know—"

"Shut up!" Bridget said. She turned to Sonny, who was visibly trembling. "Pay no attention to her, Sonny. She doesn't know what she's talking about. You go on. Don't listen to her."

Sonny Fessler climbed on his Schwinn. With an unsteady grip on the handlebars, he started to pedal away. The bike seemed to wobble a bit.

"Go ahead and run!" Mallory yelled after him. "But just remember, I'm on to you! You're going to pay for your crimes. You—"

"Shut the *fuck* up," Bridget growled.

Mallory turned to stare at her.

"How could you be so stupid and insensitive?" Bridget asked. "Sonny Fessler wouldn't hurt a soul. Why are you picking on him? What's wrong with you?"

"What's wrong with *you?*" Mallory shot back. "The only reason you're nice to him is that he's retarded. Do you think that makes you a good person or something? The only reason people are nice to *you* is that you're Brad Corrigan's twin sister. Otherwise, you'd be just as pathetic as Sonny Fessler. And you know that's true."

Mallory marched toward the supermarket door. It opened automatically. In the doorway, she swiveled around and shot Bridget one more cold, superior look. "Oh, and if I'm so *stu-*

_id_, how come I'm the one here who has an academic scholarship to the University of Washington?"

Speechless, Bridget stood by her shopping cart and watched Mallory flounce into the store.

Driving home, Bridget kept replaying the scene in her head. She kept thinking she should have said this or that—as if anything she said would ever penetrate Mallory's armor.

Bridget felt like crap. Mallory's words hurt. And the only thing that made Bridget feel better was considering the source—and fantasizing about different ways to make Mallory suffer.

When she returned home, Brad helped her unload the groceries. Cheryl, Fuller, and Olivia were also there in the kitchen, gorging on snacks and soda. Bridget found them a willing audience as she shared her fantasies of revenge on Mallory Meehan.

In fact, she commanded the room, and it was a heady experience to have Brad's pals hanging on her every word. She was so used to them treating her like a second-class citizen. Now they loved her. And they loved one particular revenge fantasy that played on Mallory's obsession for Gorman's Creek—as well as her claustrophobia.

"Oh God, that's a fantastic idea!" Cheryl said, slapping the top of the breakfast table. "Let's do it! Mallory totally deserves it. She'll get so scared, she'll shit in her pants again—like she did in fifth grade."

Sitting on the kitchen counter, Brad shook his head. "That's really juvenile. It's more like a junior high school prank. And to tell you the truth, I don't feel like getting in trouble again—just to pick on poor Mallory Meehan."

"The bitch ratted on us!" Cheryl retorted. "I had to do forty hours of community service last month because of her."

"And she stole Mom's necklace," Bridget added. "You should have seen how awful she was to Sonny Fessler. She kept calling him 'retard' right to his face, and screaming at him—"

"We got to do this, man," Fuller insisted, with a mouthful of Cheetos. "The skank deserves it."

"Shit, Bridget," Olivia said, laughing. "I had no idea you're such a kick-ass hell-raiser."

And Bridget had no idea what she'd just started.

While Brad and his friends made plans and scouted the Gorman's Creek locale, Bridget didn't take any of it too seriously. She didn't think they'd actually go through with the prank. But then Cheryl announced the date for putting their plan into action: Saturday, August 3.

It was up to Bridget to get the ball rolling. They gathered in the kitchen that Saturday afternoon while Bridget phoned Mallory and pretended to make amends. "I think you were right about the boys being killed in Gorman's Creek, Mallory," she lied. "I . . ."

Bridget hesitated. She suddenly didn't like herself for using the deaths of Andy and his friends as a way of luring someone into a trap. She wasn't enjoying this.

Brad and Olivia dragged Fuller out of the kitchen because he kept cracking up. But Cheryl took the proceedings very seriously. Sitting across the kitchen table from Bridget, she nodded and prodded her to go on.

"Um, you know how the newspapers said the boys had no shoes or socks?" Bridget continued. "I think I found something—in Gorman's Creek. There's a crawl space right by the Bowers house. Remember, I found it while we were exploring together? I saw some dirty sneakers in there. I—I didn't make the connection until I was looking over some old newspapers in the library this morning. Do you want to go back to Gorman's Creek with me tonight? Maybe there's a reward we don't know about. You and I could split it."

Mallory seemed too smart to go for the bait. Part of Bridget figured it wasn't really going to happen.

But two hours later, at 7:45, Mallory met her at the break in the barbed-wire fence along the Fesslers' property. It was still light out, with dusk just starting to creep over the horizon. They didn't have any trouble navigating the crude trail.

The plan was pretty simple. Before reaching the remnants of the Bowers house, Bridget would pretend to get scared. She'd turn and run back, screaming that Mallory could have the reward money all to herself. That was the cue for Brad, Cheryl, Olivia, and Fuller to pop out of their hiding places. They would be in disguise. Brad and his friends would grab Mallory, then drag her to the crawl space and throw her inside. The claustrophobic Mallory would freak out. They would sit on the trapdoor—for five minutes. "No longer than that," Brad had insisted. "And if she starts crying too much, let's abort. We don't want to hurt her. We're just going to scare her."

At one point, Brad had even suggested they should take off their disguises once they moved away from the trapdoor. He wanted to help Mallory out of the little bunker, then maybe take her to dinner or something. He saw the prank as a way of getting even and then burying the hatchet.

"Just how far is your head up your ass?" Fuller had retorted. "That bitch will be out for blood afterward. I say once we get off the trapdoor, we run like hell. By the time she gets her fat butt out of that crawl space, we'll be halfway home."

The disguises, it had been decided, would stay on—in case Mallory later went to the police about it. Mallory had been the victim of so many pranks by so many different classmates for so many years, the cops probably wouldn't single out the foursome she'd ratted on almost two months before.

They figured Mallory wouldn't go to the cops about this anyway, because she'd have to admit that she was trespassing on Gorman's Creek. They figured they were pretty safe if they kept their disguises on.

All their planning, plotting, and second-guessing seemed like a lot of work for a silly prank. As Bridget trudged through the woods with Mallory, it struck her as pointless. Brad's first instincts about this revenge fantasy now seemed on the money. They were five college-bound adults, cooking up a scheme barely worthy of junior high school kids.

Bridget may have had the idea, but Cheryl had become the driving force in making it happen. Bridget figured Brad went along with this scheme for Cheryl—and whatever kind of sex she'd promised him.

But as they came closer to the Bowers ruins, Bridget wondered how she could derive any pleasure from this. Yeah, for a while, she felt like Cheryl, Olivia, and Fuller considered her a friend, an equal. She felt accepted by them—not as Brad's twin sister, but as another cool member of their little group. Yet when she thought about it, they really were a bunch of jerks—not all that better than Mallory.

"You saw the corpses, didn't you?" Mallory was saying, veering off the path—toward what was left of the Bowers home. "Did you see that the boys were barefoot?"

"Yes, I saw," Bridget muttered. She kept asking herself how she could use that detail from Andy Shields's murder as a decoy in this stupid prank.

"You babysat for him. Do you remember what kind of sneakers he had?"

She remembered—after seeing those dead boys without any shoes or socks. Andy had loved his dark green Converse All-Stars.

"No, I don't remember his shoes," Bridget lied. She stopped in her tracks. "Listen, Mallory," she whispered. "Let's turn back. I made all that up about seeing some sneakers in the crawl space out here. It—well, it was an awful thing to lie about. I made that up just to lure you out here."

Mallory stared at her. "Nice try," she said with a shrewd smile. "What, did you find out about a reward or something? Did you want it all to yourself?"

"Mallory, there is no reward. There's *nothing* out here. It's all a lie."

Stubbornly, Mallory moved toward the clearing—and the remnants of the Bowers house. "You just don't want me getting any of the credit for solving these murders. Well, I'm the one who told you those boys were killed here in these woods. I'm the one who'll have a best seller writing about it—"

Bridget started after her. "Don't you understand? It's a trap. I'm trying to help you. It's all a setup."

She stopped and watched Mallory head toward the Bowerses' front stoop. "You guys!" she called. "You guys, I'm not doing this! It's a stupid idea—and I'm calling it off!"

Mallory turned and stared at her.

"Hey, guys?" Bridget called again. She kept waiting for someone to call back—or spring out from behind a tree. But nothing. Could it be that they'd all changed their minds? Had Brad talked some sense into them? Or was this a joke on her? Whatever the case, Bridget felt relieved. She let out a little laugh. "C'mon, Mallory, there's nothing here. Let's just—"

Bridget didn't finish. She saw a figure dart out from behind the Bowerses' old, crumbling brick fireplace. Bridget gasped. It didn't seem human with its distorted, brown face. After a moment, Bridget realized it was Olivia with a nylon stocking pulled over her head.

Mallory swiveled around. She let out a deafening scream.

All at once, someone in a gorilla mask came out from behind a tree. Two more people, wearing over-the-head rubber masks of Ron and Nancy Reagan, jumped out from behind some shrubs.

Bridget knew they'd be in disguise, but what she saw seemed surreal—almost funny. They all wore pale green lab coats—probably from the supply her dad brought home from the recycling plant. The maid sometimes wore them while cleaning the house.

"Get her!" someone said in a raspy voice.

They swarmed in on Mallory, who kept shrieking. She started to struggle, but the one in the gorilla mask—Fuller, probably—came up behind her and grabbed her around the waist. The force of it seemed to knock the wind out of her.

Bridget thought he might have cracked one of Mallory's

ribs or something. As they wrestled with her, Bridget caught a glimpse of Mallory's face, and she was wincing in pain.

They dragged her around the Bowers ruins toward the plateau ridge.

"Stop it!" Bridget screamed. "Don't! You guys—"

She had to refrain from yelling out their names. She didn't want to give them away.

But Fuller took care of that by announcing, "Shit, this bitch is heavy!"

"I heard you, Fuller Sterns!" Mallory cried.

They hauled her down to the plateau, past the tree tilting over the ravine. Her heart racing, Bridget ran down to the ridge—in time to see them push Mallory into the crawl space.

"No, no, no!" Mallory cried. "Please, don't—"

"Wait!" Bridget screamed. Then she heard something snap.

She was standing right behind them now. This close, she could smell that they'd been smoking pot and drinking. This close, she could see that Mallory was hurt.

She was curled up on the rotted wood floor of that tiny pit. The boards beneath her groaned and creaked. The floor started to give way.

One of the girls—Olivia or Cheryl—started laughing hysterically.

But the floor opened up, and Mallory screamed as she fell through the crater, down to the bottom of a shallow well. Suddenly, the screaming stopped.

"What the fuck? Oh my God," Fuller muttered. He was holding on to his arm, which was bleeding. Mallory must have scratched him.

Bridget stared down the opening. She could barely see Mallory—about thirty feet down, lying on her side.

"Jesus, what are we going to do?" Olivia whispered. "Did we kill her? Is she dead?"

Everyone seemed to be talking at once. They took off their masks. Brad kept telling them to calm down.

Bridget felt as if her heart had stopped. She gaped down at Mallory's crumpled body and prayed for some movement, just a little whimper, anything.

"Goddamnit, she better be dead!" Cheryl announced. Wiping the tears from her eyes, she desperately glanced around at the ground. She reached for a big stone by the tree trunk. She needed both hands to hoist it up, then struggled to carry it toward the well.

"What the hell are you doing?" Brad asked.

"I'm going to crush her fucking skull! You think she won't turn us all in? She'll make sure each one of us is screwed for life. She'll—"

"For God's sake, put that down," Brad said. "Everybody, just—take it easy. Okay?"

Brad shucked off his lab coat. He was wearing khaki shorts and a T-shirt. Bridget could see he was trembling a bit. Still, he had a calming effect on the others. They all stood by and watched Brad lower himself into the crawl space. "Mallory?" he called. "Mallory, it's Brad Corrigan, I'm coming down to get you."

Bridget had a sickly feeling that he was talking to a corpse.

Brad tried to get his footing inside the little bunker, but what was left of the rotted floor wouldn't support him. The decayed wood let out a groan. Brad scrambled back up to safety.

Bridget was looking down the well. Chunks of wood and dirt fell on Mallory, but she didn't even flinch. "She's dead," Bridget heard herself say, while Brad was catching his breath. "She must have broken her neck in the fall."

"I say we get the hell out of here," Fuller announced, still holding on to his arm.

They started arguing with each other, bickering over who was to blame for this, and wondering out loud why that crawl space was built on top of a dry well.

"Who gives a shit why they covered up the well like they did?" Brad said, finally. "And it doesn't matter who's to blame for this. We're all in it now. We're all responsible. And we need to agree on what to do. So—let's just calm the hell down—"

"We should go to the police—immediately," Bridget said. "It's the only sensible thing to do. If we just leave her here, it's like we're murderers. There's a chance Mallory is just unconscious. Maybe a couple of us can stay here while the others go to the cops. Someone should stay—in case Mallory comes to."

"Just a minute ago, you were certain she was dead," Cheryl argued. "She isn't unconscious, and she isn't ever coming to. We killed her."

"The cops aren't going to believe this was an accident," Fuller maintained. "Not when she ratted us out a few weeks ago. Look at the scratch marks on my arm. Shit, they'll throw the book at us." He sneered at Brad and Bridget. "You two may get off a little easier, because of your dad." He let out a little laugh. "Then again, maybe they'll want to make an example of the 'rich kids.' Either way, if we go to the cops, we're screwed—it's just a question of how much we'll get screwed."

"So we simply walk away?" Bridget countered. "We can't do that. We're responsible for what happened here. I don't know about you guys, but if Mallory's dead, and I don't own up to it now, this will be hanging over my head for the rest of my life. I'd rather go to the cops. I don't want to carry this inside me, keeping it secret—"

"That's right," Brad said. "We won't be able to talk about this with anyone. We all have to agree, we won't ever tell a soul about what just happened. We shouldn't even talk about it with each other after today."

Bridget turned to him. "Brad, what are you saying?"

"Fuller's right." He sighed. "All of us are planning to go away to college in two weeks. Do you think that's going to happen if we turn ourselves in? There will be inquests, hearings, maybe even a trial. And we're all eighteen. We'll be tried as adults. We could be guilty of manslaughter—or reckless endangerment—or—"

"Or leaving the scene of a crime?" Bridget said.

"Brigg, none of us will have a future. Think about it. You want to do this to Dad right now—so soon after Mom dying?" He shook his head. "No one knows Mallory came out here. We should leave her where she is, cover our tracks, and say nothing."

Bridget felt sick to her stomach. She glanced down the well. Mallory hadn't moved.

"There's nothing we can do for Mallory now," she heard Brad say. "I know it sounds uncaring, but we have to think about how we can get through this without ruining our lives. . . ."

He was very convincing. They left Mallory at the bottom of that abandoned well. Brad said it would appear as if she'd gone looking for something in there, then simply fallen in. Fuller was worried about his blood—and bits of his skin— under her fingernails.

"Maybe they won't examine her that closely," Brad replied, leading the group up the trail. They were carrying their masks and lab coats. "After all, it sure looks like an accident, doesn't it? Meanwhile, until your arm heals, you better wear long-sleeve shirts."

Bridget wanted to get a rope, a flashlight, and a first-aid kit, then come back and climb down that well. If Mallory was still alive, they could get her out of there. And if she was dead, then at least they'd know they had done everything possible to save her.

"She's dead, Brigg," Brad said. "It's too risky for us to keep marching up and down Briar Court and this trail. Someone might see us."

Brad had an answer for everything, and everyone agreed with him. Even back then, he'd shown incredible leadership skills, keeping cool under fire. He made them rally together. They were a team, all protecting each other. Each one promised they would never talk about what had just happened—not even to a priest, or a psychiatrist, or a future spouse.

"We were never here," Brad said, as they approached the break in the barbed-wire fence. "And none of us will ever come back. Okay?"

Everyone agreed—except Bridget. She turned away from her brother and gazed at the trail behind them. She figured it would be dark soon. She would definitely need the flashlight.

They passed Mallory's mother's Volare, parked halfway down Briar Court. Fuller thought they should move the car. It seemed like a blatant indication of where Mallory might be found.

"That's a terrific idea," Brad said, deadpan. "Want to go back there, climb down the well, and get the car keys out of her pocket? The car stays where it is. Makes sense that she'd leave it there before going into the woods. We're not altering anything. And none of us are going back."

One hour and twenty minutes later, Bridget was alone on the trail through Gorman's Creek. Even with a flashlight to help her navigate in the darkness, she still stumbled over tree roots, divots, and rocks along the crude path. She was weighed down with forty feet of rope she'd found in the garage, and a plastic bag with a bottle of water, a washcloth, a can of Bactine, and some old smelling salts.

The group had broken up after emerging from Gorman's Creek, all of them slinking off to their respective homes. Brad had retreated into his bedroom. As Bridget had gathered up supplies for her trip, she'd heard him in there, crying. She'd gently called to him that she was driving to the store, and did he need anything? She knew he mostly needed to be left alone.

Instead of driving to Quality Foods, she'd driven to Briar Court and parked behind Mallory's mother's Volare.

She was sweating—from the warm night, and from fear. In the heart of Gorman's Creek, Bridget could hardly see anything beyond the flashlight's illuminating beam. Everything else was just blackness. It occurred to her that she had to be insane to venture through these haunted woods alone. And what for? So she could climb down a hidden well and feel the pulse of a dead girl. Yet Bridget knew she couldn't live with herself if she didn't go back and check on Mallory.

Bushes and leaves rustled around her. Bridget wondered what kind of animals roamed these woods after dark. Or was it just her and Mallory and some ghosts out here? Bridget shone the light past the trees, hoping to spot the Bowerses' fireplace in the distance. The turnoff from the path was some place along there.

Bridget realized she would have to go to the police if Mallory was still alive. And if Mallory was dead, she would still go to the police. The others didn't need to be involved. She would tell the authorities that she and Mallory were alone when Mallory fell down the well. It was a lie that would let everyone else off the hook. And it would even soothe her conscience—if only just a little bit. Better to report Mallory's death and tell a lie than to leave her corpse out here for the coyotes.

Brad would be furious she'd broken their pact, but tough. She was doing it for him and the others—and for herself. It wasn't exactly the right thing to do, but it was the *less wrong* thing. Bridget kept stopping to direct the flashlight to her left, where she could hear the rushing water in the ravine. The beam of light made shadows sweep across the trees and bushes—so they seemed to move. Bridget couldn't shake the feeling that someone was watching her. Finally, she saw the remnants of a brick fireplace and chimney in the clearing.

Bridget headed toward the Bowers ruins, then made her way to the plateau below it. In the blackness, she couldn't see the ravine, but she knew just one wrong step would send her toppling down the hillside.

"Mallory?" she timidly called, ducking around the tilted tree. She set down the heavy rope. She planned to tie it around the trunk of the tree, then lower herself into the well. "Mallory? Can you hear me?"

She really didn't expect an answer. But calling out for Mallory gave her a little bit of hope. Bridget shone the light down at the ground. She saw the discarded trapdoor, then directed the beam to the crawl space opening. "Mallory?"

Edging closer to the bunker, she felt sick. She didn't want to look at Mallory's corpse. Wincing, Bridget forced herself to peer into the well. She directed the flashlight down there.

"Oh my God," she whispered. Bridget couldn't believe what she saw.

She saw an empty well.

Leaves rustled behind her. Bridget swiveled around and aimed the flashlight at the ravine below. She didn't see anyone. "Mallory?" she called. Then louder: "Mallory? Mallory, are you there?"

Bridget grabbed the coiled rope off the ground. Trembling, she made her way past the tilted tree and up toward the Bowers ruins. She trained the light on the broken-down old fireplace, the front stoop, and the surrounding bushes. There was no sign of anyone.

She heard leaves fluttering again, then a twig snapping. Bridget stayed perfectly still. "Mallory?" she whispered.

She couldn't see anything in the darkness. But it felt as if someone was watching her every move. "Mallory? Where are you?" she cried out. "Mallory? *Mallory, can you hear me?*"

Then she remembered something Mallory Meehan had told her during their trek through these woods last May: "There's no other place in this town where you could scream and scream, and no one would hear."

Bridget fell silent. Tears stung her eyes. With a shaky hand, she aimed the flashlight toward the trees. She had to find the path. She needed to get the hell out of there.

She heard a scream.

Bridget sat up in bed and glanced at the luminous digital

clock on her nightstand: 2:27 AM. She heard another scream. It was Eric.

Throwing aside the covers, Bridget jumped out of bed and ran down the hall to the boys' room.

David was climbing out of bed. "Hey, doofus!" he said. "Wake up, you're having a nightmare." He started toward his little brother's bed, but stopped when he saw his mother.

Bridget raced to Eric's bedside. "Honey, it's okay. . . ."

"There's a man in the room!" Eric cried. Sitting up in bed, he clutched the covers to his chest. "I saw a man!"

"You were dreaming, dopey," David said, plopping back down on his own bed. Sleepy-eyed, he ran a hand through his hair. He blindly reached for the lamp on his nightstand and switched on the light.

Bridget put her arms around Eric. He was trembling. "I saw a man creep into the room," he whimpered. "Could you—could you check the closet?"

Bridget checked the closet for him—and for herself too. She knew Eric had just imagined the intruder, but she needed to make sure. She stepped into the bathroom too, even peeked behind the shower curtain. She asked David to turn off the light again, then sat on the side of Eric's bed.

"Okay, guys, let's all settle down and go back to sleep," she said. She stroked Eric's hair. "There's nobody here but us chickens. We're safe. There's nothing to worry about. Nothing bad is going to happen to any of us."

She didn't really believe what she was saying. But she said it again. "Nothing bad is going to happen."

CHAPTER 14

He was excited about the rough, pencil sketches. He had her lying facedown with her hands tied behind her back. She was nude—except for her bra. He wanted the bra to be black. It would look so stark against her pale skin. Very kinky, the black bra and nothing else.

He didn't like overmanipulating his death scenes. But if she wasn't wearing a black bra, he'd make her put one on.

In one of the sketches, her legs were slightly spread, showing off her ass. In another, he'd drawn her legs tucked under her—as if she had slumped forward from a kneeling position. He liked that one. There was something vulnerable about it.

He'd made up his mind. Before strangling her, he would get her to kneel down.

She would die in the living room. On the end table, near where her corpse would be found, there was a framed portrait of the two boys—one of those details that fascinated him. The last time he'd broken into the house, he'd taken a close-up photo of it.

Good-looking little brats. He wanted to get their likenesses down for the portrait within the painting. It was a nice ironic touch to have the framed picture there—by the corpse.

David's and Eric's well-scrubbed faces would be smiling down at the kinky death scene in front of them.

He snickered at the notion. When he strangled her, it would be like working in front of an audience.

"I believe Ms. Corrigan has time for just one more question," the chairwoman said.

Bridget shared the stage with a stout, gray-haired woman with big glasses and a long, purple scarf draped around her neck. Bridget wore a charcoal-colored suit. They both stood behind podiums on an otherwise bare stage in the Performing Arts Hall at Roberts High School in Salem, Oregon.

Bridget's speech, sponsored by the local chapter of the League of Women Voters, had gone over nicely with the three hundred people in the audience. And so far, she'd sailed through the questions. Flashbulbs kept going off in her face, but she'd becomed accustomed to that—almost.

"I see a hand up in the back," the chairwoman said, pointing out to the audience. "You have a question?"

A woman stood up near the back of the auditorium. Bridget smiled at her, though the woman's face was in the shadows. *"Hello, Bridget,"* she heard the woman say. *"I'm Mallory Meehan."*

"What?" Bridget whispered. She felt a sudden wave of nausea.

"Could you step forward and speak up, please?" the chairwoman said.

A robust woman with black hair stepped into the aisle, cleared her throat, and spoke up. *"I'm Valerie Sheehan!"* she called. Then someone handed her a microphone. "Can you hear me now?"

Bridget managed to smile and nod. She stopped gripping the edges of the podium. "Hi, Valerie. I can hear you fine."

"I saw Jim Foley on the news this morning," Valerie continued, now a bit too loudly. She referred to some notes she'd made. "And Mr. Foley said, I quote, 'Brad Corrigan is morally unfit to hold public office. A close look at his professional record, and a closer look at his personal past, confirms what I say. He is morally unfit.' End quote." Valerie looked up from her notes. "Could you possibly answer these charges, Ms. Corrigan?"

Bridget nodded and smiled again. "I'd love to answer those charges, Valerie. But, as usual, when Jim Foley slings mud, there's never any substance to it. I can't reply to anything specific here. All we have is mud. It's dark, it's dirty, and it's murky." Bridget paused to let that sink in. "My brother's professional record is impeccable. The law firm he started has been defending people's civil rights for thirteen years. He has prosecuted everything from corrupt landlords to greedy corporations. You'd be hard pressed to find anything immoral about his professional record. As for his personal past, he's been happily married to the same woman for several years. They have a darling daughter and another child on the way. He's been a terrific uncle to my two sons and an all-around great brother to me. However, I must admit, Brad isn't perfect. And he is guilty of a crime. He stole a pack of Rainblow bubblegum from the corner grocery when he was eight. But he felt so guilty, he went back an hour later and paid for it, then volunteered to sweep in front of the store for a week—which he did."

There was some polite laughter from the crowd.

"I don't know how that compares to Jim Foley stealing the pensions from hundreds of Mobilink employees when he retired from there. But you, the voters, can decide. On election day, you tell Jim Foley just who is 'morally unfit for public office. . . .' "

As she wrapped up her speech and thanked the crowd, Bridget kept wondering what Foley's spies had uncovered about Brad's past. And why weren't they saying anything yet? Had Brad considered potential damage control?

She and Shelley had parked the minivan down the block from the school, near a playfield. Shelley was taking the rest of the day off to get together with her sister, who lived in Salem.

"You sure it's okay I'm ditching you?" Shelley asked, walking to the minivan with her.

"It's fine," Bridget assured her. "I'll crank up *ABBA's Greatest Hits* on the way home, and the time will fly. Have fun tonight."

Shelley's sister pulled up behind them in a station wagon, then tapped the horn. Bridget waved at her while Shelley got a shopping bag of clothes for her sister out of the minivan. That was when Bridget noticed a pay phone across the street—at the edge of the playfield.

She still hadn't had a chance to call Cheryl Blume.

Bridget waved at Shelley as the station wagon pulled away from the curb. Then the smile faded from her face, and she crossed the street to the pay phone. She'd gotten some quarters at Starbucks that morning. She dialed Cheryl's number in Eugene and was instructed to deposit two dollars for the first three minutes.

Bridget put the coins in the slot, then counted the ring tones. Odds weren't good Cheryl was home at eleven o'clock on a Wednesday morning. Bridget expected an answering machine to click on. But on the fourth ring, someone answered: "Yes, hello?"

"Hello, is Cheryl there, please?" Bridget said.

"This is Cheryl. Who's calling?"

"Um, hi, Cheryl. It's Bridget Corrigan."

There was a silence on the other end of the line. "Um, you know, from high school?" Bridget added.

"Yes, my brother left me a message this morning and said you called. What's going on?"

"Well, I know it's going to sound kind of crazy, but I'm a little worried. Have you noticed anyone following you around lately?"

"What are you talking about?"

"I don't know if you've heard, but I have some sad news. Fuller Sterns died a few days ago. It was a car wreck. He—"

"Yes, I heard about it. What does that have to do with me?"

"Olivia Rankin is dead too," Bridget said. "An apparent suicide a couple of weeks ago. There are a lot of suspicious circumstances behind both these deaths. And one happened practically right after the other. It's just too much of a coincidence."

There was no response from the other end of the line.

"Cheryl, I'm worried that there's a connection here," Bridget continued. "When I last talked to Fuller—just a few days ago—he was worried too. Someone was stalking him. And now it's happening to me. All of us who were with Mallory that night at Gorman's Creek seem to be targeted. That's why I'm asking if you've noticed anything strange lately—like someone following you or somebody watching your house."

"No, I haven't," Cheryl replied. "And quite frankly, I really don't appreciate this phone call, Bridget. I'm very busy and don't have time for these paranoid tales of stalkers and 'coincidental deaths.' "

"Listen, Cheryl—"

"No, you listen," she cut in. "I've put the Gorman's Creek incident behind me. Considering how much you and Brad are in the public eye right now, you'd be wise to do the same thing." She sighed. "I need to hang up now."

"Well, I'm glad you're all right," Bridget said lamely. "I'll say hello to Brad for you."

"That's really not necessary," Cheryl replied.

Bridget heard a click. Then the other end of the line went dead.

"Good-bye," Bridget said to no one. Then she hung up the phone.

"That was a good speech."

Bridget swiveled around.

Zach Matthias was smiling at her. He wore sunglasses, a pressed blue shirt, khakis, and a brown leather jacket. She hadn't noticed him in the auditorium; and she didn't know how long he'd been standing behind her just now.

"You shouldn't—" Bridget caught her breath and managed to smile. "That was a sneak attack."

He shrugged. "Sorry, I just didn't want to interrupt your phone conversation."

Bridget wondered how much of it he'd heard.

"Like I said, nice speech," he continued. "It was a lot like the one you gave in Corvallis three weeks ago. I covered that one too."

"Well, they get recycled once in a while," Bridget replied. She headed across the street toward her minivan.

"I liked how you replied to that last question," Zach said, walking alongside her. "You really gave it to old Jim Foley. I love what you said about your brother's criminal record. I thought you showed extremely good judgment not mentioning what he, Fuller, Olivia, and Cheryl did back in eighty-five."

Bridget stopped to stare at him.

Folding his arms, he leaned against the side of her van and grinned at her. "I'm talking about the great water tower scandal. *Bobcats class of eighty-five forever.* Or should I say *Forev?* Remember how it stayed like that for three days— until your brother and Fuller had to start painting over it?"

Bridget nodded and gave him a pale smile. She dug her keys out of her purse.

"Remember Mallory Meehan sending in that editorial to the *Register*? She wanted a reward for ratting on those guys— like she was turning in a crew of terrorists or something." He took off his sunglasses and squinted at her. "Hey, did you ever get your mother's necklace back from her?"

"What?" Bridget whispered.

"Kim Li told me that Mallory stole your mother's necklace—"

Bridget unlocked the car door and nodded. "Yes, that's right. And no, I—I never got it back."

He moved away from the car, then put his sunglasses back on. "You seem like you're in a hurry to get out of here."

"Yes, it was nice seeing you again, Zach. But I'm sorry, I need to get back to Portland for something."

"Really? Because I checked the Corrigan-for-Oregon Web site, and it didn't show you had anything scheduled for this afternoon."

Bridget's eyes narrowed at him. "This is something personal."

He nodded. "That's good. For a minute there, I thought you were trying to avoid me."

She opened the car door, then climbed inside. "Take care, Zach."

He stopped her before she closed the car door. "Just for the record, Bridget, I may work for a pro-Foley newspaper, but personally, I can't stand the son of a bitch. And I'm glad you nailed him today about screwing all those Mobilink employees out of their pensions. And I'd still like to take you out to lunch sometime."

Zach pulled out his wallet, then took out a business card and set it on her dashboard. "Give me a call, okay?"

Before she could reply, he smiled and nodded, then closed the minivan's door for her.

Bridget plucked the card from the dashboard and stuffed it in her purse. He unnerved her. And yes, she was attracted to him. Bridget made an effort not to look at Zach as she started up the car. She pulled away from the curb. It wasn't until she started down the street that she let herself look back at him—in the side mirror.

She saw him standing there in the distance—right over the stenciled warning: *Some objects may be closer than they appear.*

It started to drizzle during her drive back to Portland. Bridget switched on the windshield wipers and kept her eyes on the slick road ahead. *ABBA's Greatest Hits* played at a low volume.

She couldn't stop thinking about Zach Matthias. Miles

back, she'd stolen a look at his business card while at a red light:

ZACHARY MATTHIAS
Writer/Communications/Correspondent
503/555-4159

It didn't mention anything about the *Portland Examiner*. She wondered why—if he'd been covering her campaign work for at least three weeks now—she hadn't yet seen one single article he'd written. Every day, Shelley left on her desk current newspaper and magazine articles relating to her and the campaign. Certainly, she would have noticed a Zachary Matthias byline among them—if there had ever been one.

If he was lying about his job as a reporter, what else was he lying about? He came on like he still harbored that crush he'd had on her in high school. But Bridget didn't want to fall for it. She wondered what he *really* wanted. And she wondered just how much of her conversation with Cheryl Blume he'd heard.

At least Cheryl wasn't being followed, and there weren't any early warning signs that she'd been targeted. Bridget could be grateful for that.

Still, she didn't know what to make of Cheryl's hostile attitude. Cheryl hadn't seemed too concerned about the deaths of Olivia and Fuller. Nor had she seemed to give a damn about Bridget's own stalker situation. And did she really have to be so damn snotty?

Then again, perhaps more than anyone, Cheryl Blume wanted to forget about Mallory Meehan and Gorman's Creek. Although Bridget had been responsible for the revenge fantasy, Cheryl had developed it into a plan of action. She'd even wanted to crush Mallory's skull—in case Mallory was still alive in that well. And who knew? Perhaps she'd been the one who had moved Mallory's body.

Bridget remembered how terrified she'd been, returning

alone to Gorman's Creek that night. She remembered how she couldn't get out of those dark woods fast enough. Racing down the crude path to the Fesslers' fence, she'd stumbled twice. By the time she'd reached the car, Bridget was covered with dirt and sweat.

Once home, she found her father had come back from a business dinner. He'd changed into a pair of khaki shorts and an Izod golf shirt. He sat in his recliner chair with the TV remote in his hand. The light from the TV flickered across his handsome face. A glass of scotch was within reach on the side table.

Bridget wanted to throw her arms around him and tell him everything. But Brad was right. Their father had just been through hell with their mother dying. He didn't need to know about this. So Bridget just smiled and kissed her father on the forehead. "Hey, Pop."

He looked her up and down. "My God, what in the world have you been doing? Rolling around in the mud?"

She made up some lie about running into Kim and horsing around in the high school playfield. "Where's Brad?" she asked.

"He took his bike and went for a ride," her father said. "Is Brad all right, honey? Is something the matter? He was acting kind of strange."

"Oh, I'm sure he's okay, Dad," she lied.

Her father went back to watching TV and switching channels with the remote.

He was in bed by eleven. Bridget waited up for her brother. She thought about that empty hole in the ground. She wondered if perhaps Mallory had survived the fall, then pulled herself out of the well. If that was the case, Mallory would have called the police on them by now. Or had she gotten out of the well—only to have fallen into the ravine?

Bridget didn't know what to do. Going to the police at this point no longer seemed like a viable option—not without giving them a full confession.

And not without a body.

Brad returned home—looking like hell—at four in the morning. "I've been riding all over the place, just riding," he explained, hunched over the kitchen sink. He slurped water from the faucet and wiped his face with a wet paper towel. "I rode past the police station—and almost went in—three different times. . . ."

Bridget told him about sneaking back to Gorman's Creek—and about the empty well. She thought he would be furious she'd broken their pledge. But Brad just looked numb.

"It'll be light soon," he whispered, after a minute. "If she fell down the ravine after crawling out of that hole, we might be able to see her." He swallowed hard. "We should take our bikes so Dad won't hear the car."

It was strange, riding her bike alongside her twin brother for the first time in years. They'd planned to hide their bikes in the bushes at the start of the Gorman's Creek trail. As they turned down Briar Court, the streetlights started going off.

Halfway down the cul-de-sac, they both stopped. Bridget gripped her handlebars tightly. She had one foot on the bike pedal and put the other on the concrete.

"My God," she heard Brad whisper.

Mallory's mother's burnt-umber Volare was gone.

They didn't know what to think. First Mallory disappeared, and now her car had vanished.

Returning home, Bridget and Brad sweated it out. Filled with dread, they waited for that call from the police which would wake up their father. Or perhaps the cops would just come knocking on the front door.

But the police never paid a call. Bridget and Brad were like zombies the following day. Their dad kept asking what was the matter with them. Every time the phone rang, they both nearly jumped out of their skin.

One of those false alarm calls was from Fuller—at nine-thirty at night. He talked with Brad, but Bridget got on the other extension. Fuller had checked out Briar Court too. After seeing the Volare was gone, he'd driven past the Meehan house. "No Volare there either," Fuller said. "What the fuck do you think is going on?"

By Monday, Brad and Bridget wondered if perhaps Fuller had taken it upon himself to hide Mallory's car—and her body—some place else. After all, he'd been nervous about leaving the Volare parked in the cul-de-sac. Maybe he'd just been playing dumb on Sunday night.

Either that, or Mallory Meehan was alive, hiding somewhere, and having herself one hell of a laugh on the people who had tried to pull a prank on her.

By Tuesday, Mallory's graduation photo started popping up on miniposters around town—on telephone poles and in store windows. HAVE YOU SEEN THIS YOUNG WOMAN? the bulletin asked—over the photo of a haughty, bookish-looking Mallory. The police interviewed most of her classmates, including Bridget, Brad, Fuller, Cheryl, and Olivia. None of them could offer any help. The police didn't ask what they were doing the day Mallory had disappeared. No one had to resort to the cover story they'd prepared about hanging out at the Corrigan house most of the afternoon and evening.

The police already had a theory about what had happened to Mallory Meehan. The unhappy only child of a divorced, working mother had often driven that Volare to the Pacific Coast to "meditate." Most of her classmates attested to that. Maybe this time around, Mallory had decided to keep driving—down to Oregon or California. Maybe she'd run away. Or perhaps she'd been abducted in a different city—or state.

Mrs. Meehan hoped to find clues to Mallory's whereabouts from a stack of journals she'd discovered. But Mallory had written all the entries in her own special code. No one—not even the police—could decipher any of it.

Brad and Cheryl broke up over the phone that week. Everyone in the group avoided each other in what little time remained before they went off to their respective colleges.

The Corrigans moved to the Portland area during Christmas break. There was no longer any reason to associate with Olivia, Fuller, or Cheryl.

Now, twenty years later, two of those people were dead within a couple of weeks of each other. Was Brad right? Was it just a coincidence? Cheryl didn't seem to be in any danger. Bridget wondered if perhaps her stalker was just some nutcase who had seen her on TV.

Her cell phone rang.

It gave her a start. Ever since yesterday's call after that near-miss in the alley, she shuddered at the sound of the cellular ringing. Whoever this stalker was, he knew her number.

Eyes on the road, Bridget reached for her phone and switched it on. "Yes, hello?" she said.

"Brigg, it's me," Brad said on the other end.

"What happened? You sound weird."

"I feel weird," he replied, a tremor in his voice. "Um, are you on your way back from Salem?"

"Yeah, I'm in the car. What's going on?"

"It's Pop. He's in the hospital. They think he's had a heart attack."

Two video cameramen and several reporters accosted Bridget at the main entrance of Portland General. She'd had no idea they would be there. She couldn't understand why her father's heart attack warranted this kind of press coverage. For a few moments, she wondered if Brad had been letting her down easy on the phone earlier. Was he waiting for her to arrive here before telling her that their father had died?

From the car, she'd phoned Gerry at the office. To her astonishment, he'd promised to pick up David and Eric from school, then take them to his place. "I hope your dad will be okay," he'd said. After clicking off the phone with him, she'd had a crying jag that lasted several miles.

And now, as she shied away from the throng of reporters outside the hospital's main entrance, she felt the tears welling in her eyes again.

"When did you first hear about your father, Bridget?" one reporter yelled out.

"We understand a priest was called in," another said.

"Do you have any comment, Bridget?"

In the glass doors, she could see her own reflection. She also noticed someone inside, coming out to greet her. She couldn't make out his face.

"Wait a minute!" another reporter said. "Here he comes!"

The automatic sliding glass door opened. Bridget gaped at the gray-haired, ruggedly handsome man approaching her. Camera flashes went off, and video cameras hummed.

Jim Foley looked very solemn as he took Bridget's hands in his. "I just want you to know, Bridget," he announced, "that Cindy and I are praying for your dad—and your family. And if you need anything, Bridget—anything at all—don't hesitate to call on your friend Jim Foley. God bless."

Dumbfounded, she stared at him. "Um, well, thank you," she said after a moment. "I need to see my father now."

Foley suddenly looked annoyed with the reporters and photographers he must have summoned to the scene. "Don't you think we can give Bridget some privacy here, fellas?"

Bridget broke away from them and hurried to the front desk. She asked the receptionist where she could find her father. "Corrigan, Bradley Senior," she said, her voice cracking. "And could you tell me if—if he's okay? I mean, is he still alive?"

"They have your father in C-216," she replied. She didn't mention his condition. But she did give Bridget some very involved directions on how to find C-216. Bridget had to take an elevator to a sky bridge on the third floor, and then another elevator down to the second floor in another wing of the hospital. She got lost twice and had to ask two different nurses for help. She was in tears by the time she spoke to the second nurse.

After fifteen minutes of wandering around the hospital, she finally found herself in a wing marked CORRIDOR C, ROOMS 200–220. And when she saw Brad's assistant, Chad Schlund, down the hallway, Bridget actually let out a little cry of relief. Chad was a cute guy in his late twenties with a penchant for bow ties. He saw her and waved. Bridget hurried toward him. She almost wanted to hug him.

"Your dad's okay, Bridget," he said. "Brad's in there with him right now. I got a hold of Janice, and she's on her way."

According to the doctors, their father hadn't suffered an actual heart attack. He'd had an "episode," whatever the hell that meant. The doctors wanted him to stay the night for observation. Brad seemed to be holding up well under the pressure. He even found a few minutes to schmooze with the doctors, nurses, and some visitors. More votes for Corrigan.

It gave Bridget a few minutes to be alone with her dad. If she'd thought her father looked rather frail on his seventy-seventh birthday, that was nothing compared to today. He had a tube up his nose, and a bruise from hitting his head in a doorway when he'd experienced his "episode." His face looked pale and droopy, and his white hair was a mess.

Bridget sat at his bedside and smoothed his hair back in place. "Brad's out there, *campaigning*," she said with a wry smile. "I swear, he never quits."

"Good," her father grunted. He was slightly dopey from the drugs. "I told him to go talk to some of these medical people here, shake some hands, get their votes. You should go out to the hall there and do the same thing—instead of playing nursemaid to me."

"Oh, give me a break, Pop." She managed to laugh. "I just got here from a gig in Salem, the League of Women Voters."

Her father's bony hand grabbed her wrist. "You have to keep at it, honey," he said emphatically. "I thought I'd be around to see Brad become senator. But now I don't know if I'll make it—"

"Oh, now, Pop—"

"I mean it," he said.

Bridget noticed Janice in the doorway. Her blond hair was a bit mussed, and she had tears in her eyes. She'd thrown a trench coat over her maternity sweater and jeans. She held a hand over her heart.

Bridget nodded at her, then turned to her father again. "You're going to be fine, Pop," she said. "They're kicking you out of here tomorrow—if you behave yourself."

"I'm serious," he said, squeezing her hand. "I'm counting on you, sweetheart. You have to make certain Brad wins the election. You have to do whatever it takes—"

Bridget smiled patiently. "Pop, it's really up to the voters who will win in November. Now, you really need to relax and—"

"You heard what he said," Janice interjected, stepping up to the foot of his bed. She glared at Bridget. "We're going to make sure Brad wins. We'll do whatever it takes, whatever is necessary."

Janice turned to her father-in-law and started crying. "Oh, Dad! My God, how could this have happened?" She rushed around to the side of his bed—across from Bridget. Bending over, she squeezed his shoulder and kissed him on his cheek. Then she kissed him on the mouth. "I'm staying here with you tonight," she said, wiping the tears from her eyes. "You shouldn't be alone here, I won't allow it—"

"Janice, he needs rest more than anything else," Bridget said gently. "Pop is going to be okay. Let's not blow this out of proportion—"

"Why isn't there a nurse in here?" Janice interrupted. "And Christ, where's the doctor? What's going on?"

She stormed out of the room. Both Bridget and her father took a deep breath. She patted her father's shoulder. "I think *she's* the one about to have a heart attack," Bridget muttered.

Her father just chuckled.

Bridget could hear Janice down the corridor, screaming at a nurse. She sounded like a child having a temper-tantrum. Her voice was angry, yet choked with tears. "I can spend the night here if I choose to do so! And don't give me that stupid look. Do you know who I am? Do you know who my husband is? Where's the doctor who examined my father-in-law? Why isn't he here?"

Bridget could hear Brad trying to calm Janice. Then she started arguing with him—in that same weepy, demanding tone. Apparently, one of the nurses tried to get Janice to quiet down, because she cried out: "Don't shush me! Do you know who I am? Do you?"

The nurse must have said something to quiet Janice down, because Bridget couldn't hear her sister-in-law after that. Suddenly, Brad poked his head in the door. "Janice is going nuts," he said.

"Really?" Bridget replied. "Because I thought she was keeping it together rather well."

Their father let out another frail chuckle.

"Oh, screw you," Brad said to her. "So do you think it would hurt the baby if we gave Janice a sedative? She's in the restroom right now. The nurse suggested giving her something to calm her down, but when I told her that Janice is pregnant—"

"Want me to call Dr. Reece and ask?" Bridget volunteered. Dr. Reece had been Bridget's ob-gyn, and now he was Janice's.

"Yes, thanks," Brad said. He glanced over at their father. "Pop, it looks like you're getting your color back. How are you feeling?"

He nodded tiredly. "I'm okay. Go back out there and shake some hands. Get some votes."

Bridget stood by a pay phone in the visitors' lounge down the hall from her father's room. She couldn't use her cellular in the hospital. And the last thing she wanted to do was step outside to make a call, then get lost again trying to find her way back to room C-216. She rummaged through her purse for more quarters.

"Need some change?"

Startled, Bridget glanced up and frowned. "What are you doing, following me?"

Slipping his hands in his pockets, Zach Matthias leaned against the wall. "Not quite," he said. "I was called to cover Foley's appearance here. I missed him greeting you at the main entrance. I hear there wasn't a dry eye in the place."

"Yes, it was very touching," Bridget said.

"One of the other reporters told me your dad's going to be okay. I'm glad."

"Thanks," Bridget replied. "So why aren't you with the rest of them?"

Zach sighed. "Well, never one to miss an opportunity, Foley's downstairs, giving blood. It's quite the photo op. They're all down there with him, lapping it up. To commemorate the occasion, he made an AIDS joke, and I took that as my cue to leave. You can bet none of those other reporters will mention the joke in their stories."

"Will you?" she asked pointedly.

He glanced down at the floor and shrugged. "I want to keep my job. I've only been with the paper three weeks. I don't have a byline yet. I just handle 'coverage.' So even if I blew the whistle on Foley in my coverage, it wouldn't go to print."

He pulled some coins out of his pocket. "You needed some change?"

"Yes, thanks."

"So what happened? Did you use up all your quarters earlier, calling Cheryl Blume?"

Bridget stared at him. "You . . ." She hesitated. "Were you eavesdropping?"

"Not really. I might have caught the tail end of your conversation with her, that's all. How's old Cheryl doing, by the way?"

"Old Cheryl's fine," Bridget replied guardedly.

He put two quarters in her palm. "Is that enough?"

She nodded. "Thanks."

"Let's do that lunch sometime, okay?" he said. "I'm glad your dad is okay. Take care, Bridget."

She watched him stroll down the hallway, then disappear around the corner.

"Dr. Reece's office. This is Linda."

"Linda, this is Bridget Corrigan calling. How are you?"

"Great," the receptionist said on the other end of the line. "I don't have to ask how you're doing. I see you on TV practically every day, and you look terrific. What can I do for you?"

"Well, thanks. Um, I'm wondering if you or Dr. Reece could help me. My dad had—what the doctors are calling an 'episode.' Long story short, he's staying the night here at Portland General—just as a precaution."

"Oh, I'm so sorry, Bridget."

"Thanks. Anyway, Janice is taking it kind of badly, and one of the nurses here suggested we give her a sedative. But Brad and I thought—to be on the safe side—we better call Dr. Reece and see if it's okay."

"Oh, um, Bridget, I . . ." The receptionist trailed off for a moment. "Well, Dr. Reece isn't seeing Janice anymore."

"What?" Bridget murmured.

"She stopped coming by six weeks ago—very sudden. She phoned and told us that she started seeing another doctor."

"I can't believe it," Bridget said. "Did she give you the name of this other doctor?"

"No. In fact, we still have Janice's data. We've been waiting to forward it. But we've yet to hear from this new doctor. So—I gather your sister-in-law didn't tell you about the switch."

"Um, no," Bridget said into the phone. "It's a surprise to me. A total mystery."

Bridget wandered back toward her father's room. She almost ran into Brad—on his way out. "You didn't call the doctor yet, did you?" he asked. "Because it's all nipped in the bud. Janice is okay now."

"Brad, I . . ." Bridget hesitated as she noticed Janice in the room with Bradley Senior. She was holding his hand and talking in a soothing tone.

"While we were wondering if she could have a sedative, Janice was in the ladies' room taking a Valium." Brad must have read the concerned look on her face, because he let out a little laugh. "Hey, don't worry. I guess it's a real light dose. She said Dr. Reece gave her the okay. Reece said it won't hurt the baby at all."

"Are you sure she said *Dr. Reece?*" Bridget asked.

"Yeah, of course." He patted her arm. "Be right back. I need to make a few calls."

Brad headed down the hallway.

Bridget gazed into her father's room. Janice didn't look up at her. She stayed focused on Bridget's father and kept stroking his hand. "You're going to be all right, Dad," she whispered. "I'm here . . . I'm right here. . . ."

CHAPTER 15

Bridget slammed on the brakes. The minivan's tires let out a screech. Pushing back from the steering wheel, stiff-armed, Bridget prepared for the crash. She stopped just inches from the back bumper of the other car.

She hadn't noticed the Honda Accord stopped there. She hadn't even noticed the red light. Her mind was somewhere else.

It was nine-fifteen. Bridget had left the hospital only a few minutes ago. Her father was asleep. Visiting hours were over. Brad was still trying to convince Janice to come home with him.

Bridget hadn't had a chance to talk confidentially with her brother. So he didn't know about Cheryl, or Zach Matthias, or about Janice switching obstetricians. The crisis with their dad canceled everything out—at least temporarily.

Bridget was on her way to Gerry and Leslie's house to pick up the boys. Her stomach was still tied in a knot as she watched the light turn green. The Honda in front of her pulled forward, and Bridget noticed the bumper sticker: JIM FOLEY, MY FRIEND, MY SENATOR.

She let out a frail little laugh. "Huh, maybe I should have hit him," she said to no one.

She moved on through the intersection. Gerry and his girlfriend had a new house in one of those new developments with its own country club and golf course. It was out where God lost his shoes, off Route 30.

Bridget turned onto the freeway. A few drops of rain started hitting the windshield, and she switched on the wipers. Route 30 wasn't very busy this time of night. Without much traffic to navigate, she started thinking about her sister-in-law again.

She wondered about Janice and her new obstetrician, the one who wasn't interested in her previous medical records, the one who thought it was okay for her to have the occasional glass of bourbon or dose of Valium while pregnant. Who was this quack? Or did he even exist?

It might not have been any of Bridget's business what her sister-in-law did, but Brad had a right to know about the risks Janice was taking with their unborn child. And obviously, Janice was lying to him if she claimed *Dr. Reece* had approved of her using some kind of Valium lite.

Brad knew the most current figures for the state budget down to the penny, but obviously he didn't know squat about common safeguards during pregnancies.

Bridget was making up her mind to tell her brother all of this when suddenly, she felt something horribly wrong with the minivan. She glanced in the side mirror, and the image of the road behind her was shaking. In fact, everything shook and vibrated. She heard a loud rattling and wondered if something had happened to the engine. Then she realized the minivan was listing to one side.

She had a flat.

"Oh, shit," she murmured. She felt that panic-lurch in her stomach again. It seemed impossible—so soon after that blowout on the interstate two weeks ago. She'd just had two tires replaced and the other two rotated.

Trembling, Bridget switched on her flashers, then pulled over to the side of the road. All the while, she felt the car dragging in the back—on the left side.

At least there was room on the road's shoulder, but it wasn't very well lit. Trees surrounded both sides of the highway, neither a gas station nor a fast food place in sight.

Bridget switched off the motor and watched raindrops accumulate on the windshield. It wasn't raining too heavily. She climbed out of the car and took a look at the back tire.

The deflated tire's hubcap seemed to be digging into the gravel. "Lord," Bridget muttered, looking skyward, "it isn't enough my dad's in the hospital and my sister-in-law's insane. You have to give me this?"

She ducked back in the car, then called Triple-A on her cell phone. They told Bridget someone would be there within a half hour. Next, she phoned Gerry's house. His girlfriend answered the phone. Bridget could hear David and Eric laughing in the background.

"Hi, Leslie, it's Bridget. Is Gerry there, please?" she asked, trying like hell to sound pleasant.

"Oh, hi, Bridget. Yes, just a minute." There was a pause, then: "Hey, honey, it's Bridget on the phone! Sweetie?"

Bridget could still hear the boys laughing—and the television. Her family was there. Yet she felt like the outsider. When Gerry got on the line, she quickly explained that she had a flat and she'd be late picking up the boys.

"Where are you?" he asked. "I'll come by."

"No, it's okay, really. I called Triple-A, and they should be here in twenty minutes."

"Well, at least let me wait with you. It's a cold, ugly night out."

She didn't need her estranged husband being nice to her right now. "No, really, I'm fine. You stay there with the boys. Are they okay?"

"Oh, they're fine. We had pizza. And they're watching *Rat Race* on TV right now."

"They should be doing their homework," Bridget said.

"It's all done. That was part of the deal. They couldn't watch the movie until the homework was done. You sure I can't drive out there and keep you company?"

"No, I'm fine, Gerry. Thanks. See you in a bit."

Bridget clicked off. She sat in the car, surrounded by darkness. As she listened to the rain tapping the roof, Bridget had never felt so all alone.

She made up her mind, she wasn't going to cry. Still, why did the boys have to sound so happy at their place? And why did Gerry and Leslie have to sound so happy—and cozy, and lovey-dovey? Making matters worse, they were trying to be nice to her.

"Goddamnit!" she finally cried, enraged now. "Where the hell is the stupid Triple-A?"

Bridget jumped out of the car and stomped around to the back. The rain had let up a little. She opened the rear doors and started dislodging the board that covered the spare tire, the jack, and the wrench.

By the time Bridget had prepped the car to change the tire, she felt utterly miserable.

She toiled with the wrench, trying to loosen the lug nuts so she could remove the flat. Every so often a car passed, its headlights sweeping over her. When the roar of the engines faded, she could hear the nearby forest, restless with leaves rustling and rain dripping from the branches. She tried to work quickly.

Bridget was so busy, she didn't realize a vehicle had pulled over and stopped several yards behind her.

"Looks like you could use some help."

Bridget turned around and saw a man approaching. The headlights from the old Volkswagen minibus in back of him partially blinded her, and all she could see was his silhouette. He was a short, compact man, who walked with a macho swagger.

"You're just in time," Bridget called, managing a smile.

Then she saw him, and her smile faded. She'd thought he was from Triple-A. But there was no AAA logo on his leather jacket. And there was nothing professional about the way the balding little ape of a man leered at her. It was almost obscene.

"Out here all alone, pretty lady like you?" he asked. "What's this world coming to?" He licked his lips, then held out his hand. "Why don't you give me that wrench and I'll get this taken care of in no time."

She automatically took a step back. "Oh, that's okay. I've called Triple-A. They should be here soon."

Chuckling, he still held his hand out. "Bet I get it changed before they even show their faces. Gimme."

"Oh no, really, thank you, but—"

He swiped the wrench out of her hand. "C'mon, don't be stupid."

Dumbfounded, Bridget backed away from him. She watched him squat down by the tire and start working on the lug nuts. "Shit," he growled. "These motherfuckers are on here pretty tight."

She saw a squiggly vein bulge out on the side of his head. He gasped as he got each lug nut loose. He stopped and pulled off his jacket. He wore a red T-shirt that looked painted on. His muscular arms were covered with thick black hair.

"Why don't you go wait in my van while I finish this?" he said, fixing the jack under the car.

Bridget glanced back at the old Volkswagen minibus. Except for an air-freshener hanging from the rearview mirror, she couldn't see anything—or anyone—inside the vehicle. From this far away, Bridget could just make out the reflector-cartoon snake on the air freshener. The thing was grinning—with big eyes and fangs. The air-freshener was moving back and forth.

"Go ahead," the man urged her. "The door's open."

She kept staring at the darkened front seat of the minibus—and that thing dangling from the mirror. "Um, thanks," she said finally. "I'm all right here."

"Don't be silly. It's warm in there. You can listen to the radio."

"I—I'm fine, thanks," she said.

"Suit yourself," the man grumbled. He used the wrench to rotate the jack, and Bridget's minivan started tilting up on one side.

She glanced down the lonely highway and wondered what was taking Triple-A so long. She wished she hadn't left her cell phone on the front seat.

"Are you going to give me a reward for this?" the man asked, grinning up at her again.

Bridget tried to smile. "Maybe I can take you out to lunch sometime."

"Lunch, huh?" He cackled. "I had something else in mind. I bet, after this blowout, you could probably use a drink, huh? Nothing like a roadside emergency to unnerve a gal."

Straightening up, the short, muscular man smirked at her. He still had the wrench in his hand. He'd left her minivan propped up on one side. He took a step toward her.

"I have an ongoing happy hour at my place," he said, looking her up and down. "The drinks are free."

Bridget knew she couldn't take refuge in the minivan and lock the doors. Not now. Hell, she would have needed a stepladder to reach the driver's door.

She backed away from the man. "That's a very nice offer," she said. "But I—I have some people waiting for me." She looked at her watch. "In fact, one of them is on his way."

Studying her, the man cocked his head to one side. "Wouldn't the joke be on him if he got here and you were gone?"

Bridget stared at him. She kept a stony look plastered on her face. She didn't want to let him know she was scared.

At that moment, a black Honda Accord slowed down and pulled over in front of Bridget's minivan.

Squinting at the other car, the man frowned. "Is this your friend?"

Bridget had no idea who it was, but she thanked God for

their perfect timing. She watched a tall, lean man climb out of the Accord. He waved at them. Once he came out of the shadows, Bridget could see he was handsome, with brown hair, a narrow, chiseled face, and dark, intense eyes. "Looked like you guys were in trouble," he said. "Need any help?"

"It's under control," the short man said. "Thanks anyway. We don't need you."

Bridget gave the tall man a furtive, panicked look and shook her head.

He caught it, then turned and smiled at the shorter man. "Oh, I think I should stick around—just in case."

The little man changed his stance and casually brandished the long wrench. "That's not necessary. So you can get back in your car and drive to wherever you're headed. We're fine here."

"Why don't we let the lady speak for herself?" The handsome man turned to Bridget. "Ma'am, would you like me to stay?"

She nodded. "Yes, please."

"That settles it then," he said, heading toward the back of her minivan. He started to remove the deflated tire.

For a moment, Bridget wondered if the ape-faced man was going to hit him with the wrench. Instead, the little creep threw it down. The wrench hit the gravel with a clang. "Screw this," he grumbled. He swiped his jacket off the ground, then stomped back to his old Volkswagen minibus.

Bridget waited until he climbed inside and slammed the door; then she turned toward her rescuer. "Thank you," she whispered.

He set down the deflated tire. "Well, from my car, I noticed him standing there, holding the wrench—and you backing up. I figured it wouldn't hurt to stop."

"You figured right," she said, with a sigh. "He was starting to make me feel very uncomfortable." Bridget glanced back at the Volkswagen. She could see the hairy, muscular man sitting behind the wheel, watching them. She wondered why he hadn't moved on yet.

Her rescuer hoisted the spare tire over to the raised axle. "Well, don't worry, Bridget. I'll make sure he doesn't mess with you."

Bridget frowned. How did he know her name?

She watched him set the spare tire in place. "You're a life-saver," she said, stepping behind him. She picked up the wrench. "How—um, how do you know my name?"

His back to her, he was lining up the holes with the lug nut rods. "I thought I recognized you from the news," he explained. "Then I noticed the bumper sticker. And the Corrigan-for-Oregon posters here in the back of your mini-van cinched the deal."

He fixed the spare in place and smiled up at her. "My name is Clay, by the way. I'd shake your hand, but mine's dirty." He glanced down at the pavement. "Did you see where your friend left the lug nuts?"

Bridget didn't see them. She wondered if the creepy little man had stashed them in his pocket. She looked back at the old Volkswagen again. He was still in the front seat, grinning at them.

She turned toward Clay again, and noticed something in his hand.

"They should be around here some place," he said, checking around his feet.

Maybe he wanted her to look down at the ground too, but Bridget didn't take her eyes off that shiny thing hidden in his hand. At first, it looked like a silver pencil. Then she saw the sharp, slanted end glisten in the VW's headlights.

He was holding an Exacto-knife.

"You aren't helping me look," he said.

Tightening her grip on the wrench, she backed away. She heard the Volkswagen's engine starting up. Bridget glanced back as the old minibus pulled back onto the freeway. A tow truck, with its amber roof-light flashing, rolled in to take its place behind Bridget's vehicle.

"Well, your friend is gone—finally," Clay said. "I guess I

can put this away now." He showed her the Exacto-knife, then flicked a switch on the side so the razor tip disappeared inside the cylinder. "It doesn't seem like much protection, but if you hit the right artery, you can do a lot of damage. Here. You keep this." He held out the Exacto-knife for her. "My sister carries one around for emergencies—like when you have a flat tire on a cold, rainy night and the wrong guy comes by."

Bridget hesitated.

"Go ahead, take it," he said. "You never know when you might need it." He set the Exacto-knife in her hand, then waved at the tow truck.

A stocky woman emerged from the driver's side. She started toward them.

"We're almost done here," Clay called to her. "We just can't find where this guy who was helping earlier put all the lug nuts. We could use another set of eyes."

"I'm Julie from Triple-A," the woman said, approaching them.

"Hi, I'm Clay," he said. "I just stopped by to help. . . ."

Bridget barely heard him. She was studying the Exacto-knife in her hand. She flicked the switch and watched the razor pop out.

Usually, Bridget called from her cell phone about a mile from Gerry and Leslie's house. Then she could pull into the driveway and wait. No need to honk the horn. They knew she was out there, and she never had to wait long for David and Eric to come out of the house. It was a pretty good setup. Bridget didn't have to make small talk with Gerry—or God help her, Leslie. She didn't have to see the inside of their designer home or even go up to the front entrance. She'd managed to miss that—until now.

After Clay and Triple-A Julie had finished changing the tire, Bridget had tried to call Gerry, but her cellular had run out of juice. The irony didn't escape her that she'd been using *a low battery* as her excuse for using pay phones so often during the last two days.

Bridget had thought Clay might linger on after Julie's departure. Instead, he set out to leave while Julie was still filling out forms inside her tow truck.

"Well, thank you for stopping," Bridget told him, leaning out her car window. "And thank you for the razor-thingee."

"You bet," he said. "I'll vote for your brother. I hope he wins. I'll see you." Then he ran back to his car.

Julie from Triple-A had advised her to replace the spare in the morning. "From the looks of that flat," she added, "I think someone must have slashed the tire. It's a very precise puncture."

Bridget numbly stared at her.

"We've had a lot of flat tires like this lately," Julie continued. "And I've noticed something in common among many of them. The cars all have Corrigan-for-Oregon bumper stickers. Looks to me like a pretty dirty campaign. At least one side has a lot of crazy supporters."

Bridget felt sort of reassured to know that she might not have been singled out by a stalker this time. Maybe this was just someone who hated her brother. Still, as she drove to Gerry and Leslie's house, she almost felt like a moving target with that campaign sticker on the back of her minivan.

Gerry and Leslie's "cozy" two-story stucco had a courtyard atrium front entrance that seemed more suited for Southern California than Portland. Bridget walked up to the wrought-iron gate and noticed the lit flat-stone pathway through a garden area that included a Japanese maple, some sea grass, and other plants. There was also a rock garden waterfall. She could hear the water gushing. David and Eric had told her that their father and Leslie had a waterfall in their front hallway, and now Bridget knew what they meant.

The gate was locked. Bridget rang the bell. After a minute, the inside door opened and Leslie stepped out to the atrium. Bridget had met her a few times when Leslie and Gerry were still just "coworkers." But Bridget had managed to keep a cordial distance ever since Gerry had moved in with her. She was pretty, with blond hair that came down just above her shoulders. Gerry always liked curvy blondes. And Leslie fit the bill. Her tight jeans and long-sleeve T-shirt showed off her opulent figure. A catty woman might call her borderline chubby. But she had the kind of body most guys went nuts over. And Gerry was one of those guys.

"Bridget, is that you?" she called, from the doorway.

"Yes, hello!" Bridget waved.

Leslie ducked back inside and the gate buzzed. Then she reappeared in the doorway. "Well, come on in," she said, trotting down the lit pathway to meet her. "You threw me for a minute there. Gerry said you had a flat, you poor thing. We were all worried. We've been waiting for your usual call—the one you make when you're about a mile away. Gerry and the kids call it your 'five-minute warning.' "

"Well, my cell phone's dead," Bridget explained, stepping into the atrium. She tried to smile. "But the tire got changed. Um, are the boys ready?"

"They will be—in a jiff," Leslie said, turning toward the front door again. "C'mon in. You haven't seen the inside of the house yet, have you? Would you like to take the ten-cent tour?"

"Maybe some other time, thanks," Bridget said. Leslie was doing her damnedest to be perky and friendly and up-beat. Bridget didn't hate her. She just didn't need Gerry's girlfriend patronizing her.

She stepped inside and got a look at the front hallway. It was stone-tiled with a dramatic, modern stairway that curved up to the second floor. And the boys weren't mistaken about a waterfall in the front hall. Alongside the stairs was a rock wall with water gently cascading down to a pond below the stairs. And damn it to hell, they had several big goldfish in the pond. Eric had talked about how he liked to feed the fish at Daddy's house, and Bridget had imagined a little aquarium in Gerry's study or something. No, the fish were in a goddamn pond under the goddamn movie-star stairs. And the pond was lit, of course.

Bridget wondered if Leslie had patterned the layout after a lobby in a Las Vegas hotel. It had that cheesy, expensive look.

"Hey, guys!" Leslie called. "Your mom's here to take you home! Time to hustle! Move it or lose it!"

Bridget peeked into the living room—more Las Vegas chic. The carpet was a plush shag. In the corner sat a big gold Buddha. Over the red sofa with leopard-skin pillows were three Chinese fans, each in an ornate black and gold frame. The frame was much simpler for the photo portrait of David and Eric on the black-and-gold-inlay end table. Bridget imagined the boys' photo was the closest they'd ever get to setting foot inside the pristine showcase of a room. The place was dripping with money—money that used to be in her joint account before Gerry secretly transferred it all under Leslie's name.

Leslie turned to Bridget and smiled. "Oh, they're still in the den. We can't tear them away from our big-screen, high-definition TV. C'mon."

Bridget shook her head. "Um, thanks, Leslie. But I'll just wait right here by the door—"

"Don't be silly. You haven't even seen the house, and—"

"No, thank you," she said, more firmly. "I'd really be more comfortable waiting here, Leslie. It's been a long day, and I'm very tired. I just want to get the boys home and put them to bed."

Leslie's smile seemed to stiffen. "Sure, whatever," she said.

At that moment, Gerry stepped into the hall. He looked handsome and relaxed in his jeans and crew-neck jersey. Leslie went to him, grumbled something under her breath, then retreated to their state-of-the-art kitchen.

With a sigh, he frowned at Bridget. He almost looked ashamed. "The boys will be ready in a minute."

"Thanks," Bridget replied. "Please tell Leslie that I didn't mean to be rude. I just really need to get out of here."

He nodded glumly. "I understand. She doesn't. But I do."

Beep.

"Listen, it's about ten-fifteen, and I know it's late, but call me as soon as you get this. Your cell isn't answering, and I'm starting to worry."

It was the third message Brad had left. Bridget glanced at the stove clock: 10:40.

The boys were getting settled upstairs. Bridget took the cordless to the kitchen table and dialed her brother's number. He answered, and good thing too, because she was in no mood to talk with her sister-in-law. Bridget explained to him about the flat tire.

"You just had a flat last week," he said. "I don't like this."

"I'm not exactly gaga about it either. According to the woman from Triple-A, she's changed many a flat for people with Corrigan-for-Oregon bumper stickers. I guess there are some crazy pro-Foley folk out there. Slash-happy." She sighed. "Better our tires than our throats, I suppose. How's Janice?"

"Well, she was determined to stay the night at the hospital—at Dad's bedside. But I managed to convince her that it wouldn't do the baby any good, and she came home with me. Anyway, those sedatives Reece recommended must have done the trick, because she's asleep right now. We're going to have Pop stay here with us for the next couple of weeks. Janice practically insisted on it. Is that cool with you?"

"Sure," Bridget said into the phone. "Brad, I . . ." She hesitated. He'd said yesterday that their phones might be tapped. She didn't dare discuss the risks her sister-in-law was taking with Brad's unborn baby, not when friends of Foley might be listening in. "I need to talk with you tomorrow about a—a personal matter. Okay?"

"Sure," he said. "Are you okay? Should I be worried?"

"It's just something we're better off not discussing on the phone." She paused. "Oh, by the way, I got a hold of that old high school chum we were talking about the other day. I called her—from a pay phone in Salem."

"Really?" Brad said, obviously getting her drift. "How is she?"

"She's fine," Bridget said. "She wasn't exactly friendly. But the good news is, she doesn't seem to have that—*bug* that's been going around. None of the symptoms."

"I told you," Brad said. "You were worried for nothing. I ran into Zach Matthias at the hospital after you left."

"Yeah, I saw him there too. We talked. He was in Salem earlier today, covering my speech. He asked me out to lunch."

"Maybe you ought to accept," Brad suggested. "You should go to lunch with him, find out what he's after."

"You told me the other day he was *poison*," Bridget pointed out. "You want me to sit down and have lunch with *poison?*"

"Dad used to say, 'Keep your friends close, and your enemies closer.' "

"Dad never said that," Bridget whispered. "Marlon Brando said it to Al Pacino in *The Godfather*."

"Actually, it's from *The Godfather Two*, but let's not quibble. The idea is a good one."

"Well, if you think it's such a terrific idea, why don't you have lunch with him?"

"Because he didn't ask me. And I'm not the one he had a crush on back in high school. He'll have his guard up with me, but he might let it down with you."

Bridget wondered if she would be able to keep *her* guard up. She didn't trust Zach. And she didn't trust herself around him.

"I'll think about it," she said, finally.

After she hung up with her brother, Bridget emptied out her purse until she found Zach's business card. Then she clicked on the phone again and dialed his number. A machine answered, and Zach's recorded voice came on the line:

"Hi, thanks for calling. Please leave a message after the tone."

Beep.

"Hi, Zach. It's Bridget Corrigan calling. Sorry about the late hour. I—I'm free for lunch tomorrow—if you're still interested. Maybe we can try the fare in the hospital cafeteria—or somewhere else close by. Why don't you call me sometime tomorrow morning?"

Bridget gave him her number, then clicked off the line.

Some contents from her purse were in a pile on the breakfast table. She started to load them back in her bag.

Out of the corner of her eye, she saw something move in the kitchen window. Bridget gasped. Then she realized she'd caught a glimpse of her own reflection. She had the jitters.

She thought back to that time after Andy Shields and the Gaines twins had been missing and presumed dead. She'd slept with a baseball bat at her bedside, and tried to ignore Olivia's comment about someone out there bent on murdering twins.

Bridget went back to loading up her purse. She stopped to look at the razor-pen. She flicked the switch and watched the razor pop out. *"If you hit the right artery, you can do a lot of damage."*

Bridget swallowed hard. She wondered once again if she and Brad were really safe. As much as she tried to ignore it, she couldn't help thinking someone was out there bent on murdering them.

"I bend over backward to be nice to her, and she treats me like shit," Leslie complained, making herself a bourbon and water.

"Honey, she's bitter," Gerry said. "It's that simple. I know you were trying to be friendly and make her feel welcome. But I don't think she wanted to see how cushy we have it."

"So what do you expect me to do? Make her wait outside? I was just trying to be hospitable, for Christ's sake."

She sipped her drink. "That's what I should have done. I should have made the bitch wait outside while I rounded up her brats."

"Hey, watch it," Gerry said. "Those are my brats too."

Leslie picked up a copy of *To Kill a Mockingbird* from the kitchen counter. "One of them left his book behind."

Gerry glanced toward his study—off the family room. "Do you have a window open? I'm feeling a draft."

"No. And *I'm* feeling like we'll get a call in about five minutes from Her Royal Painess, wanting you to drive over with this thing, because your kid's gonna need it for school." She tossed the paperback on the counter again.

"The boys are coming over again tomorrow night. David can get his book then." Frowning, Gerry headed into the study. "What the hell . . ."

"Well, I don't mind your kids," Leslie said, between sips of her drink. "But I swear, that's the last time I'm nice to her."

"Hey, was one of the boys in here, screwing around with the sliding glass door?" Gerry called from the other room. "The damn lock is broken—"

At that moment, the front gate buzzed.

"I bet that's her!" Leslie called, snatching up the paperback. "Miss Sourpuss came back for the book." She headed for the front door. "Don't worry, I'll be nice! I'll rise above it. Just don't expect me to invite her in."

As she buzzed open the front gate, Leslie wondered why Gerry wasn't answering her—and why he hadn't come out of the study. Hadn't he heard the gate?

"Gerry?" she called, glancing over her shoulder. She opened the front door and looked toward the wrought-iron gate. No one.

Yet she could hear gravel crunching under feet. Leslie glanced around the atrium. They had gravel around the bushes near the side of the house—and along the courtyard gate. But she didn't see anyone—not at first.

Then Leslie let out a gasp. A tall, lean figure stepped out

from behind the bushes. She couldn't see his face. Then suddenly he rushed toward her.

"Oh my God!" Leslie screamed, dropping the book.

She swiveled around and headed back inside. She was about to shut the door behind her, but stopped short.

What Leslie saw in the front hall was like a freakish nightmare. It all seemed to be happening at high speed.

His forehead gushing blood, Gerry ran toward her. A short, muscular man chased after him with a pipe raised in his fist.

"Jesus, no, wait!" Gerry was yelling. "No—"

But the man slammed the pipe on the back of his head, and Gerry fell down on the stone tiles.

Leslie watched in horror. *This isn't happening, this isn't happening.*

She started to scream, but the other man slapped his hand over her mouth. It was so forceful, he almost snapped her neck back. His hand felt like rubber. She realized he was wearing surgeon's gloves. The shorter man, who now stood over Gerry, also wore them.

She heard the door slam behind her.

He twisted her around, and she could no longer see what was happening to Gerry—if he was alive or dead.

His pelvis pressed against her back, the man was almost lifting her up by her chin. Leslie could hardly breathe with his rubber-clad hand over her mouth. She stared into the living room. Gerry's sons—in their framed portrait on the end table—seemed to smile back at her.

Leslie struggled. She thought he might break her neck. One hand was firmly clamped over her jaw, and she felt his other on her belly. He tugged at her T-shirt. The rubber glove brushed against her bare skin as he pulled the T-shirt up over her bra.

"It isn't black," she heard him mutter. His warm breath swirled in her ear. "Do you have a black one?"

He lowered his hand from her mouth—just enough for her to gasp for air. "I—I can give you money," she cried.

"Please, please . . . we have cocaine here. I'll show you where it is. Take it . . . please . . . just take it and go . . ."

She managed to glance back toward where Gerry had fallen. The other man was tying Gerry's hands in back of him with some duct tape.

"Do you have a black one?" the man behind her repeated. His cheek was rubbing against hers. The whisker stubble scratched.

Leslie was crying helplessly. "A black what?"

"A black bra. Do you have one?"

Tears streamed down her face. She wondered why he would ask that. But she nodded. "Upstairs . . . my bedroom dresser . . . please . . ."

His hand came over her mouth again, tighter than before. He suddenly grabbed her arm with his other hand and wrenched it behind her back. He pushed her toward the stairs.

She glimpsed Gerry, lying on the floor, unconscious and bleeding. The shorter man darted past them to the door, and he locked it. Then he hurried to the living room window and closed the drapes. His every move seemed so efficient and passionless.

Leslie tried to breathe past the gloved hand over her mouth. The man's face was pressed against hers. Yanking at her arm, he forced her up each step toward the second floor. The lights were off up there.

Leslie looked at the darkness ahead.

This isn't happening, she kept telling herself. She felt his lips brush against her ear again, and she shuddered.

"Come on, Leslie," he whispered. "You're going to put on your black bra for me. And I'll make you immortal."

CHAPTER 16

"Where is that moron with the wheelchair?" Janice wanted to know. She nervously paced back and forth in the hospital room.

Bridget glanced over at her father. He sat on the side of the hospital bed, wearing a baggy, bright blue nylon jogging outfit with purple piping. It was zipped up around his slight turkey neck. Every white hair was carefully combed in place. But he still looked ashen and frail.

Bridget wondered if he really should be getting out of the hospital today. Or were they locked into the decision, now that the press had gathered in front of the hospital? Brad was trying to keep little Emma entertained. They'd brought her along to make the most of the photo opportunity.

Janice looked very pretty for the occasion, one of her first public appearances since the pregnancy had sidelined her. She wore a black jumper that made her appear further along than she actually was.

Bridget hadn't known this was a minor media event. Still, she'd taken too much time getting dressed this morning. Zach Matthias had called back, saying he would meet her at the hospital cafeteria for lunch, and suddenly she'd freaked out over what to wear. After changing outfits and hairstyles several times, she'd finally decided to put her hair up—and wear her sage cashmere sweater and black pants.

At the last minute, David couldn't find *To Kill a Mockingbird*, which he'd needed for class. Bridget had hunted down her own copy for him. The boys had barely made their bus. While waiting for them to replace her spare at the Firestone outlet, Bridget checked out the *Examiner*. The story was on page two: SENATORIAL CANDIDATE'S FATHER, BRADLEY CORRIGAN SR., HOSPITALIZED. They ran a photo—not of her father, but of *her* with Jim Foley. He was holding her hand, while she numbly gazed at him. The caption read:

> *GOOD SPORT: Senatorial Candidate, Jim Foley, puts aside political differences to offer his moral support to his opponent's sister, Bridget Corrigan, at Portland General Hospital yesterday. Corrigan's father was admitted to the hospital with an undisclosed illness.*

Small wonder Brad's campaign manager, Jay Corby—aka *Mr. Slick*—was turning their father's release from the hospital into a family photo opportunity.

"I think when we go out the main door, you should be pushing Dad in the chair," Janice told her husband. "I'll be at Dad's side, holding his hand, and carrying Emma. Bridget, you should be, um, let's see . . ."

"How about if I sat on Dad's lap?" she offered.

Her father chuckled. But Janice threw her a peeved look. "You're not helping."

"Sorry," Bridget said. "Actually, I'll stay in the background. This is a moment for you three and Dad. I got my picture in the paper this morning, and that's enough for me." She headed toward the door. "I'll see what's holding up the guy with the wheelchair."

She was halfway down the corridor when Brad caught up with her. "Hey, those were her raging hormones talking," he said in a hushed voice. He took hold of her arm, and Bridget stopped. "I want you in the picture, Brigg."

"No, you guys should be the focus. But you ought to be carrying Emma, on the other side of Dad. Let the orderly push Dad in the chair. It's his job."

Brad chuckled. "Well, if Janice wants it a certain way, you know that's how it'll be."

Bridget only gave a flicker of a smile. "Brad, I told you last night that I needed to talk to you about something." She glanced around the corridor. "This is as good a time as any, I suppose. It's about Janice."

Brad frowned. "What is it?"

"Well, when I called Dr. Reece's office yesterday—to ask about giving Janice a sedative—they told me Janice stopped seeing Dr. Reece about six weeks ago."

"That's crazy—"

Bridget shrugged. "Janice told Dr. Reece that she'd found another obstetrician. The nurse at Reece's office said they've been waiting to forward Janice's records to this other doctor, but they've yet to hear from him."

"But Janice just told me yesterday that *Dr. Reece* said it was all right for her to take—"

"That Valium lite, or whatever it is, I know," Bridget cut in. She sighed. "That's another thing, Brad. I think nearly every doctor and nurse here would agree with me that a pregnant woman shouldn't be taking Valium. It's a definite no-no—right up there with drinking. And as long as I'm spilling my guts, that night we got back from the fund-raiser, when I was washing dishes at your house, I noticed a glass with some bourbon in it and lipstick marks on the rim. I'm pretty sure it was Janice's shade. That was the night she'd left Emma downstairs with the boys and went to bed early."

He just stared at her and shook his head.

"Brad, I'm sorry. I feel awful telling you all this."

"Do you?" he asked pointedly.

"Yes, I do."

He just kept staring.

"I hope I'm wrong," Bridget continued. "I hope there's a perfectly good explanation. I'd love to end up apologizing to both of you for even insinuating that, well, that Janice might be taking risks with your baby."

"You'll apologize all right," he replied in a low voice. "You know, I agree with you, Bridget. Maybe you shouldn't be in the picture with us."

He glanced over his shoulder. A stocky, young orderly was coming down from the other end of the corridor with the wheelchair.

Brad turned to her again. "Janice and I can take it from here. Maybe the two of you shouldn't be around each other today."

"Brad, I—"

"I'll call you later," he said, cutting her off.

Bridget watched him head back toward their father's room. He met the orderly with the wheelchair. Brad nodded, smiled, and shook his hand. Another vote for Corrigan.

He'd been up all night. Yet he was wired. Bridget Corrigan's estranged husband and his girlfriend had quite a stash of cocaine, and he'd imbibed a bit.

Clad only in his undershorts, he stood in front of his masterpiece. Sweat, dried glue, and smudges of paint covered his skin, caking against his arm and chest hair.

Candles flickered on either side of his latest work. This one came out even better than he'd anticipated. The pale, Rubenesque young woman was nude—except for that black bra. Her wrists had been bound behind her with the same gray duct tape they'd used to tie up the man. He wasn't interested in the guy. He'd let his partner take care of him.

His subject was posed just as he'd planned—slumped forward from a kneeling position. She looked so pitiful, curled up in a little ball beside that red sofa. He'd wanted her face-down, because he didn't have much time to photograph her in the days prior to her death. He had to work without any good head shots.

He didn't see her face as he strangled her. He did it from behind, while she was on her knees. His partner had given him grief for bringing along ten feet of cord for the job. But he had his reasons—artistic reasons.

The canvas was thirty-two by twenty-four inches. Instead of getting a frame, he'd carefully glued the ten-foot cord around the edges of his masterpiece. Then he'd painted it black—to match her bra. It was the first time he'd incorporated a souvenir from his killing into his art.

He decided to call this one *Girl by a Red Sofa*.

He blew out the candles on either side of the painting. Heading toward the bathroom, he scratched his bare stomach and kicked several discarded sketches he'd tossed on the floor earlier in the week.

They were pencil drawings he'd made when he should have been focusing on his *Girl by a Red Sofa*. But he couldn't stop sketching Bridget Corrigan. He'd taken several photos of her—from newspapers and off the TV—along with ones he'd snapped himself in public—or sometimes, through a window in her home.

He'd sketched Bridget Corrigan full-face, and profile, with her hair up and down. He'd used his imagination to draw her nude. He'd made her a Madonna and a whore. He couldn't stop drawing her.

His associate said he was crazy. Maybe he was.

He'd become obsessed with Bridget Corrigan the moment he'd first set eyes on her. And he'd go on being obsessed with Bridget Corrigan—until he painted her dead.

Zach Matthias looked tired and a bit rumpled. He'd explained that he'd been up most of the night on his computer, which was hooked up on his phone line. He hadn't gotten her message until he'd signed off sometime around five in the morning.

He wore a navy blue knit sweater and gray corduroys. His wavy black hair was disheveled and he had on his black-rimmed glasses. He reminded her a little of the sweet, gawky Zach from their high school days.

In fact, it was almost as if they were back in high school again—sitting across from each other in a cafeteria with white and powder-blue tiles on the walls, and trays full of fatty, bland food on the table between them. Zach had the Teriyaki Bowl, and Bridget played it safe with a grilled cheese sandwich.

"So—what's a nice guy like you doing working for a pro-Foley rag like the *Examiner*?" Bridget finally asked, sitting back in her plastic chair.

"And providing coverage for other people's stories, no less. Talk about grunt work." Zach dabbed his mouth with his napkin. "I was desperate. I've been living in Europe for the last four years. I just got back in the States about six weeks ago, and needed a job."

"What were you doing in Europe?"

"I was an international spy," Zach replied. Then he smiled, waved the remark away, and quickly shook his head. "Actually, I did freelance stuff, writing newsletters and press releases—for museums mostly. In London, I worked for the Tate and the Tate Modern. I lived in a little flat off a canal by the Thames, and felt very continental. In Paris, I did some work for the Musee d'Orsay. My phonetic French is lousy, but I can write it okay. I really loved Paris." He shrugged and picked at some rice on his plate. "But I got homesick for the Pacific Northwest. So I moved to Portland, got an apartment in Hawthorne, bought a used VW Bug, and got a crappy job with a newspaper that supports a fascist. But when they told me I'd be covering the election, I thought, *That's cool, because I've always had a crush on Bridget Corrigan.*"

Bridget shifted a bit in her chair. She felt herself blushing. "Well, thanks," she managed to say. "That's very flattering."

"I thought you knew already," he said, grinning. "Kim Li

told me that she blabbed to you. Remember Kim? Do you know what she's doing now?"

Bridget shook her head. She'd pulled away from her best friend those last couple of weeks before going off to college. Bridget had known she couldn't stay close to Kim and not confide in her about Mallory's disappearance. It had broken her heart to phase out her closest friend like that. There had been a few letters and calls back and forth during their college freshman year, but nothing like before.

"You have this—faraway look," he said.

She blinked and sat up. "Oh, I was just thinking. It's sad, I haven't talked to Kim in nineteen years."

"I tracked her down a couple of weeks ago," Zach said. "She's a psychiatrist in Minneapolis. She's been married ten years, and has three kids. She asked about you. I've been looking up a lot of our high school classmates. It's part of a feature story idea I had."

"What kind of story idea?"

"Interviews with Brad and Bridget Corrigan's high school peers, the class of eighty-five. Some of his other friends too. Remember his buddy David Ahern? He was a class ahead of us."

Bridget felt a little pang in her stomach to hear him say the name of her old crush. "Yes. You talked to him?"

Zach nodded. "He's a Realtor in Palm Springs. He's been living with the same guy for eleven years. They're very happy."

Bridget let out a sad little laugh. "I used to have a thing for him."

"Well, maybe you don't want to hear this," Zach said. "But David admitted to me that he had it bad for your brother. He said he even made a pass at Brad during a camping overnight. Brad wasn't having any, but apparently he was cool about it and they stayed friends. Pretty amazing for a guy in high school back in 1985. David said they kept in touch—until you guys moved away from McLaren."

Tilting his head to one side, Zach studied her. "You know,

it's funny, but that was the same story with the others I interviewed. They all lost touch with you guys once you started college or moved away."

"What's so unusual about that?" Bridget asked.

"Well, it's not like you moved to the other side of the world. Portland is only, what, an hour and fifteen minutes away from McLaren?"

Bridget squirmed a bit in her chair. "What are you getting at?"

He took off his glasses and wiped them with his napkin. "I don't know. It came up with Kim, and David, and several others. They said they tried to keep the lines of communication going, but you and Brad seemed, well, unresponsive or unavailable."

Bridget frowned at him. "I still don't know what you're getting at. And I must say, I don't exactly like the idea of someone calling up my brother's and my old friends and asking questions about us."

Zach put his glasses back on, then gave her a lopsided smile. "Well, doesn't that sort of thing come with the territory when you're in the spotlight?"

Bridget shrugged. "I guess I'm not used to *the spotlight*," she said, her frown fading. "That's my brother's specialty. It's his campaign. His public relations wiz, Jay Corby, is running it. I'm just doing what I can to help."

"Huh, I have news for you. Take it from one who works with a lot of Foley insiders. You have them scared. Your brother's numbers have gone way up since you came aboard. The voters feel a real connection to you, Bridget. You're the one in the spotlight now. Hell, why do you think Foley waited around here until you showed up yesterday? He wanted to be photographed consoling *you*, not your brother."

He sat back. "Anyway, about the feature story, you can relax. I dropped the idea. I kind of lost interest when a couple of my major potential interviewees died before I got to talk with them. Brad was pretty tight with Fuller Sterns and Olivia Rankin, wasn't he?"

"Brad had lots of friends in high school," she said guardedly.

"I still think the police should have looked deeper into Fuller's death," Zach remarked—almost to himself.

Bridget glanced at her wristwatch, then crumpled up her napkin and tossed it on her tray. "Well, Zach, it's been fun, but I should be going." She reached for her purse.

"I should get cracking myself. I need to be in McLaren by two o'clock."

Bridget started to stand, but sat back down. Her eyes narrowed at him. "McLaren? I thought you were dropping the story."

"Oh, I did. I'm working on another one. See, calling up some of those people in our old class, it got me thinking about Mallory Meehan."

Bridget stared at him. She hugged her purse against her chest. "Huh, really?"

Zach nodded. "I'm going to conduct my own investigation into her disappearance. I'm seeing Mallory's mother this afternoon. She still lives in McLaren. And they're giving me access to records at the sheriff's office. I don't know what I'll find, but it should be interesting."

Bridget felt sick to her stomach. A pale smile was frozen on her face. "Huh" was the only sound that came out of her.

"Revisiting a twenty-year-old mystery," Zach said. "It should make a fascinating feature story, don't you think?"

"But you have a fund-raiser, an autumn garden tea this afternoon," Shelley said on the other end of the line.

Leaning against the wall by the pay phone in the hospital corridor, Bridget sighed into the receiver. "Which one is this?"

"Pamela St. George, formerly the host of *Portland at Seven* magazine, and currently a bitch-on-wheels. She's been a royal pain in my ass ever since she started planning this wingding. She expects fifty of her dearest friends to attend.

There's a silent auction. The tea is at her place—in her back-yard. She hired a cellist for it."

"Well, I'm sorry, but you'll have to give her my regrets. Tell her I had a family emergency."

"She'll go ballistic," Shelley retorted. "You *so* owe me for this. Is it really a family emergency? I mean, your dad got out of the hospital today, didn't he?"

"Yes, he's all right. This is something else. I'll explain later."

"You're hosting that raffle for the Northwest Children's Center tonight at seven," Shelley reminded her. "Is that still on?"

"Yes," Bridget said. She figured she'd be back from McLaren long before seven. David and Eric had after-school activities until five. She was picking them up, then driving them to Gerry and Leslie's house.

"Um, listen, Shell," she said. "Could you do me another favor? You have Gerry's new home phone number on file. Could you call my, huh, my soon-to-be-ex-husband and his, um—"

"Whore?"

"Yes," she said, with a weak laugh. "Could you call and remind them that I'm dropping the boys off at their place around six-fifteen tonight?"

"Happy to," Shelley said. "Good luck with whatever you're doing this afternoon."

"Thanks, Shelley," she replied.

Bridget hung up the phone, then took a deep breath.

She'd convinced Zach to let her come to McLaren with him. She'd feigned curiosity about his story idea, and all the while, wondered how she could discourage him from pursuing it. He was waiting for her in front of the hospital. He'd said the trip would be "part investigation, part sentimental journey." Bridget needed to be there in case he discovered anything about Mallory's disappearance. She needed to distract him, put up a smoke screen, do whatever she could to steer him away from the truth.

And she felt absolutely horrible about it.

* * *

Mallory Meehan had grown up with her divorcée mother in a little gray ranch house in the "poor" area of McLaren, not far from the town center.

Zach pulled down the street in his VW Bug. It was still a slightly shoddy neighborhood, with unkempt lawns, a few garbage cans along the edges of parkways, and cars on blocks in a couple of the driveways.

Zach had made good time on the interstate. The conversation in the car had been surprisingly effortless. Bridget liked him. Some time after crossing the bridge between Oregon and Washington, she casually mentioned that reopening an unsolved missing person case from twenty years before might be a wild-goose chase.

Later, as they turned off the interstate around Longview, she made the point again: "You know, I wonder if readers of the *Portland Examiner* will be interested in a story about a girl who disappeared in another city twenty years ago. I mean, it's old news, and doesn't even have a local angle."

"Well, I thought I'd work *you* into the story too," Zach admitted, taking his eyes off the road to look at her for a moment. "The fact that you knew Mallory—and were her friend for a while—gives the story current, local interest. You'll let me interview you about Mallory, won't you?"

Bridget turned away to gaze out the car window. "Sure, I guess," she muttered. "If you find you still really want to do this thing."

In McLaren, they passed the water tower Brad and Fuller had defaced. Bridget noticed a couple of new minimalls. Franchises like Starbucks, Hollywood Video, Kinko's, and Quiznos had invaded her old hometown.

She wasn't very familiar with Mallory's old street. Bridget had never set foot inside the little gray ranch house, which Mallory claimed had been impeccably furnished by her interior decorator aunt.

Walking up to the front door with Zach, she noticed Mrs. Meehan's lawn was freshly cut, and the potted mum plant on the front stoop still had watering instructions and a price tag attached to one of the stems.

The door swung open before they even rang the bell. Mrs. Meehan must have been watching from the living window. "Are you the reporters?" she asked eagerly.

Zach smiled and shook her hand. "Well, I'm the reporter, Mrs. Meehan," he said. "Zach Matthias. As I mentioned on the phone this morning, I was also a classmate of Mallory's. This is Bridget Corrigan. She—"

"Oh my goodness, yes," Mrs. Meehan said, grabbing Bridget's hand and squeezing it. She was a slightly chubby woman with grayish blond hair that she wore swept up on her head. "I should have recognized you. You're on the news all the time. Please, please, do come in."

She stepped aside and showed them into the living room. Mallory's interior decorator aunt must have loved Mediterranean-style furniture. The old sofa, chairs, and tables were too dark and bulky for the modest, little living room. But there were fresh floral arrangements on both end tables—and the coffee table.

"Bridget, I have to tell you," Mrs. Meehan said, her eyes watering up. "I remember how excited Mallory was that you two were becoming such good friends her senior year. She—well, Mallory always had a hard time fitting in. Your companionship meant a lot to her."

Bridget managed to smile. "Well, thank you," she said. It was her first conversation with Mrs. Meehan—ever. And she felt horrible.

Mallory's mother remained by the open door. She glanced out at the street. "Where's the TV truck?" she asked. "Isn't there a camera crew?"

"Um, Mrs. Meehan, I thought you understood," Zach said. "I'm a reporter with the *Portland Examiner.* This story is for the newspaper."

"There won't be any cameras?" she asked, crestfallen. She looked out the front door again. "No one will be taking any pictures?"

Bridget realized why Mrs. Meehan had gotten the lawn mowed and put a new plant on the front stoop. Now Bridget saw the reason for the fresh flower arrangements in the living room. No wonder Mrs. Meehan was wearing a dressy black skirt set that looked more appropriate for a night out at the theater than an afternoon at home.

She seemed so sad as she closed the door. She nervously fingered the pearl necklace that went so well with her black outfit.

At that moment, Bridget had another realization.

Mallory Meehan was dead.

After Gorman's Creek, she hadn't taken her car and driven some place far away from McLaren. Bridget had often clung to that scenario. But no, Mallory had died that night in Gorman's Creek. If she'd run away, certainly Mallory would have come back for that pearl necklace Mrs. Meehan now wore.

It was the necklace Bridget had inherited from her mother.

Bridget endured another ninety minutes in Mrs. Meehan's house while Zach worked toward reaching the same conclusion she'd made two minutes after stepping through the front door.

Mrs. Meehan showed them Mallory's old bedroom, which she'd turned into a sewing room. Framed photos of Mallory were all over the place. She'd actually been a very cute little girl. Bridget just wanted to get out of there, but Zach kept asking questions: Was anything missing from Mallory's room—or from the house at the time of Mallory's disappearance?

No, not a thing, Mrs. Meehan told them.

Did she have a bank account? Was there money still in it?

Seven hundred and twenty-four dollars, and Mrs. Meehan didn't touch the money for almost three years after Mallory had disappeared. The day she finally transferred Mallory's savings to her own account, Mrs. Meehan cried and cried. "I had to acknowledge that my baby was never coming back."

Mrs. Meehan showed them Mallory's journals, which she'd dug out of the basement. She said there were over twenty of them. Bridget and Zach took a look at a couple of the bound notebooks—all filled with pages and pages of gibberish, Mallory's own secret code.

Mallory also had a collection of news clippings—most of them about the disappearance and murders of Andy Shields and the Gaines Twins. Bridget also recognized the old *Cowlitz County Register* article Mallory had shown her twenty years ago in the library, the one about Mrs. Fessler's suicide. The clipping was yellowed, and Bridget realized that Mallory must have gone back to the library and torn it out of the volume of bound *Registers*.

"She was going to write a book about McLaren," Bridget murmured.

When they left the Meehan house, Zach told Mallory's mother that he might be back—with a photographer. Mrs. Meehan shook Bridget's hand and told her again how much her friendship meant to Mallory. "I do hope you'll both be back," she said. "I know it sounds crazy to still hope—after all these years. But if people read Mallory's story, maybe somebody out there will remember something that could help us find her. God bless."

Zach opened the car door for Bridget. After climbing behind the wheel, he just sat and stared out the windshield for a moment. "I always thought Mallory might have run away," he said, finally. "But she wouldn't have left McLaren under her own steam, not without taking money out of her bank account or collecting those private journals of hers."

"She also would have taken the pearl necklace she stole from me," Bridget said. "That necklace Mrs. Meehan was wearing belonged to my mother. It was worth about five hundred dollars."

"Jesus, why didn't you say something to Mrs. Meehan? If that was your mother's necklace—"

Bridget sighed and shook her head. "She can have it. I owe her at least that much."

Zach stared at her. "What do you mean you *owe* her?"

Bridget cleared her throat and quickly shook her head again. "Um, nothing. I just mean, I feel bad for her, that's all. Do you still want to go to the sheriff's office?"

Zach squinted at her. "Are you okay?"

"Yes, I'm fine," she said. But she couldn't look at him.

Bridget felt him staring at her for another moment. Then he finally started up the car.

At the sheriff's office, Bridget and Zach studied Mallory's missing person report. The sheriff, Bill Miller, who had been a deputy back in 1985, explained that he'd gone the extra mile to determine what might have happened to Mallory. He'd heard that she used to go "meditate" by the ocean—in Seaview. So a week after her disappearance, he'd driven to the coastal city to talk to the locals. Some regulars and a couple of waitresses at the Tides Inn Restaurant had remembered her. Apparently, Mallory always ordered the same thing there: a bacon omelet, coffee, and milk. Then she would sit in a booth, writing in her journal for hours. They all remembered the strange girl who claimed she was penning a potential best seller. But no one had seen her that August weekend she'd disappeared.

The Volare was never found. The sheriff figured Mallory'd been the victim of a carjacking, or perhaps a drifter had abducted her at a truck stop somewhere outside McLaren, then later killed her and stolen the car.

Sheriff Miller pointed out that there were seventeen other still-unsolved missing persons cases in Cowlitz County from that same year. Considering how very private and eccentric Mallory Meehan had been—to the point of creating a secret code to write in her journal—it was understandable that her disappearance had remained a mystery all these years.

In Zach's car, on the way back to Portland, Bridget suggested—once again—that a newspaper feature story about Mallory Meehan's disappearance might not be a good idea. "It looks like kind of a dead end," she said. "You heard the sheriff. There are dozens of stories just like Mallory's. And I doubt people are going to be interested just because *I* tried to be her friend for a short while. Besides, I really can't tell you much about her, Zach. Maybe I can help you with another type of feature story. Maybe I can give you some kind of exclusive—that is, if you really think people want to read about me."

Zach was watching the road. "Thanks, Bridget, that's really nice," he said. "But you know, for now, I think I'll keep looking into this Mallory thing."

After that, Zach didn't say much. For Bridget, the drive back to Portland seemed to take forever.

"Gerry? Leslie? This is Bridget. I'm in the car with the boys. We're about five minutes away. Are you there? Can you pick up? Okay, here's hoping you're home. See you in a bit. Bye."

She clicked off her cell phone.

"They're not home?" David asked, incredulous. He was in the front passenger seat. Eric was behind him, lightly kicking the back of his seat. "He forgot?" David went on. "I can't believe this. He knew we were coming over tonight. How could he totally blow us off like that?"

"I'm sure one of them is on the phone, that's all." Eyes on the road, Bridget handed her cellular to him. "Here. Could you put this in my purse for me, please?"

David took her small beaded black purse, opened it, then crammed the phone inside.

It was 6:40, and Bridget was running late. If she didn't hit too many red lights on the way, she had an outside chance of making it to the Northwest Children's Center raffle on time.

She'd returned from McLaren with Zach in plenty of time. But David's intramural basketball game had run longer than expected, and they didn't get home until six. On the answering machine was a message from Zach, thanking her for accompanying him to McLaren. He also asked her out to dinner next week: "Maybe some place where the meals don't come on trays and the utensils aren't plastic. And we won't talk about the election, or the newspaper, or Mallory Meehan. It'll be something resembling a date. How about it?"

As she got dressed for the raffle, Bridget thought about Zach. Even if she wanted to avoid him, she couldn't. She had to stay close to him, and make sure he didn't discover what had really happened to Mallory Meehan. "Keep your friends close, and your enemies closer." But she was the bad guy here. She was the one working a cover-up angle. And she hated herself for it.

Bridget's outfit—a floor-length, black satin skirt with a rust-colored, sleeveless beaded top and black satin stole—wasn't very comfortable for driving, and in a minivan no less.

"I bet you anything he forgot," David said, sticking her purse in the cup caddie between them. "Either that or something *more important* came up. This really, really sucks." He swiveled around toward his little brother in back. "If you kick my seat one more time, I'm gonna rip your leg off and beat you with the bloody limb!"

"Okay, that's enough!" Bridget hissed, clutching the steering wheel. She turned the corner and headed down Gerry's block. "Cool it, the two of you. David, turn around. Eric, stop kicking."

With her eyes on the road, she sighed and muttered under her breath—only in Spanish: "The son of a bitch better be home, that's all I can say."

"*Te digo, el hijo de puta no está alli,*" David grumbled, which roughly translated to: "*And I'm telling you, the son of a bitch isn't there.*"

Bridget glanced at him and shook her head. "Why did I ever teach you Spanish?"

"You didn't teach me *'hijo de puta.'* I picked that up on my own."

"He's home," Bridget said, seeing the house in the distance. The outside lights were on. "See? Your father's car is in the driveway. I bet they were phoning us when I was calling them. We're late. They were probably wondering where we were."

As she pulled up behind Gerry's merlot Mercedes in the driveway, Bridget kept reassuring the boys—and herself—that their father hadn't forgotten about them.

She told them to behave themselves, and be nice to Leslie. Both Eric and David gave her cheek a kiss before they climbed out of the car. "By the way," David told her, "you look really pretty, Mom."

Before she could thank him, he closed the car door, then hurried to catch up with Eric. They both trotted up to the front gate.

Bridget checked her face in the rearview mirror. She looked at David and Eric, patiently standing at the atrium gate with their fall jackets on, and their backpacks full of schoolbooks. David jabbed at the bell again. After a few moments, he turned and glanced back at her.

Bridget put the car in park and shut off the engine. "The son of a bitch," she growled. "¡*Hijo de puta*! I can't believe he's doing this." She grabbed her beaded purse, climbed out of the minivan, and readjusted the satin stole around her shoulders.

Making her way to the gate, Bridget tried to think of a backup plan for tonight. She'd bring the boys with her to the event. Maybe the Hilton could provide a hospitality room—or she could leave them in a game room or minigym, some place with a TV so they wouldn't be bored to smithereens for three hours. *Damn Gerry for doing this to them.*

"What's wrong? No answer?" she called to the boys.

"I betcha they're in the backyard!" Eric exclaimed, running around the side of the house.

David frowned at her. Bridget glanced past the wrought-iron gate at the atrium. The lights were on in the garden, but the living room drapes were closed. Bridget glanced at the mailbox beside the gate. There was a Nordstrom catalogue sticking out of the box. She pushed the lid back and noticed some letters in there too. They hadn't picked up their mail yet.

"Unbelievable," David grumbled. "The asshole totally blew us off."

Bridget pulled out her cell phone. "That's enough, David," she said steadily. "Just do me a favor, please. Round up your brother and get back in the car."

She needed to leave another message on Gerry and Leslie's machine, and didn't want David overhearing it. She was almost tempted to let David leave the message—so Gerry could hear his disappointment. She switched on her cellular and watched David head toward the back of the house.

"Mom!" Eric called. *"Mom? You guys?"*

"What is it, honey?" Bridget called back. She clicked off the phone and scurried across the side lawn—a little wobbly in her high heels. David ran ahead of her, disappearing behind the house.

The lights weren't on in the back, and Bridget slowed down to navigate her way. The boys knew the setup better than she did. She turned the corner to the backyard and passed a hot tub with a cover on it. Ahead, David was running toward his little brother, who stood in front of a sliding glass door.

Eric knocked on the glass. "Hello?" he called. "Dad?" He peeked past the door, which was open a few inches.

David reached him first. As he stepped toward the door opening, he balked, then looked under his foot at something.

Even before Bridget reached them, she could see something was wrong. "Wait just a second, you guys," she said. "Wait . . ."

Eric stopped knocking and glanced over his shoulder at her.

The door handle was broken. David had stepped on a piece of what looked like the lock mechanism. Just past the door's narrow opening, the sheer organdy drape inside billowed slightly.

Bridget felt a chill race through her. "David, Eric, go back to the car."

"I hear something!" Eric declared. Before Bridget could stop him, her younger son pushed the sliding glass door farther open and slipped inside the house.

"No, wait, don't!" she whispered urgently. "Eric!" She hurried in after him.

The room was dark, but Bridget could make out a desk and sofa, and a shelf full of books against one wall. Eric stood in the study doorway. A light came from some other part of the house, and all Bridget could see was her son's four-foot silhouette. He hesitated before taking another step.

"Sounds like water," he whispered.

She could hear it too. Maybe it was a tub overflowing. "Come here," Bridget hissed. "This instant, Eric."

David was at her side. He might have run ahead of her, only Bridget had a tight grip on his arm. She pulled him behind her. "Just stay put," she murmured, leaving him by his father's desk.

Eric backed out of the doorway, and Bridget grabbed his shoulder and led him toward the desk. "Stay right there—both of you."

She crept to the doorway. Bridget still had her cell phone in her hand. She listened to the water running, and a strange mechanical hum. Glancing over her shoulder, she saw David stepping toward her. He clutched a letter opener from his father's desk. Bridget held up her hand, indicating he should stay where he was. Then she took a step into the family room and kitchen area.

The lights were on. She didn't see anything unusual—except a drink left on the kitchen counter bar. Then she noticed the floor was wet. The water seemed to be coming from the front hallway. Bridget hiked up her dress a bit, then carefully tiptoed toward the hallway. She stopped near the threshold, where the kitchen's black and white tile ended, and the hallway's stone tile began.

The water on the floor there was pink.

Bridget swallowed hard, then continued on. She realized the splashing sound and that strange humming noise came from the pond and the waterfall wall. She gazed up at the sweeping front stairway. No one.

But when Bridget looked down again, she noticed a couple of dead goldfish on the hallway floor. They were from the lighted pond under the steps, now overflowing with pink water. Something blocked the filter in the far corner, causing that mechanical drone.

Bridget didn't see it until she was halfway to the front door.

Her husband's corpse floated in the shallow water. His hands were taped behind his back, and all around his neck the water swirled red. Someone had cut his throat.

Bridget opened her mouth to scream, but no sound came out.

She swiveled around and saw Leslie's naked body, curled up in a ball on the living room floor.

"Mom?"

She turned again—to see David paused in the kitchen doorway.

"No!" she cried. Tears brimmed in her eyes. "Don't! Get out of here! Get out!"

She raced toward him, almost slipping in the blood-tinged water. David backed away. He bumped into Eric behind him. He was still holding the letter opener in his hand. "Mom? What's wrong?"

"Get out of here!" she repeated, quickly leading them back toward the study—and the open sliding glass door. She had no idea if the killer was still in the house. The only thing on her mind was getting her sons out of there. She didn't want them to see what had happened.

She didn't want them having to remember their father like that.

CHAPTER 17

"Wednesday night's brutal murders of Gerard Hilliard and his girlfriend, Leslie Ackerman, may have been drug related," said the handsome, gray-haired anchorman. Behind him, over his left shoulder, were photos of Gerry and Leslie. "KBCQ Channel Eight News' Vita Matthews has the story."

The picture switched to a pretty reporter with short-cropped hair and light-coffee-colored skin. She wore a gray suit and a somber expression as she stood in front of Gerry and Leslie's house with her handheld microphone. Yellow police tape blocked off the front of the house.

"Thank you, Don," she said. "Portland police are now telling us that drugs could be the reason behind the heinous murders of Bridget Corrigan's estranged husband, Gerard Hilliard, and his companion, Leslie Ackerman. Early reports indicate the couple had been dead approximately twenty-four hours before their bodies were discovered here in their Portland home by Bridget Corrigan on Thursday night. Corrigan, the twin sister of senatorial candidate Brad Corrigan, had come by the house to drop off her two young sons." The reporter took a dramatic pause. "The boys were supposed to spend the evening with their father."

There was a shot of the sliding glass doors—with fingerprint dust around the broken lock. "Police believe the killers entered through this door in the back of the house."

The picture switched to a close-up of a policeman, with a caption beneath him: SGT. STEVE MOWERY, PORTLAND POLICE. "Both victims had their hands tied behind their backs," the policeman said. "Hilliard had been beaten and his throat was cut. Ms. Ackerman had been strangled. This appears to have been the work of two men. The upstairs bedroom had been ransacked, and traces of cocaine were found in the bedroom closet. It's impossible to tell at this point just how much cocaine had been there."

"Do police believe any other drugs were taken from the scene?" the reporter asked, off camera. "Any traces of heroin?"

The policeman shook his head. "I'm not at liberty to say right now."

In the next shot, the reporter was sitting in a chair—across from another woman, seated on a sofa. The interviewee was in the shadows with her back to the camera. "I spoke with a friend of Leslie Ackerman's, who has asked to remain anonymous," the reporter explained in voice-over.

"Leslie liked to party, yeah," said the woman in the shadows. "And Leslie liked her coke. She and Gerry had a few private little parties at their place. They were good hosts."

"Was cocaine used at these gatherings?" the reporter asked.

"Oh yeah."

"And heroin?"

The woman nodded. "Sure, sometimes."

"Do you know if they actually kept drugs in the house?"

Again, the interviewee nodded. "Like I say, they were good hosts. Leslie and Gerry always kept a bottle of champagne in the refrigerator too. They were always prepared for unexpected guests."

The picture switched back to the pretty reporter, standing in front of Leslie and Gerry's house with her handheld mike. "But it appears Gerard Hilliard and Leslie Ackerman weren't prepared for two unexpected guests on Wednesday night.

Police believe they now have a motive for the double homicide. But they still have no suspects. This is Vita Matthews reporting. Back to you, Don."

The gray-haired anchorman returned to the TV screen. There was a photo of Bridget—not smiling—over his left shoulder. "Gerard Hilliard and Bridget Corrigan had been married for fifteen years before their separation in May," he announced. "Bridget Corrigan was not available for comment today."

"That's because the only thing Bridget Corrigan can say right now is, 'Oh, shit,' " Bridget muttered.

She sat in her den, numbly gazing at the TV. She wore a sweatshirt and jeans, and her hair was pulled back in a ponytail. She had a half-full glass of Chardonnay on the coffee table in front of her.

It was a little after eleven o'clock on Friday night, and the boys were upstairs in bed.

Brad paced around the den with his hands crammed into the pockets of his jeans. Both of them had canceled their scheduled appearances for the day. Brad had hired someone to go through Bridget's house this morning, inspecting the locks—and checking the place for any kind of surveillance devices as well. The house was well secured and bug-free.

Brad had used his influence with the police force to have a patrol car parked in front of Bridget's house all day—and night. They were working in shifts. It was actually a welcome distraction for David and Eric, who took turns bringing their police guard snacks, coffee, or soda.

"In other news," the TV anchorman announced, "a five-car pileup on 205 left rush-hour commuters stranded for over two hours—"

Bridget grabbed the remote and shut off the TV. Then she picked up the other remote and switched off the VCR.

"Why were you recording that?" Brad asked.

"I'm watching it again tomorrow—with the boys," she said, staring at the blank TV screen. "Some of their classmates will have seen the same newscast. I don't want them hearing about this at school. They should see it with me, and if they have any questions, they can ask." She shrugged. "I don't know any other way to handle it."

The boys had been fairly lucky up until now. Except for a few isolated incidents like the National Anthem episode at David's Little League game, they'd managed to maintain a low profile during the Corrigan-for-Oregon campaign. Their last name was Hilliard, and in some degree, that had protected them from the election craziness. Not anymore. Some of their classmates knew who their mother was. But by Monday, *all* of the kids would know who David and Eric's parents were. And they would be talking about them. Bridget had to prepare her sons for what might be said.

She had more or less lost Gerry months ago. While she mourned him for a second time, and tried to get over her shock, Bridget's biggest concern right now was her sons.

Every time she stopped to think that her boys were at Gerry's house an hour or so before those killers broke in, Bridget would start weeping. It scared the hell out of her, realizing how close she'd come to losing them.

The boys had had their share of crying jags too. She'd told David about a possible drug connection to the murders after the six o'clock news had carried the story. He seemed to accept his father's alleged cocaine use as a bitter fact, just one more thing his dad had done to screw up the works for everybody.

Bridget hadn't yet told Eric about the drug-robbery angle. He was already confused enough. She would try to explain it to him tomorrow.

Brad had his usual calming effect on both boys. Thank God. He'd spent most of his day driving back and forth from his house to Bridget's. Their father was still recuperating at Brad and Janice's place, and he took the news of Gerry's murder in his stride. He'd phoned Bridget twice today, and had talked to the boys as well.

This was Brad's third visit to Bridget's place—and the

timing was perfect. The boys could go to sleep, knowing that Uncle Brad was there.

Earlier, he'd dropped off a chicken casserole Janice had made for them. Apparently, he'd had a talk with her on Thursday night. According to Janice, she hadn't told anyone about switching doctors, because she thought Bridget's feelings would be hurt. "After all, you recommended Dr. Reece," Brad had explained. "She knows how much you liked him. She wanted to like Reece too, but it just wasn't working out. She's much happier with this holistic doctor she's seeing now. And the pills she took aren't really Valium. It's a calming herb—used in teas. It's perfectly natural."

Bridget wanted to say that hemlock was a perfectly natural herb too, but she wasn't about to ingest it. She also wondered about her sister-in-law's drinking. Brad probably hadn't broached the subject with her. Well, that was Brad's business now. She wasn't going to meddle anymore. She had her own problems with spouse substance abuse.

"Do you think Gerry's cocaine habit is the 'dirt' Foley had on us?" Bridget asked, watching her brother pace around the den.

He just shrugged, and kept pacing.

"You've been very—selfless not to mention it yet, but what kind of political damage do you—and Jay—expect from this?"

"I think people will be sympathetic toward you. After all, you were separated from him—and the lifestyle he had with Leslie."

"Yeah, but I look like an idiot, dropping off my sons to stay with a couple of cokeheads." At this point, she didn't much care what people thought, but Brad couldn't afford that luxury.

"For Christ's sake, how were you supposed to know? I don't think you should worry about how it looks to people, Brigg."

"You're right," she murmured, staring down at the floor. "Thanks."

He sighed. "By the way, I really don't believe there's a connection here."

She gazed up at him. "What are you talking about?"

"You know what I'm talking about," he said. "Gerry and Leslie weren't at Gorman's Creek. You just heard them on the news. This is a drug-related killing."

"I know that," she said, reaching for her wineglass.

"Still, it's on your mind," Brad replied. "These murders don't fit the pattern—if there even is one. And I don't think there is. You told me Cheryl's fine. She's not being threatened—or *stalked*. If someone is making us pay for what happened to Mallory, why would they kill Gerry and Leslie—and leave Cheryl alone? Doesn't make sense."

Bridget just nodded in agreement.

"Anyway, I don't think anyone's out to get us. Besides, you and the boys are under police protection. I'll get them to keep a patrolman here tomorrow too."

Bridget managed to smile. "Thanks."

"Are you going to be okay?" Brad asked, his brow wrinkled. "Maybe I should have brought along a couple of Janice's herbal pills for you."

"Oh, I'm all right. I was just thinking about the memorial service on Monday," she lied. "I—I'm wondering if the press will go crazy on us there."

Brad sighed. "I'm afraid you can count on it."

To Bridget's utter amazement, the reporters and cameramen were respectful. They gathered outside the Portland funeral parlor. Although they took pictures of her and the boys walking into the front entrance, no one shoved a microphone in their faces and asked for a statement. Brad had come earlier, made a statement of his own, asking them to use some restraint.

Brad had been right about the public's sympathy for her and the boys. The funeral parlor was so crowded with flower arrangements—dozens sent by total strangers—that a couple of vanfuls were taken to Portland General for the patients there. Many people sending flowers and condolences were from different parts of the country. The bizarre murder of a senatorial candidate's brother-in-law had made national news.

Not all of the reporters remained outside. One journalist who came into the funeral parlor was Zach Matthias. "Is it okay that I'm here?" he asked, shyly approaching her. He reached out to shake her hand.

"Yes." She took his hand and held on to it for a moment. "Still, you know, we've been seeing each other at too many funerals lately."

It was a strange crowd. Bridget stood a few feet away from Gerry's closed casket, shaking hands and receiving awkward hugs. She hadn't seen Gerry's parents or his two sisters since the breakup. They'd always liked her, and now they seemed embarrassed and apologetic—as well as devastated. They seemed more at ease making a fuss over David and Eric, who looked uncomfortable in their suit coats and ties.

Old friends—who had stayed close to Gerry and written her off—now seemed rather humiliated. Gerry's new friends with Leslie had shown up too, people Bridget didn't know at all. Like the others, they seemed to have difficulty facing her.

So she was relieved to see Zach, looking so handsome in his tie and dark blue blazer. She let down her guard a little. "I'm really glad you showed up, Zach," she admitted, squeezing his hand.

But he had that same slightly uncomfortable look so many others had tonight. "Thanks, Bridget," he muttered. "I'm sorry. I—don't know if I should tell you this now. But it's not good news."

"What are you talking about?" she asked.

"Foley's on the warpath," he whispered. "I just came back from this rally in Springfield an hour ago. He's on the attack. It'll be on the six o'clock news."

* * *

"Oh, he's such a horse's ass, it makes the bile rise in my stomach just to look at him," declared Shelley. Her eyes were glued to the little black-and-white TV on the table in the funeral parlor's employee break room.

Bridget chuckled. "That's no way to talk about a close, personal friend of Jesus Christ's."

Jim Foley was on the TV. The anchorman had just announced that Foley had spoken this afternoon to a crowd in Springfield, Oregon.

Brad and Zach sat with them in the tiny, one-window room. There was barely enough space for the table and chairs, a sink, a minirefrigerator, a coffee machine, and the TV. They were pushing the maximum occupancy at four. When Bridget had asked the funeral director if there was a television on the premises, he'd shown them to this room. She'd left David in charge of his younger brother. Shelley had rounded up Brad for her.

On TV, Foley smiled at his supporters. He wore a denim shirt with the collar open, very relaxed, very folksy. "I don't know about anyone else here," he announced to a cheering crowd outside some shopping mall. "But I think most of the people in Oregon are good people, family people, church-going people, God-fearing people, people with values."

" 'People who need people,' " Shelley chimed in. " 'No more hunger and thirst'—"

Brad shushed her, but he was grinning at the same time.

"I wonder if the good people of our state want Oregon's First Family to have ties with flagrant drug abusers and pushers. I heard on the news that Bridget Corrigan's husband and his live-in girlfriend might have actually known their killers. These killers may have been guests in their house at one time—at one of their cocaine parties. This is the same house, by the way, where Brad Corrigan's nephews play—while their mother is out making campaign speeches with their uncle Brad. This isn't my idea of a good family. And they're not who I want for the First Family of this state."

"Oh, crap," Bridget muttered, over the applause on the TV.

The anchorman came back on the screen. Brad reached over and switched off the television. "Son of a bitch," he grumbled, getting to his feet. "I must have been an idiot to think he wouldn't stoop this low. Their bodies aren't even in the ground, and he's already on the attack."

"So are you going to dignify this with a response?" Zach asked.

"I don't know yet, Zach." Brad put a hand on his shoulder. "I need some air. Want to step outside with me for a couple of minutes? I could really use your advice."

Zach threw a puzzled look back at Bridget; then he shrugged. "Sure."

Brad patted his shoulder and led him out of the little room. Bridget watched them head across the hall toward a side door. Brad seemed awfully friendly to Zach all of a sudden. She was glad to see her brother warming up to him. Then Bridget remembered something Brad had said a few nights ago: "Keep your friends close, and your enemies closer."

"That Jim Foley sure knows how to bust up a party," Shelley said. Then she gently nudged Bridget. "How are you coping, hon?"

"Oh, I'm just peachy," she muttered, pushing herself up from the chair. "We should get back to the wake." Bridget linked her arm in Shelley's; then they started down the hallway toward the viewing room.

They entered the funeral parlor's lobby, a stately-looking area with a big fireplace, framed by two potted palm trees, and a pair of sage-colored velvet sofas facing each other. Sitting on one of those sofas, his restless feet not quite reaching the oriental rug on the floor, was Eric.

Bridget stopped dead.

Someone was talking to her young son. He was patting Eric's shoulder and mussing his hair.

Bridget recognized him. He was the pale, lanky red-haired "waiter" from the Mexican restaurant last week. Only this time, he was dressed in a dark gray suit.

"Excuse me!" David emerged from the crowd of mourners, then hurried toward his brother and the red-haired man.

Bridget started toward them too.

The man looked up and saw them both zeroing in on him. He grinned at Bridget for a second. "Bye, Eric!" he said, then ran out the front door.

Eric seemed to shrink when he saw his mother and brother rushing at him. "Are you okay?" Bridget asked.

Visibly frightened, Eric gazed up at her and nodded.

Bridget hurried toward the door and opened it. A couple of photographers snapped her photo, and the flashbulbs blinded her. She quickly ducked back inside.

She couldn't see where the red-haired man had gone. She couldn't get a look at his car or license plate number. She couldn't see a damn thing past the spots in her eyes.

Zach stayed on at the wake. Bridget caught sight of him every once in a while, mingling in the crowd, sometimes talking with Brad. She thought back to when she'd been so unnerved by the sight of him. Now he was no longer a stranger to her. Or was he? How well did she really know him?

He and Brad had run out to the parking lot after she told them about Eric's brush with the red-haired "waiter." But they hadn't seen anyone—only a few reporters, who snapped Brad's picture again.

Eric was a bit confused about all the fuss. He hadn't recognized the friendly man as their waiter from the Mexican restaurant. "He axed if Dad and Leslie had any parties while I stayed there," Eric said. "I told him about the fountain and the goldfish. Oh, and he axed if I ever saw you put stuff up your nose, Mom. Ha!"

Bridget wondered if the "waiter" was a spy for Foley. Was

ιe the one watching her, skulking around her house, and hiding in the alley?

She didn't want to subject David and Eric to any more strangers at this wake. Still, Bridget felt compelled to stay on for her in-laws, who were picking up the funeral parlor bill.

Brad volunteered to take the boys to his and Janice's house. He needed to go home for an emergency conference call with Jay and his public relations team—so they could discuss possible responses to Foley's Springfield speech.

"I still don't trust our buddy Zach," Brad cautioned her. "He's up to something. Do me a favor and stick close to him. Find out what his deal is. I have a real bad feeling about that guy."

Before heading out with the boys, Brad stopped to shake Zach's hand. Brad gave him the double handshake to show extra warmth and sincerity. Frowning, Bridget watched them. She hated to see her brother act so phony. Was he that way with all his *enemies*? Or was he just becoming a full-time political phony?

Zach was among the dozen or so people still at the wake when Bridget said her good-byes to Gerry's family. He asked if he could walk her to her car. In the lobby, he helped her on with her coat. "Your sons are terrific," he said. "I chatted a bit with David. He wanted to know if I was the *dude* who asked his mom out for a date. He heard me babbling on your answering machine. And he said he saw my picture in the old high school yearbook. I looked like a geek, he said."

Bridget grimaced. "Oh, Zach, I'm so sorry—"

"We had a good laugh over it," he assured her. "He's a nice kid."

Zach opened the door for her, and they headed for her minivan. The reporters must have gotten tired and left, because no one was outside the funeral parlor.

Bridget reached into her purse and fished out her car keys. "So—are you going to keep working on that feature story about Mallory Meehan?" she asked—ever so casually.

He leaned against her minivan. "Yeah, I'm still hackin
away at it."

"Really? It seems like such a dead end, Zach. Aren't yo
afraid you're wasting your time?"

There was a wounded look on his handsome face. "No—

"I didn't mean to shoot you down, I—"

"Mallory's mother didn't seem to think we were wastin
our time the other day. And Sheriff Miller thought enoug
about it that he was recalling all those details from twent
years ago. Hell, I'm just getting started. And you know,
have a feeling Mallory might have been killed in McLaren.
mean, a lot of people in that town hated Mallory, three-quarte
of our class, for starters. She wasn't easy to like. I keep think
ing about Cheryl Blume, out for blood back when Mallor
ratted on her, your brother, and the rest of them for the wate
tower fiasco."

Bridget tried to laugh. "Yeah, but are you saying she mur
dered Mallory over *that?* C'mon now . . ."

"Well, she was one of many people Mallory had pisse
off. I think it's worth talking with her. Anyway, I'm drivin
to Eugene tomorrow to meet with her."

Bridget stared at him. *"You're meeting with Chery
Blume?"*

He nodded. "Only her last name's Lassiter now."

"But—but that's silly." She tried to laugh again. "Do yo
really think Cheryl had anything to do with Mallory's disap
pearance?"

"That's what I want to find out. She might know some
thing."

"But don't you think it's a waste of time—and gas?"

"No, not at all. But you certainly seem to think so."

"Well, what are you expecting? The police interviewe
all of us after Mallory's disappearance. If Cheryl had some
thing to tell them, we would have heard about it. Do you re
ally think she'll suddenly remember something after twent
years? I mean, c'mon. Do you think Cheryl is going to si
down with you tomorrow and give you a full confession?"

"Not exactly. I just want to talk with her about Mallory." He looked at Bridget dead-on. "See, I can usually tell when a person is lying to me—or covering something up."

All at once, Bridget felt as if he could see right through her. She stepped back from him. "Well, good luck with it, Zach," she managed to say. Fumbling with the keys, she tried to unlock the minivan's door.

"What's the matter?" he asked.

"Nothing," she said, finally getting the door unlocked. She turned toward him and shook her head again. "I just—I don't understand why you're all of a sudden so interested in finding out what happened to Mallory Meehan."

He frowned. "And I don't understand why you're so opposed to the idea."

"I'm not," she lied. "I . . ." Bridget hesitated.

He was staring at her as if he didn't know her at all. He looked so disillusioned.

Bridget took a deep breath. "I really hope you—*bust this case wide open*. I mean that. Good luck with it, Zach."

She ducked inside the van, switched on the ignition, and started to pull away. She glanced at him in the rearview mirror. Zach still had the same expression on his handsome face. He was staring at her—as if she were suddenly a stranger to him.

Bridget pulled out of the parking lot. She didn't look back at him again.

She didn't get very far. Only five blocks from the funeral home, Bridget pulled over to a parking space on the side of the street—across from a Denny's restaurant.

She couldn't stop shaking. Bridget was gripping the wheel so tightly, she thought she might break it. If she kept driving, she could have gotten into an accident. Turning off the engine, and switching off the lights, she sat back and told herself to calm down. *Deep breaths, deep breaths.*

How could she tell Zach the truth?

If you like me at all, you'll stop investigating this . . .

She hated lying to him. How could she make it right? *How could she ever make it right?* For twenty years, she had been asking herself that question. Now her past was catching up with her. She always knew it would eventually.

Brad said he didn't trust Zach. But she and Brad were the ones who couldn't be trusted. Zach was just trying to get to the truth.

Bridget didn't know how long she sat in the parked mini-van while other cars sailed by. She lowered the window a few inches for some air, and glanced over at the Denny's restaurant.

Zach was in the parking lot, climbing out of his car.

Bridget numbly stared at him. Here was her chance. She could go to him and tell him everything. A full confession. She couldn't keep on lying to him. He was going to find out soon enough. She would have to trust Zach and ask him to drop his investigation.

Her stomach was tied up in knots. *Go in there, have a cup of coffee with him, and tell him.*

He glanced toward her. Bridget raised her hand to wave. But he wasn't looking at her. He was watching a Subaru pull into the lot.

Bridget realized he was waiting for someone.

She watched a man get out of the Subaru. The car beeped and its headlights flashed as he locked it with the automatic device on his key chain. He strutted over to Zach, and they started toward the restaurant together.

Bridget recognized the man with Zach.

She'd seen him earlier tonight—talking to Eric. And the time before that, she'd seen the lanky, pale red-haired man at another restaurant, where he'd been posing as a waiter.

CHAPTER 18

Cheryl Blume was late.

Zach sat at a table in the bar at Johnny Ocean's Grill in Eugene's Oakway Center. Though it was warm in the bar, Zach had a blue-and-gray-striped scarf hanging around his neck. Cheryl had asked him to wear a scarf so she could recognize him. Meeting in the shopping mall restaurant had been her idea.

He hadn't been completely honest when he'd talked to Cheryl on the phone. Apparently, the previous week, she'd put an ad in the personals, *Attractive, Sexy, Divorced, 30-Something WF Seeking 30–50-Something SWM. U-B: Professional, Handsome, Honest . . .*

When he'd phoned and told her, "Hello, my name's Zach," Cheryl immediately thought he was someone who had answered her ad.

"I called back a bunch of guys," she'd explained. "So—I'm not sure which one you are, but it doesn't matter. I only called back the good ones. Why don't you tell me what you look like?"

Zach played along. He had a feeling that Cheryl would be more willing to meet if she didn't know he was Zachary Matthias from old McLaren High.

When phoning some of his former classmates about Brad and Bridget Corrigan a few weeks ago, he'd learned that Cheryl had severed ties with nearly everyone from her old hometown. It was similar to the way Bridget and Brad had fallen out of touch with their friends once they'd moved to Portland. Though Cheryl's parents had still been living in McLaren at the time, Cheryl rarely returned there after starting college. She spent most of her school vacations with an aunt in San Diego—or with college friends. It was as if she wanted nothing more to do with the town and the people in it.

According to Mary Drollinger, who had grown up with Cheryl and stayed close to her at McLaren High, Cheryl started to pull away about three weeks before going off to college. "She broke up with Brad over the phone," Mary had told Zach. "She didn't bother saying good-bye to me or any of her other friends. I left a ton of messages too. I even wrote and called her while she was away at school. On the phone, she never had time, and as for writing me back, forget about it."

When Zach had talked with Mary, he'd hoped to get in touch with Cheryl so he could interview her about Brad Corrigan. The notion of investigating Mallory Meehan's disappearance hadn't come to him yet. But it struck him as peculiar that Mallory had vanished at just about the same time Cheryl started pushing her friends away.

Zach asked Mary if she and her former friend had ever discussed Mallory Meehan's disappearance.

"I brought it up a few times," Mary told him. "For someone who hated Mallory's guts, Cheryl didn't seem at all interested. One of the last times I mentioned it, Cheryl got really ticked off and said she was sick of me talking about it. I mean, really, *everyone* was talking about it at the time. Anyway, I never saw Cheryl after that."

Mary's parents had kept in touch with Cheryl's widowed mother. Mary didn't have Cheryl's phone number or address,

ut she knew her former friend was now living in Eugene,
and her *most recent* married name was Lassiter.

Zach sipped his Amber Ale, then glanced at his wristwatch again: 4:10. She was ten minutes late. He drummed
his fingers on the varnished tabletop and gazed at the TV
above the bar—a football game on ESPN.

"Zach?"

He looked up at her, took off his scarf, then quickly got to
his feet. She was still a knockout—with a trim, sexy figure.
She wore a black lambskin blazer, a white blouse, and form-
fitting jeans. She had a few tiny lines around her eyes, and
the straight, shaggy hair was more ash-colored than honey
blond. Still, he recognized her right away.

But Cheryl obviously didn't recognize him. They shook
hands; then she sat down and ordered a wine spritzer. She
looked across the table at Zach and smiled coyly. "Well,
Zach, I must say, I'm not disappointed."

He couldn't believe stuck-up A-lister Cheryl Blume was
actually flirting with him. She started talking right away—
exclusively about herself, but he chalked that up to blind-
date-jitters. She worked part-time in a travel agency. She'd
been divorced for five months. She and a girlfriend—another
divorcee—placed personal ads in Eugene's weekly newspaper as an experiment. The ads were free that week. She got
more responses than her friend, nineteen. She hoped he liked
kids, because she had two—Amy, eleven, and Josh, nine. They
were with their father; but she had them every other weekend and holidays.

Ten minutes went by, and Cheryl still hadn't asked Zach
anything about himself. Her cell phone went off, and she
took the call. "Hello? Oh, hi . . . Yeah, I'm fine, really fine . . .
Can I call you back?"

Zach waited until she clicked off; then he asked, "So—
was that your friend, giving you the optional 'emergency
phone call' if this wasn't working out between you and me?"

Cheryl burst out laughing. She reached over and put her

hand on top of his. "God, you see right through me! I guess I can't put anything past you, Zach."

He smiled, and hoped she was right about that.

Cheryl didn't let go of his hand. She looked directly into his eyes for a moment. "I've gone on four of these ad dates so far," she admitted. "And this is the first time I haven't exercised my escape plan."

Zach raised his beer stein. "I'm flattered."

She nudged his leg with her foot. "You should be."

"So tell me, Cheryl," he said, "where are you from originally?"

She sat back. "Oh, this three-stoplight little town near Longview, Washington."

"McLaren?"

The smile vanished from her face. "Yeah. How do you know McLaren?"

"I thought you looked really familiar," Zach said, with an appropriately stunned, isn't-this-a-coincidence laugh. "Is your maiden name Blume?"

She nodded apprehensively.

"We went to McLaren High together. I'm Zach Matthias."

"You mean, the fat kid with the thick glasses?"

Zach figured he deserved that. He laughed a little, and nodded. "Yeah, that's me, the former fat kid."

She squinted at him. "Well, you—look good. Better."

"Thanks. You know, if someone back in high school had told me one day I'd be on a date with Cheryl Blume—one in which she didn't exercise an *escape plan*—I would have said they were crazy."

She gave him a faint smile, then sipped her drink.

"Small world, huh?" he said. "I mean, I answer some ad in the personals, and it turns out to be Cheryl Blume. What are the odds of that happening?"

"Pretty slim," she muttered.

"So—have you been back to McLaren at all—recently?"

She shook her head. "Not recently. Have you?"

"Yes, I went back there last week. I've been living in Europe the last four years, and just got back to the States a couple of months ago. I was feeling nostalgic, so I took a drive up to good old McLaren."

"Uh-huh," she said, squirming a bit in her chair. Unlike Bridget Corrigan, she didn't seem interested in what he'd been doing in Europe all that time. Cheryl nervously glanced around the bar, and her gaze seemed to stop for a moment on a short, muscular, balding man, seated alone on a bench in the mall—just outside Johnny Ocean's bar area. The man wore a tight short-sleeve shirt. He was so hairy, he looked a little like a chimpanzee. He was staring back at her.

Zach caught it. "Is he someone you know?"

"Never seen him before."

"He was staring at you a minute ago."

Cheryl gave a wistful shrug. "I'm used to it. Guys have been staring at me ever since I was twelve years old."

He smiled. "I know. I was one of them."

"So—what were you talking about?" she asked with thinly veiled indifference.

"McLaren," he said. "The town hasn't changed much. I didn't see many familiar faces. Oh, but you know who I ran into there?"

"I haven't a clue."

"Mallory Meehan's mother. Remember Mallory?"

"Vaguely," Cheryl allowed. She glanced at her wristwatch. "We didn't exactly travel in the same circles."

He laughed. "Oh, c'mon, you have to remember Mallory. You hated her guts! Remember how she ratted on you, Brad Fuller—"

Cheryl was shaking her head. "You know, I don't want to talk about this."

"You don't want to talk about Mallory—or McLaren—or what?"

"Any of it," she said.

"I'm sorry. I didn't mean to upset you."

Cheryl drank her wine spritzer, draining the glass.

"I suddenly feel like I'm in a conversational minefield," Zach said. "So *Mallory* is the taboo subject, huh?"

"I'm just not interested in discussing her," Cheryl said, "okay? I hardly knew the sorry bitch."

"So when Mallory disappeared, it wasn't any big deal to you?"

She glared at him. "What are you getting at? Why are you harping on this?"

He laughed. "Why are you so sensitive on the subject?"

"Who sent you?" she asked pointedly. "This was no accident—us getting together like this. Somebody used you to set me up. Who was it?"

Zach shook his head. "I don't know what you're talking about."

"Bullshit," she hissed. "I know when I'm being set up. I'm not stupid. This is some kind of trap. And you—" She stood up and grabbed her purse. "You know something, *Zach?* You're still a loser-geek."

She snatched her coat off the back of her chair, which tipped over and fell on the floor with a clatter. Then Cheryl stormed out of the bar.

Zach watched her flounce past the restaurant's window. She was throwing on her coat. The balding, ape-faced man was still sitting on the mall bench. He was watching her too.

Zach picked up Cheryl's chair. Then he glanced out the window again. The bench where the man had been sitting was now empty.

She knew something weird was going on. For starters, her mother had called last week to tell her that Fuller Sterns died in a car accident. Sad news. But the way that son of a bitch used to drive, small wonder it hadn't happened sooner.

Then a couple of days later, Bridget Corrigan phoned her, asking all sorts of strange questions. Cheryl wasn't sure if Bridget had been trying to scare her or intimidate her or what.

And now, this afternoon, Cheryl thought she'd finally hit gold with this great-looking ad date, and he turned out to be that fat geek from McLaren High, asking all these questions about Mallory Meehan.

Yes, something weird was going on.

When she returned home, Cheryl poured herself a glass of white wine. No spritzer this time. She needed the alcohol's full, undiluted punch. She couldn't stop shaking. She had to relax.

Cheryl took her wine upstairs. In the bathroom, she turned on the water and started filling the tub. She threw in some bubble bath salts for good measure—and even lit a candle on the edge of the bathtub. If this didn't relax her, nothing would.

As she undressed in the bedroom, Cheryl glanced at the clock on her nightstand. It was almost five. She'd become hooked on the local news lately. She was closely following every development in the senatorial race. It was silly, she knew, but she couldn't help herself. She still had a thing for Brad Corrigan, the bastard.

After that debacle with Mallory Meehan in Gorman's Creek, Brad had totally pulled away from her. Whenever she'd phoned him, he got paranoid: "You didn't go back to Gorman's Creek, did you? We shouldn't be talking to each other. You didn't move the Volare, did you? You haven't told anyone, have you?"

Before going away to college, he'd broken up with her over the phone. Over the goddamn phone, for Pete's sake. End of story. She never saw him again—except on TV.

Why she still cared about him was beyond her. One minute, she wanted Jim Foley to whip Brad's ass at the polls. The next, she hoped Brad would win. Maybe she just wanted to brag to people that she'd fucked a senator. And the way Brad's old man pushed and pushed him, maybe it would end up that she'd fucked a president of the United States.

Either way, he'd certainly screwed her.

Cheryl had a mini-TV on a little shelf above the sink and

vanity. The cord was long enough to reach across the bathroom. So she moved the chair from her vanity to the foot of the tub, then set the tiny television on top of it.

Placing her wineglass on the edge of the tub, Cheryl lowered herself into the warm water. With her toe, she absently poked at the faucet. The news came on TV.

"Tonight's top story," the dapper, gray-haired anchorman, Don Gannon, announced. "Controversy in the race for senator, and a startling new development!"

Cheryl sipped her wine.

The picture switched to Jim Foley, with his blue shirt open at the collar and the sleeves rolled up, addressing the crowd outside the Springfield Mall. Cheryl had seen this footage already—on yesterday's broadcast. It was the same speech:

"I wonder if the good people of our state want Oregon's First Family to have ties with flagrant drug abusers and pushers."

"Fighting words from Jim Foley yesterday," said the anchorman over footage of Foley still pontificating. "But his speech, so soon after the brutal, drug-related murders of Bridget Corrigan's estranged husband, Gerard Hilliard, and his companion, Leslie Ackerman, drew sharp criticism all around the state—even from some Foley supporters."

"I just think it's in bad taste," a heavyset woman with short blond hair told an interviewer on the street. "These people are in mourning. Foley crossed the line."

Focused on the little TV, Cheryl slid a bit deeper into the water—so the bubbles were around her chin. Obviously, Jim Foley's little speech yesterday had backfired. Once again, Brad and Bridget Corrigan came out smelling like a couple of roses.

The anchorman was talking about some informal viewer-call-in poll: "Sixty-eight percent of the callers felt Jim Foley's remarks were inappropriate.

"However," the anchorman said, with a dramatic pause, "startling new testimony from friends of Leslie Ackerman may have a devastating effect on the Corrigan camp. Here with the breaking news story is KBCQ Channel Eight News' Vita Matthews."

Cheryl sat up in the tub. She took another gulp of wine.

"Thank you, Don," said the pretty reporter. She wore a yellow suit, which stood out against the night-shot of her in front of the Burnside Bridge and downtown Portland. "Many people feel Jim Foley's attack yesterday on his political opponent, Brad Corrigan, was ill-timed and inappropriate," she said into her handheld microphone. "*Ill-timed*, because Foley's criticism came within days of Gerard Hilliard's and Leslie Ackerman's shocking murders. *Inappropriate*, because he seemed to imply there was a connection—possibly a *drug connection*—between Brad Corrigan and Gerard Hilliard, his twin sister's estranged husband. But according to friends of the late Leslie Ackerman, there was indeed a *drug connection*—and something more—between Brad Corrigan and Ms. Ackerman."

"Holy shit," Cheryl murmured, gaping at the TV.

"Leslie and I knew each other for five years," said a woman with her face in the shadows. Cheryl remembered her from a broadcast a few days ago. "I spoke with a longtime friend of Leslie Ackerman's, who asked to remain anonymous," the reporter chimed in, voice-over.

"I met Brad Corrigan about a year ago at one of Leslie's parties. They'd been seeing each other for a while."

"Are you saying Brad Corrigan and Leslie Ackerman were having a sexual relationship?" the reporter asked.

"Oh yeah."

"Oh my God!" Cheryl said, laughing.

"Do you know if he ever used cocaine with Leslie Ackerman?" the reporter pressed.

"Oh yeah." The woman in the shadows nodded. "The three of us did coke together in Leslie's apartment once. He was into it. Anyway, he later introduced her to his brother-in-law, Gerry. And Gerry got Leslie a job at his law firm."

"Ha!" Cheryl cried, reaching for her wineglass again. "Good luck worming your way out of this one, Brad."

Suddenly, she heard a strange, grinding noise from downstairs. She clung to the side of the tub and listened intently. Was it the furnace starting up? The noise died after a moment.

She glanced back at the TV. Apparently, the reporter had introduced another one of Leslie Ackerman's friends. This one was a slender, almost-pretty, bald man with a butterscotch complexion. A caption appeared on the screen: NICO SELLERS, FRIEND TO LESLIE ACKERMAN.

"I met Brad Corrigan at a small dinner party Leslie gave in her apartment, around Christmastime last year," he said. "I'm not into drugs. But Leslie and some of her other friends were. At this party, Leslie, Brad Corrigan, and another friend of theirs slipped into the bedroom after dinner, and I know they did some cocaine in there."

"How do you know?" the reporter asked.

"Because Leslie invited me to join them."

Cheryl was toasting the TV with her wineglass when she heard another noise. It sounded like floorboards creaking in the hallway. Water sluiced from the tub as she leaned over the edge and tried to peer down the hall. She'd left the bathroom door open. She didn't see anyone in the hall. She didn't hear anything either—just the TV, and a steady drip from the faucet into the tub.

Cheryl settled back and looked at the television again.

". . . how this will affect the voters is still up in the air," the reporter was saying. "Back to you, Don."

Then the anchorman returned to the screen. "Brad Corrigan was unavailable for comment. But a representative from the Corrigan-for-Oregon committee called the remarks by Ackerman's friends 'inaccurate and reckless.' " He paused. "In the Hawthorne District, a three-alarm fire . . ."

Cheryl saw a shadow sweep across the bathroom wall. She gasped, then realized it was from the candle flickering. Obviously, she was having a hard time relaxing. She blew out the candle on the edge of the tub.

The floorboards groaned again.

"Who's there?" Cheryl called nervously.

". . . flames swept through the warehouse . . ."

She wanted to turn off the TV, but didn't dare touch it while still in the tub. Cheryl leaned over the edge again and took another look down the hallway. A shadow raced across the ceiling. Was someone in her bedroom?

She started to stand up in the tub, but the bubble bath salts had made it slippery. She grabbed a hold of the towel rack to keep from falling. A little water splashed over the side of the tub as she regained her footing.

"Shit," she muttered, grabbing a towel with a shaky hand.

". . . causing a three-mile back up on Interstate Five . . ."

Over the announcer's voice, Cheryl heard the floorboards squeaking again. Panicked, she started to wrap the towel around her. She glimpsed something in the vanity mirror—a figure coming down the hall.

She swiveled around to see a short, muscular, balding man in her bathroom doorway.

Cheryl started to scream. But as she backed away, her feet slid out from under her. She slammed against the tiled wall, then toppled back in the tub. Water seemed to splash everywhere. She tried to catch her breath to scream.

"Shut up, bitch!" she heard the man growl. He stomped toward her.

Dazed, she tried to pull herself out of the tub. But her hand slipped against the slick, soapy edges.

He darted past her, and for a brief moment, she thought he might not hurt her.

Then Cheryl saw him pick up the little TV.

"No, no, wait!" she screamed. "God, no!"

". . . check in with our meteorologist, Jason Palmer. Jason, looks like you're bringing us some rain . . ."

There was a splash. Cheryl's screams abruptly stopped.

The bathroom lights blinked on and off. And the only sound was a low, sizzling hiss.

CHAPTER 19

"Brigg, we need to talk."

"Have you talked to your wife yet?" Bridget said into the phone.

"Janice knows the whole story," her brother replied.

"Janice knows you were screwing Leslie?"

"Brigg, it's a lie. I never had anything going on with Leslie. I didn't introduce her to Gerry. And outside of getting stoned every once in a while back in college, you know I'm not into drugs. What they said on TV is all bullshit."

Bridget heard him take a deep breath on the other end of the line. "But there's something I should have told you a while ago. We need to talk."

With the cordless phone to her ear, she moved toward the family room. Through the picture window, she watched David and Eric passing around a football amid all the fallen leaves on the back lawn. Except for David occasionally calling out instructions to his little brother ("Go long!"), there wasn't a lot of yelling or laughing. It was all very subdued. They'd just buried their father today.

They hadn't seen the five o'clock news. They didn't know what was being broadcast about their father—and their uncle.

"Well, after you talk to me and make me understand what

this is all about," Bridget said to her brother, "I hope you can talk to the boys. Explain it to them."

"Why don't you bring them over?" he asked.

"See you in a half hour," she said.

The notion of eating home-delivered pizza—for about the fifth time in two weeks—and watching *The Guns of Navarone* with their grandfather sat just fine with David and Eric.

After their morning in mourning—which included a mass, a ceremony at the cemetery, and a buffet lunch their grandparents had hosted in a banquet room at the Portland Red Lion, watching an old action movie with their other grandfather and gorging on pizza was a relief. For Bridget, the ceremonies and commitments had become formal obligations that took precedence over her grief. She had to make sure the boys were dressed appropriately, that she was dressed appropriately, that they arrived at each location on time, and all the while, she had to act appropriately. Everyone was looking and judging—including members of the press— as well as friends of the slain *couple*. Maybe that was what funerals and all the formalities were about. The survivors were so busy going through the *appropriate* motions, there was no time to really reflect on their loss.

If she had a minute to think about anything at all, Bridget thought about Zach Matthias, and how he'd duped her. She kept replaying last night. She'd questioned Brad's advice not to trust Zach. It had actually mattered to her that Zach got along well with her sons. And then, she'd spotted him with that skinny, red-haired weasel. She was such an idiot.

During the funeral mass, she had a couple of emotional moments. No one knew those were tears of anger and humiliation—and yes, grief. But she was thinking about Zach Matthias, not her estranged husband. Though considering how they both treated her, they were pretty much cut from the same cloth.

Zach was meeting with Cheryl Blume that afternoon. Bridget couldn't stop him from going. She could only hope he would get the same chilly reception she'd gotten from Cheryl after phoning her last week.

She'd told Brad about Zach and his plans to interview Cheryl. Brad had merely shaken his head and rolled his eyes—as if he didn't want to hear about it, and didn't want to say, *I told you so.* Brad already had enough on his mind with Foley attacking the Corrigan family and their "drug connection" yesterday.

Then came the bombshell on the Channel 8 five o'clock news tonight. Within hours, all the other stations would be picking up the story about Brad Corrigan snorting cocaine and having sex with the woman who would ultimately contribute to the breakup of, not his marriage, but his sister's.

Bridget was impatient to hear Brad's explanation. She sat down with him on the sofa in his study. With Brad's big, ornate, mahogany desk, fireplace, built-in bookshelves, and wooden blinds on the windows, the richly paneled office looked like it might have belonged to FDR. Their father had a hand in decorating it. The fax machine, computer, and printer almost seemed anachronistic amid all the thirties and forties art deco–style trimmings.

"I guess now we know what kind of 'dirt' Foley had on us," Bridget said. "I can't see it getting much *dirtier*—unless Stab-Me-in-the-Back Zach dug up something today."

"You haven't heard from him?" Brad asked. Crossing his legs, he propped one ankle on his other knee, then fluttered his foot nervously.

Bridget just sighed and shook her head.

"Well, the story on the news tonight was about ten percent true," Brad said, frowning.

"Go ahead, I'm listening."

"I met up with Leslie last Christmas, and she invited me to that dinner party they talked about," he admitted.

"The party with the nose-candy for dessert."

He nodded. "Only I didn't participate. Everyone else

did—including that guy they interviewed on TV, Mico or Nico or whatever his name was, Mr. I-Don't-Do-Drugs. Christ, he was the worst, like a vacuum cleaner, a total cokehead—and obnoxious as hell. Actually, they all were obnoxious, but he could have taken home the prize—"

"All right, enough about him," Bridget cut in. "What were you doing there?"

"That was the weekend after Christmas, when you, Gerry, and the boys went skiing at Timberline Lodge," he said. "And I thought it was a good time to approach Leslie. I mean, you must remember, Leslie was already working at the firm at that time. The woman they interviewed on TV, the anonymous one, who was at the party—I think her name was Desiree—well, she doesn't know what she's talking about. Leslie Ackerman was working at the firm in September. I didn't introduce her to Gerry. He already knew her. Gerry was already . . ." Brad hesitated.

"*Screwing her?*" Bridget finished for him. "And you knew?"

Brad nodded glumly. "I found out from someone at the firm. I asked Gerry if it was true, and he said no. But I knew he was lying. So that Friday when you guys took off on your ski trip, I went to Gerry's firm and introduced myself to Leslie Ackerman. I got her to admit that she was indeed *involved* with Gerry. I thought I could somehow intervene, maybe make her realize she was destroying a family. I thought I was getting through to her, because she invited me over to her apartment to talk some more that evening. I told Janice where I was going—and why. Anyway, when I got to Leslie's place, the party was going on. I tried to talk to her in private, but it just didn't happen."

"So last Christmas, *Janice* knew about Gerry and Leslie too," Bridget said, vacantly staring down at the oriental carpet in her brother's study.

"I asked for her advice."

"But you didn't tell me."

"Brigg, I didn't want to ruin your life," he whispered. "I

kept hoping Gerry would come to his senses and dump her. Then you wouldn't ever need to know. I tried to talk with Leslie two more times that weekend, and it didn't take. I tried talking to Gerry too, but he just kept denying it."

What stunned Bridget most of all, oddly enough, was that her brother and Janice had known about the affair and kept it a secret from her. She wasn't really angry. After all, Brad meant well. She was just thrown for a loop. Until now, she didn't think Brad had any secrets from her. Apparently, he was very adept at keeping them to himself.

"Um, you'll need proof," she heard herself say.

"What do you mean?" he asked.

She sighed. "We need to get the employment records at Gerry's firm to prove that this Desiree woman has her facts wrong about when Leslie started working there, and when she started . . ." Bridget paused and took a deep breath. "When she started sleeping with my husband. We have to discredit this woman. You should call your public relations team together, start on damage control immediately. You have to set the record straight here."

"But I don't want to embarrass you any further."

She gave a forlorn little shrug. "It doesn't matter anymore. We buried him today. I'd still like you to help me explain everything to David and Eric. They should hear it from us—and not on the school yard." She shook her head. "But not tonight. It's too soon. Let them watch their movie with Dad."

He got to his feet. "So—you want to come to campaign headquarters with me and start gathering the troops?"

Bridget hung up the phone and waved Shelley into her office.

"We're in luck," she said, standing up behind her old, beat-up metal desk. "I just got off the horn with Doug Stutesman over at Gerry's firm. He's there working late. He always liked me, and was all apologies for missing the funeral today. Long story short, he has access to the personnel files and can get us Leslie's employment record. He'll make us a copy. He said he thinks Leslie was working there since *August* of last year, which makes the anonymous woman on TV even more of a liar. Anyway, we need to get someone over there pronto to pick up those records by eight tonight."

Shelley nodded. "I'll send Jeff."

"Thanks, Shell." She sat back down at her desk. "Are they still having their powwow down the hall?"

"Brad, Jay, and the P.R. guys? Yeah. I can hear them talking over each other in there. Looks like a long night ahead for them."

"Well, I promise I won't keep you here past eight. In the meantime, tell Jeff to ask for Doug Stutesman at the law offices, and when he gets back here he can deliver the papers to Brad in the boardroom."

"Will do," Shelley said.

She ducked back out to the main office, where three other staff members and two volunteers had come to work the phones. They were conducting impromptu surveys to get voters' reactions to the new developments. Bridget was impressed at the way they'd answered the emergency call for help.

Wes Linderman, Foley's spy, had shown up as well. Someone—not Bridget or Shelley—had made the mistake of calling him. Bridget sent him to Kinko's to have a thousand more Corrigan-for-Oregon signs printed up. She'd figured that would keep him out of their hair most of the evening.

Bridget moved down the hall to the lunchroom, which tonight served as a conference room. She knocked on the door, then stuck her head in. "Brad? You got a minute?"

He stood up at one end of the lunch table, where Jay Corby, three other men, and one woman sat. All of them looked a little haggard, and dressed for a businessperson's come-as-you-are party—except for Jay. As usual, the stocky forty-year-old was impeccably groomed, every blond hair in place.

The table was littered with bottled water, a Big Gulp container, candy wrappers, memo pads, and one laptop computer—plugged in and running.

Brad stepped outside and shut the door behind him. "These people are driving me crazy," he whispered. "What's going on?"

"We're getting a copy of Leslie's employment record from the firm to show this Desiree woman doesn't know what she's talking about," Bridget told him. "Whoever clued you in about Gerry and Leslie in the first place, he might know Desiree—or other people at that party. You should get a hold of him. We'll need someone else from that party to say you didn't take any cocaine. We have to discredit this Nico—as well as Desiree."

He nodded. "Kenny Langford is the one who told me about Gerry and Leslie. I'll talk to him." He ran a hand through his hair. "Jay is all hot on getting Janice to do some appearances with me. He thinks it'll help. I don't want to put any strain on her right now. She's been through enough with Pop getting sick, Gerry's death—and now this."

Bridget shrugged. "Well, for once, I agree with Jay Corby. It's not a bad idea—if Janice is up to it. Having her at your side would show stability—the happy, lovely wife, and a baby on the way. I agree with them." She shrugged again. "I'd stand at your side, Brad, but I'm the idiot who didn't even know her husband was snorting coke and cheating on her. You're better off doing the rounds with Janice on this one."

He let out a sad laugh. "Listen, you've been through enough today. Why don't you go home?"

She glanced at her wristwatch. "The boys have about another hour and a half of *The Guns of Navarone*. I don't want to bust that up. I can make myself useful here a bit longer."

"Thanks, Brigg," he said. Then he ducked back into the lunchroom.

Bridget headed toward her office again, then stopped in her tracks.

"Hi," Zach said. He stood by Shelley's desk with his jacket thrown over his shoulder.

"What are you doing here?" she asked.

"I heard something on the radio on my way back from Eugene," he said. "Something about a cocaine Christmas party. I swung by your place, and you weren't home. So I figured you were here."

"Well, you figured right. And we're kind of busy."

"Can I do anything to help?"

"Exactly who are you trying to help?" she asked.

He looked back at her as if she were crazy. "What do you mean?"

Bridget turned and walked into her office. Zach followed her, then stopped in her doorway. "What's going on?" he whispered. "I mean, I know you're upset about what's on the news, but why take it out on me?"

She sat down at her desk and shuffled through some papers. "I'm busy, Zach."

"You know, you started acting strange last night, when I told you I was going to talk with Cheryl. Is there something you're not telling me? Some secret between you and Cheryl?"

Bridget glanced up for a second and shook her head at him.

He stepped into the office and closed the door behind him. "I didn't get very far with Cheryl today. When I started asking her about Mallory Meehan, she became hostile. Do you know what that's about?"

"I haven't a clue," she said, focusing again on her paperwork.

"On the drive back here, I started thinking about seeing you in Salem. You called Cheryl from a pay phone there. Why?"

"Not that it's any of your goddamn business," Bridget growled, looking up at him again, "but I wanted to tell Cheryl about Fuller's death. They were close in high school. I thought she should know he'd died. Does that answer your question? Now would you leave me alone?"

"God, talk about hostile. You're almost as bad as Cheryl."

"Did you do anything last night—after I left the funeral home?" Bridget asked. She tapped a pencil eraser against her desktop and waited for him to start spinning some lie.

"Yeah. I ran into another guy from the *Examiner*. He was covering the funeral—though I didn't see him there earlier. Just as well, he's kind of a creep. Anyway, he talked me into having dinner with him—at a Denny's."

Bridget stopped tapping her pencil. She just stared up at him.

Zach sighed. "I had a Coke and a taco salad, ninety minutes of dull conversation with this jerk, and after that, I went home with a case of indigestion. That's it, that was my night. Why do you ask?"

Bridget sat back in her chair. "Can you give me a physical description of this *associate* you had dinner with?"

"A physical description of Sid the Slime? Well, um, he's about thirty years old, skinny, pale complexion, reddish hair. Not the best-looking guy in the world—"

"How did I describe the man who was bothering Eric last night?"

"Red hair, pale . . ." Zach trailed off. "Oh, Jesus, was it Sid? You were talking about Sid? My God, when I ran out to the parking lot with your brother, I was looking for some red-haired *stranger*, not someone I *knew*. And I didn't even see Sid until later—after you drove away."

"I spotted you two in the parking lot at Denny's," she said, still a bit uncertain she could trust him.

"Well, no wonder you've been acting so weird toward me tonight." He let out a stunned little laugh. "Oh, Bridget, I'm sorry. I didn't make the connection at all. And Sid Mendel fits your description to a tee—right down to interviewing unsuspecting kids to get a scoop. Sounds just like him. I thought we were looking for some anonymous *stalker*, not this slimeball I work with."

"Sid Mendel's his name?" Bridget asked.

Zach nodded. "Yeah, he's a jerk. But he has seniority over me at the newspaper. He—"

"Do you know where he lives?" she interrupted.

"No, but I could get the address from work. I can call now. I'm sure someone's there."

Five minutes later, Bridget headed out of the office with Zach. She stopped by Shelley's desk and asked her to tell Brad that she would be picking up her sons at his house in an hour or so. "After you do that, go home, Shell," she said. "If you need me, call me on my cell. I'm on my way to hunt down a certain waiter. I owe him a gratuity."

"Hey, Sid, it's me, Zach Matthias," he called into the intercom. Sid lived in a new semiswanky apartment complex in the old Waterfront District.

Zach had gotten Sid's home phone number and address from another reporter, who was working late at the newspaper. Then he'd phoned Sid from Bridget's office. Sid was entertaining some friends, but he'd told him to come on over.

"I brought a friend," Zach said into the intercom. "Can you buzz us up?"

"Yeah, man, cool. Room for one more."

The front door buzzed, and Zach held it open for Bridget. They rode the elevator to the eighth floor, then headed down the gray-and-burgundy-carpeted hallway to Sid's unit, 813. Bridget could hear rap music playing and people laughing on the other side of the doorway. She didn't care that the son of a bitch had company. If he could crash her husband's wake yesterday, she could crash his stupid little soiree tonight.

Brad rang the bell, and a moment later, the pale, thin man with red hair swung open the door. He wore jeans, a suit coat over a black T-shirt, and brandished an old-fashioned glass with some blue-colored cocktail in it. He grinned at Zach. "Hey . . ."

But then he saw Bridget and the smile seemed to freeze. Sid took a step back from the door. "What the fuck—"

"Sid Mendel," Zach said, with a hint of mock formality. "I'd like you to meet Bridget Corrigan. I believe you already know her sons."

Bridget took a step into the airy foyer that led to a living room on one side and a continental kitchen on the other. The six party guests stopped talking to stare at them. The group ranged from a pretentious-looking, longhaired young man with a scarf swept over his shoulders to a starved-thin woman with a crew cut, T-shirt, jeans, and gothic eye makeup.

Sid's place was decorated in black and gray with all sorts of techno-trash accents—including some tube lights and a couple of neon creations.

Sid backed up to the little minibar by the door. He let out an impish laugh. "So—Bridget, can I fix you a drink? Or would you rather give your nose a treat? Isn't that your brother's preference? Does it run in the family?"

Bridget heard a couple of guests laugh. She didn't see who they were. She was glaring at Sid Mendel—and his smug grin. All at once, she had to wipe it off. All at once, she slapped him across the face.

She connected with such force that Sid reeled back into his makeshift bar. One of the guests screamed. A couple of bottles and several glasses flew off the table. They smashed on the floor.

"You stay away from my sons," Bridget said steadily. "If you ever get near one of my children again, I'll kill you."

"Jesus Christ!" a guest whispered. Someone else let out a fractured laugh.

Sid Mendel straightened himself up. Bridget saw the blood trickling from the corner of his mouth, and she realized she'd caused that.

Wiping his mouth, Sid took a step toward Bridget. "You fucking bitch," he growled. He looked as if he might lunge at her.

"Hey, back off," Zach said, suddenly stepping in front of

him. He put his hand on Sid's chest. But Sid tried to get past him.

"I mean it," Zach warned, pushing him back into the minibar. Another couple of glasses sailed off the table. They hit the floor and shattered.

"You're through, man!" Sid barked at him. "I'll see they fire your ass, and I can do it! Don't even bother coming in tomorrow. You're toast, Matthias!"

"Good!" Zach shot back. "I can't stand working for that rag—any more than I can stomach being in the same office with a slime-bucket like you, Sid."

One of the party guests giggled.

Zach led Bridget out the door. He put his arm around her in the elevator. She was trembling. "I can't believe we just did that," she muttered.

"You were wonderful," he whispered, giving her shoulder a squeeze.

Outside, on the brick-paved street by the apartment building, she broke away from him. Bridget started shaking her head. "I don't think that was very smart of me," she said. "Now I've made him really angry. He'll be out for blood. He might not get near the kids, but he'll do something to smear Brad. I don't know what, but this is going to hurt Brad in the long run, I know it. I—"

"Incredible," Zach said, stepping back from her. "I give up."

She stared at him and blinked. "What?"

"Listen to yourself, worrying about your brother. You were protecting your kids. Sid had it coming. The son of a bitch deserved to get slapped—"

"You don't understand the possible backlash—"

"How it'll affect Brad? And the election?" Zach cut in, raising his voice. "Jesus, Bridget, listen to yourself! I'm not going to have a job tomorrow because of what just happened. And the only thing you give a damn about is Brad and this stupid election! You don't care about me at all, do you?"

"Zach, no, I—"

"Where are your kids?" he asked.

"What?"

"Their father was buried this morning. But instead of being at home with them tonight, you're at Corrigan-for-Oregon headquarters, working on your brother's campaign."

She gaped at him. "What makes you think you have the right to say something like that to me? You don't know—"

"I've been in love with you for twenty-two years," he replied. "That gives me some right. I might not have seen you for nineteen of those years, but I still thought about you, worried about you, and wondered what you were doing. I still replayed in my mind all the different times you talked to me in high school, and thought about what I could have said or done to make you care about me more. Now I realize there's nothing I could have done, because I'm not your brother."

Dumbstruck, Bridget stared at him.

Zach let out a sigh. "I used to watch you at Brad's basketball and football games. And afterward, he'd go off with his friends, and you'd walk back to your car alone. There were a few times I came up and talked to you. But mostly I'd just watch and wonder how you could be going home alone. I'd think, *How could this happen? She's the most remarkable person in this whole school.*"

Bridget started to reach out to him.

Frowning, Zach stepped back. "You know, tonight I felt great slamming it to that slimeball Sid. I didn't give a damn that it cost me my job, because I got to do something with you, Bridget—make a difference with you. And God, you even let me put my arm around you in the elevator. I've waited for that for twenty-two years."

She reached out to him. "Zach, I—"

He shook his head. "And when we got out here, you started talking about how this might hurt *Brad*, and how it was a mistake. You ruined it. And it was a great moment, Bridget. Why can't you see that?"

Bridget glanced down at the brick pavement. She couldn't

answer him, because everything he said was so on target. She'd always put Brad before everyone else. Gerry—and God help her, sometimes even her sons—had to take a backseat to her twin brother. It had been drummed into her since childhood that her mission in life was helping Brad achieve greatness. She remembered her father in that hospital bed last week, urging her to make sure Brad won the election.

She felt tears welling in her eyes. "I'm sorry, Zach," she whispered. "Everything you've just said is true—huh, except maybe the part about me being remarkable."

"You are," he said, gently taking hold of her arm. "It frustrates me you don't realize that." Bridget looked up at him, and he wiped her tears away. Then Zach kissed her on the cheek. He kissed her again, brushing his soft lips against hers.

Bridget kissed him back, and sank into his arms. She'd forgotten what it was like.

Zach parted his lips against her mouth. He held her tightly for a moment, then pulled back to look at her. The way he studied her face made her feel as if she were the most beautiful, desirable woman in the world.

"Twenty-two years, Bridget," he whispered. Then he kissed her again, deeply, urgently. He pressed his body against hers, and she clung to him.

There was a loud scream, and they broke apart. The scream turned into high-pitched laughter as a young woman staggered down the sidewalk, hanging on to her boyfriend.

Still holding on to each other, Bridget and Zach watched the drunken couple disappear around the corner. The woman's laughter began to fade.

Bridget rested her head on his shoulder. "You were right earlier," she said with regret. "I buried a husband today. I really should be at home with my sons." She gazed up at him. "Could you give me a lift to Brad's house?"

Zach nodded. "Sure," he whispered.

They started down the street together. Bridget didn't want to let go of him.

On their way to Zach's car, they passed an old Volkswagen minibus. There was a strange, reflecting snake cartoon on the air-freshener that dangled from the rearview mirror.

And there was someone sitting in the front seat.

But Bridget and Zach took no notice.

CHAPTER 20

He was sketching how her hands would look tied to the headboard.

This painting would be from God's point of view—looking down from the ceiling of her bedroom. He'd used this viewpoint once before—in his vertigo-inducing portrait of a man falling to his death from a Portland apartment building, a favorite piece he called *Last Leap*.

He wasn't sure what he would call this painting, but he'd started outlining Bridget Corrigan's bedroom on his canvas. The overhead perspective was a challenge. All the photos he'd taken in her bedroom had to be rendered with a vertical viewpoint.

Still, the payoff would be worth it—a full, overhead image of Bridget lying on the bed. He would position her sons on the floor—one on each side of the bed, looking like sleeping cupids.

The piece would look like a stained glass window in a cathedral. He would paint her as part Madonna, part martyr: *St. Bridget and the Children*.

As he worked on the sketches of her wrists tied to the headboard, he stopped to scribble a note to himself: *Make flesh tones extra pale, almost translucent—like sunlight is coming through them.*

The telephone rang. He sighed, put down his pencil, grabbed the cordless, and clicked it on. "Yes?"

"Do you want to be in on a job?"

He hesitated.

"It's a disappearing act," his cohort explained. "The subject is supposed to vanish. It means sticking a shovel and a bag of lime in the back of my minibus, then driving up to the mountains with somebody. Nothing fancy. No time for all your sketching, photographing, following them around, and preplanning bullshit. Still, there's a few grand in it, and all you have to do is help me dig a hole for this guy. My shoulder's been bugging me lately. I could use a helping hand."

"Take a painkiller. I'm busy."

"Are you sketching her again?"

He didn't reply. He wandered over to the bulletin board full of photos of Bridget Corrigan—along with some he'd taken on the sly of her sons.

"Never mind," his colleague said. "Forget I asked. You're going off course again. I hate it when you get like this. It's going to get you into trouble. The client had specific instructions about her. But you don't care, do you? Sick fuck."

In response, he merely chuckled. He was staring at Bridget's face in one of the photos.

"You know," his cohort continued, "I watched her last night—making out with this guy. He practically had his tongue down her throat. She's tainted goods. She isn't exactly saving herself for you, pal. You still interested?"

"Doesn't change my mind at all," he replied, settling down at his draft table. "She's still the perfect subject."

He studied his sketches of her wrists tied to the headboard. Instead of tying her up with a rope, he decided to use the same type of cord with which he'd strangled his *Girl by the Red Sofa.*

"I give up," his friend was saying. "You're on your own, pal. When you get like this, it's best just to stay the hell out of your way. I don't want to know what you're planning for her. When you're through with her, I'm sure I'll read about it in the newspapers."

"Maybe I'll let you see the painting," the artist replied. He shaded in his sketch of her arms and hands. "Have a nice drive up to the mountains. Take care of that shoulder."

The theme to *Rocky* blared over the speakers at the ice skating rink in Lloyds Center Shopping Mall. Bridget sat on a bench with Gerry's parents, watching David and Eric skate. Mr. and Mrs. Hilliard, a sturdy, sporty-looking couple in their midsixties, had wanted to spend the day with their grandsons. They lived in Minneapolis, and there weren't many other reasons to visit Portland in the future. The day's itinerary included some skating, shopping, then dinner.

Gerry's parents kept assuring Bridget that she didn't have to come along—to the point at which she almost felt unwelcome. They still seemed a bit uncomfortable around her. Understandable, since their dead son had thrown her over for a blond, twenty-something cokehead. Moreover, the local papers and news stations weren't exactly making it easy for them to ignore that fact.

Despite her in-laws insisting that she "just take the day off and relax," Bridget came along. Zach's remarks last night about abandoning her children to go work for her brother still gnawed away at her. But he was right. She didn't want to go to campaign headquarters today. All her public appearances this week had been canceled. Her place was with her kids. Still, she really was a fifth wheel.

And after watching the boys teeter on the ice for twenty minutes, her mind started to wander somewhere else—to last night with Zach.

They'd kissed in his car—in front of Brad's house.

"My dad's staying with Brad and Janice," Bridget had pointed out. "He's probably watching us." She'd felt as if she were in high school again; though she hadn't done much making out in cars back then. Neither had Zach for that matter.

Between kisses, Zach had offered to follow her home, maybe even spend the night on her sofa downstairs. He didn't like the idea of her and the boys being alone.

Bridget had assured him that they were fine. Brad had hired a pair of private detectives, who took turns parked outside the house from seven PM to seven AM. After three nights on the job, they hadn't encountered any suspicious characters—just the occasional curiosity-seeker they'd chased away. So—she and the boys were perfectly safe.

Besides the timing wasn't right for David and Eric to accept this man who clearly liked their mother as an overnight guest in their house.

But she liked that Zach was so concerned about her. Driving home from Brad's with David and Eric, she almost felt giddy. She had to contain her elation around them.

As they pulled into the driveway, the detective on duty waved at them from inside his company car, a white Taurus. It looked like Phil instead of Scott; he was the taller and friendlier one of the two. Bridget felt safe.

Once they got inside the house, David stopped to give her a long hug, then played some games on the computer. Eric brought a Coke and a bag of Fritos out to Phil, then talked his ear off about *The Guns of Navarone* for ten minutes.

She told herself that they would get through this. It no longer mattered what Gerry had done to her. She could forgive him. Gerry and his girlfriend were dead and buried.

It was easy for Bridget to move on from all the heartache, because Zach Matthias loved her. It felt right. But this man who loved her was investigating the disappearance of Mallory Meehan. She couldn't keep lying to him.

Bridget's thoughts were interrupted by Eric's cry.

"Hey, Mom! Look at me!" Eric cried, skating backward. He had his arms spread out to keep balanced on the ice.

Bridget waved at him. "That's terrific, honey!"

Her cell phone rang. Bridget dug it out of her coat pocket and switched it on. "Hello?"

"Bridget, it's me, Zach."

She smiled and mouthed the word *sorry* to Gerry's mother. "Oh, hi," she said, getting to her feet. She stepped away from the bench.

"Are you busy right now?" he asked.

"No, it's okay. I can talk." Actually, she had some noise competing with him. Gerry's mother was shouting encouragement to the boys. And the music had switched from "Rocky's Theme" to "Funkytown," and the decibel level had gone up.

"I need to see you," Zach said. "It's important. Are you free right now?"

Bridget glanced over at Gerry's parents. "Well, I'm pretty sure my in-laws wouldn't mind if I took off for a couple of hours. What's going on? You sound serious."

"Yeah, something's come up. Where are you? I'll come meet you."

"I was on the phone with the police in Eugene about an hour ago," Zach whispered.

Bridget sat with him at a table in the Barnes & Noble café. The bookstore was just upstairs from the ice skating rink in the shopping center.

Hearing him mention in the same sentence *Eugene*, where Cheryl lived, and the *police* made something sink in the pit of Bridget's stomach.

"What did the Eugene police want with you?" she asked timidly.

"I called Cheryl Blume's house and started to leave her a message, when a cop picked up. He wanted to know when I last spoke to Cheryl. They were still trying to determine a— a time of death for her."

Bridget couldn't say anything. She numbly gazed at him and shook her head.

"They found her this morning," Zach explained. "Or rather, her ex-husband did. Cheryl was supposed to pick up her kids yesterday, but she never showed. So the ex-husband went over to her house and found her in the bathtub. I guess she was watching one of those little portable TVs while taking a bath, and it fell into the tub."

Bridget put a shaky hand over her mouth. She felt sick.

"Looks like she might have slipped stepping out of the tub, then knocked it in the water." Zach shrugged. "At least, that's what the cop said. But I don't believe it. Do you?"

"No," she admitted. "So—what did you say to the police?"

Zach sipped his latte. "I told them I met with Cheryl yesterday afternoon. According to this cop, I might have been the last person to see her alive."

Bridget rubbed her forehead. She couldn't pretend that Olivia's and Fuller's deaths were a coincidence. Someone had killed them. They'd killed Cheryl too. They were killing everyone who was at Gorman's Creek that August afternoon twenty years ago.

She glanced down at the tabletop. She couldn't look Zach in the eye. "Did they—ask why you wanted to talk to Cheryl?"

He leaned forward. "You mean, did I tell them anything about Mallory Meehan?" He slowly shook his head. "No, Bridget, I didn't tell them anything."

She kept looking down at the table. His hands, in fists, rested on the edge.

"Can *you* tell me anything about Mallory?" she heard him ask.

"I don't know what you mean," she muttered.

"Yes, you do," he replied quietly. "Driving over here, I kept thinking about *Bobcats class of eighty-five forever* on the McLaren water tower. Mallory got four people in trouble for that. Then she disappeared at the end of the summer. Now three of those four people have died—all within a month of each other, two very convenient accidents and a suicide."

He reached across the table and took hold of her hand. "Bridget, why did you call Cheryl the other day?"

She glanced around self-consciously. A couple of people were staring at them. "Please," she whispered to Zach. "I—I already told you why I called her—"

"Yeah, to tell her about Fuller's death. Why didn't *Brad* call her? Cheryl and Fuller were more *his* friends than yours. You're the one who went home alone from the school games, remember? Why didn't your brother call her?"

"Brad's extremely busy—"

"Bullshit," Zach growled. "Don't answer me like I still work for the *Examiner*. I got the ax, remember? I'm asking these questions because I care about you, Bridget."

"If you really cared, you wouldn't—"

"Why did you call Cheryl from a *pay phone*?" he pressed. "Why not call on your cell—or from your house? Was it because you didn't want any record that you'd called her? Did you have a feeling Cheryl was going to die?"

"No!" Bridget yanked her hand away from his. She had tears in her eyes. "That's crazy. Please, Zach, don't ask—"

"Are you protecting your brother? Is that it? Did Brad and those three friends of his—who are *now dead*—have anything to do with Mallory's disappearance?"

"*It wasn't just them,*" she heard herself say. "*I was in on it too.*"

Zach numbly gazed at her. "What?"

"There were five of us," Bridget said under her breath. "We killed her. At least, I'm—almost certain we did."

He slowly sat back. He seemed to shrink a little in the chair. He looked at her as if he didn't know her at all.

Bridget leaned toward him. She started to reach for his hand, but stopped herself. She didn't want him to pull away. That would have killed her.

"Zach, please," she whispered. "Can we get out of here?"

* * *

They found a fairly secluded spot in the parking garage—in front of a TV-audio-video store. Bridget could talk to him there, but it was hard not to cry. As she told him about Mallory and Gorman's Creek, she'd catch Zach wincing every once in a while—or giving her that look again, as if she were a total stranger. She wondered if his twenty-two years of loving her could be destroyed in a matter of minutes.

Whenever anyone passed, Bridget would pretend to be interested in the television sets displayed in the store window. The last person to walk by recognized her. Bridget even heard the woman say to her friend, "That was Bridget Corrigan . . . the one crying . . ."

Bridget wiped her eyes and leaned in close to Zach. "I'm sorry—I can't stop blubbering," she whispered. "It's just—this has been bottled up inside me for so long. I couldn't tell anybody. Brad—he won't discuss it. I've felt all alone with this awful secret. It's why I pulled away from Kim after high school. I hated to. I miss her. But if I'd stayed friends with her, I'd have told her. I couldn't afford to be close—to anyone. For the last twenty years, I've been so afraid of someone finding out. I remember in college, a bunch of us went to get our fortunes read, and I wouldn't do it. I've always been afraid that someone will see it in me—that I've done this horrible thing . . ."

She fell silent as a couple of teenagers passed them. Bridget and Zach turned toward the store window. Brad suddenly appeared on the TV screens. He stood in front of his house with Janice at his side. Reporters thrust microphones in front of him as he made a statement.

Brad had told her this morning that the cocaine Christmas party story was killing him in the overnight polls. One of the *Examiner*'s editorials on the subject, entitled LET IT SNOW? JUST SAY NO, blasted Brad, calling him *reckless* and *morally bankrupt*.

Jay Corby had predicted it would take a while to recover from the setback, even after disproving the cocaine story. This press conference, with the pregnant and pretty Janice in tow, was one of Brad's first counterattacks against Foley and this lie.

Bridget had a hard time looking at her brother on the TV screens. What would Brad say if he knew that she'd just told Zach everything?

"Now I understand why you were so opposed to my investigating Mallory's disappearance," Zach said.

"I'm sorry," she murmured. "The last couple of nights, I've come so close to telling you the truth. I've hated myself for lying to you, Zach. I wouldn't blame you if you hate me too."

"I don't hate you," he said, leaning against the window. "I have to admit, the night of the funeral, I could tell you were holding something back from me. I figured you were protecting your brother. Now it all makes sense."

"But you must think I'm horrible—"

He shook his head. "It doesn't really change how I feel about you—how I've always felt. I mean, if it wasn't for Brad insisting everyone keep it secret, you would have gone to the police that night and told them what happened to Mallory. You would have done the right thing."

" 'Would have' and what really happened aren't the same thing," she said, her eyes downcast.

"Still, I'm glad you told me, Bridget."

"I haven't breathed a word to anyone else." She shrugged. "Except Gerry."

Zach glanced at the TV screens. "Does Brad know that you told Gerry?"

Nodding, she opened her purse and started looking though it. "Brad wasn't too happy to hear I'd spilled my guts to Gerry. But after all, he was my husband. I guess for twins, Brad and I don't operate the same way. He's never said anything to Janice."

"What are you searching for?" he asked.

She was still rummaging through her purse. "I think I've used up all my Kleenex. Plus, my head is pounding. You don't have an aspirin, do you?"

"I'm sure there's a drugstore inside," Zach said. "I also have aspirin at my place, which isn't far from here."

"Could we go to your place?" Bridget asked. "If you don't mind, I'd like to clean up a little. I must look awful."

"Not to me," he whispered. He smiled at Bridget, then gently took hold of her arm. "C'mon, let's go."

They moved away from the storefront—and all those television sets with Brad's face on them.

Zach said she was in no condition to drive. Bridget gladly surrendered her keys and he got behind the wheel of her minivan. As they pulled out of the parking garage, she figured the boys were still at the skating rink. Gerry's parents would have them for the rest of the afternoon. She had plenty of time. Maybe Zach would let her lie down at his place for a few minutes. She felt so tired and depleted.

His eyes on the road, he asked what she thought must have happened to Mallory—and her Volare. "I mean, you've had twenty years to mull over the possibilities. What's your theory?"

"I've always sort of hoped against hope that Mallory got away," Bridget admitted, her head tipped back against the headrest. "She was so unhappy in that town. I used to think she might have seen it as an opportunity to leave—and make the five of us feel horrible for the rest of our lives. God knows, we deserved that. She was a very smart, resourceful girl. She might have pulled it off. But then you and I went to her mother's, and I don't think she would have run away without her books—and some money."

Bridget cracked the window a bit for some fresh air. "Still, I can't help thinking Olivia might have spotted Mallory some place recently—and maybe that's what got her killed. Maybe it started a chain reaction of killings."

"What does Brad think?"

Bridget sighed. "He always felt Fuller had taken the body—and the car. Fuller had been worried that with Mallory's

THE LAST VICTIM 303

Volare parked on Briar Court, it would be a big clue to people where they could find her body." Frowning, Bridget shook her head. "But Fuller seemed as confused as we were about what happened to the car—and Mallory. And I think he would have said something to me—not then, but recently. He gave five thousand dollars to Olivia for that *new information* about Gorman's Creek. I think he was genuinely puzzled over what had happened to Mallory and the car."

"Mallory was a big girl," Zach said. "As big as I was. I doubt either Olivia or Cheryl could have lifted her out of that well." He kept his gaze fixed on the road. "So—if Mallory didn't crawl out of that hole herself, and Fuller didn't go back there for her, that leaves one other person besides you—"

"I know what you're about to say," Bridget cut in. "I left Brad at home and went back there—and the body was gone. Mallory's Volare was still parked on Briar Court, but the body was gone. Brad couldn't have gotten back to Gorman's Creek before me. I drove our car there."

She glanced over at Zach, who kept staring straight ahead. "Brad couldn't have gotten back there before me," she repeated.

"You said when you returned home from Gorman's Creek, he'd already taken his bicycle and left. How long was he gone?"

Bridget didn't respond. She just frowned.

"Never mind," he muttered. "You already told me. Your dad was home when you got back, and he went to bed at eleven. Brad came in at four in the morning, which means he spent at least five hours—maybe even six—riding his bike."

Bridget turned and looked out her window. She didn't want to hear any of this.

"I'm not saying he moved the body—or the car. But you need to consider the possibility—if for nothing else so we can eventually eliminate it. Maybe Brad put his bike in the trunk of Mallory's car, dumped her in the Volare, and drove it some place far away. Then he could have ridden his bike back to town."

"For the umpteenth time," she said steadily, "Mallory's

body wasn't there when I returned to Gorman's Creek! And Brad couldn't have gotten there before me."

Zach said nothing. He seemed focused on his driving—or focused on avoiding a confrontation. Maybe both.

He slowed down the car, then pulled up in front of a U-shaped apartment complex, with old brownstone row houses around a neglected courtyard. Switching off the engine, he turned toward her. "Listen, are you busy tomorrow? I mean, can you get away for a few hours?"

She shrugged. "Well, the boys—believe it or not—want to go back to school. And all my appointments were canceled this week, because of Gerry. I should be free until around three-thirty. Why?"

"I'd like to go to Gorman's Creek. You could show me exactly what you're talking about. Maybe we can go door to door on Briar Court. There weren't many houses on that street—if I remember right. Some of the residents from 1985 might still be there. It's a long shot, but maybe we can come up with an old-timer who saw someone take the Volare that night."

Bridget frowned. "Don't you think the police would have already questioned them—back when Mallory first disappeared?"

"I doubt it. You, Brad, and the others were the only ones who knew where Mallory had last parked the car. The cops wouldn't have known to question residents of Briar Court."

"Of course," she mumbled, feeling stupid.

"We should talk with Olivia's mother too," Zach continued. "Maybe Mrs. Rankin could tell us the names of some of Olivia's friends in Seattle. Olivia probably had an address book. And if her mail was forwarded to her mother, Mrs. Rankin might have her last phone bill. We can see who Olivia was calling those last few days before her death. One of her friends might know about this *new information* Olivia was trying to sell."

Bridget nodded. "I think Mrs. Rankin would help us. She

seemed to like me. At least, she was grateful I'd come to Olivia's memorial. I'll call her tonight."

"Good." Zach nodded toward the old brownstone complex. "That's my place." He climbed out of the minivan, then hurried around and opened the door for her.

They headed into the courtyard together. "I didn't mean to snap at you earlier," she said.

"It's okay," Zach replied, putting his arm around her. "He's your brother. I was out of line. You were right to snap at me."

"You didn't say anything I haven't already considered," Bridget confessed. "How do you think I had such a quick answer for you? No, Brad didn't go back there. But someone must have."

At his front stoop, Zach took out his key and started to unlock the door. "That's funny," he muttered. "I thought I'd locked the door when I left."

Not moving past the threshold, he gave the door a little push, and it creaked open. Zach hesitated, then stepped in front of her. Bridget peeked over his shoulder. The place was tidy and sparsely furnished. She noticed a tan sofa in the living room, and above it a framed Vincent van Gogh print from the Musee d'Orsay in Paris. In one corner, there was a TV set; in the other, a desk with a computer, a printer, and stacks of papers. "Is anything missing?" Bridget whispered.

Zach shrugged. "I'm not sure." He stepped inside the apartment.

Bridget walked in after him. She saw a bulletin board above the computer desk. There was an art calendar tacked to it—along with a postcard of The Three Stooges, and two flattering color photos of her carefully clipped from a recent *Northwest* magazine article.

"Well, I rank up there with Moe, Larry, and Curly, I see," she remarked.

"I didn't know you'd be coming over," he admitted. "Otherwise, I would have taken those down. Is it creepy that I have those up there?"

She laughed. "No, I'm very flattered. In fact—"

Bridget stopped talking. For a second she stopped breathing.

A man appeared in the bedroom doorway. He was short and sturdy-looking. He wore tight black jeans, a brown sweater, and a dark, multicolored ski mask that totally obscured his face. He pointed a gun at them.

Zach swiveled around and immediately stepped in front of her.

All at once, the man with the ski mask charged them. He kept the gun pointed at Zach's face. His movements were so quick and precise he almost seemed animated—and unstoppable.

Bridget screamed. Helplessly, she watched the man raise the gun up in the air, then smash it down on the side of Zach's head.

Zach crumpled down at her feet. The assailant brushed past her, then hurried out the door.

Stunned, Bridget fell to her knees and hovered over Zach.

"Jesus, that hurt," he groaned, wincing in pain. "Are you—you okay?"

"Yes." Bridget could see the blood matting down his black hair—a few inches above his left ear. "Oh my God," she whispered.

Quickly, she got up and raced into the kitchen. At the sink, she ran a dish towel under the water, then hurried back into the living room. She held the wet towel to the side of his head.

"Did you see where he ran to?" Zach asked.

"No, I'm sorry," she said, catching her breath. "Are you feeling dizzy or nauseated—or anything?"

"I'm feeling pissed off, is what I'm feeling," he grumbled. "That was *my* ski mask he had on. Son of a bitch. I loved that thing. My mother sent it to me. I wore that skiing in Switzerland last year." Sitting up, he took the wet towel from her, then pressed it to his temple. "I better call the cops, which means you better go."

"Why?" Bridget asked, still hovering over him. "What—"

"Won't look good," he said, his eyes closed. "Brad Corrigan's recently widowed sister shouldn't be caught in some man's apartment in the middle of the day. You should go before the cops arrive. In fact, it's best you were never here."

Zach unsteadily got to his feet. He checked the towel to see how much blood there was, then reapplied it to the side of his head. "I'm all right. I don't think I'll need stitches or anything."

"I'll get you some ice for that," she said.

"No. You need to go. I'll walk you to your car."

In the courtyard, Bridget kept glancing around to make sure the man in the ski mask wasn't still lurking about. Holding the dish towel to his head, Zach had his other arm around her. She stopped for a moment and pulled away from him. She hated to ask it, but she had to. "Zach, what are you going to tell the police?"

"That I walked in on a burglar—and he attacked me."

"There's more to it than that," she whispered. "Are you going to tell them anything else?"

He shook his head, then put his arm around her again. They continued walking toward her car. "Thank you," she whispered.

"You should have those guys who are watching your house at night make it a twenty-four-hour job," he said. He checked the backseat of her minivan before opening the driver's door for her.

"You sure you're okay?" she asked.

Zach nodded; then he kissed her gently on the lips. After he pulled away, Bridget touched his cheek and smiled gratefully. Then she climbed into the driver's seat.

"Listen, can you do me a favor?" he asked, leaning on the open car door. "Don't tell Brad that I know about Gorman's Creek. And don't tell him we're going there tomorrow. Don't say anything about getting together with Mrs. Rankin either."

Frowning, Bridget started to shake her head. "Zach—"

"I'm not saying Brad is the enemy here. But I think he may have someone in his confidence who's connected with these murders. Just don't say anything to Brad. I'd like to live a little longer."

With a sigh, Bridget nodded. "I promise."

He closed the door, stepped back, and gave her a little wave.

Bridget smiled at him through the window, then started up the car and pulled away from the curb.

She saw him in the rearview mirror. He was starting back toward the courtyard. Bridget swallowed hard. She prayed like hell he'd still be alive in the morning.

CHAPTER 21

There were nine houses on Briar Court, and no one was home at the first two. The third house was the smallest, but prettiest on the block—a little chalet with green shutters and flower boxes under the windows. The front yard was beautifully landscaped.

The forty-something man who answered the door was also impeccably groomed. He wore a long-sleeve T-shirt and pressed jeans. "Well, you two don't look like Jehovah's Witnesses, so I took a chance and came to the door," he announced. "What can I do for you?"

Zach and Bridget had dressed for their trek through Gorman's Creek—sweaters, jeans, jackets, and hiking boots. It wasn't such a bad day for it, chilly and slightly overcast. Most of the trees along Briar Court were quickly losing their leaves.

Bridget felt strange returning there after twenty years. She remembered that Mallory's mother's car had been parked in front of the house next door to this one. And she couldn't help thinking of Andy Shields and the Gaines twins, last seen heading down this street.

Yet the cul-de-sac seemed rather benign now. Even the

woods of Gorman's Creek at the end of the block seemed less ominous, somehow smaller, scrawnier.

Zach gave the man a friendly smile. He hadn't shaved this morning, and he looked sexy with his five o'clock shadow. He'd combed his hair to cover up the cut and the bump on the side of his head. "Good morning," he said to the man. "My name's Zach, and this is Bridget—"

"Oh my God, you're Bridget Corrigan!" the man interrupted, gaping at her.

She smiled and nodded. "Hi . . . hello."

"I'm crazy for your brother," the man declared. "My partner will be so sorry he missed you. I almost wished we lived in Oregon—just so we could vote for Brad. That Foley is such a homophobe! If he wins, God help us—and not Foley's God, please!" He opened the door wider. "I'm sorry. Do you folks want to come in?"

"That's okay," Zach said. "I'm a reporter, and Bridget's helping me with a story I'm writing about an incident that happened on this block back in 1985. I was wondering—"

"What incident?"

"Um, a missing person case from that year, a teenage girl."

"Oh, that's terrible," he muttered. "Well, we weren't living here back in eighty-five. No, my partner and I moved here in ninety. We've been together seventeen years, living here fifteen. Of course, Foley and his followers are making sure we'll never be able to get married. That's too much of a threat to families. Huh! The good news is we can still buy any number of deadly assault weapons we want to. People don't seem to have a problem with that. I mean, really, file that under C for Crazy! You just ask any person on this block if Rick and I aren't wonderful neighbors—"

"Um, yes, I hear you," Zach interrupted. "I really do. And speaking of your neighbors, do you know if any of the people on this block were living here back in eighty-five?"

The man took a deep breath, then shook his head. "Well, except for old Anastasia Fessler down at the end, I guess

Rick and I have lived here the longest. But I wouldn't bother talking to Anastasia. She's as nutty as a Clark Bar, poor thing."

"Is *Sonny* Fessler still around?" Bridget asked.

"Sonny?" The man squinted at her. "Anastasia has a kid?"

"No, this would be her older brother," Bridget explained. "He was kind of the town character—"

"Oh yeah. I remember hearing something about a brother." He shrugged. "I think he's in a rest home or in one of those assisted-care places."

"Do you know if anyone who lived on this block when you first moved here is still around?" Zach asked.

"You mean, still here in McLaren?" The man shook his head. He pointed to the house next door. "The Cronins were the old-timers when Rick and I moved here. But she died six years ago, cancer. Rick and I used to take turns driving her to chemotherapy. The husband's in a nursing home. Alzheimer's, I hear. We've lost touch with the others who moved away."

Sighing, Zach shot Bridget a defeated look. Then he smiled at the man and extended his hand. "Well, thanks, I think we've taken up enough of your time."

The man shook his hand. "I'm Lance, by the way," he said. He turned to Bridget and shook her hand too. "It was a thrill meeting you. Please, say hi to your brother for me. I'll keep my fingers crossed he beats that fascist Foley."

Zach started to back away.

The man held on to Bridget's hand and pulled her closer. "Bridget," he whispered, "if you don't mind me saying so, hold on to that Zach fella. Talk about a major dreamboat."

She smiled at him. "Thanks, Lance. I think so too."

She caught up with Zach, and they started toward the end of the block together. Bridget eyed the Fessler house. It was as dark and dilapidated as ever, almost swallowed up by overgrown bushes and trees. Bridget wondered if any kind of maintenance had been done on the place since the eighties. She thought of Sonny's sister, living there all alone now.

"Should we try Anastasia?" Zach asked, shoving his hands in his pockets. "We've come all this way. We might as well give it a shot—even if she is nuts."

Bridget nodded. "If anyone on this block noticed something that night, it would have been one of the Fesslers. They were always home."

As they approached the driveway, Bridget remembered standing at approximately that same spot with Sonny—while the police were searching the forest for Andy Shields and the Gaines twins. She noticed a sign in front of the old pathway to Gorman's Creek that hadn't been there before: NO TRESPASSING—VIOLATORS WILL BE PROSECUTED. Beneath the warning, someone had scribbled: *Eat Me.*

"Looks like we'll be breaking the law if you want to see Gorman's Creek," she remarked.

"Also looks like people don't take that sign very seriously," Zach said.

They headed up the walkway, surrounded by overgrown weeds and shrubbery, to the Fesslers' front door. Zach rang the bell. "It's kind of weird," he whispered. "I almost expect Lurch to answer."

Instead of the *Addams Family* butler greeting them, the door was opened by a thin, sixtyish woman with short-cropped beige hair. She wore a powder-blue sweat suit, sneakers, and just below her shoulder, a silver broach of a frog. "Yes?" she said, with a wary look on her wrinkled face.

"Ms. Fessler?" Zach said. "I'm sorry to drop by unannounced—"

"Oh, I'm not Ms. Fessler," the woman interrupted, slowly shaking her head. "I'm her assistant, Edna. Did you wish to speak with Ms. Fessler?"

Zach nodded. "Yes, please. We just needed to ask a few questions about . . ." He trailed off, then gave Bridget a look.

Edna didn't seem to be listening. Rather than look over her shoulder, she took small, deliberate steps until she'd made a semicircle and her back was to them. "Anastasia!" she called. "Anastasia, there are people here to see you! Do you want to see people? Anastasia?"

"What do they want? Find out what they want!" squawked a woman somewhere in the house.

Bridget peeked over Edna's shoulder and she saw a portly, old woman in a recliner chair with a remote control device in her hand. Bridget couldn't see the TV from where she stood, but there was a flickering light, so Anastasia must have had her program on mute or pause. The Fesslers' sunken living room was a large, cluttered area with a huge picture window. At the moment, the blinds were drawn, and only a dim light crept through the slats. The place was decorated with big, bulky, old furniture and too many dried flowers. Surrounding Anastasia in her recliner chair were a wheelchair, a walker, and a dainty little striped wastebasket filled to the brim with tissues and garbage. At her side sat a TV table, holding a box of Kleenex, several bottles of pills, a water tumbler, and an open bag of Pepperidge Farm cookies.

Anastasia was about seventy, but she seemed so much older. Bridget remembered the article about Mrs. Fessler's suicide, and saw the resemblance to the dowdy-looking woman pictured in that old *Cowlitz County Register*.

"We were hoping you could help us with some information about a missing person, Ms. Fessler," Zach called—over Edna's shoulder. "This was in 1985. A teenage girl was last seen heading into the woods behind your house here—"

"That's private property!" Anastasia barked.

"Yes, ma'am, I know," he said, still at the threshold and speaking past Edna. "We were hoping you might have seen something. It was a long time ago, but maybe you remember. She was a big girl with brown, frizzy hair—"

"Tell him to call the lawyers," Anastasia said.

Edna held up a finger to indicate Zach should wait a minute. Then she shuffled away from the door.

Bridget took a step into the foyer, and was hit with a blast of warm air. The place smelled a little rancid—like old, wet clothes and mold. "Anastasia? I used to live here in McLaren. My name's Bridget Corrigan. Your brother, Sonny, might remember me. Maybe Sonny or your father saw something that night, and told you about it," she went on. "It was toward the end of summer, 1985. There might have been somebody—maybe even two people—taking a girl to a car. They may have been carrying her—"

Anastasia started shaking her head. "I don't talk to anyone about things like that without my lawyer."

"Well, do you think Sonny would mind talking to me?" Bridget pressed. "He always seemed to like me. I'd love to have a chance to visit with him, catch up—"

"Edna? Give her one of the cards," Anastasia said to her assistant. "Give her one of those cards from the lawyer!"

"That's what I'm doing!" Edna shot back. She searched through the top drawer of a dresser next to the front door. "I'm looking for them right now! Hold your horses!"

"Well, they're in there, right in front of your face."

"Oh, here they are, right in front of me," Edna remarked. She shuffled over to Bridget and carefully set a business card in her hand. "You'll need to talk to the lawyers," she said. "And Sonny isn't here. He's in a rest home, and doesn't take no visitors."

"Ms. Fessler," Zach piped up, "there really isn't any reason to involve lawyers. We just thought you might be able to help us out. This was a classmate of ours who vanished without a trace. You probably remember—"

"Did you give them the card?" Anastasia interrupted, shooting a peeved look toward her assistant.

"Yes, yes, I gave it to them already," Edna retorted. "For Pete's sake—"

"I'm missing *Matlock*," Anastasia complained.

"She's missing her *Matlock*," Edna said to Bridget under her breath. "You need to go now."

Anastasia's assistant led Bridget to the door. The volume on the TV suddenly came on—quite loudly.

Bridget paused in the doorway. "I'm sorry we bothered

you, Ms. Fessler," she called—over a police siren on TV. She glanced back toward the living room.

Anastasia Fessler stared at the television set. She seemed mesmerized—almost dazed. The light from the TV flickered across her face, and her tired, old eyes were filled with tears.

Rachel Towles, Attorney
BARD & MITCHELL ASSOCIATES
Law Offices

Bridget had heard of them—through Gerry. It was a very powerful firm with a lot of rich clients and half a floor in one of Seattle's tallest buildings.

"For some reason," Zach said as she showed him the card, "I figured old Anastasia's lawyer would be some local yokel, not this big-time firm up in Seattle."

"Makes sense," Bridget murmured. "The Fesslers always had a lot of money—and a lot of problems. Just when we were leaving a minute ago, I saw her crying. I'm wondering what we said to trigger that."

Zach shrugged. "Maybe she was just upset she was missing *Matlock*."

Bridget glanced over at the NO TRESPASSING sign at the beginning of the Gorman's Creek trail. Once again, she remembered standing at this same spot with Sonny Fessler. "Maybe she misses her brother," Bridget murmured. "I wonder if Sonny did see something that night. We should have asked Anastasia's friend for the name of the rest home where he's staying."

" 'Doesn't take no visitors,' remember?" Zach said. He nodded at the sign. "Well, are you ready to trespass?"

Bridget sighed. "Sure."

She glanced at the attorney's card again, then shoved it in her pocket.

They found an opening in the barbed-wire fence—not far from the Fesslers' driveway. Walking along the pathway, Zach wordlessly reached over and took hold of her hand.

The trail was covered with fallen leaves that rustled in the chilly wind. The forest didn't seem quite so dark and menacing in the middle of the day. Still, Bridget felt the ghosts all around them.

Zach squeezed her hand and smiled reassuringly at her. "How are you doing so far?"

She nodded. This was her first time back to Gorman's Creek since the night Mallory had disappeared, but she wasn't thinking about that. Bridget was wondering if Janette Carlisle had been holding hands with her boyfriend that summer evening in the early fifties when they'd walked down this trail to go skinny-dipping in the pond.

Zach didn't say anything either. He just held on to her hand and smiled a tiny bit to himself.

No one knew she was here. She'd talked on the phone with Brad last night. Keeping her promise to Zach, she didn't say anything to her brother about their plans for today. However, she did tell him about Cheryl's freak "accident."

"Jesus, no," Brad murmured. "I really didn't . . ." He made a strange raspy sound.

Bridget listened for a moment. "Are you crying?" she asked.

"No, no, I'm okay. I—well, you just caught me by surprise. I started to remember how crazy I was about her when we were kids." Brad cleared his throat. "Listen, I should hang up and call you back."

When he called a half hour later, he was all business. He'd contacted the private detective agency and put twenty-four-hour surveillance on Bridget's house. She would have a bodyguard at her disposal, if she wanted one. He'd hired someone to start watching *his* house too. "Damn it, Brigg, you were right," he admitted. "This is no coincidence. Something's going on here. Don't take any chances. And don't say anything to anyone until we figure this out."

He phoned again this morning to make sure she was all right. He wasn't going to Cheryl's funeral—no surprise there "If you go, promise you won't drive down to Eugene by yourself. Have one of the private detectives drive you."

"It's okay, Brad," she replied. "I don't think I'm going."

He'd asked about her plans for the day. Bridget lied and said she was getting together with Gerry's sister for lunch.

Before Brad got off the line, he said that Janice wanted to talk to her.

"Listen, could you take Dad and Emma tonight?" Janice asked. "I know it's last minute. Brad had planned to go stag at this fund-raiser dinner, but now suddenly I'm coming along. They need me there for the photographers and everything."

"Sounds like a ton of fun, I don't think," Bridget said.

"It's crazy," Janice grumbled. "I swear, Foley has total control over the media. We've proven they lied about that stupid cocaine party, but it still hasn't made much difference. Jay says Brad's numbers in the morning polls haven't bounced back yet. Anyway, Mrs. Brad Corrigan has to *sparkle* tonight. So—back to my original question—can you take Dad and Emma?"

"No sweat," Bridget said. "I can even come pick them up."

"Well, I was hoping you would," Janice replied. "I don't think that's asking too much. I'm still exhausted from all those interviews yesterday. Huh, you know, it's *your* fault I have to go to this thing."

"What are you talking about, Janice?"

"Aren't you the one who was so gung ho about me making these personal appearances with Brad? It's because of you I'm suddenly in the front lines." She let out a disingenuous little laugh. "You stinker."

"Janice, I was simply agreeing with Jay and the P.R. guys. But you know, if you're feeling tired, you shouldn't go. I mean—"

"Too late, I'm going," she interrupted. "And now you get to babysit for a change."

When Bridget hung up, she wondered how—even though she was doing a favor for her sister-in-law—Janice still managed to make her feel horrible.

Or perhaps she was already feeling crummy for having lied to her brother about today. He still didn't trust Zach. But she did.

As they walked deeper into the woods, Bridget felt so grateful to have this thoughtful, handsome man at her side. After so many years of keeping Gorman's Creek a secret, she'd confided in him. Zach knew the very worst thing about her, and he still loved her. Bridget squeezed his hand.

"Is it weird coming back here?" he asked.

She glanced up at the bare tree branches hovering over them. She heard the rushing water from the creek. *The Devil's Gulch*, Mallory had called it. Bridget brushed her shoulder against his. "Just stick close to me, okay?"

"I won't let go," Zach whispered. He brought her hand up to his mouth and kissed it. Then they continued down the path.

Through the trees, Bridget saw the old Bowers place in the distance. They veered off the trail. The broken-down brick fireplace and chimney and the front stoop were just as Bridget remembered.

She wrapped her arm around Zach's as they approached what was once the Bowerses' living room. She nodded at the tree behind the house, the tilted one that precariously loomed over the ravine. "The crawl space is on a ridge by that leaning tree," she said.

As they climbed down to the ridge, she glanced at the ravine below, and the pile of rubble from the landslide. Among other things, she saw an old wicker chair, a smashed cabinet, and the remnants of a window. But the child's rocking horse was gone. She wondered if someone had taken it. Or had it just rotted and washed away in a storm?

Letting go of her hand, Zach moved along the slope, then stopped suddenly. "I see it," he announced, peeking over the tilted tree.

Bridget stepped toward him. He helped her over the tree and its tangled roots, then climbed over them himself. Bridget stared at the trapdoor on the ground. "It's not the same," she said.

"What do you mean?" Zach asked.

"Someone replaced the lid."

It wasn't the moldy, rotting wood-plank cover with the broken latch from two decades ago. This trapdoor was one piece of solid wood. It appeared a bit weather-beaten, but couldn't have been more than ten or fifteen years old.

Zach squatted down to get a closer look. He tugged at the panel. "It's nailed shut. We'd need a crowbar to get this sucker open." He straightened up and wiped the dirt off his hands. "Whoever did this, I don't think they were trying to be sneaky about it. Looks like they cleared away some shrubs here too."

Bridget nodded. "You're right." She remembered first finding the trapdoor behind a clump of bushes. She wondered why someone had replaced the lid. Had they buried something down in that hole? If that was the case, it didn't make sense to clear the bushes away.

"You said the hole is twenty to thirty feet deep," Zach said. He gazed out over the ravine. "I've never been to this spot before. At least, I have an idea of the layout now. I didn't realize there's such a sharp incline here. It's possible Mallory climbed out of the well—only to fall down this slope. Maybe that's why you didn't see her when you came back. She could have been knocked unconscious again, unable to hear you calling for her."

Bridget gazed down at the plank of wood over the hole where they'd left Mallory Meehan. She remembered what Mallory had told her: "There's no other place in this town where you could scream and scream, and no one would hear."

Bridget shuddered. "Can we go now?" she asked.

"Of course."

Zach helped her climb over the trunk of the tilted tree,

and they made their way back up to the old Bowers ruins. Catching her breath, Bridget paused by the decrepit chimney and hearth.

"Jesus," Zach murmured, looking out toward the trees.

"What is it?"

"I just saw someone out there," he whispered, still gazing at the woods.

"Where?" she asked, panicked. "Zach, if this is your idea of a joke—"

"Shhh." He pulled her behind the chimney.

Bridget resisted for a moment. But then she ducked behind the old fireplace with him. She listened for footsteps, but the rushing stream in the ravine below drowned everything out. The wind kicked up and several leaves scattered along the forest floor. Trees swayed, and everything seemed to move and shift for a moment.

"You didn't tell anyone we were coming here, did you?" Zach asked, under his breath.

Wide-eyed, Bridget stared at him and shook her head.

Zach stepped in front of her. "Damn, there he is again," he murmured.

"Where?"

He pointed toward the trail. In the distance, Bridget saw someone moving between the trees. "Oh my God," she murmured.

"Don't move," he said in a hushed voice. "Let's just see who this is. Could be anyone. Maybe a schoolkid."

But it was eleven-thirty on a Thursday morning. Most schoolkids were in school. Bridget thought about her stalker— the one playing cat and mouse with her in the alley by the Starbucks, the one skulking around her house.

Bridget watched the man—a fractured shadowy image darting between the trees. He wore dark pants and a blue jacket. "He's too tall to be a schoolkid," she whispered.

He was working his way toward them. Then he ducked behind a tree. Bridget kept waiting for him to reappear.

Zach reached for a loose brick by his feet. He straightened up and gazed toward the trail again. "Where the hell is he?"

"I don't know," Bridget murmured, clutching Zach's arm. "It's like he vanished."

Then she saw something move—several yards over from where she'd last seen him. Was it a tree swaying? The wind was starting up again.

All at once, someone emerged from behind a cluster of bushes. He was lumbering toward them.

Bridget gasped. Zach pushed her back again, and he stepped forward.

"What are you kids doing?" the man yelled.

She peeked over Zach's shoulder and recognized the tall, stocky, gray-haired man. Sheriff Miller squinted at them. "Oh, it's you two," he said.

Zach tossed the brick aside. "You gave us a bit of a scare," he admitted.

A hand on her heart, Bridget emerged from behind the chimney. "Hello, Sheriff," she said, catching her breath.

"Anastasia Fessler phoned in a report that a couple of *kids* were out here," the sheriff explained. "Didn't you folks see the *No Trespassing* sign? Old Anastasia is an absolute stickler about people coming into these woods. What are you doing out here?"

"Sorry you had to schlepp all this way for us," Zach said. "I'm researching a story idea again. I probably should have asked permission—"

"The Mallory Meehan article?" the sheriff asked. "What brings you out here for that?"

Zach hesitated, then shook his head. "Oh no, this is a different story altogether—about the Bowerses. We were just checking out what's left of the place."

Bridget touched Zach's shoulder. Now that he was carrying around her secret, Zach was lying about it too.

"Didn't Anastasia tell you that we stopped by?" Bridget asked.

The sheriff shook his head. "No, she just said there were

a couple of kids trespassing. I get a call like this at least once a month from her, and half the time it's a false alarm. Old Anastasia isn't playing with a full fifty-two—if you get my drift."

"Sorry," Bridget said. "We didn't mean to bother anyone."

The sheriff waved the apology away. "Forget it. No harm done."

"Thanks, sheriff," Brad replied. "As long as you're here, can I ask you a question? We noticed a board nailed to something on the ground along the ridge down there. Do you know what it is?"

Bridget swallowed hard. She didn't expect him to ask the *sheriff* about it. The last thing she wanted was for the authorities to investigate that well. Sheriff Miller scratched his chin for a moment, then nodded. "Oh, I know what you're talking about. A kid found a well back there about ten years ago. Must have been part of the old Bowers place. Anyway, he fell in and twisted his ankle. So we had to come out here and board it up." He shrugged. "It's always something, y'know? Anyway, we should beat a retreat before Anastasia gets her panties in a twist and calls the state police."

As they started down the trail, Bridget gave Zach a furtive that-was-a-close-call look. He reached over and took her hand.

"I guess Sonny Fessler is in a rest home now," Bridget said to the sheriff, who was walking ahead of them.

"Yeah, poor old guy," the sheriff grunted. "I've heard the place is more like a sanitarium. Anastasia couldn't take care of him anymore. Hell, she's too far gone to take care of herself."

"Do you know where this rest home—or sanitarium—is?" Bridget asked.

"Nope," the sheriff said over his shoulder. "It's weird. After they put him in there about fifteen years ago, my wife wanted to send Sonny a Christmas package. She always made Christmas cookies for Sonny and bought him a trinket. Made his day. Anyway, she asked Anastasia for the address of the place. So Anastasia gave her a card and said she should write to him care of some law firm in Seattle."

Bridget let go of Zach's hand for a moment. She dug the business card out of her pocket and looked at it again.

Rachel Towles, Attorney
BARD & MITCHELL ASSOCIATES
Law Offices

She put the card back into her pocket, and then looked at the trail ahead.

She could see the Fesslers' house in the distance, and the woods reflected against the darkened windows. No doubt, they could see whenever someone came and went out of this forest.

Bridget wondered which one of those windows was to Sonny's bedroom.

"Why did you go through directory assistance when you have the number right there on the card?" Zach asked.

"This way my phone number won't show up on their caller ID," Bridget explained.

They sat in his car, parked down the street from Mrs. Rankin's house. Bridget was on her cell phone to the law offices of Bard and Mitchell. She was on hold, listening to Willie Nelson sing "Unchained Melody."

"Do you really think Sonny might have seen something that night?" Zach asked, drumming his fingers on the steering wheel.

"It's worth a shot, isn't it?" She glanced at her wristwatch. "If this sanitarium is somewhere between here and Portland, we might have time to swing by today."

" 'Doesn't take no visitors,' remember?"

"Well, maybe we can work our way around that—"

"Rachel Towles speaking," the voice came on the other end.

"Oh, hello, I'm Cheryl—Matthias of Blooms Floral in Longview," Bridget lied. "And we have a mum plant for delivery to a Lon Fessler Junior. I was told I could get an address from you. Is that correct?"

"I'm sorry, we can't give out that information."

"Well, this is a 69.95 order, and our delivery guy's waiting in his car for an address. I understand Mr. Fessler's in a rest home. I'm calling from Longview. Is he within our seventy-five-mile delivery area?"

"Once again, I'm sorry," the attorney said. "I can't give you that information. May I ask who purchased this plant for Mr. Fessler?"

Bridget hesitated. "Well, if you're not going to help me, I don't see why I should help you," she said. "This is a 69.95 order, and now I can't fill it. Tell you what, if you give me an address, then I'll give you a name."

There was a silence on the other end. Bridget bit her lip and waited.

"Um, you said you're with Blooms Floral in Longview?" the attorney asked. "Is there a number where I can call you back, Ms. Matthias?"

"Well, I'm the only one here in the store, and I'm leaving soon. I—have to handle a big funeral this afternoon. If you can't give me an address where we can send this mum plant, I guess there's nothing more for us to discuss."

Bridget waited, hoping Rachel Towles might acquiesce and give her the name of the rest home where they had Sonny Fessler.

But there was a click on the other end, and the line went dead.

"Maybe we'll have more luck with Olivia's mother," Zach said, parking across the street from Mrs. Rankin's modest, gray ranch house. It was dwarfed by a huge evergreen tree on the front lawn.

Bridget had phoned Mrs. Rankin last night. She hadn't been sure how to approach the subject. After all, what she and Zach wanted to do was interview Mrs. Rankin—and maybe, if they could, sift through Olivia's personal effects for clues regarding her "suicide" and the "new information" she'd had about Gorman's Creek. But Bridget couldn't exactly tell Mrs. Rankin that.

Instead, she'd merely asked if she and Zachary Matthias could stop by and talk with her about Olivia. "I guess we're looking for answers too," she'd explained.

Apparently, it had been the right thing to say, because Mrs. Rankin had invited them to her house this afternoon.

She even had coffee brewed and served it to them in her living room with a plate full of Chips Ahoys that she arranged in front of them—directly from the bag. Mrs. Rankin wore a flowery print blouse and khakis. She'd made up her face— just a trace too heavily—but it didn't camouflage the fact that she looked tired. Bridget asked how she was holding up.

"Some days are harder than others," she said, sitting across from them in an easy chair.

Bridget and Zach sat on the slightly worn, beige and brown sofa. Nearly everything in the living room was beige, brown, or navy blue. Bridget had been there before on a couple of occasions back in high school. The place hadn't changed much since then. She remembered this drab living room. It had always amazed her that a wild, edgy girl like Olivia lived in such a colorless house.

"Have you talked to any of Olivia's friends in Seattle?" Bridget asked, a Chips Ahoy in her hand. "Were they any help?"

Mrs. Rankin shook her head. "Not really. Several of her friends came down for the funeral—along with her work colleagues. She was a receptionist for this group of chiropractors, you know. Very nice people, but no one was able to give me one reason why Olivia would take her own life. It doesn't make sense."

Zach leaned forward and put down his coffee cup. "This sounds like a strange question—and totally unrelated," he said. "But did Olivia ever talk to you about Mallory Meehan?"

Bridget shifted a bit on the lumpy sofa. She couldn't believe he'd just cut to the chase like that—and blurted out Mallory's name.

Staring down at the beige shag carpet, Mrs. Rankin pursed her lips. "Hmmm, you mean that strange girl who disappeared sometime after graduation?"

Zach nodded.

"No, I don't think Olivia was friends with her. Whatever happened to that girl anyway? Did they ever find her?"

"No, they didn't," Bridget said. "Um, Mrs. Rankin, I was wondering if Olivia's mail got forwarded to you. The reason I ask is that if you have her most recent phone bill, we might be able to track down some of the people she was calling near the end. Maybe they can tell us something about Olivia's state of mind around that time."

"Well, that's a very good idea," Mrs. Rankin said, reaching for a cookie. "I never thought of doing that. I have most of Olivia's mail at my office. I work mornings in the billing department at Longview Paper and Pulp."

"Do you think there's any way Zach and I could take a look at that phone bill?" Bridget asked.

"Well, I can drive back there this afternoon and fax the phone bill to you. Do you have a fax machine?"

Bridget nodded. "Yes, thank you. That would be great. I'll give you my fax number before we leave."

"Mrs. Rankin, this is another question out of the blue," Zach said.

Bridget started to squirm again.

"I was wondering," he went on. "Did Olivia ever say anything to you about Gorman's Creek?"

Mrs. Rankin had a mouthful of cookie, but she stopped chewing for a moment. Then she reached for her coffee and took a big gulp. "Um, yes," she said finally. "Olivia got into some trouble there—with the police. They caught her and some friends swimming in the pond there—without any swimsuits." She muttered the last part. "At least, that's what the police said."

"That's all?" Zach pressed. "She didn't mention any other incident there? She didn't say anything about Gorman's Creek to you recently?"

Mrs. Rankin shrugged. "Not that I recall. Why do you ask? Is there something else that happened at Gorman's Creek I should know about?"

Zach shook his head. "No. It's just that I was one of the kids who were there at the pond when the cops came. Some of the kids were naked, but not Olivia. She swam in her underwear. I remember her saying she didn't want to do anything that she might be ashamed of later. Olivia had a lot of integrity."

Mrs. Rankin smiled at him. She had tears in her eyes. "Thank you for telling me that," she said, wiping her eyes with a napkin. "You're very sweet."

Bridget sipped her coffee and watched the two of them. Zach was lying, of course. He was telling Mrs. Rankin what she needed to hear. Bridget admired how he kept a lid on the Gorman's Creek connection and managed to make Mrs. Rankin feel good about her daughter. Still, he was lying. Bridget wondered how many times he'd lied to her and told her what *she* needed to hear.

"Do you know if Olivia kept a journal, Mrs. Rankin?" he asked.

She sighed and shook her head. "No, I thought of that too. I've been through all her things. I spent last week cleaning out her town house up in Seattle. I gave away a ton of things to Goodwill. But I still have a basement full of stuff downstairs—mostly clothes and knickknacks."

"Would it be all right if we had a look?" Bridget asked sheepishly.

Mrs. Rankin took a cookie with her as she led them

through the kitchen. She switched on the light at the top of the basement stairs. "Sorry, it's an awful mess down here," she said.

They descended a creaky wooden staircase to the dank-smelling cellar. Clothes—some in dry-cleaner plastic bags—were on hangers, suspended from a pipe running along the ceiling. Boxes had been piled on top of a Ping-Pong table that also held various other bulky items. Among the odds and ends, Bridget noticed a Lava Lamp, a big stuffed rabbit, a box full of framed prints (Olivia seemed fond of Gustav Klimt), a guitar, and an open box full of Olivia's shoes. Bridget picked up a red high heel out of the group, and she felt a sudden, overwhelming sadness. She imagined Olivia, the party girl in her red pumps.

Zach peeked into one of the boxes and pulled out a couple of fat, glittery pillar candles. He gave her a furtive look, then sighed and shook his head. They seemed to be wasting their time.

Mrs. Rankin stayed by the bottom of the stairs. "Bridget, if you'd like any of Olivia's clothes, help yourself. They might be a little roomy on you. I don't know why, but I don't want strangers wearing Olivia's things. I just couldn't give them away to charity. I'd feel better if one of her friends had her clothes. Go on, take a look."

Obliging her, Bridget started looking through the clothes hanging from the pipe. She and Olivia didn't have the same taste in apparel. "This is so nice of you, Mrs. Rankin," she said. "But I don't think anything here is going to fit me."

Bridget stopped sorting through the garments as she found a couple of white nurse's uniforms. "These must be from Olivia's job at the chiropractors' office," she remarked—almost to herself.

"No, those uniforms are from her job before that," Mrs. Rankin explained.

"She was a nurse?" Bridget asked.

"Not a *registered* nurse. Olivia was a caregiver. She wore the uniforms last year, when she was working in this rest

ome in Olympia. Well, it's more like a fancy sanitarium, I
uess. Glenhaven Hills."

"Glenhaven Hills," the operator answered. "How may I
elp you?"

"Hi, this is Carol, and I'm one of the clerks from Bard
nd Mitchell," Bridget lied. She sat in the front seat of Zach's
ar, parked across the street from Mrs. Rankin's house. She
ad a couple of Olivia's sweaters in plastic bags on the back-
eat. Bridget didn't think she'd ever wear them, but Mrs.
ankin had insisted she take something.

Zach was behind the wheel, biting his lip as he watched
er.

"I wanted to check if a package arrived for Lon Fessler
et," Bridget continued. "I might be too early. We just sent it
a Tuesday."

"One minute please."

Bridget glanced at Zach. "They're checking," she said
nder her breath.

She could hear someone talking in the background:
". . wet the bed again in twenty-two-A. But I don't think we
ould . . ."

"Hello, Carol?" the woman said, back on the line.

"Yes?"

"Nothing came for Lon today."

"Well, thanks for checking. Um, one more thing. I want
 make sure we have the right room number on file here. We
ave two different numbers. Someone shows him in sixteen-
, but I don't think that's right."

"Lon's in C Ward," the woman said. "Nine-C."

"That's right," Bridget said. "That's the other room num-
er we have here. Thanks very much. Bye now."

She clicked off her cell phone. "Sonny Fessler is in C
'ard, room nine."

Zach nodded pensively. "So we think Olivia got this 'new
formation' about Gorman's Creek from Sonny Fessler while

she was working at Glenhaven Hills. And that means Son
must have seen what happened to Mallory that night." I
frowned. "It's going to be tricky getting in there to see him
he 'doesn't take no visitors,' like the lady said."

"Well, I don't think we can go there today anyway." Bridg
glanced at her wristwatch. "It's over an hour to Olymp
from here. And I need to pick up my boys from school
three-thirty."

This was their first day back to school since their fath
was killed, and she needed to be outside the school waitin
for them when the bell rang. "Maybe we can drive up the
tomorrow."

Zach nodded and started up the car. "Huh, I might ju
head up to Glenhaven Hills—after I drop you off—che
this place out."

"Do you think Sonny will talk to you?" Bridget asked.
mean, if you can get to him. Did you even know him ve
well?"

"No, but—"

"I think he might talk to me," Bridget said. "I want to g
up there with you. Let's wait until tomorrow, okay?"

Zach shifted gears and pulled down the street. "Yeah, w
can go tomorrow," he said, eyes on the road. "Still, I mig
poke around there this afternoon and see what the layout
like."

Bridget's cell phone rang. "Sorry," she said, pulling it o
of her purse. She checked the caller number, then clicked
on. "Hi, Brad. What's up?"

"Um, can you came over—right away?" he asked.

"What's wrong?"

"Janice started getting these awful stomach cramps. S
was bleeding, and . . . well, I think we've lost the baby. . .

"Oh no. Brad, I'm so sorry," she murmured.

"So—can you come over? I need you to take Emma a
Dad."

"Um, sure, of course." She glanced at the sign for Inte
state 5. "I can be there in about an hour and a half."

"An hour and a half? Where are you?"

She hesitated.

"Brigg?"

"I'm here with Zach. I'll explain when I get there. . . ."

The sign along Interstate 5 read: PORTLAND—43 MI.

Bridget couldn't even process what had happened. Yet an-
her death, this time Brad and Janice's unborn child.

Apparently, Janice's holistic doctor was at the house,
nding to her. Janice's condition was stable, but the doctor
as talking about putting her in the hospital for the night.

Bridget felt horrible, but she couldn't help wondering
out Janice's drinking on the sly, her *natural, herbal* brand
Valium, and the secrecy over her switching doctors. It al-
ost seemed as if she'd sabotaged her own pregnancy.
ridget hated herself for even thinking such a thing.

Zach had offered to pick up the boys from school, but she
dn't want to do that to David and Eric on their first day
ck. They'd only met Zach once before—a couple of nights
o at their father's wake. No, she'd have plenty of time to
to Brad's house, pick up her father and Emma, then swing
and get the boys at school.

That was easy to figure out. Deciding what to tell Brad
as the real dilemma.

"I don't want him to know what we're doing," Zach said,
s eyes on the road. "Just do me a favor and tell him we
ent for a drive along the Columbia River or something."

Bridget squirmed in the passenger seat. "Why can't I tell
m the truth?" she asked. "You know, I felt terrible lying to
m this morning. He thought I was in Portland, having
nch with my sister-in-law."

"Well, say your sister-in-law canceled," Zach said. "Then
alled you up. We had lunch and went for a drive. We were
our way to Mount Hood when he called."

"Why don't you want Brad to know what we're doing?"
ridget pressed.

"Like I told you yesterday, there might be someone Bra
has in his confidence who could be connected to the
killings."

"Who exactly?"

"It could be any number of people," he said with an exa
perated sigh. "I don't know. I just think we're better off
Brad doesn't know what we're doing."

"You're asking me to lie to my brother," Bridget said.

"Yes, I know. Will you do that for me, Bridget? Please?

CHAPTER 22

"We'll need someone to explain about the trauma parents go through when they lose an unborn child," Jay Corby said into his cell phone. "Someone who knows how to sling that psychological bullshit."

He was pacing around Brad's kitchen. He wore a blue silk shirt, black pants, and designer glasses. His short blond hair was gelled and spiked to edgy perfection. Brad's campaign manager, who routinely went in for Botox injections and chemical peels, had a perpetual "electric beach" tan, and his teeth were bleached almost too white. It always seemed to amaze people that Jay wasn't gay. At least, he *claimed* he was straight, and he had a wife and a baby boy, Cameron, to prove it.

"So get me a shrink—preferably a good-looking guy," he barked into the phone. "We'll need someone to make up for this bow-wow woman doctor who'll be explaining Janice's condition."

Apparently, Janice's holistic doctor had shown up in jeans and a sweatshirt, which was fine for an emergency house call, but it wouldn't work for a TV appearance.

Jay had summoned the press. They were expected to descend on Brad and Janice's house within the hour. He'd sent

Janice's doctor home to change her clothes for the TV interview, "and maybe if we're lucky, she'll come back looking more like a doctor, for Christ's sake."

Janice was resting in bed. Brad Senior and Emma were in the family room, watching *Mulan* together. Brad sat across from Bridget at the kitchen table, looking a bit shell shocked. There was an aspirin bottle and a tumbler of water in front of him. Under his breath, he asked Bridget—for the second time—where she'd been with Zach Matthias when he'd phoned earlier. Wasn't she supposed to be lunching with her sister-in-law today?

Bridget gave him the same reply she'd given before: "I'll explain later."

Jay clicked off his cell phone. "Bridget, I'm going to need you at Brad's side when he makes his statement. We'll tape just outside the front door—"

"Sorry, Jay, but I can't stick around." She glanced at her wristwatch. "I need to leave in about a half hour. I'm picking up my sons at school."

She reached across the table and squeezed Brad's hand. "Listen, do you want me to take Dad and Emma for the night? Because if you do, we better get some of their things packed—"

"Executive Limousines?" Jay was on his cell phone again. "Yes, I need a pickup at Lincoln Elementary School at three thirty—"

"Hey, Jay, wait a minute," Bridget interrupted. She got to her feet. "You're not sending a limo over to pick up my boys. They've probably had a tough enough time keeping a low profile today. They don't need a limo picking them up in front of God and the whole school."

"That's crazy," Jay said, still holding the cell phone to his ear. "A stretch limo with a sunroof and TV in the back. They'll love it."

Bridget shook her head. "Jay, this is their first day back to school since their father was killed. I want to be waiting there for them when the bell rings. You're not sending a limo."

Jay sighed. "I'll call you back," he said into the cell phone, then clicked it off. "Bridget, we need you on board for this. You've just been through a tragedy. And now you're here for your brother as he deals with his own terrible loss. When he makes his statement to the press, it's vital that you're in the shot with him. Brad, talk to her."

Brad got to his feet. "You guys figure this out," he muttered. "I'm going to check on Janice." He shuffled out of the kitchen.

Jay set his phone down and leaned against the kitchen counter. "Listen," he said, exasperated. "Brad's numbers at the polls are still in the toilet from this Christmas cocaine party fiasco, which—let's face it—wouldn't have happened if Brad hadn't tried to save *your* marriage. Right now, we need voters' sympathy. If it seems like I'm exploiting this miscarriage, this tragedy, well, that's exactly what I'm doing. It's essential if we want to get voters to embrace Brad Corrigan again. We need to show the family sticking together in this crisis. We need you on board here, Brigg."

Bridget scowled at him. She hated when Jay called her "Brigg," as if he were family. And it unnerved her how he automatically knew her sons attended Lincoln Elementary School. Jay Corby had known where David's Little League game was held; and he'd known before her that she would be singing the National Anthem at David's game.

She remembered what Zach had said about someone in Brad's confidence who might be involved in these recent killings. Could it be Jay Corby? He seemed to know everything. Did he know about Gorman's Creek too?

Brad came back into the kitchen. "Brigg? Janice is asking to see you." He patted her on the shoulder as he returned to the breakfast table.

Bridget brushed past Jay and headed out of the kitchen. She went upstairs to Brad and Janice's bedroom. Brad had left the door open for her.

She paused at the threshold and stared at the empty, unmade bed. She half-expected to see some blood on the sheets, but Janice's pale blue, six-hundred-thread-count designer bedding was spotless.

Janice walked across the room. She must have been at her dresser. Fussing with her hair, she made her way back to the bed. For someone who had just suffered a miscarriage today, she moved with surprisingly little difficulty.

She didn't seem to notice Bridget standing in the doorway. But Bridget noticed something as her sister-in-law passed in front of the window in her champagne-colored, lightweight nightgown. She saw Janice's slender figure through the nightgown's flimsy material. The sight of her silhouetted frame—the round breasts and that flat stomach—was a shock, especially after weeks of seeing Janice in maternity clothes.

Janice started to climb into the bed. She turned toward the door, and her eyes locked with Bridget's for a moment. "God, don't creep up on me like that!" she said, quickly pulling the covers over her stomach.

"Sorry." Bridget took a couple of steps into the room. "Brad said you wanted to see me. How are you feeling?"

"Outside of losing my baby and enduring the worst cramps of my life, I'm just dandy, thank you." Janice positioned her pillow against the headboard and settled back in the bed. "What's all the fuss about downstairs? I heard arguing."

"It's nothing," Bridget said, rubbing the bridge of her nose. "Only Jay's giving me a headache. Do you mind if I steal an aspirin?"

She ducked into the master bathroom before Janice could answer. Switching on the light, Bridget closed the door. She didn't see any bloody sheets or underclothes soaking in the Jacuzzi tub. She checked the wastebasket. Nothing—except an old tube of toothpaste, a few tissues, and the cardboard center of a used-up toilet paper roll. The hamper was empty.

And Janice was supposed to have miscarried today— after nearly twelve weeks? It was either the most immaculate miscarriage in history, or Janice was lying. Was she ever really pregnant? She must have been, because she went to Dr. Reece for a few weeks.

Bridget found the aspirin in the medicine chest—along with a bottle of Valium, the old-fashioned, nonherbal kind.

"What are you doing in there?" Janice called.

Bridget put the Valium back on the shelf, then reached over and flushed the toilet. She took an aspirin and washed it down with some water. Emerging from the bathroom, she wiped her mouth with the back of her hand. "I needed to make a pit stop," she explained. "I was going to help by cleaning up in there, but it's already very tidy—not a speck of blood, not even a wrapped-up sanitary napkin to toss in the garbage outside."

"The doctor already took care of that," Janice said, eyes narrowed at her. "If you'd been here a couple of hours ago, when Brad was hoping you'd come, you would have seen quite a mess. But it's under control now."

Bridget gave a faint smile. "That's nice."

Janice readjusted the pillow behind her back. "You know, if you're sincere about wanting to help, you might cooperate with Jay and Brad—instead of arguing with them."

Bridget rolled her eyes and shook her head. "Well, I'm sorry, Janice. Maybe it doesn't make any sense to you. But this is the first day David and Eric have been back to school since their father was murdered. I want to be waiting for them when they get out of school in—" She checked her wristwatch. "Twenty minutes. I'm going to pick them up, drive home, and start cooking dinner for them—and Dad and Emma. My boys have been through enough these last few days. They don't need chauffeured limos and press conferences. They need to start feeling 'normal' again."

"But things aren't *normal*, Bridget," she shot back. "I've just lost a baby, for God's sake. And I know you don't want to hear this, but I hold you partially responsible."

"*What?*"

"When I should have been taking it easy, I've had to look

after *your* children. I've had to look after *your* father. And because you were so gung ho for me to make all these public appearances with Brad, I've had to perform for the press. I was under a lot of stress—"

"Oh, please, Janice. You can't blame me for that. I merely agreed with something Jay had suggested—"

"The reason we've all had to work so hard these last couple of days," Janice said, cutting her off, "the reason Brad's numbers dropped, and the reason he was at that stupid party with your husband's girlfriend—it all comes back to you. Doesn't it? You're the cause of this, Bridget. I can't believe you won't even acknowledge that. I lost my baby because of you. Really, you ought to be down on your knees, begging our forgiveness—instead of throwing this attitude around. You've been asked to do a simple favor. I don't understand. In the past, you've had no problem dumping your children on me. But suddenly, you're Mother of the Year, and you need to pick them up at school—"

"You are way out of line—"

Janice spoke over her. "Your brother bailed you out when you had nothing. He rescued you, and you owe him!"

"And I've paid him back. When he brought me on board, Brad's numbers went up. Brad's a wonderful, generous guy. But he wouldn't keep me on the payroll if I wasn't valuable to the campaign. And you know that's true. Sure, I've 'dumped' my sons on you, Janice. But it was only out of dire necessity—when I was helping Brad with his campaign. Believe me, I don't enjoy leaving David and Eric with you. I don't like the way you talk to them. And I don't like the way you're talking to me right now." Bridget shook her head at her sister-in-law. "You know something, Janice? I don't like you. At all. You're not a nice person."

Janice glared at her. "How dare you say that to me—after what I've been through today!"

"I do dare," Bridget whispered. "I dare, because I don't believe for one second that you suffered a miscarriage today. You're lying, Janice."

Bridget was trembling. She'd never spoken like this to her sister-in-law. Though a confrontation was long overdue, she didn't enjoy it. In fact, her stomach was turning.

"I don't know why you're lying," she muttered. "And I don't know what really happened. But maybe it's a good thing I don't."

She glanced at her watch again. "I'm getting out of here. I need to pick up my sons at school."

Bridget hurried out of the bedroom before she or Janice could say anything else. She saw Brad coming up the hallway.

"What's going on?" he asked in a hushed voice. "Jay and I could hear you all the way downstairs."

"A difference in opinion," Bridget said coolly. "I need to pick up the boys. Do you still want me to take Dad and Emma?"

"Yes, but . . ." He hesitated. "Couldn't you just stick around for the news conference and let the limo pick up David and Eric? Then you could—"

"No, I couldn't," Bridget replied, cutting him off. She edged past him and headed down the corridor for the back stairs.

"What the hell has gotten into you today?" he called after her.

"You know, you never told me what you were doing with Zach Matthias this afternoon. Is he the reason you're acting this way?"

Bridget stopped and turned toward her brother. "Irene canceled on lunch," Bridget lied. She stared at her brother and kept her voice steady. "Zach called and asked me to go for a drive with him. I think he genuinely likes me. And no, he's not the reason I'm acting this way. I'm just *reacting* to you, Jay, and Janice." She sighed. "Anyway, Zach and I were over by Mount Hood when you called."

Brad scowled at her. He didn't seem to believe her.

Bridget told herself it didn't matter what he thought. She turned away and headed down the stairs.

* * *

A dozen pink roses, wrapped in cellophane and tied together with a white bow, occupied the passenger seat of
Zach's VW Bug. He hoped the flowers would help him get
his foot in the door at Glenhaven Hills.

The Shell station attendant in Olympia had never heard of
the place. Nor did Zach get much help from the woman at
the register inside the Texaco Stop n' Sip. But they had a
phone book and a map of Olympia, so Zach figured out how
to get to Glenhaven Drive, a little buttonhook on the map—
off a winding, hillside trail called Old Summit Road.

Dusk was looming over the landscape by the time Zach
found Old Summit Road. He had a feeling the Tip Top Kwik
& Redi Mart at the base of the mountain highway was his
last vestige of civilization for a while. Switching on his
headlights, Zach started up the two-lane trail. Through the
trees, he could see the state capitol building below as he
climbed higher and higher. He tried to imagine Olivia zip-
ping up and down this lonely, narrow road on her way to and
from work every day.

He wondered what kind of "new information" Sonny
Fessler had told her about the Gorman's Creek incident. Had
Sonny witnessed the disposal of Mallory Meehan's body?
Had he seen someone walking her to her car? Or perhaps
Mallory had already been dead when she'd taken her last
ride in her mother's tan Volare.

For Zach, it didn't take a lot of guesswork to figure who
had disposed of Mallory's body and her car. He was convinced Brad Corrigan had lied to his sister about that. Bridget
said Brad couldn't have returned to Gorman's Creek and
gotten rid of the body before she'd driven back there in the
family car. Zach was pretty sure Mallory Meehan had pulled
herself out of that well. Bridget may have called out her name
several times. But Mallory would have had good reason to
ignore her. Bridget had already led her into one trap. Why
answer her call and be duped again? After Bridget had found
the well empty and fled the scene, her brother must have re-

turned there on his bike. He could have found Mallory. Perhaps there was an altercation and he accidentally killed her. Or maybe Brad used his charms on Mallory and convinced her to let him walk her back up that wooded trail to her car. Maybe he insisted she was in no shape to drive, and after loading his bike into the Volare, he would have driven her out of town to some remote spot. Once he killed Mallory Meehan, he would have gotten rid of her body and her car. Then he could have ridden home on his bicycle. That would explain why Brad had gone on a "bike ride" for over six hours that night.

Obviously, Sonny Fessler had seen part—or all—of what had happened, and he'd told Olivia Rankin about it. But Olivia had quit working at Glenhaven Hills over a year ago. Why had she waited so long before trying to peddle this "new information" to Fuller Sterns? Had she approached Brad Corrigan too? Was that why she'd been killed?

Zach imagined Olivia's murder setting off a chain reaction of killings by Brad or someone in his camp. Olivia's suicide, Fuller's car accident, Cheryl Bloom's freak mishap in the tub—they were all part of a housecleaning expedition. All the witnesses to the senatorial candidate's twenty-year-old crime were being eliminated. Part of that housecleaning must have included the "drug-related" murders of Gerard Hilliard and Leslie Ackerman. Hadn't Bridget said Brad was unhappy that she'd told her husband about Gorman's Creek?

Bridget didn't see any of this as a possibility. How could she—without acknowledging that her twin brother was a murderer?

Zach wondered what Brad had in store for her. She was the only other remaining witness to the Gorman's Creek incident. She was valuable to his campaign. But wouldn't her "untimely death" so close to Election Day win him thousands and thousands of sympathy votes?

Zach's ears popped as the VW Bug continued its ascent. Dusk had surrendered to night. The road had leveled off, and he passed about a dozen estates, all set back from the winding, tree-lined road. Zach kept looking for the turnoff for Glenhaven Drive. For five minutes, he drove by a dark forest preserve. He could hardly see anything past the beams of his headlights. He had to slow down, because too often the road took him alongside a cliff—with nothing but a short guardrail between his car and the sheer drop below. "Jesus," he muttered, keeping a tight grip on the steering wheel. "Where is this godforsaken dump anyway?"

Had he passed it? Was Glenhaven Hills one of those estates a few miles back? Zach had a sickly feeling in the pit of his stomach.

He saw some light ahead—by the side of the road. "Please be it, please be it," he whispered. Drawing closer, he saw a pair of open wrought-iron gates and a lamppost with a sign: GLENHAVEN HILLS. Beside the front gates stood a darkened guardhouse. Though no one appeared to be on duty, there was a camera trained on him.

Zach turned down the driveway, lined with trees and neatly pruned hedges. He studied the building at the end of the drive—a sprawling, three-story beige brick structure from the twenties. At least, to Zach, it looked like something out of *The Great Gatsby* era. There was a resemblance to the White House—with pillars in front of the main section, and two wings. Very stately. An ugly iron statue of three deer stood on a big stone pedestal on the lawn in front of the main doors. The grounds were well lit and beautifully maintained. Yet the place looked imposingly creepy. As Zach got closer to the building, he noticed two floors on the left wing had bars on the windows.

A black sign with gold letters pointed him to VISITOR PARKING, and he pulled into a lot by the facility's right wing. Considering all the secrecy about Sonny Fessler residing at this place, Zach had expected more security. Then again, it was only 6:20. They were probably between shifts, and just finishing up the dinner hour.

He parked his car, grabbed the bouquet of pink roses, and

stepped outside. Zach walked up a set of steps by a wheel-chair access ramp. He followed the paved pathway to the main entrance.

Zach stepped into the lobby, a comfy, spacious area decorated with rustic-chic furnishings. The sofas and easy chairs were covered with a Native American–patterned weave. Autumn-theme fake flower arrangements were strategically placed throughout the room, and a fire blazed in the stone hearth. The place resembled the lobby of a slightly cheesy mountain resort—except for the buzzer that went off as Zach stepped over the threshold. There was also a plump young nurse on duty behind a sliding glass window along one wall.

As Zach approached the window, he noticed a couple of cameras up near the ceiling.

The nurse slid the window open and smiled at him. She'd laid on the mascara a bit too thick, and had long blond hair in corkscrew curls. "Can I help you?" she asked.

Zach held up the roses so she could see them. "Yes, hi. I understand Olivia Rankin works here. Could I see her for a minute—if she isn't busy?"

"You want to see Olivia?"

He nodded eagerly. "Could you tell her Zach from McLaren High would like to talk with her?"

The chubby receptionist twisted her mouth to one side. "Um, I'm sorry, but Olivia hasn't worked here for about a year now. She—um, well, she doesn't work here anymore."

Leaning against the window frame, Zach tried to look appropriately crestfallen. "Is there anyone here who knows how I can get a hold of her? I've come a long way. See, Olivia and I dated in high school, and I haven't seen her in years."

She nervously cleared her throat and reached for the telephone. "Let me see if Monique has a couple of minutes to talk with you. She knew Olivia pretty well. Why don't you have a seat over by the fire?"

"Thanks very much," Zach said. Turning away from the

window, he looked up at one of the security cameras, pointed at him. A little red light was blinking beneath the lens.

"Monique?" he heard the receptionist say under her breath. "This guy's here, asking for Olivia. He brought flowers . . . No . . . No, I didn't have the heart to tell him. They were high school sweethearts . . . Well, you knew Olivia better than anyone else . . ."

Suddenly, the nurse poked her head out the window opening. "Um, Zach, if you'll just have a seat over there," she said, pointing to the sofa by the fireplace, "someone will be right with you."

He nodded, and then retreated toward the couch. He passed by a set of double doors and wondered if they led to the C Ward. He looked around for another door and saw another single door in the corner. A black placard with a single gold C on it was on the door. There was also a numerical security device by the door frame, the kind airports use for personnel-only areas. Zach realized that was the left wing, the one with the bars on the windows. If Glenhaven Hills was a combination rest home and sanitarium, as Sheriff Miller had said, then Sonny Fessler was residing in the sanitarium part. Zach wondered how they were going to get in there to see Sonny when he "doesn't take no visitors."

He sat down with his flowers and stared at the fake logs in the gas fireplace for a few minutes.

"Zach?"

He quickly stood up, and was a head taller than the short, round, coffee-colored nurse with shiny, ironed-flat shoulder-length hair. "I'm Monique," she said with a crisp Jamaican accent. "I used to work with Olivia."

Zach shook her hand. "Hi. I was hoping to surprise her. But I guess the surprise is on me. Do you know how I can get in touch with Olivia?"

With a sigh, Monique motioned toward the sofa. "Why don't you sit down, Zach? I have some bad news for you."

He put on a concerned, confused look, then sat down on the sofa arm. "What is it?"

Monique grimaced for a second. "Um, Olivia's dead. She committed suicide a few weeks ago."

"Oh my God," he murmured, gaping at her.

She shrugged. "I can't tell you much more about it. After she quit here last year, Olivia moved to Seattle and we fell out of touch. I'm sorry to be the bearer of bad news."

Zach shook his head. "I can't believe it," he said. "Could you—well, can you tell me what it was like working with Olivia?"

"I beg your pardon?"

He gave her the flowers. "Oh, here. Maybe you'd like these. Or you can give them to a patient. Maybe you can give them to Lon Fessler."

"Lon Fessler?" she asked, eyes narrowed at him. She tentatively held the bouquet of roses.

"Lon was this quirky guy from Olivia's and my old hometown," Zach explained. "This friend of mine who told me about Olivia working here said that Lon was one of her patients. Is he still here?"

"Yes," she replied, frowning. "Lon's still a patient here."

"I hate coming all this way for nothing," Zach continued. "I haven't seen Olivia since high school—twenty years ago. She was always a lot of fun. And she was no stranger to trouble, believe me. But she could be awfully sweet too. Can you tell me what she was like? Was she still the same girl I knew in high school?"

Monique shrugged. "I don't know what to tell you. Olivia and I weren't especially close. We just worked together."

"Anything at all that you remember," he said. "I just want to hear about Olivia. I know she was no saint. You don't have to sugarcoat it. Can't you tell me anything about her? Was she a good nurse?"

"Well, she wasn't a registered nurse," Monique said. "She was a caregiver." Monique glanced over her shoulder, then checked her wristwatch. "Listen, can you step outside with me? I want to have a cigarette."

They went outside. Monique set the roses down on a

bench by the front window, then pulled a pack of Marlboro from the pocket of her nurse's uniform. The three iron dee watched them as Monique lit up a cigarette.

"So—was Olivia a good *caregiver?*" Zach asked.

"Not really," Monique admitted, after a long drag on he Marlboro. "You want the truth about Olivia?"

He nodded. "Sure."

"Well, I don't mean to burst your bubble, Zach. But Olivi was kind of a screwup. Many of our regular patients com plained about her being rude and incompetent."

"So—they fired Olivia?"

"No, they put her in C Ward, where we keep the nutcase: The patients don't complain so much over there. And that when Olivia ran into Lon Fessler, and the girl fell into a tu of butter. They'd been on the verge of firing her, and sud denly they started treating her like the Queen of fuckin Sheba."

Zach let out a little laugh. It was startling to hear Moniqu say "fuck" in her precise Jamaican accent.

"The girl got to come and go whenever she damn wel pleased," Monique groused, puffing on her cigarette. "Sh could be an hour late for work, and no one raised an eye brow. She called in sick at the last minute, no sweat. The gave her a raise and more vacation time. I tell you, Olivi had it made."

"How did she rate this royal treatment?" Zach asked.

"Lon Fessler is how. The Fesslers donated nearly a mil lion dollars to this place. Lon is our number-one patien And Lon apparently liked Olivia. I have to be honest wit you, Zach. He was the only one here who liked her. She g away with murder, and the rest of us resented it. That in cludes several of the doctors on staff. Finally, the Fessle family lawyers got involved, and Olivia was offered a ver sweet buyout. I remember her bragging to all of us about i They gave her a full year's pay, plus another month of vaca tion. Last I heard, after moving up to Seattle, she wer through all that money in less than eight months. I don know if it went up her nose, or what." Monique took one last puff of her cigarette, then dropped the stub on the pavement and stepped on it. "Then the next thing I heard was a couple of weeks ago, when someone read in the newspaper that Olivia had shot herself."

"Did Olivia spend a lot of time with Lon?" Zach asked.

Monique leaned toward him. "Olivia spent a lot of time in the employee lounge. She claimed Lon liked her, which just goes to show how crazy he is. Anyway, Zach, I'll tell you this much about your old high school girlfriend. Olivia made me laugh sometimes. She had a wicked sense of humor. I didn't like her, but the girl could make me laugh."

"Did she tell you anything about Lon?" Zach asked. "Anything he might have said to her?"

Monique squinted at him. "Why do you ask that?"

"What's going on out here?"

A short, slight, balding man with glasses had come out the front door. He wore a navy blue business suit. Though he looked very meek, he had a prissy, authoritative tone. He scowled at Monique. "Ms. Wilson, why aren't you in B Ward?"

She grabbed the bouquet of roses from the bench. "This gentleman was a friend of Olivia's," she explained. "He thought she was still working here. I was just explaining to him that she's no longer with us."

"In more ways than one," Zach added glumly.

"You can go back to your duties now, Ms. Wilson," the officious little man said.

A uniformed security guard held the door open for her. Monique turned to Zach. "Thanks for the flowers," she muttered. Then she hurried inside.

The tall, stocky, pug-faced security guard stepped outside. He hovered behind the little man like a bodyguard. "I take it Ms. Wilson has already explained to you that Ms. Rankin doesn't work here anymore," the man said to Zach. "If you have no other business here, I think you should leave. We close the front gates here at Glenhaven Hills at seven o'clock."

"I was going to ask if you gave tours of the facility," Zac said. "It's such a beautiful spot—"

"Tours are only available by appointment, Mr.?"

"Matthias, Zach Matthias. Could I make an appointment Do you have a business card, Mr.?"

"I'm Mr. Jonas," he said, pulling a business card from in side his suit coat pocket. "All tours are private and arrange through me. If you call me during business hours, M Matthias, I'll see what I can do to help you." He glance over his shoulder. "Robert, will you escort Mr. Matthia back to his car? See that he's able to leave before lockin the gate."

"And then this goon of a security guard followed me the gate," Zach explained over the phone. "I don't think I ca show my face there tomorrow, not without raising th creepy little guy's suspicions."

"Then I'll just have to go there alone," Bridget whispere She sat on her bed with the phone to her ear.

The boys, Emma, and their grandfather were downstai parked in front of *Hoosiers* on cable-TV. Before dinner, they all watched Brad's press conference on the local news. Sl and her father had done their best to answer David's an Eric's questions. She'd cooked spaghetti, and everyone ha been rather subdued around the dinner table. Bridget ha been washing the dishes when Zach had called. She'd ru upstairs to talk with him in private.

"I'll drive up to Olympia tomorrow," she said into t phone. "I have all day. One of David's friends is having birthday tomorrow. His little brother is in Eric's class. S they've both been invited to go bowling after school, an then dinner and cake. I'm free until eight-thirty tomorro night."

"Well, I don't like the idea of you driving all the way there alone."

Bridget glanced out the bedroom window. She gazed down at the white Taurus parked in front of her house. She could ask for an escort, but the private detectives had been hired by Brad. Zack didn't want Brad to know about their interest in Glenhaven Hills. And now *she* didn't want Brad to know about it either. "I'll be all right," she told Zach. "I'll call this Mr. Jonas and schedule a tour tomorrow."

"Schedule it for late morning or early in the afternoon," he said. "You shouldn't be driving up and down that winding, hilly road at night. It's pretty dicey. Right now, I'm calling from the parking lot of this little dump at the base of the hill, the Tip Top Mart. I was glad to have made it here alive. I almost kissed the pavement when I got out of the car."

"I'll see if I can get in there before two," she said. "From what you tell me, this place would love housing the father of a senatorial candidate. I'll tell Mr. Jonas we're looking for a place for my dad. The name Corrigan still has some clout in that part of Washington State. I think Glenhaven Hills will open their doors to me."

"Well, see if you can't get them to open the door to Ward C," Zach said. "You might use your Corrigan clout to ask for a list of other residents. Then when you see Lon Fessler is there, maybe use the fact that you knew Lon way back when to get in to see him. It's a long shot, but worth a try."

"Brigg?" It was her father, coming up the second-floor hallway.

"I've got to go," she whispered into the phone. "Call you later."

Bridget was hanging up the receiver when her father poked his head in the bedroom. In his navy blue cardigan and madras shirt, he actually looked rather spry tonight. Bridget was surprised he hadn't nodded off in front of the movie yet.

"Who were you talking to?" he asked.

"Barbara Church," Bridget lied. "She's giving this birthday party tomorrow. The boys are going to it. How's the movie?"

"Terrific. There's a commercial right now." He let out a sigh as he sat down beside her on the bed. "How are you holding up, sweetie?"

"I'm okay, Dad," she replied, patting his bony thigh.

"You know, I couldn't help overhearing you and Janice going at it earlier tonight."

"Sorry," Bridget muttered, rolling her eyes. "I didn't know we had the volume up so high."

"Well, while you were rounding up the kids, I stopped in on Janice and asked what all of the ruckus was about. She told me. What makes you say she was—faking this miscarriage today?"

Bridget didn't want to get into this with her father. She sighed. "It's a lot of things, Dad. I mean, even at the press conference tonight, that holistic doctor said Janice was nine weeks pregnant. You and I both know it's been at least twelve. Why lie about something like that?"

Her father cleared his throat and glanced down at the bedroom carpet.

"She should have gone to a hospital today," Bridget went on. Now that she'd started, she couldn't stop. "Maybe that's why they said Janice was less far along than she's been telling us. A woman losing a baby after twelve weeks, there can be complications. That's not home-healing holistic stuff. I don't mean to be gruesome, but there should have been a lot more blood. I didn't even see a box of sanitary napkins in the bedroom or bathroom. And Janice was wearing a lightweight nightgown this afternoon. I could see through it when she was standing against the window. Janice looks more like she has spent the last twelve weeks in an aerobic class—not Lamaze. No one loses baby weight that fast. I don't know how she's been fooling Brad. But I think something happened about six weeks ago, when she suddenly stopped seeing Dr. Reece."

"That's when she lost the baby," her father whispered.

"What?"

Her father's shoulders slumped a little. He was still staring down at the carpet. He looked so forlorn and defeated. "It happened while Brad was out of town—in D.C. Janice was actually eight weeks along. The campaign was going so well. You were on board, and making a difference. And it certainly helped that everyone knew Brad's wife was pregnant. Janice didn't want to muck that up. She didn't want Brad to know. She was thinking about the campaign."

"That's crazy," Bridget murmured.

"That's Janice, doing what she felt was necessary to help Brad become senator," her father said. "She called up that gal who was at the house today, the home doctor on the news. She's a friend of Janice's. She took care of her, looked after Emma too. You talk about blood. We thought for a while we'd have to take her in for a transfusion."

"You were in on it?" Bridget asked. "You knew?"

He nodded. "We decided it would be best for the campaign if Janice went on being pregnant for a while. And then she'd have the miscarriage when it could do some good."

" 'When it could do some good?' " Bridget echoed, incredulous.

"Brad's numbers at the polls dropped drastically after that cocaine party lie, and they weren't bouncing back. But they should be back up very soon—now that the people know about Janice losing the baby."

Bridget stared at her father. "I don't believe this. Dad, how—how could you be so calculating? Who else was in on this? Does Brad know?"

"No, and don't say anything to him."

"Did Jay mastermind this?" she pressed.

"He doesn't know a thing about it," her father replied. "This is something your sister-in-law and I decided on. And I'd appreciate it if you lay off her for a while, Brigg. She's got your brother's best interests in mind. Hell, Janice even let you take the spotlight, because she realized how good you were for the campaign. If that isn't selfless, I don't know what."

Bridget shook her head. "I don't understand any of this. How could Brad not know? I could tell Janice hadn't been pregnant recently just by seeing her in her nightgown today. Is Brad blind? Don't they sleep together?"

Her father frowned. "They haven't for a long while."

She let out a stunned laugh. "Well, how did this baby happen?"

"It was an accident," he replied soberly. "It was someone else's. Once Janice found out she was pregnant, she briefly rekindled things with Brad. She wanted to have this baby. And she wanted him to think it was his."

Dumbfounded, Bridget numbly stared at her father.

"She was thinking about the campaign," he said.

"It's insane," she murmured. "How—do *you* know all this, Dad?"

"Janice confides in me. We think alike. We both want to see Brad succeed."

"She wants to see him succeed while she's sleeping around with someone else?" Bridget got to her feet and started pacing around the bedroom. "Who's the father?"

"It doesn't matter anymore, just as long as Brad keeps thinking it was his child."

Bridget couldn't look at her dad. She always knew her father was the one pulling the strings for Brad's political career. But she had no idea it went to this extreme. And her dad had found a kindred spirit in Janice. Poor Brad didn't know how much he was being manipulated by them. He truly wanted to do good in the world, help people, and make a difference. Yet the people closest to him were so ruthless and scheming.

"Is Emma his?" Bridget asked, finally.

"Of course she is," her father replied, sounding a bit annoyed.

"Well, I'm sorry, but I don't know what to believe anymore," she retorted. "That Christmas cocaine party, did it really happen the way Brad said? Or is that a lie too? Was he involved with Leslie?"

"Brad was telling the truth," her father said. "He didn't say anything to you about Gerry and Leslie, because he was looking out for your best interests. And in regard to what's been discussed here tonight, I don't want you saying anything to him—for the same reason. It's in Brad's best interest that he doesn't know any of this."

Rubbing her forehead, Bridget let out a sad laugh. "My God . . ."

"Brigg, I want you to promise you won't say anything to him."

"What about your *episode*, Dad, the one that landed you in the hospital? Was that faked too? Something you and Janice cooked up for voter sympathy?"

"No, it was real," he growled. He pushed himself off the bed and got to his feet. "I don't know how much longer I'll be around. That's one reason why Brad has got to win this election. I don't think I'll be here to see him try again. That's why you have to promise you won't say anything to Brad about this."

"Yes, we have to protect Brad, and make sure he succeeds," she muttered. "It's always been my purpose in life—as far as you're concerned. Isn't that right, Dad?"

"Promise you won't say anything to him," he pressed.

"I won't say anything. I don't want to hurt Brad." She stared at her father and shook her head. "But if you really think you and Janice are doing right by him, then I'd say your priorities are awfully screwed up, Dad. And I guess I should thank God that I'm the child you didn't give a shit about."

Gaping back at her, Bridget's father had that startled, feeble look on his face which made him look so old. With a shaky hand, he touched his right temple. "I'm tired, Brigg," he said, finally. "I'd appreciate a ride back to Brad's house, if you don't mind."

"Go on down and get ready," she said listlessly. "I have another call to make. I'll be down in a minute to take you and Emma home."

Bridget watched her father shuffle out of the room; then she sat down on the bed. She wondered just how far her father—and Janice—had gone to determine Brad would win the election. Did either one of them know about Gorman's Creek? Zach had said that someone in Brad's confidence might have been behind the recent murders. Was it her father?

She reached for the phone, then dialed a number she'd written down on a scratch pad several minutes ago. An answering machine picked up on the other end of the line. She was instructed to dial O if she wanted to talk with an operator. Instead, Bridget waited for the beep.

"Yes, Mr. Jonas," she said into the phone. "I'm Bridget Corrigan. My bother is running for senator here in Oregon. You might have read in the newspaper that my father was taken ill recently. He's recovering now, but I'm starting to look at rest home facilities. Glenhaven Hills has been highly recommended. I'm wondering if you have some time tomorrow in the morning or early afternoon to take me on a personal tour . . ."

Bridget left her home phone and cell numbers, then hung up the receiver.

She took a deep breath and got to her feet. She still couldn't fathom the conversation she'd just had with her father. Maybe it would all sink in tonight when she was trying to sleep. For now, she was just in shock.

She took another deep breath and wandered out of the room.

An empty bedroom.

He'd finished it—down to the last detail. Bridget Corrigan's bedroom was rendered from God's point of view on a thirty-six-by-forty-inch canvas. A lot of time and effort had gone into this piece so far, but the real work hadn't yet begun. That was tomorrow.

Right now, it was just an empty bedroom. But soon, he would fill it—with three bodies.

CHAPTER 23

He drove by her house. Brad's private detective was sitting in a white Taurus, parked in front of Bridget's cedar shaker. He could only see the detective's silhouette in the car, but knew the guy was looking at him. He wasn't sure whether or not the detective was the same one from the night before last. Maybe he recognized his VW Bug—and figured him for Bridget's stalker.

Zach wondered if driving by a woman's house at night on a semiregular basis was *stalking* her—especially when he was finally establishing a real relationship with her. Besides, this was more concern for her safety than an obsession. Okay, so he was a bit obsessed, but he also wanted to make sure Bridget and her sons were all right.

The drive back from Olympia had taken two hours. Zach had periodically checked his rearview mirror to see if he was being followed. Fuller Sterns had died in a car accident. Zach didn't want to meet the same fate. He knew he was on someone's hit list.

The break-in at his apartment yesterday was no random burglary. That man had been sent there to kill him. Zach figured if he hadn't walked in with Bridget Corrigan, he would have been a dead man. The intruder in *his* ski mask had slammed the butt-end of a gun on his head. But he hadn't touched Bridget. Obviously, Bridget Corrigan was not to be harmed—not yet.

So, after a brief, depressing dinner alone at a Subway in Vancouver, Washington, he'd driven on to Bridget's place to make certain she was okay. It was nine-thirty, and he could see some lights on inside the house. Brad's guard was on duty—and vigilant. Zach figured she was safe.

The guard seemed to be watching as Zach drove away. Zach thought about waving good-bye, but he kept both hands on the wheel.

Zach found a parking spot about a half block from his apartment complex. He didn't see any other vehicles slowing down or stopping on the street. No pedestrians either. He climbed out of the car and walked toward the U-shaped compound of old brownstone row houses. He saw a few lights on in his neighbors' apartments. But the neglected courtyard was still dark and gloomy—with only a couple of dim lights near the ground illuminating the walkway.

Zach glanced over his shoulder as he stepped into the courtyard. Every few units, there was a walk-through between the apartments. Approaching his own place at the end of the square, he kept an eye on those little passageways. Zach noticed the carriage lamp was broken above the alcove to the laundry room—two doors down from his apartment.

Something moved in that shadowy niche.

Zach suddenly stopped. He backed up, and then ducked into one of the walkways between the units. With his back pressed against the wall, he spied the laundry room foyer. After a few moments, a figure emerged from the dark alcove. Zach heard something crunch, and he realized the man had stepped on some glass from the carriage light he'd broken. It was too dark to see his face, but he was short and balding. He seemed to be holding on to something in the pocket of his windbreaker. He looked around the courtyard, then stepped back into the shadows.

Zach was almost certain it was the same man who had attacked him yesterday—the same build, the same quick little movements.

He kept his eyes glued to the laundry room alcove across the courtyard. Taking a step back, he nearly tripped over something. A cat let out a loud screech, then scurried around his feet and slammed into an empty garbage can. The lid fell off and hit the pavement with a loud clatter that seemed to echo through the apartment complex.

Zach ran for the opening at the other end of the passageway. It led to a fenced-in sidewalk area, where people set their garbage cans and recycling bins. There was even a plastic kiddy pool, tilted up against the side of the building. Zach ducked behind the plastic pool and caught his breath. He tried not to make a sound.

He heard footsteps, then a low, little cackle. "Hey there, kitty-cat?" the man called softly. "Kitty, kitty, kitty?"

Zach knew damn well he wasn't talking to the cat.

He slowly crept toward the end of the walkway. He heard a tinny clatter and realized the man must have accidentally kicked the garbage can lid in the passageway. Or was it an accident? Was he playing around with him—making a game of it?

Zach ducked into another walk-through and sprinted to the courtyard. Then he ran for the street. He quickly hid behind an SUV parked across from his apartment complex. His heart was racing. He watched the man emerge from one of the compound's alcoves. He stood in the middle of the courtyard, looking to his right and left. He kept his hand in the pocket of his windbreaker. He was grinning. "Hey, kitty, kitty, kitty," he called again.

Zach didn't move.

He thought the man might come out to the street, but he remained in the courtyard. After a few minutes, he retreated toward the laundry room alcove again.

Zach realized he wasn't going to leave his post—not until he'd accomplished his mission. The guy probably figured his prey would have to come home eventually.

But Zach wouldn't be going home tonight. He crept back to his VW Bug, started it up, and drove away. He didn't switch on his headlights until he was two blocks from his apartment complex. He kept checking his rearview mirror, and didn't see anyone following him.

Forty-five minutes later, Zach was standing in front of a vending machine by the ice dispenser in the Best Western Airporter Inn. He slipped two dollars into the machine, pressed a button, and watched the little overnight kit—disposable razor, toothbrush, toothpaste, and shaving cream—pop into the receptacle tray.

He would take his chances and go home in the morning.

"The fax was waiting for me last night when we got back from dropping off my father and my niece," Bridget said into the phone. "Mrs. Rankin scribbled a note on the cover page, saying she was grateful for our interest and it was nice to see us. Anyway, she sent Olivia's phone bill, and I recognized a few of the numbers Olivia called during the last couple of weeks of her life."

Bridget sat at her computer desk in the basement. The boys used the computer more than she did, which was evident from all the cookie crumbs, gum and candy wrappers, and the two empty Coke cans left on the desk. Between the small, high basement windows, David and Eric had plastered posters on the walls—everything from the Portland Trail Blazers to *Star Wars* to *Dodgeball*. There was also the older TV and a Foosball table to keep them entertained.

Bridget had installed the fax machine when she'd started working on Brad's campaign. The boys were under strict orders to leave it alone.

"Fuller's phone number is on here," Bridget continued, studying the faxed document. "Olivia called him four times. She called Brad's line at Corrigan-for-Oregon headquarters twice. Both times she must have left messages, because each call was less than a minute. And I got curious about this one number she called three times in the beginning of the month. Brief conversations, but she certainly must have talked to someone. I dialed the number and got Edna."

"Who?" Zach asked on the other end of the line.

"Edna, the woman who works for Anastasia Fessler," Bridget explained. "She's the one who answered when I phoned. You know, that loud, slightly crazy voice of hers? '*Fessler residence, Edna speaking*!' "

"That confirms what the nurse at Glenhaven Hills was telling me," Zach said. "Olivia had some kind of special connection with the Fesslers and their lawyers because she got chummy with Sonny. We need to find out what exactly he told her about Gorman's Creek."

"Mr. Jonas called me back this morning," Bridget said. "I'm getting a private tour of Glenhaven Hills at two o'clock today."

"I'll go up there with you," Zach said. "There's a camera at the gatehouse. But you can let me out before we get to the gate, and I'll wait down the road for you. It's a two-hour drive, so I'll come by your house around eleven-thirty. And I don't mean to freak you out or anything, but we have to keep something in mind."

"What's that?" Bridget asked warily. She put down the fax sheet.

"The 'new information' about Gorman's Creek that Sonny Fessler gave Olivia got her killed. We have to make sure the same thing doesn't happen to us."

"Well, Zach, thanks a lot," she said sarcastically. "That doesn't freak me out at all."

She heard him chuckle on the other end of the line. "I'll see you in about an hour, okay?"

"See ya, Zach," she said. Then she hung up the phone.

Bridget sat back and glanced at Olivia's phone bill again.

She heard a noise upstairs, and quickly stood up. It sounded like someone had bumped into something. Or was it just the house settling? Noises like that in the middle of

he day seldom bothered her before. But things were different now. She waited and listened for a moment. Nothing.

Bridget crept up the stairs. She checked the kitchen, the
den, and the living room. She glanced at the front door. The
dead bolt lock was still in place. For the last few days, she'd
been using the dead bolt all the time.

She glanced outside the living room picture window. The
guard, Scott, was standing outside his car, smoking a cigarette. He was a stocky black man in his early thirties. Scott
was all-business, and taciturn—almost to the point of gruff-
ness—but the boys were thawing him out.

He seemed to catch Bridget looking at him. He nodded,
and she waved back at him. Scott gave her a little smile.

Bridget told herself that she was going to be all right. For
the time being, she was going to be all right.

Zach pulled out of the parking lot of Elmer's Steak and
Cake House by the Best Western. He'd eaten breakfast there,
then talked to Bridget on the pay phone outside.

They would be in a car together for four hours today. He
needed to change his clothes. He'd been wearing them since
yesterday morning. Last night he'd showered at the Best
Western, but it had hardly done any good, since he'd just
climbed back into the same old clothes. He couldn't avoid
his apartment forever. And he felt safer going there during
the daytime.

Zach slowly drove around the block twice to get a good
look at his apartment complex. The maintenance man was
sweeping the courtyard walkway. Zach didn't notice anyone
else.

He parked the car a block away and looked over his shoulder several times on his way to the apartment compound.
Lester, the maintenance man, was in his late twenties and
something of a burn-out. Today, he had his long black hair in
a ponytail, and wore a jacket-vest over his short-sleeve

T-shirt, displaying the multicolored tattoos that complete[l]
covered both arms.

Listlessly sweeping the walkway, he glanced up at Zac[h]
"Hey, man," he muttered.

"Hi, Lester," Zach said.

"Some a-hole busted the light outside the laundry roo[m]
last night," Lester grumbled. "There was glass all over th[e]
place. Did you see who did it, man?"

"No. I wish I had," Zach answered. "But you know, some
thing weird is going around, because I couldn't get into m[y]
apartment last night. The lock's screwed up—or maybe it[']
my keys. Can you come take a look at it with me?"

Lester shrugged. "Sure."

Zach doubted his assailant would have stuck aroun[d]
while Lester was sweeping the compound. Still, he ke[pt]
glancing back and forth at the different walk-through pa[s]
sageways in the U-shaped complex as they approached h[is]
front door. Zach wanted someone else with him as he e[n]
tered his apartment. There was safety in numbers—even
his backup man was a perpetually stoned janitor.

He pulled out his key, then purposely fudged with th[e]
lock for a moment before he got the door open. "Hey, it[']
working," he said.

Lester just nodded and scratched his head.

Zach peeked inside his apartment. Nothing seemed [to]
have been disturbed, and he didn't see anyone. But he didn[']
want to take any chances. "Could you use a Coke?" h[e]
asked.

Lester let out a little laugh. "Shit, yeah, man."

"Hold on, I'll get it for you." Zach left him in the doo[r]
way. He went into the kitchen and grabbed a can of Coke o[ut]
of the refrigerator. He looped around and peeked into h[is]
bedroom and bathroom. Then he returned to Lester at th[e]
front door and gave him the can of soda. "Here you go, Les[.]

Lester frowned. "Oh, *a Coke*," he mumbled with disa[p]
pointment. "I get it. Well, thanks." He opened the Coc[a]

Cola, took a swig, then headed toward the front of the courtyard, dragging his broom behind him.

Four minutes later, the dead bolt was on the front door, and Zach was in the shower. It was the fastest, most frantic, most paranoid shower of his life. He kept the bathroom door open, and his map-of-the-world shower curtain half-open. Water was getting on the floor, but he didn't care. It was more important to have a clear view—in case someone was creeping up on him. He couldn't get it out of his head that Cheryl Blume had died in a bathtub.

He dried off and dressed in a hurry. For every minute he spent inside his apartment, it was another minute Zach felt he was pushing his luck. He wanted to be long gone by the time his assailant showed up.

He glanced out his front window before stepping outside. Lester was nowhere to be seen. Zach hurried through the courtyard. This was one of the few times he wished he owned a gun. Not that he was any match for someone who knew how to use one; still, having a gun right now would have given him a little peace of mind.

Zach breathed a bit easier once he was on the street—and out of the confines of that slightly dilapidated courtyard, where his assailant had set traps for him twice already. Zach headed down the sidewalk at a brisk clip.

For a moment, he couldn't see his car, and he slowed down. But then he realized his VW Bug was hidden in back of a big, old VW minibus. The other Volkswagen hadn't been there before.

Zach took another look over his shoulder, then continued toward his car. He reached into his pocket for the keys. Just as he passed by the minibus, he saw someone out of the corner of his eye. Zach spun around.

All at once, the little man grabbed him by the collar. The guy was almost a head shorter than him. Zach felt a surge of adrenaline rush through him. He drew back his fist and slugged the guy in the face.

The balding, muscular man barely flinched. "Fucker!" he growled.

All of a sudden, Zach felt something slam into his crotch. The little ape-of-a-guy had just kneed him in the groin. Zach could barely comprehend anything else beyond the excruciating pain. Doubling over, he tried to get a breath. He thought he might pass out.

"Hey, kitty, kitty, kitty," he heard the man say, followed by a low cackle.

Zach heard a car door opening. The man grabbed him by the hair. Still bent over in pain, Zach automatically moved where he was being led—into the back of the VW minibus. He couldn't see anything, and he still couldn't breathe. The man threw him on the floor of the backseat.

"There you go, kitty-cat."

Zach hit the floor with a thud that was mere muted pain compared to the utter agony overwhelming him. But his vision started to right itself, and he saw what was piled beside him in the back of the old minibus. His assailant had a shovel, a pick, a pair of thick rubber gloves, and a minidrum labeled with a hazardous material warning Zach couldn't quite read. But he was able to focus on the product name: *E-Z CHEM Lime Solution.*

Zach realized it was for him—or rather, for his burial.

Unlike the others before him, he wouldn't be the victim of an accident, or a suicide, or a murder. No, he would simply disappear. A shovel, pick, and one gallon of lime solution would help make that happen.

Zach let out a cry of protest. He tried to pull himself off the floor of the minibus. He saw the ape-faced man snarling at him. His lip was bleeding, and Zach figured he must have done that to him. The little man had something in his hand. It looked like a blackjack. "Shut the fuck up!" he growled.

Zach recoiled. He saw the leather-cased little weapon coming at him. It was the last thing he glimpsed before he fell back against the minibus's floor. Then it was only blackness—and one more sound.

"There now," he heard the man say through the thick darkness. *"There now, kitty-cat."*

"Okay, it's noon, and this is my second message for you. I'm officially worried."

Bridget was dressed in a black suit with a white silk blouse and pearls. The outfit smacked of affluence and good pedigree—the kind of qualities she hoped would help her get her foot in the door at Glenhaven Hills.

She was on the phone in the kitchen, throwing some last-minute things into her purse. "So where are you?" she continued—onto Zach's machine. "We were supposed to meet here at my house a half hour ago. Anyway, Zach, I need to leave now if I expect to make it to Olympia by two. Don't worry about me going alone. Scott, the private detective on duty here, he's driving me. I'll be all right. I'm just worried about you. Call my cell—or my house—as soon as you get this message. I'll keep checking in. Please, let me know you're okay."

Bridget clicked off the phone. She threw on her trench coat, grabbed her purse, hurried out the door, and double-locked it behind her.

"I'll ride shotgun," she told Scott, who was opening the back passenger door for her. "Unless you want me in back."

"Up front's fine," he said, shutting one door and opening the other for her.

"Thanks, Scott." She paused before climbing inside the white Taurus. "Promise me again, you won't tell my brother about this trip to Olympia."

"I said I wouldn't, and I won't," he replied, unsmiling.

"Good, thanks." She ducked into the passenger side.

Once they started on the road, she asked if he could swing by an address in the Hawthorne District. Bridget had only been to Zach's apartment once, but she was able to give Scott accurate directions.

Within fifteen minutes, she was walking up the courtyard

of the apartment complex. Scott was at her side. Bridge
knocked on Zach's door and rang the bell. She tried the door
Locked. She even peeked into the front window, but she didn'
see anything suspicious.

"Pardon me, ma'am," Scott said. "But if you want to
make it to Olympia by two, we're already running pretty lat
right now."

She took a piece of paper out of her purse and scribble
on it: *Where are you? Call me—B. 12:20.* She stuck the slip
of paper between the door and its frame.

Returning to the car, Bridget phoned Glenhaven Hills and
got Mr. Jonas. "My driver and I ran into some traffic here in
Portland," she explained. "We'll be arriving closer to two
thirty. I hope that won't be inconvenient."

Mr. Jonas said it would be fine. After she clicked off the
phone, Bridget turned to Scott. "Sorry about that 'my driver
crack. I was trying to sound rich and important."

Eyes on the road, Scott smiled a little. "You *are* rich and
important," he said. "Okay if I play some music?"

He popped in a tape cassette, and Vivaldi's *The Fou
Seasons* came on. Bridget hadn't taken him for a fan of the
classics. Then again, she didn't know Scott very well at all
In a way, she was glad it was quiet, brooding Scott driving
her to Olympia—and not the more friendly guard, Phil. She
would have felt obliged to make conversation with Phil. And
right now, all she could think about was Zach. He should
have called by now. Where in God's name was he?

Scott stayed quiet, kept his eyes on the road, and made
good time on the interstate. While passing through Longview
Washington, Bridget left her third message on Zach's cel
and home phones. Forty minutes later, in Centralia, she
checked her home line for any voice mails from him. Nothing
Bridget phoned Zach again when they reached Olympia
This time, she hung up when she got the machine.

She'd printed directions to Glenhaven Hills off the com
puter. When Scott drove past the Tip Top Kwik & Redi Mar

at the base of Old Summit Road, Bridget knew they were close. Zach had called her from that spot last night. He'd been right about the winding, hilly road up to Glenhaven Hills. Bridget felt her ears pop just before the road leveled off. "Should be along here some place," she said, glancing at the Mapquest.com printout.

Her stomach had been in knots for the last three hours, because she was worried about Zach. It was even worse now, and she felt sick with nervousness. She had a half-baked plan for getting in to see Sonny Fessler and wasn't sure she could pull it off.

They turned onto Glenhaven Drive and drove past the gates. Bridget gazed at the beige brick building at the end of the long, tree-lined driveway. It looked stately, yet a bit sinister too. Something about those iron deer in front of the main entrance gave her the creeps.

"Can I go over this again with you?" she asked Scott.

"Yes, ma'am, suit yourself," he replied, watching the road.

"You'll call my cell phone a half hour after I step inside the place," she said. "If I can't sneak away while I take your call, you'll need to phone the front desk and ask for Mr. Jonas."

Scott nodded. "I ask for Mr. Jonas. It's an emergency concerning one of his patients. Matter of life and death. I can't call back."

"And once you get him on the phone—"

"I'll ask him a lot of questions about the hospital and keep him on the line as long as possible. I know." He pulled into the parking lot. "I'm a private detective, ma'am. I do this kind of shit all the time."

She gave him a nervous grin. "Thanks, Scott. I don't know how long I'll be in there. It may be an hour—maybe two."

"I'll be waiting," he said.

Scott parked the car, then hopped out of the driver's side

and got the door for her. "I'll walk you into the lobby," he said. "It'll make you look even more respectable. And be sure to dismiss me in front of him."

Bridget nodded. "Thanks, Scott," she said again.

They started up some steps by a wheelchair-access ramp. Bridget paused along the walkway to the main entrance. She pulled out her cell phone and tried Zach's number one more time. She got a recording again. "Damn," she muttered, clicking off the phone. "Where is he?"

With a sigh, she put the phone away and let Scott escort her to the main doors.

He heard his cell phone go off.

Zach opened his eyes and saw only blackness. He realized an old blanket was covering him from head to toe. He wanted to pull it off, but his arms were asleep. He couldn't move them—or even feel them. Every part of him ached, and he felt sick.

He stirred restlessly and managed to shake the blanket off his face. For a moment, everything was blurry. He felt as if he were a kid again—without his glasses.

Even before things came into focus, Zach realized what had happened to him. The blanket had been covering him—so no passing truckers and minivan drivers would see him on the floor, in the back of that little creep's VW minibus.

They must have been driving over a bumpy road. He kept getting jostled back and forth. Even with the blanket, he felt cold, and Zach realized that somewhere along the line, after knocking him out, the goon had stripped him down to his T-shirt and undershorts. He couldn't feel or move his arms because the blood wasn't circulating in them. When the guy had taken away his clothes, he must have also tied his hands behind him. Zach's feet were tied up too. And his shoes were gone.

"Your girlfriend just called again," said the man at the wheel. "You awake? You still out, numb-nuts?"

Zach didn't answer. He thought he might be better off playing possum—until he figured out what to do. His vision began to correct itself. He looked up at the minibus's windows and saw trees looming above. They seemed to be in the mountains some place. Obviously, that was where the guy planned to bury him—in a mountain forest.

Zach looked around for the shovel, the pick, and the drum of lime solution. Maybe he could use something to defend himself—once he wiggled out of the binding around his wrists and ankles. But all the burial apparatus had been shoved to the far back of the minibus—out of his reach.

Frustrated, he looked beneath the seats for something that might have accidentally dropped under there. Nothing.

Zach tried moving his hands back and forth. It felt like tape around his wrists. It pulled and pinched at the hairs above his hands. He turned on his side and tried to reach back for the tape around his ankles. All the while, he did his damnedest not to bump into the back of the driver's seat. He had to bend and make contortions within such a limited space. He merely grazed the tape around his ankles with his fingertips.

"I feel you moving back there, fuck-face," the man said in a singsong, chiding tone. "Have a good nap?"

Zach froze. He didn't answer him.

"Well, just sit tight, asshole. We're almost there."

Zach kept trying to scratch at the tape around his ankles. All the while, he heard the man in the front seat humming. The car seemed to accelerate. Zach looked up at the minibus's window and saw the trees whooshing by.

He told himself that he wasn't going die in some god-forsaken woods. He wasn't just going to disappear. That might have happened to the very first victim from the Gorman's Creek incident. But it wasn't going to happen to him.

CHAPTER 24

She looked for Sonny among the Glenhaven Hills residents wandering around the neatly manicured grounds. An iron "nature sculpture"—obviously by the same artist as the deer monstrosity in front—desecrated the back lawn. This piece had two huge bears on a stone pedestal. One bear was on all fours, and the other stood on its hind legs with a fish in its mouth.

A croquet game was heating up on the lawn. Along the winding trail, Bridget noticed nurses pushing people in wheelchairs. There was a cluster of old ladies, huddled by the dahlia garden with their kneepads, spades, work gloves, and sunbonnets—even though the skies were overcast. About a dozen senior citizens sat in wheelchairs on the back veranda, but Bridget didn't see Sonny Fessler among them. Of course, she might not be able to recognize him without his hunting cap and his Schwinn. And he was in his seventies now.

"Have you ever seen a more beautiful setting?" Mr. Jonas asked. He was a persnickety little man with glasses and a blue three-piece suit. "These grounds stretch nearly a half mile. If your father likes to take walks, this is the place for him. What you see here is just a preview to the many activities that we have at Glenhaven Hills. Would you like to take a look at our nature trail?"

Bridget glanced at her wristwatch. Scott was supposed to call her cell phone in five minutes. "No, thank you," she said. She'd adapted a slightly haughty, *please-me* tone with Mr. Jonas. She hated the snooty way she sounded. But he seemed to lap it up, and hung on her every word.

"You're right though, it's a perfectly lovely setting," Bridget continued. Then she turned toward the building. "I'm very impressed with what I've seen so far. But I'm wondering about that area with the bars on the windows. You haven't shown me that wing yet, have you?"

"No, but your father wouldn't be staying there. That's Ward C, where we house residents who need constant, special attention. The bars on the windows are just a precaution. We needn't concern ourselves with that particular area." He turned and made a sweeping gesture with his hand. "During the summer, we have picnics on this lawn. If you—"

"Actually, I'd like to take a look at Ward C," Bridget interrupted.

"I beg your pardon?"

"Well, in addition to looking for an assisted-care residence for our father, Brad and I are also looking for a private institution in which we can invest a—well, a rather *sizable* donation. I'd like to see *all* of Glenhaven Hills."

Mr. Jonas seemed a bit perplexed. "I'm sorry, Ms. Corrigan, but we're simply not prepared for a tour of Ward C. We don't—"

"Are you implying that you have to *make preparations* for tours here?" she asked. "You're not hiding anything from me, are you?"

"Of course not," he said.

She gave him a cool smile. "Mr. Jonas, I'd hate to tell your board of directors that my request for a complete tour here was denied."

His eyes narrowed at her from behind his glasses. "No,

we wouldn't want that, Ms. Corrigan. If you'll follow me, I'll take you to C Ward. We have nothing to hide here at Glenhaven Hills."

Bridget glanced over at the section of the building with the bars on the windows, then followed him into the building.

She was running late, and hoped Scott's call wouldn't come until she was well inside C Ward. She'd planned to use the call as her excuse for "a little privacy"; then she would slip away from Jonas and start looking for Sonny's room, 9-C.

Jonas led her down a long corridor. "You'll find the conditions in Ward C are no different from Ward A," he said. "But the residents in C Ward have special needs and special problems."

"Are some of the patients there mentally ill?" she asked, stealing a look at her wristwatch.

"Some are challenged in that area, yes," he allowed.

Bridget wondered if Sonny Fessler would even be able to communicate with her—once she found him. Maybe he was catatonic—or in a padded cell somewhere.

"I'm going to ask that you remain close by my side for this part of the tour, Ms. Corrigan. We don't want to disturb any of the residents." He stopped by a closed door and punched some numbers in the keypad by the door frame.

Bridget tried to sneak a look at the code. Out of four numbers, she only caught a 1 and a 7.

The lock clicked, and then Jonas pushed the door open and held it for her. Ward C smelled more like a nursing home than the other wing—bedpans and body odor. It was also at least five degrees warmer in there, almost oppressive. The hallway had tan linoleum tile on the floor, and starkwhite walls. Bridget heard a TV going in one of the rooms. The only other people in sight were a nurse and an elderly man whom she led down the corridor. He wore a striped robe and kept rattling his head back and forth as if he had a spasm.

As Mr. Jonas closed the door behind him, Bridget noticed another keypad by the door frame. She wondered how she was going to slip away after talking to Sonny. "So—you can't get in or out without the code?" she asked.

"That's correct," he said. "Not without setting off a security alarm in our control center."

"What if there's a fire or some other emergency?" she pressed.

"Then the doors automatically unlock," he said. "This way, please."

He led Bridget down the corridor. She looked at the room numbers by the doors as she passed. C-32 . . . C-30 . . . C-28. Some of the doors were open. The units were different from the little studios in Ward A, which resembled snug one-room apartments. These were hospital rooms—with hospital beds, some of which had fleece-covered wrist and ankle straps to restrain the patients. From the grounds, she'd seen the bars outside the windows. But she hadn't noticed that inside, chain-link-fence-style screens prevented the patients from getting at the windows in their rooms. There were no mirrors in the rooms either. Obviously, the residents in Ward C weren't trusted around glass.

She didn't see any raving maniacs. Most of the patients strapped in their beds—or slumped to one side in their wheelchairs—were quiet and docile. Bridget noticed another corridor that branched off this one, and a small placard on the wall: C-1 THRU C-9.

Her cell phone went off. "Oh, pardon me," she said, reaching into her purse. She pulled out her phone and glanced at the caller-ID pad. "Oh, I really need to take this in private," she said, edging toward the other hallway. "Do you mind?"

"As a matter of fact, I *do* mind, Ms. Corrigan," he replied in an officious tone. "Use of cell phones is prohibited here inside Glenhaven Hills."

"Oh, well, then I'll make it quick." She clicked on the phone. "Hello—"

"Ma'am?" Scott said on the other end of the line.

"Ms. Corrigan!" Mr. Jonas hissed. "Please!"

"Um, I'm sorry," she said into the phone. "Call back later."

"Call *you* back?" Scott asked. "Or call his number?"

"Yes, call the other number and leave a message for me."

"You mean, leave a message for *him*?" Scott asked.

"Yes. Thanks very much. Good-bye." She clicked off the phone and shoved it back in her purse. She smiled at Mr. Jonas. "My apologies. I'm afraid the more we tend to use our cell phones, the ruder we become to those around us. Do you have an activities room in this ward? If you do, I'd like to take a look at it."

Jonas gave her a pinched smile. "Why, certainly."

He began to lead her down the hallway—in the opposite direction from C-1 through C-9. Bridget glanced back at the other corridor, where Sonny Fessler had his room. She reluctantly followed Mr. Jonas. At least she would know where she might look for Sonny if he wasn't in his quarters. So far, she'd passed several empty rooms. She heard a TV set blaring, and figured they were getting closer to the activities room.

Mr. Jonas abruptly stopped in his tracks. "Excuse me," he muttered. "I'm being paged." He pulled the little pager off his belt, and then glanced at it. He must have had the mechanism on vibrate, because Bridget hadn't heard a sound. "I need to answer this," he grumbled.

"First, could you point me to the restroom?" she asked.

"There's an employee restroom near the nurses' station, where I'm answering my page," he said. "It's just this way."

"Terrific. Thank you."

They continued down the hallway toward a nurses' desk. He stopped, took out a set of keys, and unlocked a door marked STAFF ONLY. "Here you go, Ms. Corrigan," he said. Then he nodded toward the counter only a couple of doors farther down the hallway. "I'll be right over there."

"Thanks," she said, ducking into the bathroom. She closed the door behind her. She'd been hoping to give him the slip, but the damn nurses' station was less than forty feet from the bathroom door.

Bridget glanced around the small, white-tiled lavatory—one toilet, one sink, no other door, and no window. With a sigh, she turned the knob and pulled the door open half an inch. She peeked through the crack—toward the nurses' station. Mr. Jonas was leaning on the counter with the phone to his ear. He was staring right back at her.

She shut the door again. "Shit!" she whispered. She waited a few moments, then pried the door open another half inch and peeked toward the nurses' station again.

Mr. Jonas was fussing with a spot or something on his tie while he talked on the phone. Bridget could hear him: "Who? What kind of emergency? Well, all right, put him on."

She waited until he turned away. Then Bridget opened the door wider. Still eying him, she crept out of the restroom—and almost ran right into a heavyset woman. Bridget let out a gasp.

The woman was about sixty, with gray-brown hair and listless eyes. She wore a periwinkle-blue robe. "Have you been inoculated yet?" she asked.

Bridget quickly shook her head, then ducked inside an empty room.

"There's someone here who hasn't been inoculated!" the woman declared. "We have a young lady here in our hallway and she hasn't had her inoculation! This is serious! No one should be allowed here without the proper documentation and an inoculation. . . ."

Bridget held her breath and listened to Mr. Jonas on the phone, trying to talk over the woman. "Well, what kind of emergency are you talking about?" he said loudly. "What's the name of the patient? Just a second—Sandra, can you take her down to the activities room? I can't hear myself think. Now, which patient has the emergency?"

Bridget poked her head out of the doorway. Jonas was on the phone—with his back to her. A nurse was walking the hefty, middle-aged woman farther down the hallway. Bridget stepped out to the corridor and crept in the opposite direc-tion—toward the wing of rooms marked C-1 THRU C-9. As she turned the corner, she glanced back at Jonas one more time to make sure he hadn't seen her. He was facing her, but still on the telephone and fussing with his tie again.

Bridget hurried down the hall to room C-9. The door was open just a few inches. She tried to catch her breath, and then knocked softly. No one answered. She knocked again. After hesitating for a moment, she pushed the door open all the way.

Sonny wasn't there.

"Oh no," she whispered. She couldn't go looking for Sonny in the activities room, because she'd have to walk past the nurses' station—and Jonas—to get there. He was proba-bly off the phone now, and wondering why she was taking so long in the lavatory.

Bridget heard footsteps behind her. She quickly hurried inside Sonny's room and closed the door halfway. She lis-tened to the footsteps coming closer. Then, whoever it was passed by. Sighing, Bridget turned and took a look at Sonny Fessler's quarters.

The room had bars on the window—and the chain-link screen so he couldn't touch the window. But that was where the similarity to the more dreary, hospital-like rooms in Ward C ended. Bridget felt as if she'd stepped into a time warp—and into the bedroom of a young boy in the early fifties. On the walls were framed prints of ships, railroad en-gines, and several black-and-white shots of Guy Madison from the old *Wild Bill Hickok* TV series. There was also a photograph of Mrs. Fessler, the same one the *Cowlitz Country Register* had printed when they'd run the story about her sui-cide. None of the frames had glass in them.

On the bureau, she noticed another glassless framed photo, which seemed anachronistic compared to the others. It was of Christopher Reeve as *Superman*. Also on the bureau were a View Master with several round slides, an antique piggy bank, and a bust of Lincoln. The bust looked like bronze—

until Bridget touched it and realized it was made of cheap plastic and had a coin slot on top of Lincoln's head.

There was also a stuffed rocking chair with a throw pillow that had a hula girl on it. The bedspread on the half-made bed was off-white—probably from age and wear—with a mallard design. At least there were no restraint straps on the bed. The room smelled awful—like sour milk.

Bridget noticed a series on the Old West from Time-Life Books on his bookcase. She pulled out one of the volumes and found an old *Playboy* from 1984 hidden between the books. Sonny must have smuggled it out of his old bedroom—from the Briar Court house. Most everything in this room had probably come from there.

She returned the book to the shelf and tucked the *Playboy* back in its hiding place. Then Bridget wandered over to the window. Past the interior screen and the outside bars, there was a sweeping view of the grounds. She thought about Sonny in his old bedroom with its view of Gorman's Creek. How much had he seen from that window?

Bridget heard the door creak open behind her, and she swiveled around.

Staring back at her was an unshaven, gray-haired man in a pale blue cardigan sweater and dilapidated madras slacks that hit him at the ankles. He was wearing a pair of beat-up tennis shoes. He smiled at her. His milky blue eyes appeared a bit vague. He wasn't wearing his hunting cap or his old merit badge. But Bridget recognized Sonny Fessler.

Zach's hands and wrists were bleeding.

For the last fifteen minutes, he'd picked and scratched at the tape around his ankles until he'd managed to shred a section of it. He didn't dare tear it off all at once, because that would have made a ripping sound, and the creep in the front seat would have heard. Zach still hadn't spoken a word to him. But the guy kept taunting him every few minutes: "I know you're awake back there, asshole . . . You aren't fooling me . . . Don't you want to know where we're going? C'mon, fuck-face, talk to me. . . ."

So Zach tore the tape off his ankles a little section at a time. It hurt like hell—slowly pulling the hairs off his lower legs. But he kept thinking that he wasn't going to die somewhere in these woods. He wasn't going to let that malignant little creep put a bullet in his head and call him "*fuck-face*" or "*asshole*" while he was doing it. Those weren't going to be the last words he'd ever hear.

Zach was able to break the heavy-duty electrical tape around his ankles. Some of it still clung to one ankle, but it didn't matter as long as he could move his legs.

He was working on the tape around his wrists now—and it was a far more delicate and painful task. Because the guy in front was so short, he'd pulled the car seat up close to the wheel—leaving the back part of the runner-grooves on the floor exposed. The edges were sharp. Zach tried to slice at the tape by rubbing against those grooves. But he kept cutting his hands and wrists in the process. Blood covered the tape and ran down his arms.

The road was rough and full of potholes. He got thrown around the minibus's floor several times. "Hey, feel that last one, numb-nuts?" his driver asked, over the sound of gravel and rocks deflecting off the underside of the vehicle.

A section of the tape was in tatters, and he kept wiggling his wrists and trying to pull his hands apart. He could feel it loosening. But he also felt the minibus slowing down. Zach looked up at the window, and saw the trees looming overhead. They were deep in the forest, driving on a dirt road now—he could tell. He worked frantically to tear the tape apart.

The minibus came to a stop.

"What the hell are you doing back there?" his driver asked. He switched off the engine.

Zach kept trying to slice at the tape. Sweat was running down his forehead—into his eyes. He heard the front door open. The little creep was humming.

The tape broke. Zach turned and twisted his wrists to free them.

The door opened behind him. Zach looked up. From his perspective, the ape-faced man was upside down—and slightly out of focus. But Zach could see he had a gun in his hand, and he was smiling.

"C'mon, asshole," he said. "You and I are going for a walk."

"Hi, Lon. I don't know if you'd remember me, but I'm Bridget Corrigan—from McLaren."

Sonny stared at her with a dazed, childlike smile frozen on his unshaven face.

"I—I came to visit you," Bridget continued. She stayed by the window screen. She didn't want to step toward him—for fear she might scare him away. "I hope you don't mind visitors. I wanted to talk with you."

"You're the lady they're looking for in the hallway."

Bridget swallowed hard and nodded. "Could you close the door? I don't want them to spoil our visit. I—I came such a long way to see you, Lon."

"It's against the rules to close the door—unless we're in our rooms with a doctor or nurse." He glanced over his shoulder, suddenly distracted.

"Is someone coming?" Bridget whispered.

He nodded.

"Please, don't tell them I'm in here!" Bridget said in a hushed voice. She rushed toward the opposite corner of the room—so anyone poking their head in the doorway wouldn't see her unless they actually stepped into the room and turned toward that corner. Bridget pressed her back against the wall.

"Lon?" Bridget recognized Mr. Jonas's voice. "Did you see a lady around here? She's wearing a black suit and a white blouse. She's very pretty with brown hair."

Sonny looked at her and giggled. Then he turned toward

the doorway again. "No, I didn't see any lady around here."
He turned toward her once more and grinned.

Bridget shrank against the wall.

"Okay, thanks, Lon," she heard Mr. Jonas say distract-
edly. "Good Lord, I can't believe this . . ." His voice faded—
along with his footsteps as he moved on down the corridor.

"Thanks for covering for me, Lon," Bridget whispered.
"Only—I think they'll be coming back. Do you know a
place where we can sit and talk, where no one will disturb
us?"

His face lit up. "Like a secret place? I have a secret place
where I go, and no one knows about it."

"You do?" Bridget managed to smile. "Well, that would
be good, Lon. Do you think we could get there without anyone seeing us?"

He nodded eagerly, then took hold of her arm. Bridget let
him lead her toward the door. He glanced up and down the
hallway. "The coast is clear!" he whispered. "Come on!"

He pulled her across the empty corridor to a stairwell
door. It had a punch-code keypad by the doorway frame. Without hesitation, Sonny pressed four numbers, then pushed the
door open. He chuckled.

Bridget ducked into the dim, cinder-block stairwell. "You
knew the code," she murmured.

Sonny nodded. "I've been here a long time. I know a lot
of the codes. I peek over their shoulders when they don't
think I'm looking."

Bridget glanced around—at the cement stairs, and the
harsh pools of light at every landing. It was a gloomy, cold
place. She backed away from the door and leaned against the
banister. "Well, I guess we can talk here."

Sonny shook his head. "Oh, but there's a nice room down
in the basement, and no one ever uses it. That's my secret
place. We can go and talk there. They have a candy machine
and a machine that makes hot chocolate. Do you like hot
chocolate?"

Bridget nodded. "Sure."

He gave her a shy smile "I   I'll buy you a hot chocolate)kay?"

"Well, thank you. That's very sweet, Sonny   I mean, .on."

His face seemed to light up. "I like being called *Sonny*. It nakes me feel like I'm back home."

Bridget's heart broke for him. "Then *Thank you, Sonny,* 'd love some hot chocolate."

"Okay. I'll just get some quarters I saved in my bank." He urned toward the door.

She reached out and grabbed his arm. "Oh no," she whis-•ered. "You don't have to do that. I'll treat you."

He scowled at her. "You said you'd let *me* buy it," he said, aising his voice a little.

"But I don't want to take any chances—"

"I'll be right back," he said. "I promise. Cross my heart." Then he opened the stairwell door and stepped out to the allway.

Bridget waited alone in the dismal, windowless stairwell.)n the other side of the door, she heard footsteps in the all—then a woman's voice: "Lon, we need you in your oom. The security people are looking for someone, and the allways have to be cleared."

Biting her lip, Bridget listened for Sonny's response, but he didn't hear anything. There were more footsteps. It ounded like a few people. "Well, she couldn't have gotten •ut of C Ward without setting off an alarm," she heard Mr. onas say. He seemed to be right on the other side of the loor. "I can't understand how she could just wander off like hat."

Someone mumbled a suggestion to him. Bridget only eard part of it: ". . . unless we check every room."

"I doubt it," Jonas replied, sounding annoyed. "Wait a ninute. I don't know why I didn't think of this before. Let ne borrow your cell phone . . ."

Bridget crept closer to the door. Now Jonas was mutter-ng something under his breath. ". . . then maybe she can tell

me where the hell she has wandered off to," she heard hi
say.

"In the meantime, we'll start a room-to-room search
the east end of C Ward, and we'll work our way—"

Suddenly, her cell phone went off. Startled, Bridg
bumped against the cinder-block wall. The phone was insid
her purse, but the sound still echoed in the stairwell. She r
alized Jonas was just on the other side of that door—callin
her.

Hugging the purse to her chest to muffle the soun
Bridget quickly crept down the stairs to the next landin
Once far enough away from the door, she opened her purs
and switched off her cell phone. The silence was glorious–
but probably too late. They certainly had to have heard th
phone go off. Bridget tiptoed down a few more steps unt
she was in the stairwell's shadows. She gazed up, waiting t
see if they'd come. She listened for the stairway door t
open, but there wasn't a sound—only a mechanical hur
from some machinery in the basement, maybe the furnace c
a boiler.

Bridget didn't know how long she waited, but she bega
to get a crick in her neck from looking up toward the first
floor landing. Was it possible they hadn't heard her phone
She was beginning to think they hadn't, when she heard th
stairwell door's lock click. A shaft of light hit the gray cinder
block wall. Bridget froze. She saw someone's shadow mov
across that wall—until the door closed again, and darknes
wiped away the image.

"Hello?" Sonny Fessler called in a timid, quiet voice.

Bridget let out a sigh. "I'm down here, Sonny!" she whis
pered.

He peeked over the banister and smiled at her. "Hi. I'r
coming down to meet you."

Lon crept down the stairs. "There's a couple of guards i
the hall looking for you," he whispered. "I had to wait unt
they were gone. C'mon, follow me."

He opened the basement door, and a mechanical roa

greeted them. Bridget wasn't sure if they were in the furnace room or the boiler room—or both. There were several big contraptions that resembled hot water heaters, and they made a loud racket. The place was dimly lit and hot—at least eighty degrees.

Sonny took her hand and pulled her along a grated walkway. Following him toward a door at the end of the long room, Bridget was glad she had on her low heels today. She tried to ignore the uneasy feeling in the pit of her stomach. Here she was in a dark basement with a mental patient. She kept having to remind herself that Sonny Fessler was harmless.

They stepped into a long, empty hallway with yellow walls. Sonny pulled her past a couple of janitor's closets, then stopped at another door, put his ear to it for a moment, and slowly opened it. Except for a couple of lighted vending machines against one wall, the room was dark. One of the machine lights must have had a short, because it kept flickering. "This is the janitors' break room," Sonny whispered. "Only they don't use it much."

He switched on the fluorescent overheads, but one of them wasn't working—so half of the room remained dim, except for that strange flickering light. There were two small, high windows—with no view outside because of some bushes. The furniture was old and broken down: a worn sofa, a tattered easy chair, and a portable TV with a bent antenna. Some Gary Larson *Farside* cartoons had been taped on the yellow walls—along with scribbled reminders that were posted: KEEP THIS ROOM CLEAN, TURN OFF LITE WHEN THRU! and NO SMOKING. A large table and five mismatching chairs were near the vending machines. Sonny gestured toward a chair, and then quietly closed the door behind them.

Bridget sat down near the head of the table, while Sonny fished a couple of quarters out of his pocket. "They have good hot chocolate here," he said.

The HOT COFFEE! machine looked like something out of the sixties. It was the one with the faulty light. The other machine had Twinkies, chips, pretzels, and chocolate bars—al of which had to be beyond their expiration dates.

"You don't want coffee or chicken soup, do you?" Sonn asked. "They have those too, but the hot chocolate is th best."

"Well, I'll have that then," Bridget said. "Thank you Sonny."

He seemed to get a big kick out of putting the coin in th machine, making his selection, and watching the little card board cup fill up. Biting his lip, he carefully brought the ho chocolate to the table and set it in front of her. The cup had playing card design on it—some tie-in with a *collect then all* poker contest.

"So, Sonny, you didn't say whether or not you remembe me from McLaren," Bridget said, while he got some ho chocolate for himself. "I'm Bridget Corrigan. You know Brad's twin sister?"

He was so intent on the workings of the vending machin that he didn't seem to be listening to her. "Don't drink you hot chocolate just yet, because it can be awfully hot," he saic carrying his cup to the table. Sonny sat down next to her a the head of the table, and he chuckled nervously. "Could yo check the hall and make sure no one's coming?" he asked. " thought I heard someone."

Bridget hadn't heard anything—except the old vendinj machine cranking out hot liquid. She shrugged. "Sure Sonny." She got to her feet and went to the door. She opene it, then peeked up and down the hall. No one.

When Bridget stepped back into the break room, she sav Sonny fanning the vapors from her cup of hot chocolate fo her. "We're okay for now," she said, returning to her chai "Thank you for cooling it off for me. You're a real gentle man, Sonny."

He blushed, and chuckled. Then he leaned over his cu; and blew into the hot chocolate.

"You know, I was friends with Olivia Rankin," Bridge said. "Do you remember Olivia? She used to work here."

He nodded. "Yes, she was blond and kind of fat."

"Did you spend much time talking with her?"

"Oh yes. We even had hot chocolate down here once, but she had coffee instead."

"What did you talk about with Olivia?"

He shrugged. "Stuff." He went back to blowing into his hot chocolate.

"Did you talk about *stuff* that happened in McLaren?"

He nodded. Then he sipped his hot chocolate, and winced. "Ouch, too hot, too hot!" he said, fanning his mouth.

"Are you okay?" she asked.

He nodded, then sighed.

"Did you talk about Gorman's Creek?"

"I lived right by there," he said.

"I know. You probably saw a lot of things that happened there. Remember the night you and I stood outside your house, watching the police look for Andy Shields and the Gaines twins?"

"They had flashlights," he said. He blew into his drink again.

"That's right. Do you remember anything else that might have happened in those woods?" Bridget leaned closer to him. This close, she could see the dandruff in his receding gray hair—along with the food stains on his cardigan sweater. "Do you remember a girl named Mallory Meehan?" she asked.

"She was the fat girl who was mean to me," he muttered, pouting. "She yelled at me. She was just as mean as those boys, only she didn't throw any rocks at me."

Bridget frowned. "What boys? What are you talking about, Sonny?"

"She fell down a well," he said.

Bridget reached over and took hold of his hand. "That's right. Mallory fell down a well. Then you saw it. What happened after that?"

"Well, I really didn't see her fall in, but I heard some noise by the old house. Then I saw her climb out of the well."

"And you told this to Olivia?" she asked anxiously. "You were there?"

He nodded.

"What happened then? After Mallory climbed out of the well, what happened?"

"She was crying," Sonny said. He took another sip of his hot chocolate, and this time he smiled. "This is good. Try some."

Bridget took a swig of the hot chocolate. It scalded her mouth, and tasted awful, but after her initial grimace, she worked up a smile. "Delicious. So—what happened after Mallory pulled herself out of the well? You said she was crying."

He nodded. "She was limping too. I think she hurt her foot. I came up and asked her if she needed help. And she started to call me names again, and telling me to stay away from her." He sipped his hot chocolate. "I used to carry my Boy Scout knife with me for emergencies. They won't let me keep it here, but I had one back then. Anyways, the fat girl kept yelling at me and calling me names. So I took my hunting knife and cut her throat."

Sonny sipped his hot chocolate again, and then he licked his lips.

"So—are you working for Brad Corrigan?"

"Yeah, that's right, asshole." The short man chuckled. "I work for ol' Brad. You cold? Well, don't worry. You'll be working up a sweat soon."

Zach was shivering. Shoeless, and dressed only in his T-shirt and undershorts, he walked in front of the ape-faced little man. They'd left the VW minibus parked off a dirt road along the mountain ridge. At gunpoint, Zach had obediently wrapped the digging tools in the blanket, then started along a crude, overgrown path through the forest. The guy had loaded the drum of lime solution and thick gloves into a bag. He carried the bag in one hand and held a gun in the other.

Zach dragged the blanket on the ground behind him, hoisting it up every once in a while. The pick and shovel kept clanking against each other, and their four-foot wooden handles stuck out of the blanket's folds. Zach guessed that no one had used the trail in weeks. His feet were killing him—blistered, bleeding, and near-frozen.

The little creep was right. Zach was indeed working up a sweat, but he was still cold and shivering. He kept telling himself that he wasn't going to be killed in these woods. Exactly how he would get out of this, he wasn't sure yet.

"What's going to happen to Bridget Corrigan?" he asked, staggering along the trial.

"Oh, I wouldn't worry about your girlfriend," he heard the man say. "You two will be together again soon enough."

"Brad's going to have her killed too?"

"Let's put it this way, she's as good as dead."

Zach glanced over his shoulder for a second, then moved on. "That doesn't make any sense—unless Brad is waiting for the 'right time.' You could have killed us both when you broke into my apartment the day before yesterday, but you didn't. That was you, wasn't it?"

"Smart guy. Go to the head of the class."

"Why didn't you kill us both then?"

"I was only waiting for you. She wasn't part of the equation."

"And yet, she's going to die anyway?" he asked, stopping for a moment.

"Get moving, asshole."

Zach forged on through the woods. "What's going to happen to her? What's Brad planning?"

"Huh, Brad Corrigan has no control over the situation," the man replied. "There's no hit on her. We're only supposed to watch her. But my work partner has a crush on your girlfriend, and that's bad news for her."

"What are you talking about?" Brad asked warily.

"I've seen it happen before. He gets obsessed and goes off on his own. We had a job together down in San Diego a few years back. This attorney needed to disappear. And my pal got a hard-on for the guy's eighteen-year-old daughter. He started following her around, and even set it up so he could 'accidentally' meet her and talk with her. And all the while, he was sketching her. That's his thing. He thinks he's this great artist. Anyway, he ended up killing this girl, broke her neck. Then he hung her from a ceiling beam in her parents' living room. Police thought it was a suicide. So he painted her like that—in her bra and panties, hanging from her neck. Quirky son of a bitch."

"What does that have to do with Bridget Corrigan?" Zach asked.

"Maybe you're not as smart as I thought." Zach heard the man chuckle. "I just told you, numb-nuts. My pal has got it bad for your girlfriend. He's already sketched her at least fifty times. He set up an accidental meeting with her too. He slashed her tire, then helped her on the roadside. He even got me to play along on that charade. Paid me five hundred bucks. Talk about crazy, all this elaborate planning, just so he could talk to the bitch. You should have seen him with his hands in his pockets half the time to hide his hard-on. He could have killed her that night, but it's not how he wanted to paint her."

Stopping, Zach turned around and stared at him.

The short, ape-faced man nodded. "Keep moving. We're losing our sunlight. Veer to the left. There's a clearing up ahead."

Zach's teeth started to chatter. He pressed on. "What— what's he going to do to her?" he asked. "How is he going to—*paint* her?"

"Why do you care?" the man replied. "You'll be dead."

Zach staggered into a clearing—a little bald spot in the forest. Through the trees, there was a beautiful, panoramic view of the mountains.

"Okay, this is good, right here," he heard the man say. "Start digging."

* * *

"*You* killed Mallory?"

Sonny nodded sheepishly. "Are you mad at me?"

She stared at him and shook her head. "No, Sonny," she whispered. "I'm just trying to understand." She stole a glance at the door. She was much younger than him—and much faster. But Bridget wasn't going to run out of there—not until she found out exactly what had happened on that night twenty years ago.

"Don't you like your hot chocolate?" he asked.

She sipped a little more. "It's great, thank you. So, tell me what happened after you—you killed her?"

"Then *you* came by with a flashlight. So I dragged her into the bushes and hid."

"And you heard me calling for her," Bridget said.

He nodded. "After you left, I dragged her to her car. She was awfully heavy. I knew it was her car, 'cause of that time she started yelling at me outside the supermarket. I remembered how she came out of that tan car and called me a 'retard.' I'm not retarded." He stopped and gazed at her cup of hot chocolate—and then at her.

Bridget drank some more. "What happened after you took Mallory to her car?"

He smiled. "I found the keys in her pocket, and I put her on the floor in the backseat. Then I—then I . . ." Sonny seemed to be getting excited as he told the story, and he couldn't catch a breath. "Then I got my bike and loaded it in the trunk, and I drove out of town. There's—there's this marsh outside of town. I took my bike out, and I—I pushed the car into the marsh. I did it all by myself too."

"You drove?" Bridget asked. "You can drive?"

"Yeah. It's a secret." He chuckled. "I don't have a license. But I taught myself to drive."

Numb, Bridget stared at him. "Did you—ever drive to the Oxytech plant outside of town?"

He nodded shyly.

"You said earlier that some boys threw stones at you. Were they the Gaines twins and Andy Shields?"

"The twins were the mean ones. I told them they weren't allowed in the forest, and they threw rocks at me and called me names. So—I hit them, real hard, and knocked them out. I wasn't going to hurt the other one, the one with red hair, but he kept screaming. So I hit him too. And while they were sleeping, I tied them up and took their shoes so they wouldn't run away."

"That night you met me outside your house and we watched the police look for those boys, you knew all along where they were."

Nodding, he smiled at her, and then he had another sip of hot chocolate.

"You'd already taken them to the railroad yard in that deserted plant, and you'd killed them," Bridget whispered.

He nodded again. "Aren't you going to drink your hot chocolate?"

Bridget took a swallow. "Mallory was right then," she murmured. "You killed those boys. Did you talk about this with Olivia?"

"Yes. I told her just like I'm telling you."

Bridget felt a little dizzy. It was all starting to make sense. Yet her head was whirling. This was the "new information" Olivia had tried to sell to Fuller. How did Fuller put it? She had "stuff that would rip the lid off what went on at Gorman's Creek." Olivia couldn't tell Fuller—or Brad—that this new information actually exonerated them from a crime they thought they'd committed twenty years ago. If she'd divulged what she knew, Olivia couldn't have hoped to make money off them. So she was holding out.

Bridget remembered the sad, hopeless look on Anastasia Fessler's face as she and Zach left her house yesterday. Anastasia knew. It explained all the secrecy behind where they'd sent Sonny. And obviously, Olivia had contacted Anastasia after getting an earful of Sonny's activities in

Gorman's Creek. She was tapping Anastasia for money—and special treatment at Glenhaven Hills.

Bridget felt a little sick. The room felt as if it were spinning. Sonny kept looking at her with those guileless, milky blue eyes. Behind him, the light from the coffee machine continued to flicker. She thought of something that made her laugh—and the same time, tears welled up in her eyes.

She and Brad, Cheryl, Fuller, and Olivia—they were all innocent. They hadn't killed Mallory. And Mallory had been right about Sonny all along. Bridget used to regard him as the town's Boo Radley. But he was really the town's Ed Gein.

"Was there anyone else, Sonny?" she heard herself ask. "Did you kill anyone else in those woods behind your house?"

He nodded. "All together, nine people. I buried three of them, and no one ever found them. And these two teenagers, this boy and girl, I hung them from a tree. . . ."

Bridget squinted at the feeble old man next to her. Sonny's voice seemed to be coming at her through a fog. She wished the light behind him would stop blinking. "My God, Janette Carlisle and Frank Healy," she murmured. "You must have been—around their age, seventeen, eighteen . . ."

"I caught them swimming without any suits on in our pond," Sonny said. "They were naked. And he got real mad when he caught me peeking. He called me all sorts of names, and he even hit me . . . and she was laughing at me . . . but I'm not a pervert . . . told them . . ."

Bridget felt herself drifting off. What was wrong with her? She couldn't focus, and Sonny's voice kept drifting in and out. She reached for the hot chocolate—for a jolt of *something*.

Then she saw the eager look on Sonny's face. He giggled. "Are you tired yet?" he asked. He reached over and touched her hair.

Bridget would have shrunk back, but she realized she couldn't move. She had another awful realization. This mental patient who had killed nine people—some of them, children—had put something into her hot chocolate. No wonder he was so anxious for her to drink it. She remembered how—after serving up the hot chocolate—he'd asked her to check the corridor.

Bridget sat there in a stupor while his hand moved down from her hair to her shoulder to the front of her blouse. "Sometimes they give me pills to help me sleep," she heard him say through the fog. She tried to focus on him against the sputtering light. He was smiling. "I saved some of my pills for you, young Corrigan lady."

She let out a moan of protest and started to shake her head. "No . . ."

He pulled his hand away, then reached inside his shirt pocket. "Look what else I have."

Bridget felt herself slipping away. She could barely focus on what he'd taken out of his pocket. Her body was shutting down. She felt so helpless.

Just before she lost consciousness, Bridget saw the razor blade in his hand.

CHAPTER 25

The ground in the forest clearing was hard. Swinging the pick, Zach had spent a half hour breaking apart the topsoil. Then he'd gone to work with the shovel for another hour. Now he stood in a narrow hole that was about two feet deep. At the edge of the pit, the ape-faced goon looked down at him with the gun in his hand and a smug grin on his face.

The sun was setting, and a chilly wind kicked up. Zach felt goose bumps rise under the clammy layer of sweat that covered him. His back ached from all the digging. He'd lost the feeling in his toes, and his feet stung. Both his heels were bleeding, because he often had to use the bottom of his bare foot to force the shovel deeper into the ground. His executioner seemed to enjoy watching him wince in pain every time he had to give the shovel that extra push.

Zach still wasn't sure how he was going to get out of this. He hoped to come up with something before this guy ordered him to stop digging.

He needed to catch him off guard. One little distraction and he could pitch a mound of dirt in his ape face and charge him with the shovel. But whenever Zach glanced up, the man was staring down at him—and smirking. He seemed to know his vigilance was being tested.

"Listen," Zach said, hoisting a pile of dirt over his shoulder. "If I'm going to die anyway, why not just tell me? What's he planning to do to her?"

"Oh, give it up already, numb-nuts. I told you, she's as good as dead. Leave it at that."

"So why not tell me what he's going to do to her? It's not like I'll have far to go—carrying the secret to my grave."

The goon chuckled. "Good one. For that, I'll give you an honest answer. I don't know what the hell Clay has planned for your girlfriend—"

"*Clay?* He's the painter? The artist?"

"Likes to think he is. Anyway, I figure he's going to finish her off tonight—or tomorrow. Hell, maybe he's even doing her right now—I fucking hope so. It's getting to the point at which she's all he thinks about, and he's useless. He went AWOL on our last job, because he was so preoccupied with that Corrigan bitch. It's why he's not here with us now. Like I told you, I've seen it happen to him before. He's not going to focus on anything else until she's dead—and he can paint her."

Zach stared at him and shook his head.

"Keep digging, asshole. You'll be able to rest soon enough. Huh, *eternal* rest."

Zach went back to work with the shovel. "So—what's Brad Corrigan going to say?" he asked. "Don't you think your employer will be upset when his sister ends up dead?"

The man didn't answer. Zach glanced up at him.

"What makes you so sure I work for Brad Corrigan? Keep digging."

"It's a pretty easy deduction," Zach replied, scooping out another mound of dirt. "Brad needs me to disappear. I've been asking too many questions about Mallory Meehan and Gorman's Creek."

Zach scooped up another shovelful of loose earth and hurled it over his shoulder. "That's quite a body count you and your buddy Clay have going," he remarked, breathing hard. "The newspapers said the 'drug-related' murders of

Bridget's husband and his girlfriend looked like a two-man job. Makes sense now. And it must have taken the two of you to set up Fuller Sterns in that car crash. What about Olivia and Cheryl? Were you both working those jobs?"

"We handled the girl on the beach together," the man grunted. "Clay wanted to paint her, so he's the one who shot her. But I fried that juicy bitch in the tub all by myself. Like I told you, Clay went AWOL on that hit. He was too busy finalizing plans for your girlfriend."

"All of this because Brad Corrigan wants to be senator," Zach muttered with disgust. "So he has to get rid of everyone who was there at Gorman's Creek twenty years ago, everyone who knows about his crime—"

"A little less talk, and a little more work, asshole."

Zach ignored him and kept muttering to himself while he dug. "And now, one of the apes he hired to pull these hits has decided to go off on his own and murder Bridget. Jesus—"

"I told you to shut up, fuck-face."

"Hey, hit man," he retorted, glaring up at him. "You can call me *Zach*, okay? Calling me *fuck-face* or *asshole* every time you address me is getting kind of old. You're a walking cliché of your profession, using that kind of defense mechanism."

"What the hell are you talking about?"

"I'm talking about you, and the little tricks of your trade. You're trying to maintain this contempt for me, so it'll be easier to kill me. Hit men and professional burglars fall back on that to ease their consciences."

The little man let out a defiant laugh.

Zach went back to digging. "I read an article about it in a psychology magazine. It's why some burglars trash a house when they rob it. By having contempt for the victim, it justifies what they're doing. Even if I'd been your good friend up to this point, you'd suddenly start calling me *fuck-face* and *asshole* right now—so it'll be easier to put a bullet in my brain without feeling bad about it."

"That's fascinating, asshole."

Zach felt something sting his shoulder. It burned. Wincing in pain, he suddenly straightened up. He realized the guy had just thrown a small rock at him.

"That's just a defense mechanism too, *Zach*," the man said. "Now shut the fuck up and keep digging."

Zach rubbed his shoulder and went back to digging his grave. It dawned on him that he'd just missed an opportunity. The little creep must have taken his eyes off him for a couple of moments to pick up that rock. Zach figured if he could make him angry again, the guy might go looking for another rock. Then maybe he could catch him off guard.

"So—do you have a name, hit man?" he asked, shoveling the dirt.

His executioner didn't respond. Zach glanced up. The man just smirked and shook his head.

"C'mon, you have a name, don't you?" Zach went on. He kept staring up at the guy while he dug. "Or maybe a nickname? *Monkey Man?* Did anyone ever tell you that you look like an ape? Well, actually, you look more like a real *short* ape—a chimp."

The man let out an irate laugh. "That's right, funny man, keep it coming . . ."

"Did the kids in school call you *Cheetah*?" he said, scooping up another mound of dirt. "Or maybe *Bonzo*?"

"Fuckin' asshole," the man muttered. He looked down at the ground, then bent down and started to pick up a rock.

Zach swung the shovel upward. Dirt flew in the air. Zach connected with the backside of the shovel and hit the man square in his ape face. He heard a hard smack and felt a jolt vibrate through the shovel handle.

The man howled in pain. It was like the sound of a wounded animal—echoing through those woods. Blood gushed from his nose and mouth. Somehow, he'd managed to hold on to the gun. He waved it erratically and staggered back from the grave. He wouldn't stop screaming. The man cursed at Zach between his anguished cries.

Zach started to charge toward him with the shovel.

A shot rang out, and then another.

The screaming abruptly stopped. And the forest was quiet again.

She swallowed, and it felt as if she had ground glass in her throat.

Bridget tried to move, but she couldn't. Her body was still asleep. She was somewhere between a terrible nightmare and consciousness. She wanted so much to wake up. She hated this helpless, paralyzed, *trapped* feeling. Bridget wanted to scream, but no sound came out.

The last thing she remembered was this same awful, powerless feeling—and Sonny Fessler showing her a razor blade.

Now she was in a bed—somewhere—and someone had stripped her down to her bra and panties. Her head was aching, and she was afraid to swallow, because it hurt so much.

"Ms. Corrigan? Bridget? Can you hear me? Bridget?"

Her eyes fluttered open. She realized that she was in one of the more "homey" hospital rooms Mr. Jonas had shown her in Ward A of Glenhaven Hills. Bridget suddenly sat up. Her head throbbed.

A wry-faced nurse with white hair was hovering over her. "You'll be okay," she said, adjusting the pillow behind her. "Just take it easy." She gently pushed Bridget back against the pillow, then pressed a button that raised the mattress up to a sitting position.

"Oh God," Bridget murmured, rubbing her head.

"I've got you covered," the nurse cooed. She put a cold washcloth on Bridget's forehead, then reached for a plastic tumbler of water on the side table. She bent the flexible straw in the tumbler and raised it to Bridget's lips. "Wet your whistle first. Then I have some aspirin for you—industrial strength."

Bridget drank, took the pills, and then drank some more. All the while, she looked at a woman, seated in an easy chair across the room. She was about fifty-five with short blond hair and a still-attractive, suntanned, sun-wrinkled face. There was something very elegant about her—or maybe it was just her black suit and the Hermes scarf. She seemed to be studying Bridget.

"What time is it?" Bridget asked, her voice hoarse. "How long have I been out?"

"A couple of hours," the nurse said. "It's just about five-thirty. You sit still, and I'll get you some coffee." She headed for the door.

"Um, I have a man who drove me here," Bridget said, half sitting up. "He's—"

"He's in the lobby," the nurse said. "He knows you're all right. I'll be back with your coffee in a jiff."

"Thank you," Bridget said, taking the washcloth off her head.

"Get me a coffee too, will you, Cecilia?" the woman finally piped up. "Industrial strength."

"Okeydoke," the nurse replied. Then she ducked out of the room and closed the door behind her.

Bridget took another sip of water and noticed her purse on the night table. She grabbed it, opened it up, and pulled out her cell phone. There were three new messages—all the same area code, 360. She listened to the voice mail. It was Mr. Jonas, asking where she was.

Frowning, Bridget dialed her home phone to retrieve her messages. Nothing. No one. Zach still hadn't called.

She sighed, tossed the phone back in her purse, and set the bag on her nightstand. Then she locked eyes with the woman who sat across the room from her.

The woman leaned forward in the chair. "So—how are you feeling, Ms. Corrigan?"

Bridget put the cool cloth on her head again. "Lucky to be alive, I guess. Did they—pump my stomach? It sure feels like it."

"No, you pumped it for them. Apparently, you were out for a few minutes. Then you suddenly came to, stuck your finger down your throat, and threw up. Talk about survival instincts. Your clothes are down in the laundry right now. They should be done soon. Anyway, you scared the hell out of Sonny."

"Well, Sonny scared the hell out of me," Bridget muttered. She tried to smile. "I'm sorry. Who are you?"

"You don't recognize my voice?" the woman said. "I should be offended, Bridget. Or would you rather I call you *Cheryl*?"

Bridget squinted at her.

"Cheryl Matthias of Blooms Floral in Longview?" the woman said. "That was you who called my office yesterday trying to get an address for Sonny Fessler, wasn't it? Talk about a red flag. I knew there was going to be trouble after that call. Sure enough, just when I thought I'd sneak out of the office early today, I get a call from Glenhaven Hills. And I had tickets to Benaroya Hall tonight too. Anyway, ninety minutes later in rush-hour traffic, here I am."

She got to her feet and walked over to Bridget's bedside. She grabbed Bridget's hand and shook it. "Rachel Towles, Bard and Mitchell Associates. I'm the attorney for the Fessler family—and Glenhaven Hills."

The nurse returned, pushing a cart with a thermal pitcher, two cups, a creamer, and packets of sugar. She poured their coffees for them and announced that the doctor wanted to give Bridget another quick examination before they sent her home.

"Where's Sonny?" Bridget asked, setting aside the cool cloth.

Rachel gave the nurse a look. "Thanks, Cecilia. Give us a few minutes, okay?"

She waited until the nurse left and closed the door behind her. Then Rachel took a deep breath. "Sonny's back in his room in C Ward. And he's very sorry. He told us everything that happened."

"Well, maybe you can tell me," Bridget said over her coffee cup. "I missed part of it. Last thing I remember was Sonny showing me a razor blade. What did he do with it?"

"He carved your name on the tabletop," Rachel replied, frowning. "And I'm sorry, you might as well know. Sonny admitted that he touched your hair. He also touched your breasts over your blouse. According to Sonny, he was cutting off the buttons to the front of your blouse when you suddenly woke up—and made yourself vomit. Like I told you, it scared the hell out of him. Sonny ran back up to C Ward and confessed everything to Mr. Jonas.

"Apparently, he gave you four sleeping pills. The doctor who examined you earlier thinks you got them out of your system. But I wouldn't operate any heavy machinery for the next few hours if I were you. I know that ruins your plans to drive a forklift tonight, but that's the way it goes."

Bridget gave her a pale smile.

The Fesslers' attorney shrugged uneasily. "Anyway, they found the missing buttons from your blouse. They're sewing them back on down in the laundry."

Bridget nodded. She took another gulp of coffee. Her head and throat were feeling a bit better. "Did Sonny tell you what we talked about?" she asked.

Rachel frowned. "Yes. Sonny can spin some pretty fantastic stories—"

"Something like this happened before with Olivia Rankin, didn't it?" Bridget cut in.

Rachel nodded. "Sonny mentioned you were a friend of Olivia's."

"We weren't that close," Bridget admitted. "Olivia was hitting up Anastasia Fessler for money, wasn't she? She'd gotten an earful of Sonny's 'fantastic stories.' So Olivia received special treatment around here for keeping quiet—and finally, they gave her a nice severance package. But that wasn't enough for her, was it?"

Rachel glumly shook her head. "How do you know all this?"

"A friend of mine did some snooping yesterday. Olivia's mother faxed me a recent phone bill. Olivia was still calling Anastasia only a few weeks ago. What happened there?"

Rachel took a sip of coffee. "We advised Ms. Rankin to stop harassing our client."

"And when Olivia didn't stop, you had her killed," Bridget murmured.

"God, no," Rachel replied, staring at her as if she were crazy. "She committed suicide. And that was practically three weeks after we last talked to her."

"What kind of talk did you have?"

Rachel Towles let out a wary sigh. "When we first started dealing with the 'Olivia situation,' we had private detectives following her—investigating her. After several months, we let her know that we had enough on her to—ah, well—put her on the receiving end of what she was doing to the Fesslers. That's when we had Glenhaven Hills offer her a generous severance package. When Olivia started contacting Anastasia again last month, we tactfully reminded her that she was in no position to threaten us. And that was the end of that."

"What kind of information did you have on her?"

"Let's just say, Olivia Rankin was no saint, and we had enough on her that she took us very seriously. No reason to go into it now. No reason to speak ill of the dead."

Bridget just nodded, then sipped her coffee.

"Sometimes, keeping things secret is the best choice," Rachel Towles said, getting to her feet. "Sonny told you some stories tonight—stories about people who have been dead for a long, long time. Anastasia Fessler and this rest home would rather not have these stories repeated."

"But they're not just *stories*," Bridget argued. "Sonny didn't make all that up. *He killed nine people.* They had families—"

"Many of whom have since died or moved on with their lives," Rachel Towles interjected. Then it must have been the lawyer in her who quickly added: "That is—*if there is any truth to Sonny's stories.* Listen, Bridget. Do you think these families really want to relive their tragedies from over twenty years ago—all so a seventy-one-year-old mentally ill man can stand trial? Where do you think Sonny would end up?

They'll put him in a sanitarium. What difference would it really make? Sonny would just have to endure much worse living conditions, and the state would be paying for him to stay there. This way, if you forget about what happened today and what Sonny told you, then at least he'll remain comfortable here at Glenhaven Hills, where his sister pays for his room and board. And no one is hurting."

She put her hand on the side rail to Bridget's hospital bed. "Ms. Corrigan, I want to apologize for what happened to you. This incident you've just had with Sonny is a very isolated case. He's really harmless. He's kept in a private, locked area of this facility. What happened today was an exception. We'll learn from it. We'll change the codes and keep him on a tighter leash. Please, Ms. Corrigan, forget about what happened today—and what Sonny told you. I assure you, he's never going to leave this place. It's his prison, and it's his home."

Bridget tipped her head back against the pillow. "You know something, Ms. Towles? You're a pretty damn good lawyer. Could you give me twenty-four hours to deliberate?"

Rachel Towles seemed to work up a smile. "Sure, take all the time you want," she said. "Sonny isn't going anywhere."

No service available came up on the cell phone's little screen.

Standing in the forest clearing, Zach looked out through the trees—at the mountain wilderness. He'd figured he wouldn't have any cell phone service out here, but it was worth a shot.

He glanced down at the half-naked man, lying beside the unfinished grave.

Norbert J. Siegel was still breathing—bloody and unconscious, but breathing. That second hit in the head with the shovel had knocked him out. Zach wasn't sure if Norbert J. Siegel was the little ape's real name, but that was what it said on the driver's license and credit cards in his wallet. Zach

ad also found in the billfold some pieces of scratch paper
ith addresses scribbled on them. One of the addresses was
ach's apartment in the Hawthorne district. Another was for
meone named *Lassiter* on Van Buren Street in Eugene,
nd he realized it had been Cheryl Blume's address. There
as no address or phone number for someone named Clay.

Zach wondered if this *Clay* character had gotten to Bridget
et. His first order of business was getting to a phone and
alling her.

Zach had taken Siegel's shoes and socks—as well as his
cket and shirt. He'd figured he couldn't fit into the short
an's jeans. As for the size 8 black Reeboks, Zach wore
em like flip-flop slippers—with his sore, bleeding heels
ticking over the smashed back edges. He'd removed the
ces and used them to tie up Siegel's wrists. Zach had also
ken Siegel's belt and strapped his feet together with it.

He left Norbert Siegel where the hit man had intended to
ave him—alone in the forest clearing. He would call the
olice and tell them where to find the son of a bitch. Siegel
ould be all right there for a while—unless some forest
reature decided to make an early dinner out of him.

Zach took Siegel's gun, wallet, cell phone, and keys with
im as he made his way through the darkened woods. He
oped he was headed in the right direction. It was hard to
avigate the overgrown trial. Threading through shrubs, and
tepping over rocks and tree roots, Zach kept looking for a
irt road ahead. Once he found the Volkswagen minibus—*if*
e found the minibus—he would still have to figure out
here the hell he was. He'd been unconscious during most
f the drive here. From the floor of the minibus, he hadn't
een able to see any landmarks or signposts. He could be
ver by Mt. Hood, or up near Mt. St. Helens, or maybe
omewhere near the coast. He had no idea. But Zach forged
head and tried not to trip in Siegel's little shoes.

At last, he saw a clearing through some trees ahead. But
e had to walk around a gully and stream that didn't look at
ll familiar. This wasn't the way he'd taken with Siegel. Still,

as he emerged from the thicket, Zach found a dirt road. He must have wandered off the trail and overshot where the minibus was parked. He tried the cell phone again, but still no service.

He treaded up the dirt road. Siegel's little shoes had become more a hindrance than help, so Zach kicked them of He spotted the VW minibus parked down the mountain lan in the distance, and he started running.

Inside the minibus, he found his cell phone and his pant on the floor—by the passenger seat. He tried the phone. N service there either.

Zach quickly put on his pants, started up the car, an drove down the dirt road. He had no idea where he wa headed. He just knew he couldn't go too fast, because h came upon one hairpin turn after another through the hill forest. There were also several intersections with other dir roads—none of them with signposts. Leaning forward, h kept a white-knuckled grip on the steering wheel, and staye on the same road. All the while, he prayed he'd soon com upon a paved highway—and some directional sign tellin him where the hell he was.

He kept thinking of Bridget. She'd had that tour of Glenhaven Hills today at two o'clock. He hoped she hadn driven by herself up there. It was a two-hour trip each way According to Norbert Siegel, this *artist,* Clay, had alread stalked her in her car once before. Perhaps that was how he planned to trap and kill her.

He had to get to a phone, and hoped he wasn't too late.

"Oh, thank you, sweet Jesus!" Zach called. Just whe he'd thought he was driving around in circles, he saw the dir path dip down and merge onto a paved road. But there wa no signpost, so Zach just took a chance and turned right. Fo all he knew, he could be driving *back* toward where he'd lef Siegel. He was going by sheer intuition. One thing for cer tain, he was pretty high up in the hills. From this section o the mountain highway, he had a view of the trees and th river trails—and the last vestige of a beautiful sunset.

Zach was still looking for a signpost on the roadside
hen he passed a little inlet and spotted a couple of hunters,
rapping a dead deer to the front of a Jeep. He hit the brake,
en backed up, rolled down the window, and called to them.
Excuse me! Please? Could you help me? I'm totally lost
re."

The older, stockier of the two men frowned at him. He
ld a rifle, and wore a hunter's hat, boots, and a camouflage
cket. He seemed to be supervising his buddy on how to tie
their kill. The younger fellow, wearing a baseball cap,
wn vest, and Doc Martins, didn't seem to be having a ter-
fic time. It was the young guy who stopped what he was
ing and approached Zach.

"Where are you headed?" he asked. Behind him, the
der man remained by the Jeep with his rifle in his hand. He
ed Zach suspiciously.

"I'm going back to Portland," Zach explained. "But I got
tally lost and turned around, and now I don't have a clue
here I am."

"Well, we're near Rocky Top, at about 2,400 feet." He
dded down the highway. "If you keep heading in that di-
ction, you'll see the sign for Detroit Lake and State Twenty-
vo. Follow the signs to Twenty-two West. That'll get you
ck to the interstate."

"Thanks, do you know the name of this road here?"

He nodded. "Rocky Top Road, Route 319."

"One more thing," Zach said. "Is there a grocery store
earby?"

"C'mon, hurry it up!" yelled the older man.

The younger man rolled his eyes. He nodded at Zach.
About fifteen minutes down the road, you'll find a little
om-and-pop store called Rudy's. Good luck."

"Thank you very much," Zach replied. "Good luck your-
elf."

"I need it," the man mumbled. "This son of a bitch is my
oss. Thinks he's Davy Friggin' Crockett with a rifle. He's
riving me crazy."

"Take care," Zach whispered. He waved at him as [he]
peeled away down Route 319. At least he knew where [he]
was going now. And he could make some calls from Rudy['s.]
He'd be able to give the state police a pretty good idea [of]
where they could pick up Norbert Siegel.

Rudy's Last Stand Grocery & Fish & Tackle had li[ve]
worms, "ammo," an espresso machine, Rudy's own hom[e-]
made beef and pork jerky, and by the entrance, a phone boot[h.]
Zach still wasn't getting any service on either cell phon[e.]
But he found that Rudy's phone took AT&T credit card call[s.]
He tried Bridget's home first, and got her answering m[a-]
chine.

"Are you there?" Zach asked, after the beep. "Bridget, i[t's]
Zach. If you're around, please pick up. If you're there alon[e,]
make sure that guard on duty isn't asleep at the wheel. Yo[u]
could be in a lot of danger. Listen—just be careful. I'[m]
going to try you on your cell. I'm out of a service area rig[ht]
now. But leave a message on my cell if you get this. Bye."

He tried her cell phone number next. While counting th[e]
ring tones, he nervously tapped his foot.

"Hello?" he heard her say on the other end.

"Bridget? Thank God!"

"Zach? Are you okay?"

"I'm—alive, which is good. Listen, where are you?"

"Well, we just passed the Longview-Kalama exit, so I'[m]
about forty-five minutes from home. What happened to you[?]
I was so worried . . ."

Zach told her about his run-in with Norbert Siegel. H[e]
also warned her about the hit-man *artist* named Clay. "Who[-]
ever's going to be guarding the house tonight, let him kno[w]
about this guy. I'll see if I get a last name on him and trac[k]
him down. I'll come over later."

"Please be careful," she said. Bridget paused; then he[r]
voice dropped to a whisper. "So—this other hit man, he ju[st]
outright told you that they'd killed Gerry and Leslie, an[d]
Fuller—"

"And Cheryl and Olivia," he finished for her. "Yeah. H[e]

gured I wouldn't be repeating it to anyone. I also found out at he and his pal were—well, they were working for Brad."

She didn't say anything on the other end. He just heard er sigh.

"I'm sorry, Bridget," he murmured. "If it's any consola-on, the way I understand it, you and the boys weren't sup-sed to be harmed. This Clay character is acting on his own. isten, did—Sonny say anything? Were you able to talk with im?"

"I'll tell you about it later tonight." She whispered again: Zach, are you sure these men were working for Brad?"

"Well, I asked the guy if Brad hired him. And he replied, eah, right, I work for ol' Brad Corrigan.'" Zach took a eep breath. "But later, he asked me why I was so sure he orked for Brad. Maybe he was jerking me around, I don't now. Anyway, I'm calling the police to go pick up this Siegel uy. This means you'll see your tired old sin made public, nd I'm sorry, Bridget. I can't think of any other way—"

"You don't have to worry about that," she cut in. "It's not n issue anymore. I'll explain it all to you tonight, Zach. You etter make that call to the police."

After Bridget hung up with Zach, she called Barbara hurch on her cell. In the background on the other end of e line, Bridget could hear music and the din of crashing owling pins. "Would you mind taking David and Eric back your place?" she asked her friend. "Then I'll swing by and ick them up around nine. I hate doing this to you, Barb. But 's kind of a family emergency."

Her friend said it wouldn't be a problem. Bridget thanked er profusely.

After she hung up, she turned toward Scott. They had the ar windows cracked open—to keep the air circulating. It vasn't so much to keep her awake as to neutralize the fake fresh breeze" scent the laundry had used on her clothes. At east they were cleaned and pressed.

"Can you take me to my brother's house, Scott?" she asked.

He nodded. "No problem."

Bridget speed-dialed Brad's home phone. Her father picked up. "Dad, it's me, Brigg," she said coolly. "Is Brad home?"

"Just a minute," he grumbled.

She heard him put down the phone. Things weren't right between her and her father—not after what had been said the previous evening. Bridget didn't think things between them would ever be right again.

Brad came on the line. "Brigg? What's going on?"

"I need to talk with you, Brad," she said steadily. "Can I come over?"

"What is it? You sound awful, Brigg."

"Yeah, I'm feeling pretty awful," she whispered. "I'll see you in an hour, Brad."

"You can find him in a forest clearing off a dirt road near Rocky Top, Route 319, at about elevation 2,400 feet," Zach said into the pay phone outside Rudy's. He'd already given the police Norbert J. Siegel's name, address, and driver's license number. He'd told them that Siegel was a hit man involved in the murders of Gerry Hilliard and Leslie Ackerman. All the while, Zach was holding Siegel's cell phone and scrolling through the directory.

"I'm sorry I can't give you more exact directions," he said. "That's the best I can do. You might want to bring along an ambulance. He could be hurt pretty badly. I hit him with a shovel a couple of times."

"I see here you're calling from a pay phone in the area," the state police dispatcher said. "What's your exact location, Mr. Matthias?"

The name *Clay* popped up on the cell phone's little screen—with a Portland area code.

"Mr. Matthias?"

"Um, I need to hang up," he said. "You have my home phone. We'll talk later."

"Wait, just a minute—"

Zach hung up the pay phone. He made yet another call, this time to the city desk at the *Examiner*. He asked for Tina, an editor there. They'd had lunch a couple of times.

"This is Tina," she answered.

"Hey, Tina, it's Zach Matthias, how are you?"

"Missing you and hating work. What's going on?"

"I need a favor. Do you still have that reverse directory for the Portland area?"

"I sure do."

"I'm looking for a name and address for a Portland resident."

"Okay. Go ahead. Give me the number."

Zach looked at the screen on Norbert Siegel's cell phone, and he read her the number for *Clay*.

Ten minutes later, Zach slowed down to sixty miles an hour on Highway 22. A cop car was speeding toward him in the other lane. Its flashers were going. The patrol car whooshed by. It was headed toward Rocky Top Road.

Zach checked his rearview mirror. He noticed a Jeep straggling behind him. But he was more interested in the patrol car, which eventually disappeared from view.

The two state police officers were investigating a report made at 6:47 PM. Some joker had called in from a pay phone, claiming he'd captured and "hurt pretty badly" a hit man named Norbert J. Siegel. Apparently, one of Siegel's jobs had been on Bridget Corrigan's estranged husband and his girlfriend. The police had already chalked up dozens of false leads on that double homicide. But when they ran a check on *Norbert J. Siegel*, they came up with a list of priors and a couple of aliases.

So Officer Susan Rose and her partner, Edward Kelly,

were on their way up to Rocky Top Road, Route 319, elevation 2,400 feet, for what they figured would be a wild-goose
chase. Even with the information they had on this alleged *hit
man*, the two officers had a feeling they'd be wandering
around the woods for two hours, and totally wasting their
time.

At just past 2,400 feet along Route 319, they did spot a
dead deer off the side of the road.

Then they noticed the two men lying beside it.

They looked dead too, beaten and bloody. On the ground
near one of the bodies, there was a shovel.

CHAPTER 26

"I paid a visit to Sonny Fessler today," Bridget said.

Sitting on the edge of his big mahogany desk, Brad squinted at her. "What?"

They were in his late-thirties-style study. Brad had a bottle of Amstel Light in his hand. He'd offered Bridget something to drink, but she'd declined. Her back straight, she sat on his sofa. She still had a bit of a headache from Sonny's pills, but after about a gallon of coffee, she felt wide-awake. In fact, she was tense and on-edge.

"Sonny's in a rest home up in Olympia," she explained. "I went there to talk to him, because I thought he might have seen what happened that night with Mallory at Gorman's Creek."

Frowning, Brad sighed, then took a swig of beer.

"Olivia Rankin worked at this rest home, and I figured Sonny might have told her something. In fact, I was right. He told her quite a lot."

"Brigg, I—"

"We didn't kill Mallory," she said, cutting him off.

"What?" he whispered.

"I don't know if she was unconscious—or merely playing dead," Bridget explained. "But after we left, Mallory pulled

herself out of that well. She ran into Sonny Fessler, and
Sonny slit her throat."

"Jesus," he murmured.

"Sonny told me all about it today. A couple of years ago,
when Olivia was working at this rest home, he admitted the
same thing to her. Olivia used what she knew to tap
Anastasia Fessler for money. Eventually, Anastasia's lawyer
persuaded her to back off. And that's when our friend Olivia
tried to sell this 'new information' about Gorman's Creek to
Fuller Sterns. She tried to sell it to you too, Brad, didn't
she?"

Her brother shook his head. "It doesn't make sense."

"Olivia held out on you and Fuller—and the rest of us
who were at Gorman's Creek that night. We all left there
thinking we'd killed Mallory Meehan. Olivia was offering
you and Fuller exoneration—only she tried to put a price on
it. Fuller paid her five thousand dollars. But Olivia never got
a chance to tell Fuller of his innocence, because someone
put a bullet in her head."

Brad appeared dazed. He moved as if in a stupor, retreating behind his desk. He plopped down in his big leather
chair. He seemed unable to look her in the eye.

"Don't you see, Brad? For a measly five thousand dollars,
you could have learned you were innocent—after all these
years. You wouldn't have had to cover up any crime or get rid
of any witnesses. Don't you see what a senseless waste it
was? You—" Bridget felt sick. She took a deep breath and
tried to continue in a steady voice. "You had all those people
murdered—for no reason."

He shook his head at her. "Bridget, you're wrong. That's
crazy—"

"I know you were behind all those killings, Brad," she
said angrily, her voice quivering. "Don't lie to me. I know it
was you."

"Brigg, I swear to God—"

"You had Olivia killed, because you thought she was trying to blackmail you. And Fuller, he made the mistake of

ying to see you and dredge up Gorman's Creek again. So
our hit men arranged a car accident for him. You got rid of
erry and Leslie, because you knew I told Gerry about
orman's Creek. You couldn't have anyone around who
ight come forward and say the *future senator of Oregon*
ad committed manslaughter—or second-degree murder—
venty years ago. So you had Cheryl killed too." Tears were
a her eyes, but she let out a crazy laugh. "And it was all so
oddamn unnecessary! Because you didn't kill Mallory!
one of us did."

Brad got up from his chair. "Brigg, please, calm down.
his is insane. You're talking nonsense—"

"You tried to have Zach killed because he was digging
oo deeply into what happened to Mallory. You—"

The study door opened. Bridget fell silent.

Their father stepped into the room. He wore a madras
hirt and khaki slacks. His white hair was carefully combed,
ut his face looked ashen. He shut the door behind him.

"Pop, could you leave us alone for a second?" Brad
sked.

"I heard everything you two were saying," he said in a
aspy voice. He made his way across the study and braced
imself against the desk with a shaky hand. He turned to-
vard both his children. "Bridget, back when your brother
ecided to run for senator, he told me about this bad busi-
ess at Gorman's Creek. And I made myself a vow right
here and then, that if anyone got in Brad's way—or even
hreatened to get in his way—I'd cut them down."

Brad sighed. "Pop, please—"

Their father waved him away.

"At least sit down," Brad pleaded. "You shouldn't—"

"I'm fine!" he growled. "I want to stand for this." He
ointed a finger at Bridget. "I heard about that gal, that Olivia,
vho wanted money from your brother. So I hired those fellas
o get rid of her—"

"Jesus, Pop, no," Brad said, wincing. "Please, don't—"

"And because I didn't want to run into any more like her

later on, I had these guys take care of the others. Like I said, no one is going to get in your brother's way—not on his way to the senate, or his *way* to the White House, if he wants."

"You mean, if *you* want," Bridget retorted. She stared at her father with wonder and pain. Now she knew what the big man had meant when he'd told Zach that *old Brad Corrigan* had hired him. She'd misunderstood at first. So had Zach. But now she understood everything.

"My God, I don't know you at all," she said to her father. "And you certainly don't know me, Dad. Zach said I wasn't supposed to be harmed. Okay, so what did you think I was going to do? With so many people dying, sooner or later, I was bound to figure out what was happening. What did you expect me to do?"

"I expected you to support your brother," he replied, glaring at her. "And keep his best interests in mind. I did what was *necessary*, Brigg. Now it's your turn. There's no reason any of this should ever come out."

"What are you talking about? You had people murdered!"

"What happened to your husband and his girlfriend, the police are calling a 'drug thing,' " her father said. "The other deaths looked like accidents, didn't they? Let it stay that way. No one has to know any different."

Bridget slowly shook her head, and then she turned to her brother. "God, listen to him, Brad. Can you believe it?"

Brad stared at her for a moment. He shoved his hands in his pockets, then looked down at the oriental rug and sighed. "So what *are* you going to do, Brigg?" he asked in a cold voice that sliced right through her.

"You want me to be a part of this?" she asked, incredulous. "Did you know what he was doing?"

"Of course not," Brad whispered. "But if it gets out, we're ruined."

"Don't muck it up, honey," her father whispered. "I'm sick. I'm not going to be around much longer. The doctor at the hospital gave me less than a year. I want to see my son become senator before I die. Nothing is standing in our way now."

"That's part of your vow, isn't it?" Bridget said. "And if I stood in Brad's way, you'd get rid of me too. Isn't that right? Is that how much I matter to you, *Dad?*"

"Your brother asked you a question. What are you going to do?"

She shook her head. "I'm not doing anything," she said, standing up. "The police are already doing it. You're both too late. Dad, your hit man—the one who was supposed to get rid of my friend Zach today—he failed in his mission. The police have him by now. I'm sorry I made *a muck of it*, Dad, but your dream is going to die before you do. Brad's political career is over. And you're the one who ruined it."

Her father let out a frail cry, then staggered toward the sofa. Bridget watched him put his head in his hands and sob.

She stepped out of the study—and almost bumped into Janice. Her sister-in-law backed away from the door. Obviously, she'd been listening in on the conversation. A day after her fake miscarriage, she still carried on the charade by wearing an oversized blue sweater. She had a drink in her hand. Bridget frowned at her. Janice might have had to keep pretending she had a "tummy" for another week or two, but at least she didn't have to drink on the sly anymore.

Bridget brushed past her.

"Why don't you just take a knife and stab him in the heart?" Janice said in a low voice.

At the front door, Bridget glanced back at her.

"You know, he's really dying," Janice said. "It's cancer, and it's inoperable. He's dying, and you don't give a damn. How did such a great man end up with a bitch like you for a daughter? He told me some of the hurtful things you said to him last night. After all he's done for you—"

"Well, he gave me an earful about *you* last night too," Bridget retorted. "I can't believe how for the last ten weeks, you've dished out all that *crap* about having *Bradley Corrigan the Third*, and how it just *had to be a boy*—"

"It was a boy!" Janice growled. "I *felt* it. I knew!"

"Okay, Janice, it might have been a boy," Bridget allowed.

"But one thing we know for sure. He wasn't Brad's son. Tha wasn't my nephew you were carrying around."

Janice let out an irate laugh. "No, it wasn't. You're right It wasn't your nephew, Bridget. It was your *brother*."

Bridget numbly gazed at her.

"It was your baby brother, and I wanted to keep him, Janice whispered. She had tears in her eyes as she glared a Bridget. "Your father has only one child worthy of him. thought he deserved another—another child to make up fo his *disappointment of a daughter*."

"Oh, Jesus," Bridget murmured. She backed away an bumped into the door. She felt so disgusted, she just wante to get out of there. "I—I'm sorry, Janice," she heard hersel say. "But lucky for that poor baby, it died."

Janice slapped her across the face. The drink slipped ou of her hand, and the glass smashed on the floor.

Dazed, Bridget barely felt the blow. Though the side o her face stung, it was if Janice had merely grazed her. Sh just couldn't feel anything right now. Bridget turned towar the door.

She left her brother's house and headed for the car.

Clay hadn't planned on being there for the changing c the guard.

He was parked halfway down the block from Bridget house. He'd come dressed and prepared for tonight's activ ties. He wore a black turtleneck and black jeans. His sup plies were in a little knapsack on the floor in the front seat c his car: a set of skeleton keys, .45 revolver, hunter's knife Polaroid camera and extra film, heavy-duty tape, and fift feet of the same type of cord he'd use to strangle his *Girl b a Red Sofa*.

Clay had been sitting there in his car for the last twenty five minutes. No one was on duty in front of the darkene house. But Bridget's minivan was in the driveway.

He knew the routine by now. The guards switched shif

at seven in the morning and seven at night. The detective agency must have gotten some deal on white Tauruses, because that was all they drove. Most of the time, the same two guards were on duty: a tall, white dude with thinning brown hair; and a stocky, tough-looking black guy.

Finally, a white Taurus pulled up in front of the house. Clay watched the black guy help her out of the car, then walk her inside. Some lights went on in the gray cedar shaker. The guard must have been giving the place the once-over or using the can or something, because he stayed in there a good ten minutes. Meanwhile, the other guard finally arrived, but he stayed in his car.

Seeing the two white Tauruses parked one in front of the other struck Clay kind of funny. He didn't know why. Maybe it was the realization that they were going to so much trouble working out their shifts, checking the house every time she came and went, always dressing up in their business suits, and driving cars that matched. It was pretty damn funny. They were going through all those formalities to guard her, and Bridget Corrigan would still end up dead tonight.

After emerging from the house, the black guy talked to his colleague, got into his car, then drove away.

Clay waited. Obviously, the boys weren't home. And he'd already planned on using the little brats in his painting, *St. Bridget and the Children.* It wouldn't work without them.

So for now, he just sat and waited and watched.

Janice's slap had left a red mark on the left side of Bridget's face. She stood in front of the bathroom mirror and camouflaged the fresh welt with some makeup. It felt a little sore. But she didn't have time to fuss over it. She just needed to cover up the damn thing so David wouldn't see and ask about it.

She didn't want to answer any questions tonight—or explain anything to anybody. Too much had happened in the last few hours. Maybe Sonny Fessler's pills weren't completely out of her system, or perhaps it was what Rachel Towles called her "survival instincts" at work again. Whatever the case, Bridget wasn't allowing herself to feel anything at the moment. She was just numb.

She threw on her coat, grabbed her purse, and stepped outside. After double-locking the front door, she waved at Phil. The detective stepped out of his car and met Bridget in the driveway.

"I'm just going to pick up the boys at a friend's house, Phil," she explained. "They're only a few blocks away. I shouldn't be more than ten minutes."

"Well, let me drive you," he offered.

"Thanks, but I'm expecting a friend. His name's Zach Matthias. I want someone to be here in case he shows up while I'm gone. I'll be right back."

She unlocked the door to her minivan, and he held it open for her. "Thanks," she said. "By the way, Phil, my friend, who's pretty reliable, he heard about some nutcase who's obsessed over me. He might try something later tonight. I don't know any details, but—"

"A little extra vigilance wouldn't hurt?" he finished for her. "I hear you. I'll keep my eyes peeled, Ms. C."

She nodded. "Thanks, Phil. See you in a bit."

He closed the minivan's door for her. Bridget started up the engine, then backed out of the driveway. As she started down the street, she passed a black Honda Accord, parked along the curb. Bridget thought she saw someone sitting alone in the darkened car. She stepped on the brake and checked her rearview mirror. Now the Accord looked empty.

Bridget figured it must have been the streetlight reflecting on the windshield, or perhaps it was merely her imagination. She drove on.

The address for Clay Hendricks was a converted warehouse in Portland's Pearl District. Zach had parked the VW minibus and walked two blocks to the building. He'd made good time driving back from Rocky Top—an hour and a half. For a while, he'd thought a Jeep was on his tail, because it had lingered a distance behind him on Highway 22; then he'd spotted it a couple of times on the interstate. But after taking the Portland exit, he didn't see the Jeep again.

There was a lot of foot traffic in the trendy Pearl District. Zach knew he looked pretty damn strange, trotting down the sidewalk in his stocking feet and a jacket that was way too small for him. A few people stared. But Zach was unfazed— just as long as they didn't notice the gun concealed in his ill-fitting jacket.

He needed to see this *artist's* studio and confirm what Norbert Siegel had told him about his colleague. Maybe Clay had some of his *death paintings* on display. Or maybe he had some files with records of past and present employers, something to remove any lingering doubts about Brad Corrigan's complicity in these recent murders. Once he found the evidence he needed, Zach would call the cops.

He realized he also might find Clay Hendricks at home. That was why he'd brought the gun with him.

Norbert Siegel had a hell of a lot of keys—at least two dozen. Zach hoped one of them would get him into Clay's lobby, and another into his apartment. It was a long shot that Siegel kept keys to his work partner's place; still, it was worth a try.

But it wasn't worth seventeen tries. None of the keys were working. He'd been trying to get the lobby door open for way too long, and people on the sidewalk were starting to notice.

He stepped away from the door and studied the keys on the ring. He'd seen enough movies to recognize skeleton keys, and Norbert Siegel had several. Siegel must have used one of them to enter Cheryl Blume's house while she was in the tub.

Zach was still studying the keys when a young couple came out of the lobby. The girl was laughing, and they didn't seem to notice him. Zach grabbed the door before it closed again; then he ducked inside.

C. HENDRICKS – 6-B was on the metal mailbox. Some ugly abstract art hung on the lobby walls. Zach wondered if Clay had created it.

He took the elevator up and saw that six was the top floor. The lift let out a loud *clink-clink* noise making its ascent. Zach didn't want Clay to know he was coming. He quickly pressed 5. Getting off on the fifth floor, he listened to the elevator *clink-clink* its way up to six. He found the stairwell, and then waited it out a couple of minutes. He didn't hear any sounds from above.

Zach crept up the dark, musty-smelling stairwell to the sixth floor. There were only two units. Hendricks must have had a genuine *artist's loft*. Zach put an ear against the big, clunky metal door. It didn't sound like anyone was home. He tried Siegel's keys again—this time, one of the filed-down skeleton keys.

With the third key he tried, he heard a click.

Zach cautiously pushed open the door and saw the lights were on in the apartment. Maybe Clay Hendricks was home. Zach hesitated for a moment, then stepped inside. He got a waft of oily paint and turpentine fumes. The spacious loft had a high ceiling, a bare hardwood floor, and exposed brick walls. He skulked past the kitchen and living area—with its sleek, cold, modern furnishings. Everything was black and stainless steel. In contrast, the "studio" area was an explosion of color and clutter.

Track lighting illuminated the big, multihued paintings that covered the walls. But Clay Hendricks had also left a few candles lit—including a couple of tall fat tapers on ornate stands. It didn't look like he was home; still, he must have been planning to come back soon. Only a crazy person would leave lit candles unattended in an apartment crammed with oil paints and thinners. Then again, this *artist* was pretty insane—and an obvious risk-taker.

Zach took a closer look at Clay's artwork. They were vivid, disturbing images of dead people. Among them, a young woman, dressed in a bra and panties, hanging by the neck from a ceiling beam. Obviously, this was the San Diego girl Norbert Siegel had told him about.

Zach thought he recognized the man falling from a rooftop in a *Vertigo*-inspired painting, but he didn't linger over it.

Hendricks's gruesome rendering of a car wreck was undoubtedly Fuller Sterns's death scene. Zach had passed that BRAKE FOR COFFEE sign on the highway a few times.

As he turned to look at the image of a dead blonde—slumped on a park bench with blood soaking the front of her green dress—Zach remembered what Siegel had said about Olivia Rankin's murder: "We handled the girl on the beach together. Clay wanted to paint her, so he's the one who shot her."

Backing away from the picture, Zach bumped into a large worktable completely covered with cans of paint, turpentine, and rags. Nearby, there were three easels. One held a huge canvas with a bird's-eye-view painting of an empty bedroom. The painting looked like a work in progress.

Zach checked out the other two easels in Hendricks's work area. They held large corkboards, crammed with photos and sketches of Bridget—and her sons. Several snapshots were of furniture and knickknacks that filled the bedroom Clay had painted on the big canvas.

Staring at the sketches, Zach shuddered. One rendering had a boy asleep, curled up in a little ball. He looked like an angel. There was a dark circle around his head and neck, resembling a halo. Another sketch was a close-up of a woman's hand tied to a bedpost. Clay had done a similar rendering of a woman's foot tied to a bedpost. In still another drawing, a woman—unmistakably Bridget—was sprawled over the bed—the same bed in the big painting. She wore only a bra and panties. Her hands and feet were tied to the bedposts. She had a dark circle around her head and neck as well. It was a pencil sketch, but Clay had colored the *halo* red. Zach realized those circles around their heads weren't halos; they were pools of blood.

"Oh, Jesus," he murmured. This was how Clay Hendricks planned to murder Bridget and her sons. He was going to cut their throats and lay them out in the bedroom. Then he would finish his latest *masterpiece*.

Suddenly, Zach heard a muffled *clink-clink* from the elevator. He swiveled around and knocked over an open can of paint thinner. It spilled across the floor.

He stepped over the puddle and took the gun out of Siegel's jacket. Moving toward the door, he listened to the elevator as it worked its way up one floor after another. *Clink-clink, clink-clink.* Then it stopped—but not on the sixth floor. He could tell someone was getting off on five.

Zach saw the telephone on a table over by the window. He didn't have to look for any more evidence of Clay Hendricks's crimes. He didn't have to second-guess what Hendricks intended to do to Bridget—and her sons. Zach set the gun on the table, picked up the receiver, and started to dial.

"Put it down, fuck-face."

Zach turned around. His heart stopped for a moment.

Norbert Siegel stood in the doorway with a hunting rifle pointed at him. The army camouflage jacket he'd stolen off the hunter's corpse was too big for him, and he had the sleeves rolled up. His face beaten and swollen, Siegel smiled at him. "Just toss the phone on the floor, and don't even think about going for that gun, asshole."

Zach dropped the receiver, and it landed on the floor by his feet.

"Get away from the window," Siegel whispered.

Watching him, Zach moved toward the studio area. "How did you get in?" he asked.

Siegel shut the door with his foot, then stepped into the room. "I've come over here enough to know the building's side door is a piece of shit, and Clay keeps a spare key behind the fire extinguisher in the hallway. And when I want to surprise him, I never take the elevator all the way up."

Looking at him, Zach saw he'd done some serious damage to Siegel's face. The gash on his nose and mouth had stopped bleeding, but his eyes were puffy and discolored. Still, he was grinning.

"I'm a little upset with you, asshole," he said. "We dug a nice hole back there in those woods, and I never got to fill it."

Phillip Tuttle thought he saw something.

He was leaning against his white Taurus, smoking a cigarette. Out of the corner of his eye, he'd caught some movement near the bushes at the side of the house.

Phil tossed his cigarette on the ground, then reached into his coat pocket for his gun. He didn't take his eyes off the house—and the hedges along that south side. Bridget hadn't returned yet from picking up her kids. She'd asked him to be extra vigilant tonight. Maybe her words of caution had made him a little jumpy.

After staring at the gray cedar shaker for a couple of minutes, he gave her front yard the once-over. Nothing unusual. Phil sighed and scratched his head.

Suddenly, a dark figure darted in and out of the hedges again. "What the hell?" he muttered. It didn't look human. It was something on all fours.

Phil quickly opened the car door and pulled out his flashlight. He thought about calling Scott for a backup, but decided to hold off until he got another look at this thing. Switching on the light, he moved toward the bushes on the south side of the house. In his other hand, Phil had his gun ready.

He crept around to the backyard. He didn't see anything—or anyone. No sign of a break-in either. The north side of the house was all clear too. Phil kept expecting to see a raccoon or a dog prowling around. Whatever it was, he must have scared it away. He returned to the front yard, then glanced up and down the street. Nothing.

Sighing, he switched off the flashlight and put his gun away. Then he climbed into his car and tossed the flashlight on the passenger seat. A shadow swept across the windshield. He wasn't sure what it was—maybe just his own reflection in the glass.

He quickly shut the car door, so the light would go out and he could see more clearly. The street in front of him was empty.

His eyes shifted to the rearview mirror. "Oh God," he whispered.

A man was in the backseat, staring at him.

It happened so fast. Phil didn't even see the hunter's knife. He only felt something tickle the soft spot just above the back of his neck.

Then Phillip Tuttle felt nothing at all.

"Honey, please, don't make me tell you again," Bridget said, glancing in the rearview mirror. "Quit bouncing up and down back there. It's driving me crazy."

Eric giggled, then settled back and gently kicked at the back of the passenger seat.

Bridget shot a look at David, sitting across from her. "Talk about *wired*. He'll be bouncing off the walls tonight. How much candy and cake did he have anyway?"

"Two pieces of cake, a root beer float, Milky Way bar, and about twenty red vines," David replied. "And that was just dessert."

Sighing, Bridget once again turned her attention to the road ahead. "Swell."

"Are you okay, Mom?" David whispered. "Something's the matter, I can tell."

"I'm fine," she muttered. "I'm just tired, that's all."

Bridget made the turn down their street. She figured she'd talk to the boys in the morning. Right now, she had no idea what was going to happen. The authorities were probably already investigating her father's connections to these *hit men*. Brad and she might be facing some minor charges for leav-

the scene of an accident twenty years ago. His career in
tics was over, of course. She felt sorry for him. At the
e time, she couldn't get over the way he'd so quickly ac-
ed their father's role in the murders, then without any
tation started discussing how to cover it up. And he'd ex-
ed her to go along with it.

t was too bad. Despite everything, he would have made a
n good senator. And now the people of this state would
 to endure six years with that fascist Jim Foley.

addest of all was what would happen when news of
ny Fessler's murders became public. All those old wounds
 had healed over twenty years ago would be reopened.
 for what? So a confined, elderly, mentally ill man would
attacked and demonized; then they'd ship him from a
, clean sanitarium to a substandard one. That lawyer,
hel Towles, was right. The ghosts in Gorman's Creek
ld have been best left undisturbed.

Bridget drove up the block. "By the way, my friend Zach
oming over a little later tonight," she announced.

The guy we met at Dad's funeral?" David asked. "What—
 your boyfriend now?"

No, right now, he's just a friend," she replied coolly. "Is
 okay with you? Do you mind if I have a *friend*?"

It's fine," he muttered. "Jeez, I was just asking."

They pulled into the driveway. "There's Phil!" Eric said,
ing at the white Taurus parked in front of their house.
y, Phil!"

The shadowy figure in the driver's seat waved back at

.

"Clay isn't here. You know what that means, don't you?"
Zach stood near the easels with his hands half-raised in
air. "What does it mean?"

"Means he's being a bad boy," Siegel replied. "He's with
r girlfriend. I bet tonight's the night."

Zach glanced back at the corkboard—and that penc
sketch of Bridget sprawled over the bed, her hands and f
tied to the posts. He felt a sickly pang in his gut.

Siegel kept the rifle pointed at him as he moved tow:
the window. He picked up the handgun from the teleph
stand, where Zach had left it. "What did you break in h
for anyway?" he asked. "Are you a big art lover or somethin;

"I thought I might find some records connecting you w
your employer," Zach admitted.

Siegel chuckled. "We don't keep shit like that. Hell, v
would we—for tax reasons? If you're looking to incrimin
somebody, Sherlock, you won't find any *evidence* sitt
around my place—or here."

Zach nodded toward the paintings on the wall. "What
you call that?"

He chuckled again. "I call it fucking weird. But then, l
damn good at his job." Siegel made a sour face. "Shit, g
whiff of the chemical stink in here. Did you go into his da
room? It's like a fucking laboratory—with all the soluti
and ethanols and crap. I bet he has some kind of acid stu
could use."

"Use for what?" Zach asked warily.

"Well, if I can't bury you out in the woods, I gotta f
some other way for you to disappear." He moseyed tow
Zach, keeping the gun trained on him. "You stupid son (
bitch. You could have had a quick little burial out in th
pretty woods. Now all you've done is made a lot of work
me. I hate to chop up people. It's messy, and the acid sti
And I'll probably stain his tub too. Clay's gonna be pisse

Zach glanced down at the floor. He just now noticed
Norbert Siegel was still shoeless. He did have on a pai
socks—with extra room in the toes. He must have st
them from one of those hunters.

"Shit—" Siegel was just now noticing something too. I
stepped into a puddle of paint thinner.

And once again, for a moment, Zach caught Norbert Si
looking down.

He knocked over one of the tall candlestick holders—and
then the other. They each hit the hardwood floor with a loud
clatter. One of the candles went out. But the other flame survived. A burst of fire raced across the puddle on the floor—
spreading out in little snakelike rivulets. Suddenly, Norbert
Siegel let out a shriek. He dropped the gun and tried to
cover his face. The fire seemed to crawl up his body, and he
blindly stumbled into a wall of flames that lashed up from
the floor.

Zack staggered away from him. He felt a blast of heat
across his face. Choking on the black smoke and the smell of
burning flesh, he backed into the worktable. Siegel's screams
seemed to fade under the crackling blaze. Zach couldn't
even see him anymore.

Suddenly, flames rushed across the worktable. The tops
popped and flew off small cans of paint, and a dozen rags fu-
eled the incendiary wave. Fire swept over Clay Hendricks's
unfinished painting—along with the sketches and photos he
had displayed on the corkboards.

Zach glimpsed that image of Bridget tied to the bed. The
paper started to burn and curl.

"What do you think Phil would like?" she asked. "Fritos
Sun Chips?"

"Phil likes Sun Chips!" Eric declared.

Working up a smile, Bridget handed her younger son a
small bag of Sun Chips. Then she went to the refrigerator
and took out a can of Coke.

Eric hadn't gotten the chance to even say hello to Phil—
less, talk his ear off—when they returned home a few
minutes before. Eric had had a bathroom emergency. Once
inside the house, he'd raced for the bathroom. Sulking,
David had lumbered into the den and switched on the TV.

Now Bridget handed Eric a napkin. "Tell Phil I can make
him a sandwich if he wants one."

She walked Eric to the front door and opened it for him.

Carefully holding the chips, Coke, and napkin, I headed down the walkway toward the white Taurus.

Bridget waved at her night watchman, then stepped side. She left the door open a crack, then wandered into den. Folding her arms, she frowned at David, who slouched on the sofa.

"I'm sorry if I got a little snippy with you in the car," said. "I've had a pretty awful day today. I don't want to into it right now. But we need to have a long talk tomorr

"Am I in trouble?" he asked.

"No, honey. You're fine—you're terrific." She manage smile at him. "And about Zach Matthias, you have ev right to ask about him. The truth is I like him a lot—"

Bridget fell silent. The way David stared at her, he seen utterly horrified. It took Bridget a moment to realize he wa looking at her at all. Puzzled, she glanced over her shoul

Eric stood at the edge of the den. Tears streaked down face, and his lower lip was trembling.

A man hovered behind him. He held a hunting k against Eric's throat.

The inferno encircled him. Coughing, Zach looked aro for a way to escape. He was suffocating. He kept thinking had to get to Bridget before it was too late.

The fire alarm went off with a shrill ring.

In all the smoke, he wasn't sure where the door was. I he decided to run toward the sound of the alarm b Blindly, he raced through the fire. Wretched fumes filled mouth and nostrils. He felt the heat burning his hair.

But Zach kept running until he slammed into a w Frantic, he felt around for the door and burned his fingers the bricks. It was as if he were inside an oven. He could t his skin cooking.

*   *   *

"Let go of him," Bridget said in a low voice.

She recognized *Clay,* the man who had helped her that
ght she'd been stranded with the flat tire. She remembered
s chiseled features and those intense eyes. Even when he'd
me to her rescue that evening, she'd felt a bit uneasy
ound him. If Triple-A hadn't shown up when it had, would
have used that Exacto-knife on her? She now realized
'd only given her the little knife because she'd caught him
ing to conceal it.

The knife he held against Eric's neck was not little at all.
had a six-inch blade and a serrated edge.

"I said, *Let go of him!*" Bridget repeated.

Clay seemed astonished—and a bit amused—by her au-
oritative tone. He grinned at her and pulled the hunting
ife away from Eric's throat.

Crying, Eric ran into her arms. "He killed Phil! Phil's
ad! I saw him lying in the backseat of the car!"

Bridget hugged her younger son. She glanced over at
avid, who had gotten to his feet. He stood by the sofa, with
s eyes riveted on their intruder.

Clay put away his knife, and within a second, he pulled
t a gun. He chuckled. "Thanks for the Coke and the chips.
I have them later. Right now, we're all going upstairs."

"You don't want these boys," Bridget said, trying to breathe
ght. Her heart was racing. "You just want me. So why don't
u send them upstairs? They won't go anywhere. You and I
n be down here—alone. Wouldn't that be better?"

"Mom, no—" David said.

"*Sí!*" she hissed. "*Tu y Eric peuden escaparse por la ven-
na del baño y bajarse por el árbol. Ambos lo han hecho
tes.*"

"Mom—"

"What the hell did you just say to him?" Clay asked.

She'd told David that he could escape with his brother out
e upstairs bathroom window, then climb down a nearby
e. He'd done it before.

"I told him to be quiet," Bridget explained, shooting
quick look at David. Then she stared at Clay, and her voi
dropped to a whisper. "I also said that you weren't going
hurt him. Now, you're not interested in either one of r
sons. So—don't you think it would be better if you and
were alone?"

"No, Bridget. This will be *fun for the entire family*."
nodded toward the front hall. "C'mon. Upstairs, single fi
Eric takes the lead, followed by Mom, then David in front
me—and my gun."

Bridget shuddered. How did he know all their name
How long had he been planning this?

"David, think you're going to have a cigarette upstairs
he asked.

Bridget glanced back at her son.

"Put down the goddamn ashtray, kid," Clay continue
"What—did you plan to *hurt* me with that thing?"

"It was worth a try," David answered defiantly, glari
back at him. He held the heavy marble candy dish out in t
open now.

"Put it down—unless you want to be carrying a couple
your fingers in it."

"You heard what he said," Bridget whispered.

David returned the candy dish to its spot on the cofi
table.

Clay motioned toward the front hall, and they filed out
the den. Bridget kept her hands on Eric's shoulders. H
whole body shook. She could tell he was trying not to c
But every so often a scared, heartbreaking little whimp
came out of him. "We're going to be okay, sweetie," she sa
under her breath. "We'll be okay."

Yet she knew they were heading up those stairs to th
doom. She'd already seen what this man had done to Gei
and Leslie. All she could think about was getting her be
out of there. But right now she had no idea how she w
going to do that.

* * *

His jacket was on fire.

Zach staggered out to the hallway, where the fire alarm
ll was deafening. The overhead sprinklers had been acti-
ted. But the water hadn't yet dowsed the flames crawling
his sleeve. Because Siegel's jacket was so small and tight
him, Zach couldn't struggle out of it until he was halfway
wn the first flight of stairs. He flung the burning garment
hind him and kept running down the steps.

The shower of water felt cool against his hot skin. But he
s still coughing and gagging—until finally, he spat up
me black mucuslike liquid. Then he relentlessly continued
wn the stairwell.

Once outside, Zach threaded through the crowd of people
o had gathered in front of the building. He heard the fire
gine sirens blaring. He stopped and tried to catch a breath.

Zach realized he'd left his cell phone in the pocket of
egel's jacket. He needed to call the police—and Bridget.
thought about borrowing a phone from someone on the
eet. But a couple of onlookers gasped when they saw him.
one would get near him. His face was red, some of his
ir had burned off, and smoke soot covered his clothes.

He broke away from the crowd and ran down the block to
ere he'd parked Siegel's minibus. In his pants pocket, he
ll had Siegel's keys. As he hurried toward the car, Zach
ticed the skin on his left arm was scorched. He knew he
d to get to a doctor soon.

But he had to get to Bridget first.

"Well, well, Bridget, since you've done such a terrific job
th the boys, you can tie up your ankles for me." He tossed
hree-foot section of cord on the bed. "I'll watch and make
e you do it right."

Bridget sat with her feet up on the bed. She was trem-
ng. She didn't want to start crying in front of him—or the

boys. Still, tears filled her eyes. He'd made her take off he
shoes. And for some reason she thought about Andy Shield
and his green Converse All-Stars. They'd found him an
those other two boys without their shoes.

She glanced over at her sons.

Clay had made them lie facedown on her bedroom floo
Then he'd given her sections of cord to tie their hands behir
their backs—and bind their stockinged feet together. Fir
David, then Eric. He'd tested her work, pulling at each cor
and making sure it was tight enough.

Now he stood at the end of the bed, watching her tie th
cord around one ankle. "Okay, take the other end of the cor
and tie it around the bedpost here—nice and tight."

She obeyed him. She listened to her younger son. Poo
Eric couldn't stop whimpering.

"That's right," Clay said. "Only put the cord ends th
way—so they stick out. There, that's the way I want it." Cla
tested the cord around the bedpost. "Good girl. Now start c
the other ankle."

She couldn't understand why the knots had to *look* a ce
tain way. But Bridget figured he was going to tie her hand
to the headboard posts in a similar fashion. Maybe she cou
surprise him while he was doing that. Bridget started
wrap the cord around her other ankle. "David, rememb
your mother loves you," she said, her voice cracking. The
she added, *"Necesito que me lo distraigas. ¿Esta bien?"*

In English, it roughly translated to: *"I have a plan. I
need you to distract him for me. Okay?"*

"*Sí*," he replied. "I love you too, Mom."

"Lie back," Clay whispered.

Bridget reclined on the bed. She was still shaking. Sh
watched him pull at the cord around her ankle. Her leg
spread as far as her skirt would allow. With a flicker of
smile, he stuck his gun in his belt, then took out his hunte
knife. He slowly cut a line on the taut fabric between h
legs—until he reached her thighs. Tucking the knife away,

gave the cord around her ankle a yank and quickly tied the other end to the post.

"David," she said. "*Cuando le digo, 'Te daré mi bolsa,' quiero que comiences a toser y fingir que te estàs a hogando. ¿Entiende?*"

"Hey, that's enough of that shit," Clay growled.

"*Sí, entiendo, la Mama,*" David said defiantly.

Clay took out another piece of cord. Bridget eyed the gun in his belt. As he grabbed her hand and started to tie the cord around her wrist, she ever so subtly slipped her other hand beneath the spare pillow.

She had told her son to start coughing and feign a choking fit once she gave him the cue, "*. . . when I say to him, 'I'll give you my purse.' "*

Clay started to tug one end of the cord toward the bedpost.

Tears in her eyes, Bridget looked up at him. Her free hand felt around under the pillow. Where was it? She'd had it hidden there the last few nights—the same way she'd kept a baseball bat by her bed back in high school, when she'd thought someone might be murdering twins.

"Listen, you don't have to do this," she said. "You and I can go downstairs now. If it's money you want, I'll give you my purse. I think there's a couple hundred dollars in it—"

Suddenly, David started coughing and gagging.

"My God, I think he's choking!" Bridget cried. "Please, could you—please, just turn him on his side."

But Clay didn't even glance over his shoulder at David's expert convulsions. He fastened the knot around the bedpost.

All the while, David was relentless. He kept coughing and making raspy noises. It started Eric up too. He began to cry out loud.

Bridget frantically groped under the pillow. Damn it, where was it?

Clay wouldn't take his eyes off her. "Let him choke to

death," he muttered, taking out his hunter's knife. "He's gonna die soon enough anyway." Clay drew another cord from his knapsack, then reached for her other hand.

David's coughing got even louder.

Clay hesitated and sneered down at him.

Bridget found it. For a minute, she'd thought the Exacto-knife must have rolled out from under the pillow and fallen behind the bed. But no, thank God, she had it in her hand now. She remembered what Clay had said when he'd given it to her: "It doesn't seem like much protection, but if you hit the right artery, you can do a lot of damage."

"Can it!" Clay growled, past David's exaggerated coughing fit. He was still looking down toward him. "You're faking," he muttered, brandishing his knife. "I'll shut you up, you little shit."

With his head turned away, Clay didn't seem to notice Bridget pulling her hand out from under the pillow. He couldn't have seen the silver penlike weapon in her grasp.

But he certainly must have felt the exposed blade as it slid across his throat.

When Zach drove up the street, he saw the white Taurus parked in front of her house. He figured everything was all right. But then he got closer, and the private detective's car looked empty.

He parked the minibus, jumped outside, and ran up to the Taurus. Zach noticed streaks of blood on the driver's window and then saw the crumpled body on the floor of the backseat. "Oh God, no," he murmured.

He turned and started to run toward the front door. But Zach saw something in the upstairs window that made him stop in his tracks. Through the sheer, organdy drapes, he saw the silhouette of a tall man. He was staggering toward the window, touching his neck, and flailing his hands in a strange way. Reeling around, the man entangled himself in the drapes. Bloodstains bloomed on the delicate fabric.

Zach could see him now. The man's eyes were rolled back. Blood gushed from a slash across his throat. It splattered against the glass.

Suddenly, Clay Hendricks flopped over and crashed through the window. Zach jumped back from the explosion of glass. Hendricks's body hit the stone walkway. There was a loud crack.

Zach figured Clay Hendricks must have broken his back. He lay faceup with his eyes wide open. His twisted body kept convulsing for another few moments.

And then—with a dead stare fixed on his face—he became perfectly still.

He looked like someone in a Clay Hendricks painting.

EPILOGUE

When Bridget telephoned the police, she informed the 9-1-1 operator that she'd killed an intruder. She knew it was just one small part of a very long story she would have to tell them.

"God, I don't want to rat on my father," she whispered to Zach.

He still smelled of smoke and soot. Bridget still had a piece of cord tightly knotted around one ankle. They were both perspiring and trying to catch a breath. Bridget had managed to remain calm in front of the boys. But David had taken Eric into the bathroom to wash his face, and now she let down her guard with Zach. They stood in the upstairs hallway. In the distance, they could hear police sirens.

"I don't want to be the one who turns him in," she said under her breath. Her voice started cracking. "Can't we pretend we don't know anything? I just wish this—*nightmare* could end now. Haven't David and Eric been through enough already?"

She didn't want to see her frail, dying father endure scandal, a trial, and imprisonment. She didn't want to see her brother's career ruined. As much as she couldn't forgive them, they were still her family.

Still, several murders had been committed, and she was

involved. She couldn't remain silent. She loathed the idea of keeping this horrible secret for the rest of her life.

It was like Gorman's Creek all over again.

Bridget noticed the red strobe light flashing through the front windows. At that moment, the phone rang. On the other end of the line was a very somber Brad.

"This isn't a good time, Brad," she told him.

"I know you don't want to talk to me right now, Brigg. But we're waiting for the ambulance here. I think Dad's had a stroke."

After she hung up the phone, Bridget put her head on Zach's shoulder and cried.

Downstairs, the police were knocking on the front door.

"Oh, God help me," Bridget whispered. "I don't want to turn him in."

"We might not have to," Zach assured her.

The state police had a record of Zachary Matthias's call from a pay phone at 6:47 Friday night. He'd told them he'd been abducted by Norbert J. Siegel, and claimed Siegel was a hit man, responsible for the murders of Leslie Ackerman and Gerard Hilliard.

At 7:22, state patrol officers Susan Rose and Ed Kelly found the bodies of two hunters along Route 319. Both of them had been shot. Theodore Liming, fifty-seven, was dead. His coworker, Sean Donovan, thirty-four, was rushed to the hospital in critical condition. Donovan remembered giving directions to Zachary Matthias. From a driver's license photo, Donovan identified Norbert J. Siegel as the "crazy little creep" who had sprung out of the woods and attacked him and his boss with a shovel. Siegel had gone after the older man first. He'd taken away his rifle, then shot them both. The Jeep he'd stolen belonged to Sean Donovan. It was found—in good condition—parked in a loading zone in Portland's Pearl District.

Half a block away, a fire had broken out on the top floor

of a six-story apartment building. Siegel's wallet and license were discovered in his partially burnt jacket, which had been discarded in the building's stairwell. Siegel's dental records helped identify the scorched skeletal remains found in Unit 6-B.

The fire caused an estimated $48,000 in damage. The only other casualty was the man who admitted to starting the blaze. Zachary Matthias sustained second-degree burns on his left arm, and some minor smoke inhalation.

A thorough search of Siegel's residence—a two-bedroom house in Vancouver, Washington—uncovered a small arsenal, enough porn to open his own adult video store, $17,000 in cash, and several fake identification cards. Police also discovered a pound of cocaine, which matched with residue samples taken from Leslie Ackerman and Gerard Hilliard's bedroom closet. They uncovered no records of the hit man's jobs or his various employers. "Much as we tried," one cop later confided to a friend, "we didn't find a record of Norbert Siegel's Greatest Hits."

Siegel could only be linked with the murders of Theodore Liming, Gerard Hilliard, and Leslie Ackerman—as well as the *attempted* murders of Sean Donovan and Zachary Matthias. The only way the police could connect him with Clay Hendricks was from testimony by Zachary Matthias. They spoke with Zach for three hours at the downtown precinct office—after he'd been released from the emergency room at Providence Hospital. He was exhausted, and still wearing his sooty, smoky clothes. His arm was in a bandage, and his face, neck, and hands had been covered with ointment to prevent infection from the minor burns.

The authorities had difficulty understanding—and believing—his story about Hendricks's penchant for painting his victims. They were also a bit fuzzy on exactly how this hit man became obsessed with the estranged wife of his alleged victim, Gerard Hilliard.

Only two of Hendricks's paintings survived the blaze. All the others were completely destroyed. One surviving piece sustained some water damage, and the top right corner had been burned beyond repair. But the undamaged portion of the painting clearly showed a middle-aged businessman sitting at his desk with a bullet in his head. On a hunch, one of the detectives interviewing Zachary Matthias photographed and faxed a copy of the painting to the San Diego Police Department. Twelve hours later, SDPD informed them the "painting" matched crime scene photos taken of Wallace Stanton, from his unsolved murder three years ago. They confirmed what Zachary Matthias had said about Hendricks's obsession for the victim's daughter. Eighteen-year-old Jessica Stanton had been found three weeks after her father's death, hanging by the neck in her parents' living room, an apparent suicide.

The painting and the San Diego connection gave credence to Zachary Matthias's story of Hendricks's strange obsession. One detective, who had grown fond of Zach, told him off the record: "You're not as full of shit as we first thought you were."

The other painting that survived the fire—with only a few burn marks along the right edge—was the one that caused such a scandal. Without a doubt, it had an effect on the race for senator.

Hendricks had named the painting *The Last Leap*, and it had been one of his favorites.

Zach had thought the man in the piece looked vaguely familiar. A couple of detectives concurred with him. The bird's-eye-view rendering of the man's fall from a rooftop looked like a scene from Hitchcock's *Vertigo*. But the locale in this painting was undoubtedly Portland. One of the cops pointed out that the street below the victim was Park Southwest, not far from the statue of Lincoln—the same spot where two years ago, Mike Nuegent, a nine-year employee at Mobilink, Inc., had committed suicide.

Rumors still circulated that Jim Foley had the Mobilink clerk murdered for spitting in his face. The story was Nuegent became disgusted after Foley had spoken to a group of clerks, comparing himself to a Native American warrior who rides his horse until it's dead, and then he eats it. "You people are like my horse," Foley had concluded.

The police unearthed some photos of Mike Nuegent, and there was no mistaking it. He was the man in Hendricks's painting.

Zach found it terribly ironic that Brad Corrigan Sr. had hired the same hit men that Jim Foley had once used. He didn't share this with the authorities. Nor did he tell them about his three former classmates from high school, who had been murdered by these hit men. He feigned ignorance when asked why he'd been targeted by Norbert Siegel. "The guy didn't explain why he was going to off me," Zach told them. And that much was true. Siegel hadn't actually given him a reason for the hit. Zach had done most of the talking back in those woods.

Asked if he had any enemies, Zach admitted that he'd recently had an altercation with a former coworker at the *Examiner*, who had been harassing Bridget Corrigan and her children. "His name's Sid Mendel. He threatened to get me fired. I doubt he was mad enough to take it up a notch and hire a hit man. But he's pretty damn sleazy. Maybe you want to check him out."

One of the detectives questioning Zach thought it odd his would-be killer would offer no explanation for the hit on him—and yet run at the mouth about his role in the Gerard Hilliard, Leslie Ackerman murders—and his partner's fixation on Bridget Corrigan.

Zach gave an evasive shrug. "Well, he seemed to be bragging about the Hilliard, Ackerman murders. They got so much coverage on TV. As for Ms. Corrigan, I was worried and asked if she'd been targeted too. That's when he told me about his friend and his weird 'artistic obsession' over her. I think he was trying to torment me with the information. I wasn't sure if he was telling the truth or not. That's why I went to Hendricks's loft—to see if it was true."

"Why would you ask about Bridget Corrigan?" the cop pressed.

"Because I'm in love with her," Zach replied.

He was so in love with Bridget that he'd been willing to lie
r her. But Zach didn't have to go that far during the rounds
police questioning. He'd merely left out huge chunks of
e truth.

If a dark cloud seemed to loom over the Corrigan family
at weekend, Brad's numbers at the polls were the silver lin-
. People couldn't help feeling sympathetic.

And people couldn't help wondering about Jim Foley's
ssible affiliation with these hit men. Although Portland
lice reopened the investigation into Mike Nuegent's "sui-
e," they found nothing beyond circumstantial evidence
plicating Foley. Still, scathing accounts of his "warrior
ef" speech and Nuegent's suspicious demise began to re-
culate. There was also talk that Foley may have arranged
hit on Gerard Hilliard and Leslie Ackerman to expose a
aine connection to the Corrigans. Some even went as far
to say that Foley had put a contract out on Bridget
rrigan, his opponent's sister and *secret weapon*.

A week before the election, the *Examiner* ran a survey that
ed: *Do you really believe Jim Foley has ever hired hit men
ill for him?* The response was 61 percent yes, 29 percent
and 10 percent don't know. The pro-Foley newspaper had
ected a different response, and didn't print the survey re-
s. But the statistics accidentally showed up on the
miner's Web site for about twenty minutes before being
ked off.

im Foley never acknowledged any of the accusations. In
speeches and interviews, the "Nuegent matter" was a
oten subject. But Foley talked more and more about
prayer influenced his life. He said that God wanted him
senator.

wo days before the election, the senatorial candidates
in a dead heat.

rad asked Bridget to make some eleventh-hour appear-

ances with him. She refused. She didn't want to be a pa
his campaign anymore, not when people were being
dered so he could win. Brad might not have been behin
murders, but he didn't seem at all troubled that they'd
committed for his political gain. Despite everything, Bri
still considered him a better candidate than Foley. But a
point, her brother merely seemed like the lesser of two

Considering what she'd been through, people tho
they understood why Bridget Corrigan had stopped wo
for her brother and started spending more time with
sons. Though the Corrigans weren't seen together in p
anymore, people assumed Bridget, Brad, and their fam
still spent time together in private. The assumptions
wrong.

A week after the election, Bridget sold the house. The
time she'd considered putting the place on the market, D
and Eric had been ready to commit mutiny. But now
were as eager as she was to get out of there.

They were making a fresh start—up in Belling
Washington. Since she'd made her first splash working
her brother, Bridget had been receiving offers from all
A congressman from Washington State wanted her as
chief of staff in the Bellingham office. He'd been impre
with her work for Brad, and there was a large Spanish-sp
ing population in his district. For Bridget, it seemed li
good fit. She bought a three-bedroom, redbrick house—
a nice yard. They would be moving the week after Tha
giving.

Bridget got a head start packing things in boxes. E
drawer and closet she cleaned out was full of memories.
browsed through her high school yearbook again, stud
the photos of those classmates who had died. A disapp
ance, a suicide, and two freak accidents—none of them w
be investigated any further. She found several items
Gerry had missed when he'd moved out earlier in the y
among them, an ugly brass paperweight with his frater
letters on it, some cards she'd written to him, and a copy

atcher in the Rye with *Gerry Hilliard—English/3rd period—Mrs. Kinsella* scribbled on the inside front cover. Bridget couldn't throw any of his things away. She packed them up for the move.

Another keepsake she couldn't toss out was the picture Andy Shields had drawn of her. She'd tried to talk with Andy's dad three weeks ago—shortly after that awful Friday night. Of all the people who had lost someone connected to Gorman's Creek—the old murders as well as recent—the one person she'd wondered about most was Mr. Shields. Would he really want to know the circumstances of Andy's death? Would that information heal old wounds—or merely open them up again?

She'd learned that Mr. and Mrs. Shields had moved to Santa Rosa back in 1986. Bridget had left two messages at their home, and was leaving a third when Mr. Shields picked up. "I'm sorry we haven't called you back, Bridget," he explained, his voice a bit strained. "I—well, Karen—*Mrs. Shields* and I—we thought you might want to talk about Andy. And it's just too painful. I don't mean to be rude or make you feel bad. But I associate you with that day he disappeared. Don't get me wrong, Bridget. You were perfectly wonderful. But every time we see you or Brad on the news, I think of the day we lost Andy, and it still hurts. So, Bridget, if you called to talk about my son, I—I simply can't. I'm sorry."

Mr. Shields had answered her questions. The ghosts of Gorman's Creek—old and new—were best left undisturbed.

A week before Thanksgiving, Bridget was still cleaning closets when an old friend from out of town dropped by. They had coffee and sat in the den, amid trash bags full of Corrigan-for-Oregon paraphernalia and other junk Bridget was throwing out. Through the picture window they could see Zach tossing around a football with David and Eric in the backyard.

Kim Li hadn't changed much since high school, except she'd gotten rid of the pink streaks in her hair. She also had glasses now, very chic-looking. She'd told Zach that she wa coming to town, and he'd arranged the reunion.

Bridget told her everything.

"I think I made the right decision," she said. "Gerry's par ents don't want to hear anything more about his death. The just want to move on. I doubt Mrs. Rankin would like t know about Olivia blackmailing people. And Mrs. Meeha doesn't need to hear how her daughter was killed after taun ing a mentally ill man—"

"You don't have to justify it to me," Kim said, patti Bridget's arm.

Bridget slouched farther back on the sofa and sighe "God, I shouldn't even be telling you any of this. If it ev came out that you knew—"

"Oh, relax. I'm a shrink. We'll call this a session. Ever thing you say falls under the sanctity of doctor-patient con dentiality."

"I'm so sorry I pushed you away after high schoo Bridget admitted.

"Me too," Kim whispered. "You know, you could ha told me about Mallory. I would have kept your secret."

"I didn't want to burden you with it. And Brad was adamant about us not telling anyone."

"How are things with you and Brad?"

"Strained," Bridget replied. "We're cordial to each oth and that's about it. Still, he's my brother, and I love hi We'll always have that connection. But right now, we doing our best to avoid each other. That might change so time down the line, but I doubt it."

It certainly didn't help matters that Janice refused to h Bridget in their house. Bridget didn't tell Kim the awful tails about Janice's pregnancy. There were some family crets that couldn't be shared with anyone.

Her father was a stranger to her now. Bridget reme bered when she was a child, how much she and Brad worshipped him. She remembered making all those welco home signs they posted on the block whenever their fa

turned from one of his business trips. Now, whenever she
sited him in the rest home, Bridget would bring him flow-
s, then sit at his bedside. She couldn't think of anything to
y to him. So usually she just sat there saying nothing. But
least, he knew she was there.

Kim glanced out the window. "Well, the kids look like
ey're doing okay," she said.

Bridget smiled as she watched Eric, trying to block a long
ss Zach threw to David. "They've sure latched on to Zach.
ey're really crazy for him."

"You too, I guess," Kim said. "It's about time you caught
 to what a catch he is. Don't forget, I had a crush on him
y before he became officially cute."

Bridget just smiled. Her old friend had always been very
ght.

He sat alone on the park bench. Through the chain-link
ce, he had a good view of the playground of St. Catherine's
ementary School. He watched Bridget's younger son,
ying with some other third graders on the monkey bars.
 could hear them laughing and shouting in the distance. In
t, Eric was so busy having fun that he apparently had no
a someone was watching him.

"Sorry I'm late," Bridget said, coming around and sitting
the park bench with him. She wore a trench coat and car-
d a Subway bag. "I had to interview clerks, and it took
ger than I expected."

Eying the playground, she handed Zach the bag. "I got
 plain turkey on Italian bread, and a root beer. What did I
s?"

"Eric's having a good time," Zach said. "Didn't you get
 lunch for yourself?"

'I'm too nervous to eat," she said. Bridget spotted Eric,
ying with the other kids, and she smiled. She scooted
er to Zach on the bench.

When she'd told him about her job at the congressional

district office in Bellingham, Zach had started looking f
work at Western Washington University and the *Bellingha*
Herald. He'd landed on the staff of the Living Arts section
the *Herald,* and found himself a small apartment eig
blocks from Bridget's new home. Zach had moved the we
before.

Bridget had just relocated this weekend. She hated pluc
ing the boys out of school in the middle of the year, but t
congressman wanted her working for him that first week
December. She knew she was being overprotective—spyi
on them during recess on their first day in the new scho
But they'd been through so much recently, she needed
make sure they were getting along all right.

The recess bell rang, and the younger students started
file back into the school building. Eric was among them
couple of boys were talking to him. *Good,* Bridget thougl

From another set of double doors, the older stude
came out to the playground in waves.

"I don't see David yet," Bridget whispered. "Do you
him?"

"Not yet," Zach said, over his sandwich. "You know, *if*
sees us, he'll be really ticked off."

Bridget spotted him, wandering out those double do
by himself. He walked with his head down and should
slouched. He kept his hands tucked in the pockets of
windbreaker. Someone yelled out, "Maul ball!" and a gr
of boys started running in a pack, tossing a ball around.

David leaned back against the brick building and watc
them. Bridget's heart was breaking for him. "Why doesn'
go join them?" she muttered.

"Well, he's *new,*" Zach said, his eyes on David. "I
checking things out, that's all."

"You'd think one of those little jerks would go over
talk to him—or invite him to play. They ought to make
new kid feel welcome."

The screams and shouts from the playground grew lou
The crowd playing maul ball got bigger and more rov

stayed propped up against the building, looking down
feet. He was still all by himself.

h, I hate this," Bridget whispered.

ait, look," Zach said.

o boys wandered over to David and began to talk to
Both boys were shorter than David. One was very hefty,
e other, his exact opposite—a gangly stick of a teenager.
her, the two boys resembled the number 10. Biting her
ridget anxiously gazed at them. "Oh, I don't know," she
ured. "It sounds mean, but they look kind of geeky."

ch nudged her. "Hey, I was a geek, remember?"

e leaned over and kissed him on the cheek. "Sorry."

e round boy said something that made David laugh.
a few moments, the three boys looked like old friends.
atching them, Bridget smiled. "Well, he seems to be
okay."

ch put his arm around her. "Yeah, I think it's going to
right."

e staff at Glenhaven Hills always made a fuss when-
Brad Corrigan, the senator from Oregon, came to visit
ther.

nice Corrigan was at the rest home twice a week. The
s had grown to hate her. They felt sorry for Brad. His
were infrequent. He always came alone, and stayed
a few minutes. It was touching to see the handsome,
g senator sitting at his father's bedside, holding the old
bony hand.

adley Corrigan Sr. was dying, and drugged up with
illers most of the time.

ey'd put a fake little Christmas tree in his room that
mber afternoon the senator came to visit. Brad Corrigan
ed the nurses and thanked them for the festive decora-
Then they left him alone with his father.

ad pulled up a chair, sat down, and took hold of his fa-
hand. "Well, you look good, Pop," he lied.

He glanced at the side table—at a Christmas bouque
Janice must have brought, and a drawing Emma had r
Brad didn't spend much time with them nowadays. Wi
his trips to Washington, D.C., it was becoming more
home now.

"On the way here today," he told his father, "I was t
ing about all the sacrifices you've made for me, Pop. W
am today, I owe to you."

He leaned forward. "I've avoided talking to you .
this," he whispered. "But I think you know anyway.
night you had the stroke, when Brigg and I were in my s
I didn't expect—"

Brad shook his head. He looked down at his father's
so drained of color and expression. But his eyes twi
with a sort of understanding.

"You must have been listening to our conversatio
quite a while," Brad said in a hushed voice. "And whe
came in and told Brigg that you'd hired those guys to k
all the Gorman's Creek witnesses, I was in shock. I co
believe what you were saying, Pop. I just couldn't believ

A little smile came to his father's pale, lopsided fac
opened his mouth. When he spoke, his words were sl
but Brad understood.

"But . . . Brigg . . . believed, didn't she?" the old man

Brad nodded and squeezed his father's hand. "Yeah,
he whispered. "She believed you. Thank you for lying."

His father didn't try to say anything else, and neithe
Brad. He sat there, just holding his hand for several
minutes.

He stayed longer than usual. Finally, Brad got to his
He bent down and gently kissed his father on the fore
"I'll be back to see you again real soon, Pop," Brad sa
promise it won't be so long until the next visit."

But even as he made his promise, Senator Brad Cor
knew he wouldn't keep his word. He wouldn't be by
for several weeks. What he'd said was a lie.

Still, he told himself that his father would understan